MRS. H

ORVILLE COLLEGE

Elibron Classics
www.elibron.com

COLLECTION

OF

BRITISH AUTHORS.

VOL. 916.

ORVILLE COLLEGE BY MRS. HENRY WOOD.

IN ONE VOLUME.

TAUCHNITZ EDITION.

By the same Author,

ORVILLE COLLEGE.

A STORY.

BY

MRS. HENRY WOOD,

AUTHOR OF "EAST LYNNE," "THE CHANNINGS," ETC.

COPYRIGHT EDITION.

LEIPZIG

BERNHARD TAUCHNITZ

1867.

CONTENTS.

ORVILLE COLLEGE.

CHAPTER I.

In the Plantation.

THE glowing sunset of a September evening was shining on the fair grounds around Orville College, lighting up the scene of stir and bustle invariably presented on the return of the boys to their studies after the periodical holidays. A large, comfortable-looking, and very irregular building was this college. But a moderate-sized house originally, it had been added to here, and enlarged there, and raised yonder, at different times as necessity required, and with regard to convenience only, not to uniformity of architecture. The whole was of red brick, save the little chapel jutting out at one end; *that* was of white brick, with black divisional strokes, as if the architect had a mind to make some distinction by way of reverence. The Head Master's house faced the lawn and the wide gravel carriage-drive that encircled it; the school apartments, ending in the chapel, were built on the house's left; the sleeping-rooms and domestic offices were on its right. It was only a private college — in fact, a school — founded many years ago by a Dr. Orville, and called after him; but it gradually became renowned in the world, and was now of the very first order of private colleges.

Situated near London, in the large and unoccupied tracts of land lying between the north and the west districts, when the college was first erected, nothing could be seen near it but green fields. It was in a degree isolated still, but time had wrought its natural changes; a few gentlemen's houses had grown up around, and a colony of small shops came with them. The latest improvement, or innovation, whichever you like to call it, had been a little brick railway station, and the rushing, thundering trains, which seemed to be always passing, would occasionally condescend to halt, and pick up or set down the Orville travellers. In want of a name, when the houses spoken of began to spring up, it had called itself Orville Green — which was as good a name for the little suburb as any other.

Dr. Brabazon, the head master, stood at the door to receive his coming guests. It had been more consistent possibly with the reserve and dignity of a head master, to have ensconced himself in a state-chair within the walls of his drawing-room or library, and given the boys a gracious bow as each introduced himself. Not so the doctor. He was the most simple-mannered man in the world — as these large-hearted and large-minded men are apt to be, — and he stood at the hall door, or went to it perpetually, with a hearty smile and outstretched hands for each fresh arrival. A portly, genial man he, of near sixty years, with an upright line of secret care on his brow that sat ill upon it, as if it had no business there.

The boys on this occasion came up, as was usual, to the front, or doctor's entrance; not to their own entrance near the chapel. The number of students altogether did not exceed a hundred. About forty of

these were resident at the head master's; the rest —
or nearly the rest — were accommodated at the houses
of other of the masters, and a very few — eight or
ten at the most — attended as out-door pupils, their
friends living near. No difference whatever was made
in the education, but these last were somewhat looked
down upon by the rest of the boys. They arrived
variously; some driven from town in their fathers'
handsome carriages, some in cabs, some used the new
rail and walked from thence, some had come by
omnibus. Dr. Brabazon received all alike, with the
same genial smile, the same cordial grasp of the hand.
He liked all to make their appearance on the eve of
school, that the roll might be written and called: the
actual business beginning on the morrow.

A pair of beautiful long-tailed ponies, drawing a
low four-wheeled open carriage, came round the gravel
sweep with a quiet dash. The driver was a well-grown
youth, who had entered his eighteenth year. He had
high, prominent features of an aquiline cast, and large
sleepy blue eyes: a handsome face, certainly, but spoilt
by its look of pride. His attention during his short
drive — for they had not come far — had been absorbed by his ponies and by his own self-importance
as he drove them. It was one of the senior boys,
Albert Loftus. By his side sat another of the seniors,
a cousin, Raymond Trace, a quiet-looking youth of no
particular complexion, and his light eyes rather sunk
in his head; eyes that he had a habit of screwing together when at his studies. He had been reading a
book all the way, never once looking up at his cousin,
or the road, or the ponies, and answering in civil
monosyllables when spoken to. Behind sat another

college boy, younger, Master Dick Loftus. Master Dick possessed very little pride indeed, and was a contrast to his brother. He had amused himself, coming along, with a pea-shooter, and hung out a flag behind — all to the happy ignorance of the driver and Mr. Trace. A groom in plain livery, nearly bursting with suppressed laughter, made the fourth in the pretty carriage.

"Well, Loftus, I'm very glad to see you: you're rather late, though, considering you are so close," was the doctor's greeting. "How are you, Trace? Dick, you rebel, I hope we shall have no trouble this term."

The doctor laughed as he said it. Dick, a red-faced good-humoured boy, met the hand and laugh readily. He knew he was a favourite, with all his faults.

"Sir Simon's compliments to you, sir, and he will do himself the pleasure of calling shortly," said Mr. Loftus. "Dick, take those things away."

Mr. Loftus had slightly altered the phraseology of the message: "My respects to Dr. Brabazon, and I'll give him a look in soon," was the one sent. The groom had been depositing a few things on the ground, and Dick was loading himself, when a close carriage drove in. A lady sat inside it in solitary state, and a young gentleman sat on the roof backwards.

"Halloa! It's Onions!"

The remark came from Mr. Dick Loftus. He dropped the things summarily, went out, and began a dance in honour of the new arrival. Loftus the elder seized on a square parcel done up in brown paper, and disappeared, leaving the other things to their fate. "Onions" got down by the chariot wheel, and shook hands with Dick.

They called him Onions as a sort of parody on his name, "Leek." The college was in the habit of bestowing these nicknames. Joseph Leek, at any rate, did not mind it, whatever others, thus distinguished, might do; he would as soon be called Onions as Leek, at any time. Nothing upset his temper or his equanimity. He was one of the coolest boys that ever entered a school, and was a universal favourite. His father, General Leek, was in India; his mother, Lady Sophia, whom Dr. Brabazon was now assisting from the carriage, was an invalid in the matter of nerves, and always thankful to get her son to school again the first day of term.

The pony carriage drove off; Lady Sophia Leek's carriage was not long in following; other carriages, and cabs, and flies came up and went; and there was a lull in the arrivals. Dr. Brabazon was standing at his drawing-room window (a light pretty room on the right of the hall) and was trying to call to mind how many were still absent, when he saw some one else approaching, a small black travelling-bag in one hand, and dressed from head to foot in a suit of grey.

"Who's this?" cried he to himself. "It looks too tall for Gall."

Too tall certainly for Mr. Gall, who, though the senior boy of the college, was undersized. And too old also. This gentleman looked two or three-and-twenty; a slender man of middle height, with pale, delicate features, and a sad sort of look in his pleasant dark eyes.

"It must be the new German master," thought Dr. Brabazon: and he hurried out to meet him.

The new German master it was, Mr. Henry. There

was a peculiar kind of timid reticence in his manner which seemed foreign to himself, for his face was a candid, open face, his voice frank. Dr. Brabazon put it down to the natural shyness of one who has resided abroad. Mr. Henry, of English birth, had been chiefly educated in Germany. He spoke German as a native, French also: for some few years he had been a professor at the University of Heidelberg, and had come thence now, strongly recommended to Dr. Brabazon.

"I am very glad to see you," said the doctor, taking his hand in his simple, cordial manner. "Welcome to England! I have been expecting you since the morning."

"We had a bad passage, sir; the boat was late by many hours. It was due at ten this morning, but we only got in an hour or two ago."

The words were spoken without any foreign accent. Not only that: the tone was that of a refined Englishman. The fact gave satisfaction to Dr. Brabazon, who liked his pupils to be surrounded by good associations in all ways.

"Will you kindly tell me where I am to lodge?"

"Here, for a few days," said Dr. Brabazon. "As you were so complete a stranger, we thought you might like best to fix, yourself, upon lodgings. It is some years since you were in England, I think?"

"Nine years, sir."

"Nine years! Dear me! You have not many friends, then, I conclude, in your own country?"

Mr. Henry shook his head. "Few men are much more friendless than I am."

And the accent sounded friendless. There was something singularly attractive about this young man, in his gentle manner, his sensitive, shrinking shyness (for so it seemed), his sad, earnest brown eyes: and Dr. Brabazon's heart went out to him.

"You shall be shown your room, Mr. Henry," he said, "and then my daughter will give you some tea."

Later, Dr. Brabazon took him through the passages, on either side of which were rooms appropriated to particular studies, to the lofty hall, which was the chief school-room. A long room, with high windows on one side of it; the masters' desks in the angles of the room, and the long desks of the boys ranged against the sides. Dr. Brabazon's place was at the upper end, in the centre, facing the door, so that he commanded full view of all. Three masters lived in the house: the Reverend Mr. Jebb; Mr. Baker, the mathematical master; and Mr. Long, who took English generally, some of the natural sciences, and was supposed to superintend the boys out of hours. Mr. Jebb assisted Dr. Brabazon with the classics, and the latter took divinity. The other masters lived out. Dr. Brabazon introduced Mr. Henry to the clergyman and Mr. Long, and left him. Mr. Baker was not there.

The boys were renewing private friendships, telling tales of their holidays, hatching mischief for the coming term, criticising a few new-comers, and making a continuous hum. Their ages varied from ten to eighteen. On the whole, they seemed a rather superior set; for one thing, the terms were high, and that tended to keep the school select.

A sudden "Hiss-is-s," from the lips of Master Richard Loftus — or, as he was called in the school, Loftus minor — suppressed almost before it was heard, caused the group, of whom he was the centre, to look round.

"What is it, Dick?"

"Don't you see?" whispered Dick. "A nice amount of brass *he* must have, to show himself here again! Look at him, Onions; he looks more of a sneak than ever."

Onions lifted his eyebrows in his cool, but not ill-natured manner, as he surveyed the boy coming in. It was Edwin Lamb. His hair was of a glowing red, and his eyes had a kind of look as if they were not quite straight. Not for that did the boys dislike him, but because he had been found out in one or two dishonourable falsehoods: they brought it out short, "lies:" and was more than suspected of carrying private tales to Mr. Long. They called him "Le Mouton," "the Sneak," "Jackal," and other pleasant names. In short, there was a great amount of prejudice against him; more, perhaps, than the boy really deserved.

"Don't let any fellow speak to him! Don't let's——"

"Hold your tongue, Loftus minor. Allow bygones to be bygones. Time enough to turn against Lamb when you find fresh cause."

The rebuke, spoken civilly, came from Raymond Trace, who happened to overhear the words, and who never willingly offended anybody. Not that Trace was a favourite in the college; none of them liked him much, without being able to explain why. Dick Loftus turned with a quick, scared look, wondering whether Mr. Trace had also overheard a private colloquy he had been holding with a very chosen companion, Tom Smart. He did not answer Trace; as a rule the younger fellows had to obey the seniors.

At the sound of a bell, they began to hurry into a

small place, called the robing-closet, where their caps and gowns were kept. Putting on the gowns, and carrying the caps in their hands, they went to the call-room, waiting there to be marshalled into chapel. The caps, or trenchers, were used always; the gowns were worn in chapel and on what might be called state occasions, such as the examinations, also at lectures; sometimes they wore them out of doors, but not in school ordinarily, nor when they were at play. The masters' gowns, worn always in public, were of the same make as the boys': the caps were all alike in form, but the masters' were distinguished by a scarlet tassel in addition to the black one.

It was a small pretty chapel, the size of an ordinary room, the lectern slightly raised, and a standing desk for the lessons. The senior boys, meaning those of the first desk, read the lessons in turn. Part of the service was intoned, part read, part sung. Mr. Long, a good musician, took the organ to-night, and Dr. Brabazon, as was mostly usual, was in the reading desk. Mr. Loftus, as first senior present, left his place to read the first lesson. He read very well; clearly and distinctly, though somewhat coldly. Raymond Trace read the second lesson. His voice was subdued; its accent to some ears almost offensively humble — offensive because there was a ring in it of affected piety that could never be genuine. No such voice as that, no such assumption of humility, ever yet proceeded from a truly honest nature.

"That young man is a hypocrite!" involuntarily thought the new master, Mr. Henry. "Heaven forgive me!" he added, a moment after; "what am I that I should judge another?"

He did not know the name of the reader; he did
not know yet the name of any one of the boys surrounding him; but he had been studying their faces,
as it was natural he should do, considering that he
had come to live amongst them.   Instinct led Mr.
Henry to study the human countenance — to be
studying it always, unconsciously; and he was rarely
deceived in it.

On ordinary evenings the supper was served immediately after they came out of chapel; but on this,
when neither things nor scholars had shaken down into
their routine, there appeared no signs of its being
ready.   Several of the fellows were expected yet, and
the discipline, obtaining customarily, had not com-
menced.   Two of them, at any rate, took some undue
advantage of it.   Going out after chapel was against
the rules; perhaps Mr. Dick Loftus considered he
might, on this night, break it with impunity.

Hanging up his gown in its place, he went stealing
along the passages again towards the chapel, carrying
a brown paper parcel, which he tried to cover with
his trencher, lest curious eyes might be about.   His
friend Smart went stealing after him, and they turned
off through a door into an open quadrangle; on three
sides of which ran a covered gallery or passage, with
a brick floor and Gothic pillars, called the cloisters;
on the fourth side were the great gates that formed
the scholars' entrance. A truck of luggage was coming
in from the railway station; Dick and the other slipped
past it.

Now what had these two got in that parcel, guarded
with so much care? Mischief, you may be sure. It
was the parcel that Loftus major had picked up on his

arrival, and taken off to his room; and it contained nothing less than a pair of pistols. Mr. Loftus had recently purchased these pistols; he thought their acquisition one of the greatest feathers his cap could display, and he had not resisted the temptation to take them with him to show his compeers. Of course some secrecy had to be observed, for Dr. Brabazon would as soon have allowed him to bring a live bear into the college, and the case they lay in had been well wrapped in wadding, and otherwise disguised. Loftus minor, Mr. Dick, who was burning to finger these pistols, and had not yet obtained the ghost of a chance to do it, thought he saw it on this evening. He found out where his brother had placed them, brought them down, hid them while he went into chapel, made a confidant of Smart, and the two stole out with them. They had no particular motive in taking the pistols abroad, except that there was little opportunity for a private leisurely view indoors.

Crossing the wide road, they plunged into what was called the plantation: a large plot of ground intersected with young trees; or, rather, trees that had been young, for they were getting of a sheltering size now. A cricket-field lay to the left, beyond the chapel end-window; the station was in the distance; houses were dotted about; none, however, in the immediate vicinity. It was a beautiful moonlight night; and the boys chose an open place amid the trees, where there was a bench, and the beams were bright. There they undid the parcel, and touched the spring of the box.

Bright beams beyond doubt; but not so bright to the four admiring eyes as the pistol barrels. Never had such pistols been seen, although Loftus major —

as Mr. Dick communicated in open-hearted confidence
— had only given an old song for them at some pawnbroker's. They lifted, they touched, they stroked,
they cocked, they took aim. The caps were on; and
it was only by an amount of incomprehensible self-
denial, that they did not fire. But that might have
betrayed all; and Dick Loftus, though daring a great
deal in a harmless sort of way, did not dare that.
Dick fenced with the one, Smart with the other; they
were like a couple of little children, playing with
make-believe swords.

All in a moment, Dick caught sight of a trencher,
poking itself gingerly through the trees, and regarding
them. A master's trencher, too, for the two tassels,
one over the other, were distinctly visible. With a
smothered cry of warning to his companion, Dick
vanished, carrying his pistol with him. Smart, nearly
beside himself with terror when he comprehended the
situation, vanished in Dick's wake; but in his confusion
he dropped his pistol into the sheet of wadding on the
bench.

The coast clear, the spy (an unintentional spy, it
must be confessed) came forward. It was not a master;
it was one of the boys, who, in coming out, had un-
wittingly caught up a master's trencher in mistake for
his own. He took up the pistol and examined it —
he turned over the wadding on which it lay, and the
brown paper, and the case; scrutinizing all carefully in
the moonlight, and coming on a written direction at last.

"Oh, indeed! 'Albert Loftus, Esquire'! What
does he want with pistols? Is he thinking to shoot
any one of the fellows? And Mr. Dick has stolen a
march on him, and brought them out, has he?"

He took up the pistol, looked at it again, critically held it for a minute before him; then took aim, and fired it off. The answer to this was a human cry and a fall; the charge — shot or bullet, which ever it might be — had taken effect on some one but a few paces off. The culprit remained perfectly still for one minute, possibly scared at what he had done; he then quietly put the pistol on the case, crept off on tiptoe amidst the trees, and — came face to face with the new master, Mr. Henry.

Mr. Henry was on his road to the station to order his luggage to the college. He had left it on his arrival, not knowing where he was to lodge. Dr. Brabazon had offered to send a servant, but Mr. Henry coveted the walk in the cool, lovely night; he and his head were alike feverish from the effects of the sea voyage; so they directed him through the plantation, as being the nearest way.

Face to face. But only one glimpse did Mr. Henry catch of the meeting face, for the boy's hand was suddenly raised to cover it, even while he took flight. A moan or two, and then a loud shout for assistance — as if the sufferer, on second thoughts, deemed it would be better to shout than to groan — guided Mr. Henry to the spot. He was lying close by, in an intersecting path of the plantation, a boy of some sixteen years, whose trencher showed he belonged to Orville College.

"Who is it?" asked Mr. Henry.

"Talbot," shortly answered the boy. "I say, though, who are you? How came you to shoot me?"

"It was not I who did it. I heard the shot as I came up. Where are you hurt?"

2*

"In my leg, I think. I can't move it. I only got in by this train, for I missed the one in the afternoon, and was running through here, full pelt, when somebody takes a shot at me! Cool, I must say!"

The master raised him, but the right leg seemed nearly helpless, so he laid him down again, and ran to the college for assistance. But as Mr. Henry was turning away, the white wadding on the bench caught his eye, and he found the pistol and its accessories. These he carried with him.

Dick Loftus, hiding in the distant trees, could bear the suspense no longer. Something was wrong; some untoward event had occurred; and he came forward in disregard of Smart's prayers and entreaties. Dick was of an open honourable nature, in spite of his pursuit of mischief and his impulsive thoughtlessness: he never hesitated to take his escapades on himself, when real necessity arose.

"I'm blest! Why, it's the earl!" he shouted out. "Smart! Smart! come here. It's the Earl of Shrewsbury!"

"Is that you, Dick?" exclaimed the wounded boy, looking up as Dick bent over him in the moonlight. "Did you do it?"

"No, I didn't," said Dick. "I say, old fellow, is it much! I wish his pistols had been buried before I'd brought 'em out!"

"How was it all? Whose are the pistols?" questioned Talbot. And Mr. Dick, in an ecstasy of contrition, but vowing vengeance against the shooter, whoever it might be, entered on his explanation. To do him justice, he gave it without the least reserve. And Tom Smart, shivering amid the thickest trees, at

a safe distance, daring to stir neither one way nor the
other, lest he should be seen, and who had not heard
the salutation, wondered whether Dick would keep his
word, and not mention his name in connection with
the calamity.

A fine commotion arose in the college when Mr.
Henry got back with the news. One of the gentlemen
had been shot in the plantation! — shot by a fellow
student! It was incredible. Mr. Henry, breaking away
from the throng, quietly gave Dr. Brabazon an account
of the whole, as far as he was cognizant of it: how
that he had heard a shot quite close to him, followed
by a cry, and had caught a glimpse of a youth stealing
away. He gave no clue as to who the youth was;
apparently did not know; and of course could not
know positively that it was he who had fired; he recognized him as belonging to Orville College by the
cap. It was but a hurried explanation; there was no
time to waste in question and answer; Talbot must be
seen to.

He was brought in on a hurdle, and a surgeon
summoned. On the first day of this boy's entrance at
the college, when Dr. Brabazon, the roll before him,
asked his name, the answer was, "James Talbot."
"James Talbot, Earl of Shrewsbury?" jokingly responded the doctor, in allusion to one noted in English history; and from that hour Talbot had gone by
no other name in the school. Of a good-natured,
generous disposition, he was ever ready to do a kind
action, and was liked immensely. Not that he had
much to be generous with in one sense: his father was
a banker's clerk; very poor; struggling with life; and
pinching himself in all ways to keep his son at Orville.

Not during the first confusion did a suspicion, that the offending pistol could have any connection with a certain brown paper treasure-parcel upstairs, penetrate to the brain of Loftus major: not until Dick's name arose into prominence. Up to his room stepped Mr. Loftus, six stairs at a stride, pulled open a drawer, essayed to lay his hands upon the parcel, and — found it was not there. He could not believe his own eyes; he stared, he felt, he stood in a mazed sort of bewilderment. Meddle with *his* things! that wretched Dick, who was nearly three years his junior, and held at arm's-length accordingly! — with his new pistols, that were only brought en cachette! When Loftus major recovered his equanimity sufficiently to think, he came to the conclusion that hanging would be too good for Dick.

CHAPTER II.

The New Boy.

THE Rev. Mr. Jebb and the new German master stood over the bed of James Talbot. The surgeon had been busy; he had extracted the shots from the leg, and pronounced the injury to be not material. Talbot must be kept quiet, he said, both in mind and body.

"It's a very strange affair," murmured the clergyman into Mr. Henry's ear. "Dr. Brabazon's opinion is, that it must have been Loftus minor, after all, who fired off the pistol."

"It never was, then," unceremoniously spoke up the patient. "When Dick Loftus says he didn't do a thing, I know he *didn't.*"

"You are not to talk, Talbot," interrupted Mr.
Jebb: and the two gentlemen moved away from the
bed. Mr. Henry began to ask who Dick Loftus was.

"He is brother to the second senior of the school,"
was the clergyman's reply. "You may have remarked
Loftus major in chapel, from the circumstance that he
read the lesson."

"Which of the lessons? I noticed the readers of
both."

"The first lesson. The second was read by Trace."

"Trace?" echoed Mr. Henry.

"You are thinking it an uncommon name. Raymond Trace; he is cousin to the Loftus boys. There's
quite a romance attaching to their history," proceeded
the clergyman, who was a bit of a gossip, and he
dropped his voice as he spoke. "The two fathers were
in partnership in Liverpool, stock and share brokers,
quite a first-class house, and much respected. Unfortunately they took in a partner, and before two
years were over he ruined them. He issued false
shares, put forged bills in circulation —I hardly know
what he did not do. They were quite ruined; at least,
it was ruin compared to what their former wealth had
been. The house was broken up; all its debts were
paid; and Mr. Loftus retired to the Isle of Wight upon
a small private property. He had lived there previously, never having taken a very practical part in
the business. The other partner, Mr. Trace, went
abroad, hoping to carve out a second fortune. I hear
he is doing it."

"And these are the sons?" observed the German
master, after a pause.

"These are the sons. Mr. Loftus has several

children, Mr. Trace only this one. Mrs. Loftus and
Mrs. Trace were sisters. Their brother, Sir Simon
Orville, a retired city man, lives here close to the
college; he is some distant relative of its founder. The
three boys were placed at it two years ago, and it is
thought Sir Simon pays for them. They spend their
vacations generally at his house: Trace always does.
He has no other home in England: Mrs. Trace is
dead."

The injured boy stirred uneasily, and Mr. Henry
hastened to him. "Do you feel much pain?" he
kindly asked.

"Rather sharpish for that," was the answer. "I
say, sir, you — you don't think I shall die?" and the
bright brown eyes looked wistfully up at the master's,
as the sudden anxious question was whispered. "It's
my mother I am thinking of," added Talbot, by way
of excuse.

"So far as I believe, there's no danger," replied
Mr. Henry, bending down to him and pushing the
hair off his hot brow. "Only put yourself trustingly
into God's care, my boy — have you learnt to do it?
— and rely upon it, all shall be for the best."

Miss Brabazon and a nurse came into the room
and the gentlemen prepared to leave it. Mr. Henry
went first. Talbot put out his hand and detained Mr.
Jebb.

"I say, sir, who *is* that?"

"The new foreign master. Do you keep yourself
tranquil, Talbot."

With the morning came the discipline of school
rules. Talbot was going on quite favourably, and all
outward excitement had subsided. The breakfast hour

was half-past seven; from eight to a quarter-past the pupils from the masters' houses arrived, also those who lived altogether out of bounds, with their friends or in lodgings; slightingly called by the college, these latter, "outsiders." During this quarter of an hour the roll was called, and the boys did what they pleased: it was recreation with them. At a quarter-past eight the chapel bell called all to service.

The boys stood in groups this morning in the quadrangle, not availing themselves of their liberty to be noisy during this quarter of an hour, but discussing in an undertone the startling events of the previous night. Dick Loftus had openly avowed the whole; and somebody, not Dick, had contrived to betray Mr. Smart's share in it. Dick protested that whoever had peered at them was a master: he judged by the cap. It appeared equally certain that it could not have been a master: the only masters arrived were Mr. Jebb and Mr. Long, and they, at this very self-same hour, had been with Dr. Brabazon in his private study. But it was easy for any one of the senior boys to have taken up a master's trencher by mistake, or to have gone out in it wilfully to mislead. Had the boy, whoever it was, purposely shot Talbot? The opinion, rejected at first, was gaining ground now; led to, possibly, by the appropriation of the master's cap. Altogether it was a very unpleasant affair, enshrouded in some mystery.

William Gall was there this morning, the senior of the school; a slight, short young man, the age of Loftus major, with an undoubted ugly face, but an honest one, and dark hair. There was not much good feeling existing between Gall and Loftus, as was well known, but it had never broken into an open explosion. Gall despised Loftus for his pride and his fopperies, his assumption of superiority and condescension; and Loftus looked down on Gall and his family as vulgar city people. The Galls lived at Orville Green, but the son was an in-door scholar. Mr. Gall was in some mysterious trade that had to do with tallow. There was plenty of money; but Loftus thought, on the whole, that it was out of the order of right things for the son of a tallow-man to be head of the college and senior over *him*.

Three or four new scholars came straggling in during this quarter of an hour, and they attracted the usual amount of attention and quizzing. One of them was a tall, agile, upright boy of sixteen, or rather more, with a handsome, open countenance, dark chestnut hair, and bright grey eyes. He stood looking about, as if uncertain where to go. Mr. Long went up to him.

"Are you belonging to the college? — a new student?"

"Yes."

"If you pass through that side of the cloisters and turn to the left, you will find the call-room. Mr. Baker is there with the roll, inscribing the new names as they come in, and he will add yours. What is your name?"

"Paradyne."

There was a free, frank sound in the voice, though the words spoken had been but two; and the boy lifted his hat (he would not get his cap and gown for a day or two) with somewhat of foreign courtesy as he turned away to the cloister. Mr. Henry, who had heard the name, hastened after him and overtook him in the cloister passage.

"You are George Paradyne?"

"Yes. And you are ——"

"Mr. Henry."

Their hands were locked together; they gazed into each other's face. "I don't think I should have known you," said the boy.

"No? I should have known you anywhere. It is the same face, not changed; but you have grown from a little boy into a great one."

"*Your* face is changed. It is thinner and paler, and — somehow ——"

"Well?" said Mr. Henry, for the sentence had come to a stop midway. "Speak out."

"It is a sadder sort of face than it used to be. Are you quite well?"

"Yes, I am well. I don't know that I am strong. Good-bye for now," hastily added Mr. Henry. "Mr. Long has told you where to go."

The boy continued his way up the cloister, and another ran up to Mr. Henry — a second-desk boy named Powell.

"I say, sir, do you know that new fellow?"

"I used to know him," replied Mr. Henry. "But I have not seen him for several years."

"Lamb says he thinks he is an outsider. I like the look of him. Where did you know him, Mr. Henry?"

"At the Heidelberg University. He was a young pupil there, when I was a junior master."

Mr. Powell's face grew considerably longer. "At the Heidelberg University! Does he speak German?"

"He used to speak it perfectly. I dare say he does still."

"That's blue, though," was the rejoinder. "I'm going in for the German prize: but who can stand against a fellow who has been in Germany? He's sure to be at our desk. What's his name, sir?"

"You will learn it in good time, no doubt," called back Mr. Henry, who was hastening away as if he were in a hurry. And Mr. Powell vaulted over the open cloister wall into the quadrangle: which was against rules.

A few moments, and the chapel-bell rang out. The boys got their caps and gowns, and went into the call-room. Dr. Brabazon came up in his surplice and hood, and they followed him into chapel.

Possibly it was because Mr. Trace had no duty to perform — for Gall and Loftus read the lessons — that his sight recreated itself with scanning the new scholars. Not so much the whole of them, and there were nine or ten, as one — George Paradyne. It was not a stare; Trace never stared; his eyes were drawn together so closely that even Paradyne himself could not have known he was being looked at; but nevertheless, so intent was Trace's gaze, so absorbed was he in the new face, that at the end of the *Te Deum* he quite forgot to sit down, and remained standing, to the amusement of his friends.

"I wonder if it *is*," spoke Trace to himself, as they left the chapel. And he inquired of two or three what that new fellow's name was, but could not learn it.

"He's some crony of the new master's," spoke Powell; "I saw them shaking hands like mad. It'll be an awful shame for him to be put in our class, if he *is* up in German."

Trace had not waited to hear the conclusion; the boys were hastening to take their places in school.

On this morning, until their state of advancement could be ascertained, the fresh boys were ordered to a bench opposite the first desk. Trace, who sat next to Loftus, directed his attention to this new boy.

"Do you recognise him, Bertie?" he asked in a whisper.

"Recognise him? no," drawled Mr. Loftus, as if it were entirely beneath him to recognise any new fellow. And he could think of nothing but his pistols. Which Dr. Brabazon had taken possession of.

"Look at his face well," continued Trace. "Can you see no likeness to one you once knew?"

"Not I." And this time Mr. Loftus did not speak until he had taken a good look at the boy. "Don't know the face from Adam."

"Well, perhaps I am mistaken," mused Trace. "It's a long while since I saw the other."

But, nevertheless, in spite of this conclusion, Trace could not keep his eyes off the face, and his studies suffered. The boy went up to Dr. Brabazon for examination, as it was usual for a new scholar to do; and Trace's ears were bent to catch the sound of the voice, if haply it might bear recognition for his memory. The head master found the boy thoroughly well advanced in his studies, and a suspicion arose in the school that he would be placed at the first desk. Loftus heard somebody say it, and elevated his eyebrows in displeasure. When the school rose, Trace went up to Mr. Baker.

"I beg your pardon, sir; would you allow me to look for one minute at the roll?"

"At the roll? — what for?" returned Mr. Baker, who was a little man with a bald head.

"I think I know one of the new boys, sir. I want to see his name."

There was no rule against showing the roll, and Mr. Baker took it out of his desk. Trace ran his finger down the new names — which were entered at the end until their places should be allotted — and it halted at one.

"*George Paradyne!*" he mentally read. "Thank you, sir," he said aloud, with the quiet civility characteristic of him: and Mr. Baker locked up the roll again.

For once in his college life, a burning spot of emotion might have been seen on Raymond Trace's cheek. A foul injury, as he regarded it, had been done to his family and fortune by the father of George Paradyne; and he deemed that the son had no more right to be receiving his education with honest men's sons, as their equal and associate, than darkness has to be made hail-fellow-well-met with light. He went in search of Loftus. Loftus was leaning over the open wall, his legs in the cloisters, his head in the quadrangle, and his arm round a huge pillar, ruminating bitterly on the wrongs dealt out to himself, on Dick's wickedness, and the ignominy of possessing pistols that one can't get at.

"I thought I was not mistaken in the fellow," began Trace. "It is George Paradyne."

"Who?" cried Loftus, starting round, aroused by the name.

"George Paradyne: Paradyne's son."

"No! Do you mean that fellow you asked about? It can't be."

"It *is*. I knew him, I tell you; and I've been

looking at the name on the roll. Your memory must be a bad one, Loftus, not to have recognised the face also."

Loftus drew a deep breath, as if unable to take in the full sense of the words. But he never *displayed* much surprise at anything.

"I don't suppose I saw the fellow three times in my life," he presently said. "We did not live on the spot, as you did; and it is so long ago."

"What's to be done? He can't be allowed to stay here."

Loftus shrugged his shoulders, French fashion, having no answer at hand. "Brabazon is not aware of who he is, I suppose?"

"Impossible; or he'd never have admitted him. One can overlook some things in a fellow's antecedents; but *forgery* — that's rather too strong. If the rest of the college chose to tolerate him, you and I and Dick could not."

Mr. Loftus threw up his condemning nose at the latter addition. Dick, indeed! Dick seemed to be going in for something too bad on his own score, to be fastidious as to the society he kept.

"What's the matter?" inquired one of the first-class boys, Irby, coming up to them from the middle of the quadrangle, and leaning his arms on the cloister wall, to talk face to face.

"That new fellow, Paradyne — do you know which of them he is?" broke off Trace.

Irby nodded. "A good-looking chap, don't you mean? Well up in his classics."

"Well up in them by the help of stolen money, I suppose," spoke Trace, an angry light for a moment gleaming in his eye. "You have heard, Irby, of that dreadful business of ours at Liverpool, some four years ago, when Loftus & Trace, the best and richest and most respected firm in the town, were ruined through a man they had taken in as partner?"

"I've heard something of it," said Irby, wondering.

"This new fellow, Paradyne, is the man's son."

Irby gave a low whistle. "Let's hear the particulars, Trace."

And Trace proceeded to give them. Irby was a great friend of his, and there were no other ears in view. Loftus drew himself up against the pillar, and stood there with his arms folded, listening in silence; all of them unconscious that Mr. Henry was on the other side of the pillar, taking a sketch of the quadrangle and the door of the chapel.

You heard something of the tale, reader, from Mr. Jebb last night, and there's not much more to be told. Trace, speaking quietly, as he always did, enlarged upon the wrongs dealt out to his father and Mr. Loftus, by the man Paradyne. It was the most miserable business that ever came out to the world, he said, blighting all their prospects for life; never a rogue, so great, went unhung.

"And he had only been with them a couple of years," he wound up with; "only a couple of years! The marvel was, that he could have done so much mischief in so short a time—"

"The marvel was, that he could have done it at all without being detected," interposed Loftus, speaking for the first time.

"Yes," corrected Trace; "people could not understand how he contrived to hoodwink my father. But that came of over-confidence: he had such blind trust in Paradyne."

"Why did they take him in partner at all?" asked Irby.

"Ah, why indeed!" responded Trace, pushing his trencher up with a petulant jerk, as if the past transaction were a present and personal wrong. "But the business had grown too large for one head, and Mr. Loftus was almost a sleeping partner. Who was to suppose it would turn out so? If we could only foresee the end of things at the beginning!"

"Let it drop, Trace," said Loftus. "It's not so pleasant a thing to recall."

"The fellow called himself Captain Paradyne; he came introduced to them grandly," resumed Trace, in utter disregard of the interruption. "Of course he dropped the 'Captain' when he joined them."

"Was the man hung?" questioned Irby.

"Neither hung nor transported; he saved himself. On the evening of his first examination before the magistrates," continued Trace, "after he was put back in the cell, he took poison."

Irby's eyes grew round with awe. "What a wicked simpleton he must have been to do that! Poor fellow, though," he added, a feeling of compassion stealing over him, "I dare say he —"

"When you undertake to relate a history, gentlemen, you should confine yourselves to the truth. Mr. Paradyne did not take poison. He died of heart disease, brought on by excitement."

The interruption was Mr. Henry's. He quietly put his head round the pillar, and then came into full view, with his sketch-book and pencil.

"How do you know anything about it?" demanded Trace, recovering from his surprise.

"I do happen to know about it," was the calm answer. "The case was bad enough, as Heaven knew; but you need not make it worse."

"It was reported that he took poison," coldly persisted Trace.

"Only at the first moment. When he was found dead, people naturally leaped to that conclusion, and the newspapers published it as a fact. But on the inquest it was proved by the medical men that he had died from natural causes. I think," added Mr. Henry, in a dreamy kind of tone, "that that report arose in mercy."

The three boys stared at him questioningly.

"To his friends the business of itself was cruel enough — the discovery that he, whom they had so respected as the soul of honour, was unworthy," pursued the master. "Then followed the worse report of his self-destruction, and in that shock of horror the other was lost — was as nothing. But when the truth came to light on the following day — that he had not laid guilty hands on himself, but that God had taken him, — why, the revulsion of feeling, the thankfulness, was so great as to seem like a very boon from Heaven. It enabled them to bear the disgrace as a lesser evil: the blow had lost its sting."

"Did you know him?" questioned Trace.

"I knew him in Germany. And these particulars, when they occurred, were written over to me."

"Perhaps you respected him in Germany?" cynically added Trace, who could not speak or think of the unfortunate Captain Paradyne with his usual degree of equable temper.

"I never respected any one so much," avowed Mr. Henry, a scarlet spot of hectic arising in his pale cheeks.

Trace made no rejoinder. To contend was not his habit. It was impossible he could think worse of any one than of the unhappy man in question, and nothing had ever convinced Trace fully that the death was a natural one.

"He has been dead four years," gently suggested Mr. Henry, as if bespeaking their mercy for his memory. "As to his son, it must be a question for Dr. Brabazon of course whether or not he remains here; but I would ask you what he, the boy, has done, that you should visit the past upon him? Can you not imagine that the calamity itself is a sufficient blight on his life? Be generous, and do not proclaim him to the school."

"It would be more generous not to do it," candidly avowed Irby, who had a good-natured, ready tongue. "Of course it was not the boy's fault; we shall lose nothing by it."

"Lose!" repeated Mr. Henry. "If you only knew the gain! There's not a kind action that we ever do, but insures its own reward; there's not a word of ill-nature, a secret deed of malice, but comes home to us four-fold, sooner or later. Look out carefully as you go through life, and see whether I do not tell you truth."

"Young Paradyne is free for me," said Loftus, speaking up frankly. And Irby nodded his head in acquiescence.

3*

"Thank you greatly; 1 shall take it as a kindness shown myself," said Mr. Henry. He turned and looked at Trace.

"Of course, if Mr. Henry wishes the thing to be hushed up, and Dr. Brabazon to be left in ignorance ——"

"Stay," said the master, interrupting Trace's words. "You heard me say a moment ago that it must be a question for Dr. Brabazon whether or not Paradyne remains here. But I think that Dr. Brabazon would, in either event, counsel you not to denounce the boy publicly."

"I am not given to denounce my companions publicly; or privately either: as you perhaps will find when you are used to us," was Trace's rejoinder, delivered with civility. "If the doctor condones the past, why, let it be condoned; I can't say more. But the sooner the question is decided, the better."

"Undoubtedly."

Mr. Henry turned round with the last word, and applied himself to his drawing. Loftus and Irby strolled away, and Trace besought an interview with Dr. Brabazon. It was at once accorded; and he told him who Paradyne was. To do Trace justice, he spoke without prejudice; not alluding minutely to past facts, but simply saying that the new scholar, George Paradyne, was the son of the man who had committed all sorts of ill, and ruined his father and Mr. Loftus.

"And you and Loftus think you can't study with him!" observed the doctor, when he had listened, and asked a few questions.

"I did not say that, sir: it is for you to decide.

We shall get over the unpleasantness by degrees, no doubt, if he does stay on."

"Very well, Trace; I'll consider of it. Keep a strictly silent tongue about it in the college."

The interview did not last many minutes. Soon after its termination, an authoritative cry was heard down the cloisters for Loftus major.

"Here," shouted Loftus from the other end of the quadrangle.

"You are to go in to the Head Master."

Away went Loftus in his indolent fashion; he rarely hurried himself for anything. Dr. Brabazon met him at his study door: he put into his hands a parcel tied with string, and sealed at the ends with the doctor's seal.

"Your pistols, Loftus. I shall have something to say to you later, in regard to them and the calamity you have most unjustifiably been the means of causing. Take them back at once; and make my compliments to Sir Simon, and say I particularly wish to see him. Perhaps he will oblige me by coming over: to-day, if possible. You'll be back to dinner, if you put your best foot foremost."

Mr. Loftus flung on his gown and cap, and went away with the parcel in an access of private rage. It was so mortifying! it was the very acme of humiliation! — a dog with a burnt tail could feel jolly, in comparison. Some of the middle-school boys, leaping over the road from the plantation, came right upon him. That incorrigible Dick was one of them, and he recognized the parcel.

"It's the pistols," proclaimed Dick. "Brabazon has turned them out. I say, Bertie, though, that's not so bad; we had bets that he'd confiscate them."

"A pity but he could confiscate you," was the scornful retort thrown back.

Dick laughed. The throng echoed it. But Mr. Loftus went on his way, and made no further sign; his fine figure drawn to its full height, and his nose held in the air.

CHAPTER III.

Hard and Obstinate as Nails.

DR. BRABAZON sat at his desk-table, birch in hand. Not often were the whole of the boys assembled in hall as on this afternoon; there were smaller rooms appropriated to particular branches of study. A huge birch, apparently made out of ten besoms. The stump rested on the table, the pointed end with its tickling twigs, tapered aloft in the air. This formidable weapon, meant to inspire wholesome awe, had never been used within memory. Very rarely was it taken from its receptacle to be held *in terrorem*, as now, over the different desks, running down the side walls of the long room, and along the end of it.

The shooting of James Talbot the previous night in the plantation: was it an accident, or was it done of deliberation? This was what the Head Master wanted to get at: and he very particularly wanted to get at the gentleman who did it. Dick Loftus had made a clean breast of it, offhand; for it was in Dick's nature so to do. But, in spite of all the questioning; private, individual, and collective; — in spite of putting the school upon its honour; — in spite of the offered promise that the boy, if an accident, should be held harmless, nobody came forward to confess; the whole lot remained, as the Doctor in his vexation expressed it, "hard and obstinate as nails." So then the birch was got out.

"Gentlemen, I feel sure it was a pure accident, and I could extend my free forgiveness to the offender if he will only come forward in honour and avow himself. Talbot is going on well; will be amidst us again, I hope, in a few days; there's no earthly reason for his refusing to acknowledge himself. Mrs. Talbot, sitting now with her son, says she forgives him heartily. She is a Christian woman, gentlemen, and she is sorry for the boy, instead of angry with him, because she knows how sorry he must be himself for this. 'Accidents and moments of thoughtlessness happen to us all,' she has just remarked to me: and so they do. Come! I hope there's some honour left amidst us yet."

The appeal elicited no response. And yet, that one of the boys present had been guilty, there could be little doubt; or that he had gone out in a master's cap by accident or design. In the confusion of the news the previous night, when a rush was made to the robing closet, the caps of the two masters, then arrived, were found hanging there. Upon the boys being mustered, all who were known to have returned to school answered to their names. There was no confusion, no sign of guilt observable in any one of the responders: nevertheless, the offender must have made a run, as if for his life, sneaked in, replaced the cap, and mingled with the others.

"*Won't* you speak?" reiterated the Doctor, casting his eyes around in anger.

But not one answered.

Up went the birch, and came down again on its

hard end. Dr. Brabazon was by no means a choleric man; but he could be so when greatly provoked.

"Mr. Henry—no, don't rise, don't quit your place—of what height was the boy you saw running away?"

The Doctor's voice — a sonorous voice at all times — went rolling down the spacious room to the opposite corner, where Mr. Henry sat behind his desk. The latter hesitated in his reply, and the boys turned their eyes from the Head Master to him.

"I cannot say positively, sir," was the foreign master's answer. "It was so momentary a glimpse that I caught."

"Yet you met him — as I am given to understand — face to face!"

"I did; but he glided aside at once amidst the trees. He was of a good height."

"Tall enough for a senior boy?"

"Yes, certainly: I think so."

The birch agitated itself gently, as if the Doctor's hand shook a little, and he looked full at the first desk, regarding those seated at it in individual turn.

"I thought I could have *trusted* you all; I deemed there was not one of you that I might not have relied upon. Gall, did you do this? I ask you chiefly for form's sake, for you had not come back to college. Did you fire, by accident or design, this pistol off in the plantation last night?"

"No, sir, I did not," replied Gall, slightly rising in his place to answer.

"Did you, Loftus major?"

The exceeding satire of the question, as addressed to him, the wronged owner of the abstracted weapon, nearly struck Loftus major dumb.

"Of course I did not, sir," he said, after a pause.

"Did you go out of college after prayers?"

"No."

"Trace, did you go out of college after prayers, and fire off this pistol?"

"No, sir." And Trace's usual civility of tone was marked by a dash of remonstrance at being asked. Suspect him, Mr. Trace, the model fellow of the school! What next?

"Irby, did you?"

"I, sir! No, sir. It wasn't me, sir."

"Fullarton, did you?"

"I did not get back until this morning, sir."

"True. Brown major, did you do it?"

Brown Major, a simple fellow in most things, but with a rare capacity for Latin and Greek, opened his eyes in pure wonder. "Please, sir, I never fired off a pistol in my life, sir. I shouldn't know how to do it, sir."

And so on. Not a boy at the first desk acknowledged it; and they numbered twelve. The Doctor glanced at the second desk; some tall boys were there; but he said no more. Perhaps he thought suspicion did not lie with them; perhaps he would not afford them opportunity of telling a falsehood.

"It seems, then, I am not to be told. Well," — and he turned particularly to the seniors — "I must believe that some mystery attaches to this affair, and that not one of you is guilty. I will trust you still, as I have ever done: only — do not let it come to my knowledge later that my trust is a mistaken one."

He flung up the lower compartment of his table, put in the birch, and shut it down with a bang. An uncomfortable feeling was on the Head Master that day.

A thirteenth boy had been added to the first desk, in George Paradyne. Mr. Baker had directed him to take his place at it after morning school, in accordance with some words let fall by the Head Master, of the boy's proficiency. The first desk was a very exclusive desk, not to be invaded lightly by a new-comer, and the decision, an unusual one, did not find favour. Paradyne was greeted with a stare of surprise, and the desk turned its back upon him.

The afternoon studies proceeded as on other afternoons; but neither masters nor boys felt at ease. Trace, especially, was in a state of inward commotion, calm as he appeared outwardly. He supposed that Dr. Brabazon had decided to retain Paradyne in the college, and he resented it utterly. Mr. Trace had also one or two private matters of his own troubling him, that it would not be convenient to speak of.

Loftus, as you perceive, was back in his place. He had walked on to his uncle's before dinner, when despatched by the Head Master, carrying the banished pistols in all the ignominy of the position. Sir Simon Orville's residence was about half a mile from the college. Pond Place it was called; an appellation that was supposed to have originated from a large pond in the vicinity, and was excessively distasteful to Mr. Loftus. A lovely spot, whatever it might be called, with the brightest and rarest flowers clustering on the green slope before the low white house. Sir Simon happened to be tending some of these flowers, as it was his delight to do, when Loftus entered, and that young gentleman was a little disconcerted at the encounter.

In his present frame of mind, he really did not want the additional humiliation of having to explain to his uncle.

"Halloa!" cried Sir Simon, in surprise. "What brings you here?"

He was a little round man, with a red, kind face, shaped not unlike the head of a codfish, and light hair that stuck up in a high point above his forehead: one of the most unpretending, outspeaking men ever known, who could not conceal that he had been "born nobody," imperfectly educated, and had made his fortune laboriously and honestly by the work of his hands. Now and then he burst out with these revelations before the schoolboys, to whom he was fond of declaring his sentiments, to the intense chagrin of Loftus major and the dancing delight of Dick. Sir Simon, an old bachelor, was very kind and good, hospitable to everybody, and making much of his nephews. He was fond of Albert Loftus, distinguishing the really good qualities of the boy's nature, though ridiculing his pride and self-assumption. "He'll get it taken out of him," Sir Simon would say: and to do the knight justice, he spared no opportunity of helping on the process of extermination.

Twitching at his grey garden coat, which caught, with the suddenness of his turning, in a beautiful shrub that bore white flowers, Sir Simon looked in his nephew's face: not quite so lofty a face as usual.

"What's the matter, Bertie? What's in that parcel?"

So Bertie Loftus had to explain: he had taken a brace of pistols to school, and the Doctor had despatched them back again. Sir Simon enjoyed the information immensely; that is the "despatching back" portion of it. He knew very little about pistols himself; could not remember, like Brown major, to have handled one in his life; and regarded them rather in the light of a dangerous animal that you were never sure of.

"I should have buried them in the ground, had I been the Doctor, instead of giving them back to you. You'll come to some mischief, Mr. Albert, if you meddle with edged tools."

"I'd as soon he had buried them, as sent me back with them in the face of the school," avowed Loftus, in his subdued spirit. Very subdued just now, for there was more behind. Too honourable not to tell the whole, he went on to disclose the calamity that the pistols had caused. Sir Simon was horrorstruck.

"*Albert!* You have shot a boy?"

"It was that miserable Dick," returned Loftus, looking as chapfallen as it was possible for him, with his naturally proud face, to look. "I'm very sorry, of course; I'd rather have been shot myself. But it was not my fault, and Dick ought to be punished."

"No; you ought to be punished for taking the things to school," rebuked Sir Simon. "It would be punishment enough for my whole life, sir, if I had been the means of putting a fellow-creature's life in danger. Here, stop! Where are you going now?"

"To put the pistols away," answered Loftus, who was turning to the house.

"Are they loaded?"

"No, sir; not now."

"I'd not permit a loaded pistol to come inside my house, look you, Albert. You'll shoot yourself, sir; that's what you'll do. And it's poor Talbot, is it? I knew his father when I lived in Bermondsey."

Away went Loftus, feeling no security that the
pistols were not going to be confiscated here. He
locked them up in the room he occupied when staying
at his uncle's, and came forth again directly, de-
livering the Head Master's message as he passed Sir
Simon.

"Very well; I'll come, tell Dr. Brabazon. I suppose he is going to complain of this underhanded act
of yours."

Mr. Loftus supposed so too: had supposed nothing
else since the message was given him.

"Here; stop a bit; don't stride off like that. I suppose you must *eat*, though you have done your best to
kill a boy. Will you have some dinner? There's a
beautiful couple of ducks."

"I can't stay, Uncle Simon: the Head Master
ordered me back at once. Thank you all the same."

Sir Simon nodded, and Bertie set off back again;
leaving Pond Place behind him, and the cherished
pistols that had come altogether to grief.

Sir Simon Orville knew the hours at the college,
and he timed his visit so as to catch Dr. Brabazon at
the rising of afternoon school. The Doctor took him
into his study: a pleasant room, with a large bay window at the back of the house, partially overlooking the
boys' playground, with its gymnastic poles. The middle
compartment of the window opened to the ground,
French fashion.

Sir Simon spoke at once of the unhappy accident
that his nephews had been the means of causing; asking what he could do, how he could help the poor boy,
and insisting that all charges should be made his. He
then found it was not on that business Dr. Brabazon

had sent for him, but on the other annoying matter relating to George Paradyne. The doctor stated the
circumstances to him: that one of the new scholars,
entered that day, had been recognized by Trace to be
the son of the defaulting man, Paradyne.

"It vexed me greatly," observed the master, when
he had concluded his recital. "Somehow the term seems
to have begun ungraciously. I suppose there's no doubt
that the boy is the same?"

"I daresay not," replied Sir Simon, standing up by
the window. "Raymond ought to know him."

"Ay. Well, it is a very vexatious matter, and
one difficult to deal with. Just at first, while Trace
was speaking, I thought there could be only one course
— that of putting Paradyne away. But the cruel injustice of this on the boy struck me immediately, and
I could not help asking myself why we should visit on
children the sins of their fathers, any more than —
than ——" Dr. Brabazon seemed to hesitate strangely,
and came to a long pause — "any more than we visit
the sins of children on their parents."

Sir Simon brought down his stick with a couple of
thumps. It was a thick stick of carved walnut-wood,
that he was rarely seen without, and he had a habit
of enforcing his arguments with it in this manner.
Dr. Brabazon understood this as meant to enforce his.

"And so I decided to do nothing until I had seen
you. I would not have assigned him his place in the
school, but Mr. Baker did so before I could stop it.
But for your nephews being here, I should not think
of taking notice of the matter; I should let the boy
remain on. As it is, I must leave it to you, Sir Simon.
If you consider he ought not to be in the same establish-

ment as your nephews — their companion and associate — I'll put him away. Or, if you think it would be very objectionable to themselves ——"

"Objectionable to them!" cried Sir Simon, bringing down his stick again in wrath. "I can only tell you this, doctor, that if my nephews were mean enough and illnatured enough to carry out those old scores upon the boy, I'd disown 'em."

"Trace, I am sure, will not like the boy to stay, though he may silently put up with it. I saw that."

"Trace has got his silent crotchets just as much as anybody else," cried Sir Simon, a shade of deeper anger in his tone. "I'll talk to him; I'll talk to the three. Treat Paradyne as you do the rest, Dr. Brabazon; I would ask it of you as a personal favour. *I* turn the boy away! I've just as much right to do it as he has to turn me out of Pond Place. Deprive the lad of an education; of the means by which he'll have to make his bread? No; a hundred times over, no," concluded Sir Simon, in an explosive tone, the stick descending again.

"Very well; he shall stay. And if circumstances force me to put him away later, — that is, if the facts become known to the school, and the boy's life is thereby rendered unhappy, why — but time enough to talk of that," broke off the speaker. "It might happen, however, Sir Simon; and there's no knowing how soon."

Sir Simon saw that it might. "Who knows of it?" he asked.

"Your two nephews and John Irby. I have strictly charged them, on their honour, not to speak of this: I called them in before afternoon school. Dick does not appear to have heard the name yet: but I shall speak to him. It is unfortunate the name should be so peculiar — Paradyne."

Sir Simon nodded. "What an odd thing it is the boy should have come to this particular school," he exclaimed. "Is he one of your boarders?"

"No; he is an out-pupil; not in any master's house at all. About five weeks ago," pursued the head master, in explanation, "I received a letter from the country, from a l dy signing herself Paradyne — I remember thinking it an uncommon name at the time — asking if there was a vacancy in the college for a well-advanced out-door pupil, and inquiring the terms. There happened to be a vacancy, and I said so, and sent the terms; in a few days she wrote again, saying her son would enter. She has come up to live here. I asked Paradyne this morning where he was going to live, and he said close by, with his mother."

"They never much liked her, I remember," observed Sir Simon, who was casting his thoughts back. "Mrs. Trace used to say she spent too much."

"I suppose they lived beyond their means, these Paradynes."

"No; it did not appear so; and the mystery never was cleared up where the abstracted sums (enormous sums they were!) had gone, or what they had gone in. Mrs. Trace, my poor sister Mary, was of so very quiet a disposition herself, caring nothing for dress or show; and Mrs. Paradyne, I suppose, did care for it. I remember my brother-in-law, Robert Trace, observed to me after the explosion, how glad he was that he and his wife had lived quietly; that no blame on that score could attach to him. The Loftus's were different; they spent all before them; not,

however, more than they had a right to spend. I suppose you know the particulars, doctor?"

"Not at all. I never heard them."

"Then I'll tell you the story, from beginning to
end, in a few brief words. My brother-in-law, Robert
Trace, who was always up to his eyes in business —
for Loftus would not attend to it — had some matters
to transact for a Captain Arthur Paradyne, — the
selling out of shares, or the buying in of shares, I forget which; and an intimacy grew up between him and
his client. Paradyne had come into some money
through the death of an aunt in Liverpool; previous to
that he had lived in Germany, on a very small income,
as I understood. He seemed a thorough gentleman,
and, I should have said, an honest, open-dealing man.
In an unlucky hour Robert Trace — who had been
hankering after a third partner for some time, though
Loftus could not see what they wanted with one, as
they kept efficient clerks — proposed to Captain Paradyne to invest his money — two or three thousand
pounds I think it was — in their concern, and take a
share. Paradyne consented. Mr. Loftus murmured at
first, but at last he consented; and the firm became
Loftus, Trace, & Paradyne. Things went on smoothly
for two years, or thereabouts, though Paradyne proved
an utter novice in business matters, as your military
men, gentlemen by birth and habit, often do; and
Trace grumbled awfully. Not publicly, you know;
only in private to me, whenever I was down at Liverpool. Then came the crash. Paradyne was discovered
to have played up Old Harry with everything; the
money of the firm, the shares of customers, all he
could lay his hands on. Strange to say, it was Loftus,

the unbusiness man, who was the one to make the first
discovery.   Only think of that!"

Dr. Brabazon merely nodded.   He was listening
attentively.

"Mr. Loftus had gone to Liverpool for a few days.
Something struck him in looking over the books, and
he called Robert Trace's attention to it.   That night
in private they went into the thing together, and saw
that some roguery was being played.   The next day it
was all out, and ruin stared them in the face.   On the
following morning Mr. Loftus caused Paradyne to be
arrested, and telegraphed for me.   When I got down
at night, the man was dead."

"Dead!" exclaimed Dr. Brabazon.

"He was dead, that poor Arthur Paradyne.   Ah!
when Loftus met me with the news, it was a shock.
He had been taken before the magistrates for examination, was remanded, and put in a cell in the lock-up,
or whatever they call the place.   One of the clerks, a
young man named Hopper, was allowed to have an interview with him; half an hour afterwards Paradyne
was found dead in his cell.   Of course it was assumed
that he had taken poison, and the report found its way
to the newspapers.   But when the doctors made the
examination, they found he had died of disease of the
heart; — a natural sequence to the events of the day,
for one whose heart was not sound."

"It was very shocking altogether."

"Ay, it was.   And with his death ended the investigation.   'Why pursue it?'   Trace asked; 'let it drop,
for the wife and children's sake.'   Robert Trace was
a hard man in general; but I must say he behaved
leniently in this case.   It did not, so far, touch his

pocket, you see; for all the investigation in the world would not have brought back the wasted money, or undone the work. The concern was wound up; Mr. Loftus had to move into a small house, and otherwise reduce his expenses; Robert Trace went to America with a little money I lent him; and Mrs. Paradyne disappeared."

"It was a dreadful thing for *her*," spoke Dr. Brabazon.

"Very. People, in their indignation against Paradyne, could not think of her; but I did, and I went to see her. She was very bitter against her husband; I could see it, though she said little."

"Did she tell you how the money had gone?"

"She did not know. The discovery that he had been using it came upon her with the same shock of astonishment that it had upon the rest of us. One thing she could swear to, she said to me — that it had never been brought home, or used in any way for her or his children. I can't quite recollect about the children," broke off Sir Simon: "there was one, I know, for I saw him — a fine boy; I suppose the one now come here; but I have an impression there were more."

"Had she nothing left — the mother?"

"I asked her the question. She told me she had a small income, nothing like enough to keep her. I wonder how they have lived?" continued Sir Simon, after a pause.

"The son has been to a thorough good school," observed Dr. Brabazon. "Did Mr. Paradyne acknowledge his guilt?"

"He denied it utterly, so Loftus told me; made believe at first to think they were accusing him in joke."

4*

A sudden light, something like hope, appeared in Dr. Brabazon's eyes as he raised them to Sir Simon.

"Is it possible that he could have been innocent?" he eagerly asked.

"No, it is not possible; there was no one else who could have had access to the shares and things," was the avowal. But Sir Simon looked grieved, and was grieved, to have to make it.

And so it was decided that George Paradyne should remain.

CHAPTER IV.

Sir Simon Orville's offered Reward.

IN the comfortable apartment which was made the family sitting-room, where Miss Brabazon might usually be found by anybody who wanted her, sat a young lady on this same afternoon. A laughing, saucy, wilful girl of thirteen, with short petticoats, and wavy brown hair hanging down. It was Miss Rose Brabazon. Dr. Brabazon had married two wives and lost them both: he had several older children, all out in the world now, but this was the only young one, and spoilt accordingly. That is, all out in the world save his eldest daughter, whom you will see presently. Miss Rose was supposed to be at her studies. Sundry exercise-books were before her on the square table, covered with its handsome green cloth, in the middle of the room; in point of fact, she was inditing a private letter, and taking recreative trips to the window between whiles, — a large, pleasant window, looking out on the gymnasium-ground, with a view of the Hampstead and Highgate hills in the far distance. At least seventeen of the boys were madly in love with Miss Rose, and Miss Rose reciprocated the compliment to a large proportion of them.

The door opened, and Miss Brabazon came in: a middle-sized, capable, practical young woman of thirty, with a kind, good, sensible face. She was the prop and stay of the house; looking after everything; to the well-being of the large household, to the comfort of her father and of the boys, and to the education of Rose. Her dark hair was plainly braided on her face, and she wore a dress of some soft blue material, with lace collar and cuffs. Crossing over to a side table, she laid down a book she was carrying, and then looked at the address of two letters in her hand, which had just been given her by the postman as she crossed the hall. Miss Rose, all signs of everything unorthodox hidden away, was diligently bending over her studies.

"Is that exercise not done yet, Rose?"

"It is so very difficult, Emma."

"You have been idling away your time again, I fear. Have you practised?" continued Miss Brabazon, glancing half round at the piano.

"Not yet, Emma."

"Have you learnt your French?"

"I've not looked at it."

"What *have* you been doing?"

"Miss Rose Brabazon lifted her pretty face, and shook back her wavy hair from her laughing blue eyes.

"I thought you'd perhaps give me holiday this afternoon, as you were so much occupied up-stairs with Lord Shrewsbury and his mother."

"Now, Rose, you knew better. And be so kind

as to call the boys by their right names. I wish you'd be a steady child!"

Rose laughed. "Sir Simon Orville's here, Emma. I saw him at the study window just now with papa."

"Of course! That's the way you get your lessons done, Rose."

Miss Rose tossed her pen-wiper into the air and caught it again. She had the peculiar faculty of never listening to reproofs. At least, of listening to profit.

"Whom are those letters for, Emma."

"Not for you," answered Emma. "You may put the books away now, and go and wash your hands. It is tea-time."

Books, exercises, pens, ink, were all hurried into a drawer in the side-table, and away went Rose, meeting Mr. Henry at the door, for whom Miss Brabazon had sent. He no longer wore his grey travelling clothes, but was in a black surtout coat, looking, Miss Brabazon thought, very entirely a gentleman, with his quiet manner and refined face.

"Is this for you?" she asked, holding out one of the letters, which bore a foreign post-mark. "It is addressed to Doctor Henry."

He took it from her with a smile. "Yes, thank you; it is for me. Is there anything to pay?"

"No. Are you really Dr. Henry?"

"Oh, Miss Brabazon, it is only my degree at the Heidelberg University. I drop it here. I see this is from one of the professors. He forgot, I suppose: I wrote down my name for them all, 'Mr.' Henry."

"But why should you drop it?"

"It is much better to do so. Fancy a young man like I am being called doctor here! The masters

would look askance at me, and the boys make fun of
me in private.   Please don't mention it, Miss Brabazon."

"Certainly not, as you wish it.   I do not quite
see your argument, though.   Here's papa."

Dr. Brabazon came in with a quiet step.   He
threw himself into a chair, as one in utter weariness,
speaking sadly.   "Oh, these boys, these boys!"

"Is anything the matter, papa?"

"Not much, Emma; save that I feel out of sorts
with all things.   Don't go, Mr. Henry, I want to speak
to you."

Mr. Henry had been leaving the room.   He turned
back, and the doctor sat forward on his chair.

"You are acquainted with young Paradyne, I hear,
Mr. Henry."

A sort of bright hectic flashed into Mr. Henry's
face.   Miss Brabazon noticed it.   When she knew him
better, she found that any powerful emotion always
brought it there.   "Yes, sir, I knew him in Germany.
He is a very clever boy."

"Ay, he seems that.   I like the boy amazingly, so
far as I have seen.   What about his past history?"

Dr. Brabazon looked full at the German master.
Mr. Henry understood the appeal, and found there
was no help for it; he must respond.   But he had an
invincible dislike to speak of the Paradynes and their
misfortune.   And the doctor was not alone.

"You allude to that unhappy business in Liverpool,
sir?"

"I do.   I am *very* sorry the boy has been recognised here.   You may speak before my daughter,
Mr. Henry," — for the Doctor saw that he had glanced

uneasily at Miss Brabazon. "I told her of it to-day; she is quite safe. It seems almost a fatality that the boy should have come to the very place where Trace and the Loftuses were being educated."

"Yes it does," was the sad response: and Dr. Brabazon little thought how bitterly that poor sensitive young German master was reproaching himself, for he had been the means of bringing young Paradyne to Orville College.

"I'd not hesitate to keep the boy a minute, if I were sure —"

"Oh, sir, don't turn him out!" interrupted Mr Henry, his voice ringing with pain. "To dismiss George Paradyne from the college, now that he has entered it, might prove a serious blight upon him; a blight that might follow him everywhere, for the cause could not fail to be noised abroad. Better let him stay and face it out: he may — it is possible he may — in time — live it down. I beg your pardon, Dr. Brabazon; I ought not to have said so much."

"My good friend," — and the doctor was a little agitated also, — "you never need urge clemency on me. Heaven knows that we have, most of us, secret cares of our own; and they render us — or ought to — lenient upon others. If I could wipe out with a sponge the past as regards young Paradyne, I'd do it in glad thankfulness. He is to remain; it is so de-cided; and I hope the past will not ooze out to the school. That is what I fear."

"In himself he is, I think, everything that could be wished," said the usher in a low tone; "a good, honourable, painstaking boy, with the most implicit trust in his late father's innocence."

Dr. Brabazon lifted his eyes. "But there are no possible grounds to hope that he was innocent! Are there?"

"Not any, I fear."

"Well, well; better perhaps that the son should think it. You were not in Liverpool when it happened?"

"I was in Germany. The account of it was sent to me."

"By whom? — if I may ask it."

"By Mrs. Paradyne."

"*She* does not believe her husband to have been innocent?"

"Oh, no."

"Has Mrs. Paradyne enough to live upon?" pursued the doctor, whose interest in the affair had been growing.

"Her income is, I believe, very small indeed."

"Then how does she give the boy this expensive education?"

"I fancy some friend helps her," was the reply. "And I know that a considerable reduction was made in the terms of the last school, on account of the boy's fluency in French and German."

"I suppose you have kept up a correspondence with them, Mr. Henry?"

"Yes; though not a very frequent one."

"When you knew Mr. Paradyne, was he an honest man?"

"Strictly so; honourable, upright, entitled to every respect. I have never been able to understand how he could fall from it."

"One of those sudden temptations, I suppose," observed the doctor, musingly. "Beginning in a trifle;

ending — nobody knows where. I won't detain you
longer, Mr. Henry."

Mr. Henry left the room with his letter. Miss
Brabazon found her tongue, speaking impulsively.

"Papa, how strangely sensitive he seems to be,
this new master of yours! Did you see the hectic on
his face?"

"Poor fellow, yes. He is very friendless; and, to
be so, gives us a fellow-feeling for the unfortunate,
Emma."

"Are you aware that he is Dr. Henry?"

"Is he? He took honours abroad, I believe. We
don't think much of that, you know."

"He drops the title over here; does not care that
it should be known. Did it strike you, papa, while
he was speaking, that he must have some secret trouble
of his own?"

"No. I was thinking, Emma, of somebody else's
secret trouble."

Miss Brabazon evidently understood the allusion.
Her countenance fell, and she turned her face from the
doctor's view.

"I thought Sir Simon was here, papa."

"So he is. Sir Simon's gone up to see Talbot.
He will take tea with us, Emma."

The tea and Sir Simon came in together; Emma
Brabazon was always glad to see him. Miss Rose
followed, and the conversation was general, on account
of the young lady's presence; otherwise it must have
fallen on the Paradynes. Sir Simon was in spirits;
Mrs. Talbot, sitting with her son, had assured him the
doctor said all would be well.

But Sir Simon had something to do yet. When

tea was over, he said farewell to his friends and went in search of the boys, who were in the cricket-field. He called aloud for Trace and for Loftus major. When the rest of the boys came flocking up with a shout — for it was a red-letter day when they could get Sir Simon — he sent them away again.

"I want only these two graceless ones," he said: "you all be off," and the boys went, shouting and laughing. "Yes, you, Irby; you may stop."

Gathering the three around him, he entered on his business, and talked to them for a few moments very plainly and earnestly. Loftus was the first to respond, and he did it with frankness.

"I have already said, sir, that Paradyne is safe for me. I will keep my word."

"I'll never tell upon him, Sir Simon," added Irby; "I'll make him my friend, if you like."

"Is the fellow to stop?" asked Trace.

"Yes, sir, he is to stop," replied Sir Simon, turning sharply upon the speaker. "It is Dr. Brabazon's pleasure that he should stop, and it is mine also. What have you to say against it?"

"Nothing at all," quietly replied Trace.

"That's well," returned Sir Simon, in a cynical tone of suavity. "And now, mind you, Trace — all of you mind — if unpleasantness does arise to this unlucky boy through either of you, I'll — I'll — by George! I'll make him, young Paradyne, my heir."

He turned off in the direction of the plantation, curious to examine the scene of the last night's outrage. Quite one half of the college had gathered there, and the rest ran up now. Sir Simon laid his hand upon Dick Loftus.

"So! This was your doing!"

"Don't, uncle," said Dick, wincing; "I'm as vexed about it as you can be. I'd rather have been shot myself."

"That's what Bertie says. A pretty pair of nephews I've got!" continued Sir Simon, using his stick on the ground violently, to the admiration of the surrounding throng. "The one smuggles pistols into the school, and the other brings 'em out and shoots a boy!"

"I didn't shoot him," said Dick.

"You were the cause of it, sir. If Talbot dies, and the thing comes to trial, were I the judge on the bench, I should transport you for seven years, Dick Loftus, as accessory in a second degree."

"Talbot isn't going to die," debated hardy Dick.

"And serve him right," put in Mr. Loftus, answering the semi-threat of Sir Simon. "Transportation for seven years would be just the thing Dick deserves. What right had the young idiot to meddle with my pistols?"

"What right had you to have pistols to be meddled with?" cried Sir Simon, retorting on Bertie. "And to keep 'em loaded? And to put 'em where Dick could get to them? I'd transport *you* for fourteen."

Mr. Loftus did not like the tables being turned on him. He drew his head up with a jerk.

"And you the senior, save one, of the school, who might have been expected to be a pattern to the rest!" added Sir Simon, mercilessly. "You'd not have done it, would you, Gall?"

The senior boy, quietly looking on, lifted his eyes at being addressed. "I don't think I should, Sir Simon."

It was an inoffensive answer enough, in regard to
words; but the quiet tone of condemnation, the half
compassionate smile that accompanied it, angered
Loftus out of his pride and his prudence.

"It's not likely he would. Pistols would be of no
use to him. What do those city tradespeople want
with pistols?"

The insolent retort was not lost on Sir Simon, for
it gave him an opportunity that he was ever ready to
seize upon; ever, it may be said, watching for — that
of putting down the lofty notions of his otherwise
favourite nephew.

"Those City tradespeople," he echoed, making a
circular sweep with his stick, as if to challenge the
attention of the crowd. "Hark at him! Hold your
tongue, Gall; I'll talk. Has he changed ranks with
Talbot, do you know, boys, and become a lord? City
people! I'm his uncle; but he ignores that. I wasn't
in the City; never aspired to it; I was only in Bermondsey; a tanner. A tanner, boys, as some of your
fathers could tell you; Orville & Tubbs it was. Tubbs
is there, tanning still; Tubbs & Sons; and a good snug
business they've got. *I* wasn't born with a fortune in
the bank, as some folks are; I had to make my way
by hard work, and with very little education, and I
did it. I had no Orville College to learn Latin and
Greek and politeness at; though they do tell me I'm
related to its founder. Perhaps I am; but it's only a
sixteenth cousin, boys."

A shout of laughter: the boys' satisfaction had
grown irrepressible. Sir Simon laughed with them.

"We were thirteen of us to get out in the world,
boys and girls, and our father a clerk on three hundred

a year. It seemed a fortune in those days; because a
man's children expected to go out and work for themselves. I went out at twelve, boys; my father put me
to a fishmonger, and I didn't like it; and he gave me
a flogging for caprice, and sent me to a tanner's. I
didn't like that — you should have smelt the skins! —
but I had to stick to it. And I did stick to it, and in
time made a business for myself, and when it got too
large I took in my young foreman, Tubbs, and gave
him a share. I was a common-councilman, then; and
a very grand honour I thought it to be such; but I
didn't leave off work. Up early and to bed late, and
making my abode amidst the skins in my yard, was I.
Fortune came to me, boys; it comes to most people
who patiently work for it; and they made me a sheriff
of London, and in going up with an address to Court,
the Queen knighted me: and that brings me with the
handle to my name, which I assure you I'm not at
home with yet, and for months afterwards couldn't
believe that it was me being spoken to. I retired
from business then, and I bought Pond Place up here.
I didn't buy it because it was near the college, and
that Dr. Orville had been a sixteenth cousin, but because it suited me; and the situation and the air
suited me. And that's how *I* come to be Sir Simon
Orville: and what I've got I've humbly worked for.
Mr. Loftus there was born a gentleman, as his father
was before him, and he'd like me to go in for rank,
and for quarterings on my carriage, and crests on my
spoons, and to make believe that I'd never heard
there was such a low thing as tanning amidst trades.
Yah, boys! I hate pretension: and so does every
sincere nature ever created. It's only a species of

acted falsehood; it won't help us on the road to heaven."

A murmur of applause, and a slight clapping of hands. Sir Simon lifted his stick again.

"He despises the Galls, that lofty nephew of mine; he lets you know that he does. Boys, allow me to tell you, that there's not a better man in all London than Joseph Gall, the head of the respectable firm of Gall & Batty. Substantial, too, Mr. Loftus."

Loftus stood like a pillar of salt, stony and upright, showing no sign whatever of his intense annoyance. These periodical revelations of Sir Simon's, given gratuitously to the boys on any provocation, were the very thorns of his life. At such moments it would have puzzled Loftus to tell which he despised most — the Galls as a whole, or his uncle as a unit.

"And now about this shooting business," resumed Sir Simon. "Where was the pistol fired from?"

"Just from this point, Sir Simon," spoke Leek, who was one of the greatest admirers Sir Simon possessed. "And here" — running a few paces onward — "is where the earl dropped."

It was growing too dusk to distinguish objects; the moon as yet did not give much light; but Sir Simon stooped, and peered about with the utmost interest. Suddenly he rose and confronted them.

"Now, look here, you fellows! I dare say it was an accident; the boy got fingering the pistol, and it went off; he's not so much to blame for that. What he is to blame for, is the not confessing; it's dishonourable, mean, despicable; and for that he deserves no quarter. Try to find him out, boys; hunt him up; run him down; surely a stray word or a chance look may

guide you to him. And whoever succeeds in bringing
the truth to light, may come to me for the handsomest
gold watch that is to be bought with money."

A deafening shout arose. In the midst of it the
three strokes of the great bell were heard, calling the
boys to evening study. They set off with a bound,
all except Trace, who found himself detained by the
hand of his uncle until the rest were out of hearing.

"Raymond, if mischief comes of this matter, it will
be through you."

"Through me!" repeated Trace, taken thoroughly
aback. "Can you suppose, sir, I went shares with
Bertie in buying the pistols? Or that I knew of his
bringing them to school, loaded?"

"Not that. I am speaking of the other matter —
Paradyne's. You are bitter against the very name of
Paradyne; and I don't say you have no cause. But
now, take my advice, Raymond. Do you hear me?"

"Yes, sir."

"Don't be the one to stir up the past against the
boy. I have a feeling against it."

Sir Simon, leaving his words to tell, walked away
towards home, and Trace stood looking after him,
resenting the injunction. He was not a favourite, and
he knew it; even that despicable Dick was preferred
to him. As a matter of affection, perhaps Trace did
not regret this; but his policy in life was to stand well
with all. The tolerating of George Paradyne was an
uncommonly bitter pill to swallow; and Trace would
have given the world to reject it. But he scarcely
saw his way clear to do this, if he wished to keep
friends with his uncle. And Trace threw a gratuitous
and by no means complimentary word at the un-

fortunate boy, as he went off to be in time for his studies.

Scarcely was he out of sight, when Miss Brabazon came quietly up through the trees. She had put on a cloak and hood; and, as she threw back the latter her face looked white with a curious fear. Searching here, bending there, she seemed to be seeking for some traces of the last night's work. Now she bent her ear and listened, now she knelt down by the bench, feeling under it and about it. One might almost have thought she was seeking for a letter. So pre-occupied was she as not to hear the sound of footsteps.

"What are you looking for, Emma?"

The interruption was from Dr. Brabazon, who happened to be passing through the plantation. Emma started up with a cry.

"What is it, my dear? What are you doing here?"

"I — I — was thinking who could have done it, papa," she answered, in a frightened whisper. "I mean that dreadful thing last night. If the boys all deny it — why, perhaps they are really not guilty. It — it was so very easy for a stranger, coming by chance through the plantation, to have picked up the pistol that Smart dropped, and fired it off without thought of harm. Without thought of harm, papa."

How pleadingly, yearningly the last words were spoken, Dr. Brabazon's own heart told him. He answered cheerfully, although it was beating with pain.

"Emma, I see what you are thinking of. But it could not have been. It was one of the boys beyond doubt, for he wore the college cap. Why do you let these fancies trouble you? Run home, child; run home."

CHAPTER V.
Mother Butter's Lodgings.

THE term had begun, as the Head Master expressed
it, ungraciously. The mysterious and disagreeable accident to James Talbot was leading to endless discussion and dissension. The first desk utterly repudiated
the notion that it could have been one of them, and
tacitly, if not directly, accused the second; the second
desk threw back the insinuation with all the insolence
they dared to use. Lamb was one of these, and his
name got mentioned (failing somebody else to fix it on)
in connection with the charge. The suggestion spread,
although Brown minor, rather a crony of Lamb's, was
ready to testify that Lamb had never stirred out of the
hall that night after chapel; and did testify to it, in
fact, with some confirmatory words of unnecessary
strength. Lamb, a tall, thin fellow, was in a terrible
rage; could not have been in a worse had he been
guilty. Gall, the senior boy, said little; not having
returned at the time, he did not consider it was his
province to interfere; but Loftus, smarting personally
under the affair, made himself exceedingly busy. And
it was a very unusual thing for Loftus to do.

The boys, at their evening studies, sat at the low
table in the well-lighted hall — a long table on trestles
that ran down the middle of it, with benches around.
They were ostensibly preparing their lessons for the
morrow; in reality were discussing and bickering among
themselves in an under-tone. You heard the bell ring
for them in the last chapter, when they were in the
plantation with Sir Simon Orville. Mr. Long sat at

his desk in a remote corner, paying no attention. Great in science, he always had his near-sighted spectacles buried in some abstruse book, and his ears also.

"Look here," spoke Loftus minor, who was burning to get at the offender quite as hotly as his brother Bertie, "when my uncle says he'll give a gold watch, why, he *will* give it; there's no sham; so if any of you fellows do know about this, just go in and earn it. It'll be a shame to let a watch go begging."

"It's an awful shame that a gold watch, or any such bribe should be needed," called out Loftus major. "Who but a sneak would shoot a fellow, and then shrink from avowing it, letting suspicion fall on the rest indiscriminately? A sneak, I say."

"Do you mean that for me, Mr. Loftus?" spluttered Lamb, who was sitting opposite to Loftus at the table. "Because if you do —"

"There you go, Lamb, you and your corky temper," interposed good-humoured Leek.

"You be quiet, Onions. I say that if he does, I'll make him prove his words."

There was a smothered laugh. The notion of Lamb's making a senior prove anything, was good, especially Loftus.

"I don't mean it for Lamb in particular, unless he chooses to take it to himself," coolly drawled Loftus. "I have no reason for supposing he can take it."

The semi-apology did not satisfy Lamb. He knew that he was called the "sneak," par excellence; he knew that he did many little underhand things to deserve it. Consequently he always strove to appear particularly white; and to have this grave suspicion thrown upon him was driving him wild.

5*

"I believe that Loftus knows I was no more out last night than he was," said Lamb, giving his Virgil a passionate wrench, which tore the cover — "that you all know it."

"As far as I can understand, not a soul of you went out, except Smart and Loftus minor," observed the senior boy, who really wished to heal the general discomfort. "None of you were missed."

"And that's true," said Lamb. "And if it comes to that, who is to say that it was not that new fellow did it, after all? Took up the pistol and shot it off by accident, and went and said what he did to screen himself."

"What new fellow? Do you mean Paradyne?" quickly asked Irby, following out some association of ideas in his mind.

"Paradyne, no! What could Paradyne have had to do with it? I mean the new master; that German fellow with an English name."

"Nonsense, Lamb!"

Lamb nodded his head oracularly. "It might have been."

It was a new phase of the question, and the boys looked up. Lamb continued. "Trace says he thinks he's a regular spy."

"By the way, where is Trace?" asked Gall, who had suddenly noticed that Trace, usually so punctual at studies, was not present.

"It couldn't have been him," said Leek, regardless of the question as to Trace. "He saw the fellow making off; he said he wore the college cap."

"Your tongue is ever ready, Onions," was the rebuke of the senior boy. "It's not at all likely to have been Mr. Henry; but neither is it obliged to have been the fellow he saw making off. And if it was, the fellow might not have come out of the college; he may be an outsider. Get on with your work; there's really no cause to be worrying over it and suspecting each other."

The words acted as oil on the troubled waters, and they began to settle down to their books and exercises. But it's pleasanter to gossip than to learn.

"Why does Trace think the German's a spy?" asked Loftus minor.

"He's not German; he's English. A German would have his face covered with hair; this fellow shaves."

"Of course he's not German by birth," returned Dick; "anybody can see that. Onions said ——"

"What's all that talking about?" roared out Mr. Long, suddenly becoming awake to the noise. "Is that the way you do your lessons?" And for a few moments, at any rate, silence supervened.

Where was Trace? I think I shall have to tell you. After digesting Sir Simon Orville's words in the plantation, he set off quickly, to be in time for the evening study, which was the preparation of lessons for the next day, and rarely lasted more than an hour. Running full pelt into the cloisters, he ran against one of the masters.

"I beg your pardon, sir," he said, thinking it was Mr. Baker; for the cloisters were in almost total darkness.

It was Mr. Henry; and when Trace became aware of the fact, his spirit rose up in rebellion at having called him "sir." A feeling of dislike to this new master was rife within him, having its source no doubt

in the past friendship the stranger had avowed for the
unfortunate Captain Paradyne, and in his present evident
intention to befriend the boy, and defend him against
surreptitious lance-shafts. Trace was apt to be so prejudiced.

"Is it you, Trace?" cried Mr. Henry, recognizing
the voice. "I would say a word to you."

"Be quick, if you please, then," was the half-dis-
courteous answer. "We have only one hour to prepare
everything, and I am late as it is."

"You have heard probably that George Paradyne
is to stay here," began Mr. Henry, leading the way
into the open quadrangle, where it was lighter, and
there could be no danger of eaves-droppers.

"Yes; and I am surprised at Dr. Brabazon. My
uncle, Sir Simon Orville, sanctions it too. He—he——"

Trace stopped. The generally cool voice seemed
overflowing with passion; and Mr. Henry looked at
him in the light of the rising moon.

"You do not like the decision!"

"*Like* it!" repeated Trace; "I think it is an infa-
mous thing. And we are put upon our honour not to
tell! It is the first time I ever knew it was right to
conceal crime."

"The boy has committed no crime, if you allude to
him."

"His father did."

"And his father expiated it with his life. Should
not this be sufficient for you?"

Trace answered by a gesture of contempt. Mr. Henry
threw his luminous eyes on him, their sad expression,
so namelessly attractive, conspicuous even in the subdued
light.

"I have had a great deal of trouble of one sort or another," said the master, in a low tone. "It has taught me some things: and, amidst them, *never* to add, by act of mine, to the grief of others. Oh, Trace! if you did but know the true, tender compassion we feel for them, when dire trouble has fallen on ourselves! if you could but see how cruel their life is, without additional reproach!"

"And did Paradyne — the man — bring no trouble upon us?" burst out Trace. "Did he not ruin my father, and drive him into exile, and break up our home, and kill my mother? She died here; here at my uncle's; and you may see her gravestone in the churchyard hard by. Trouble! Did the man not bring enough upon us?"

"Heaven knows he did," was the sad answer. "I do not seek to depreciate it; but the boy is innocent. He does not deserve to have it visited upon him."

"Doesn't he!" retorted Trace, utterly angered out of his usual civility.

"Why no, of course he does not," rather sharply resumed Mr. Henry, feeling now how hard must be this contending nature. "Look at the thing dispassionately; imagine for a moment the case reversed: that your father was the guilty man, and Paradyne's the one on whom the blow fell: should you not think it cruelly unjust and unjustifiable if he pursued revenge on you?"

Trace became half-speechless with indignation. "I cannot imagine anything of the sort, sir," he haughtily said, using the "sir" as he might have used it to an offending footman. "I think you are forgetting yourself: we are gentlemen at this college."

"I did not wish to offend you; only to put the matter in the light that it should, as I think, be looked at. What had young Paradyne done — a lad of twelve, then — to invoke this evil on himself? He was not responsible for his father's actions; he could not hinder them."

"It appears to me that we have had enough of this," observed Trace. "Perhaps you will tell me why you are detaining me from my studies to say it?"

"To bespeak your kindness for the boy, — your silence, in fact; that he may be allowed to pursue his course here unmolested. It will be repaid to you many-fold."

"Then you can make yourself easy; I am not going to betray him. Dr. Brabazon has put us on our honour."

The acknowledgment was not graciously expressed, but Mr. Henry saw he should get nothing better. "And now, Trace," he continued, "I have a question to ask you on a different subject. When that pistol went off in the plantation last night, I met a boy, supposed to be one of the seniors, stealing away. Was it you?"

There had been many little points in the interview not palatable to Mr. Trace; but all put together were as nothing compared to this. His complexion was peculiar, apt to turn of a salmon-colour on occasions of rare provocation, as it did now; but his reply was cold and calm.

"You had better take care what you say, Mr. Henry! *I* in the plantation at the time! stealing away! No, I was not. It is against rules to go out after prayers, and I am not in the habit of breaking them.

I wish I had been there! and dropped upon those two juniors who were fools enough to take out a loaded pistol."

"Hush, that's enough: I would not do you an injury for the world," said Mr. Henry, in the gentlest and kindest tone. "I did think it was you; but I kept it to myself, as you perceived."

"Thank you," said Trace, half in allusion to the wish, half ironically. "I suppose I may go in now."

"Yes," said Mr. Henry, "that is all. Good night, Trace."

He went out at the great gates as he spoke. But Trace, instead of hastening in to his studies, that he seemed so anxious over, came to the conclusion to delay them yet a little longer. He had a mind to track Mr. Henry.

Following him at a safe distance, keeping under cover of any bit of shade cast by the moon, he saw him pass the front of the college, and make for some houses round by the shops. Mr. Henry was looking about him as if uncertain of his geography; finally he paused before a row of small "genteel" dwellings, and entered one of them.

"Number five!" exclaimed Trace, taking his observations. "I'm blest if that's not the place where the Paradynes live!" he continued with sudden conviction, for he had been gathering a little information for himself in the course of the afternoon. "A nice lot to know! Birds of a feather. I shouldn't wonder but he had a share of the spoil in Liverpool! He confesses to having known them well. If ever a firebrand came into a school, it's this same German master. I'll look after him a bit."

And, having so far set operations afloat, Mr. Trace galloped back to school as fast as his legs would carry him.

Skirting the playground at the back of the college, nearly opposite the large bay window of the master's study, and of the boys' dormitories above it, was a small dwelling-house of rough stone, known amidst the boys as "Mother Butter's." Mother Butter, a tall spare angular lady of fifty, kept a cow and a donkey, and a good many fowls. She sold a little butter, she sold poultry and fresh eggs; she sold choice herbs, mushroom ketchup; lavender, and other sweet dried flowers to scent drawers. Formerly she used to make "bullseyes" for the junior college boys; small square delectable tablets, composed of butter, treacle, and peppermint, and did in this a roaring trade. But differences arose, beginning at first with long credit, and going on to open rupture, and one day last term she flung her treacle saucepan amidst the crew, vowing she would make no more. The saucepan struck Gall's trencher, denting it in and blackening his ear, nearly stunning him besides. Smarting under the infliction, he issued on the spot a general order that no more bullseyes were to be consumed of Mother Butter's, though she "made them till she was blue." Since then there had been open and perpetual warfare. Mrs. Butter carried tales of them to the masters: the boys entered on a system of petty annoyance: their palates suffering under the deprivation of those choice sweetmeats, it was not likely they would spare her. They painted her cow green; they cut off the plume of a handsome cock, the pride of the whole poultry; they tied a bell to the donkey's tail when it was charged with two panniers of eggs, thereby causing the startled animal to smash the lot; and they laid a huge tin plate across the top of her low kitchen chimney. Nearly all these miseries were securely effected at night; and as Mrs. Butter watched vigilantly and detected nothing, her surprise equalled her rage. Dr. Brabazon had levied a contribution for the value of the eggs; but that did not stop the fun.

It was a pretty place to look at, this dwelling-house of Mrs. Butter's, with the clematis on its stone walls, the bright flowers before it, and the little paddock behind; and it so happened that Mr. Henry, seeking for lodgings, heard there were some to let here. He found a neat plain sitting-room, and a closet opening from it which just held the bed and wash-hand stand, with space for his portmanteau, if he put the chair out. Mrs. Butter said she would cook and wait upon him; the rent asked was low, and he made the bargain, unconscious man, offhand. The previous occupant had been an outdoor servant of the college, and you may imagine the effect Mr. Henry's choice produced on the school. Not until he moved into it was he aware of the contemptuous feeling it excited, and then not of its extent. "It suits me," said he, quietly and decisively.

He saw no reason why it should not suit him. It had been done up nicely afresh, and was convenient for the college. He might have thought it good enough, even though he had not been obliged to look at every sixpence that he spent. The boys might have thought it good enough, but for its being in the house of the obnoxious Mother Butter, and for a servant's previous occupation of it.

You know the old saying, my friends: "One man must not look at a horse, while another may leap over the hedge." Just so was it here. Had somebody great and grand — a duke, let us say, for example — taken a fancy to that room, and come and occupied it, the boys would have been seized with a sudden sense of its desirability as a lodging, had its photograph taken as a model of beauty, and extolled it abroad; they might even have relaxed a little in their polite attentions to Mother Butter; but as one whom they were half-way prepared to regard as an enemy entered upon it, the case was different. In truth, a strong feeling, independent of this, was setting in against the foreign master.

The declining sun shone full on Mr. Henry, as he sat at the window of his room. He had taken possession of it some days now, and things were settling down into ordinary routine. James Talbot was nearly well again, and the commotion had subsided; but the affair remained in the same doubt, none of the boys had confessed, and suspicion was partially diverting itself from them. This room of Mr. Henry's faced the college and playground, and he liked to draw his table to the window. He was dotting down on a piece of paper his probable expenses; was calculating how little it would be possible for him to live upon, and how much save out of his hundred and twenty pounds a year salary. He had applied to a house in Paternoster Row for some translation to do: his idea had been to get private teaching in his free hours, but he found Orville Green too small a place to admit of the probability of much. The answer from the Paternoster Row house had just come in: they would give him the translation of a scientific German work; but the terms offered with it were very poor indeed. He intended to accept them; he said to himself that he had no other resource but to accept them, and they were being put down in his pencilled calculation.

Lodgings, food, laundress, clothes, and sundries. The lodging and laundress must be paid, the sundries must be found, those hundred and one trifles that arise one knows not how; in the clothes he could not stint himself, for he must appear as a gentleman: indeed, it would have been against Mr. Henry's natural instincts not to do so. But the food! — ah! he could deny himself there as much as he pleased; and the "much" seemed to be unlimited. To a young man these self-denials in prospective seem so easy.

He laid down his pencil, and leaned his head upon his hand. In his face, as he looked upwards; in his sad dark eyes fixed on the blue of the sky, but seeing it not, there was an expression that seemed to speak of utter friendlessness. A great care was upon him that evening; care of one sort was always upon him, but a different one had suddenly arisen to make itself heard. *Was his health giving way?* Doubts of it had occurred now and again in the past few weeks and been driven away without much notice; but since crossing over to England, his strength was as a mere reed. What if the capability to work were taken from him? Certain words came into his mind, — "Cut it down, why cumbereth it the ground?" Was *he* destined to be one of these useless trees, bearing no fruit? doing no good in his generation? The hot tears came into his eyes, and he breathed a silent word to One who was seated beyond that bright blue sky.

George Paradyne dashed in. "I say, Mr. Henry," began he, without preliminary ceremony of any description, "I shan't like this Orville College."

"Why not?" asked Mr. Henry, putting his paper into a drawer, and his pencil into his pocket.

"There's something up against me. The fellows won't let me join in their play."

"Oh, nonsense, George."

"But it isn't nonsense. They were at a fault just now for one to make up a game — it's that noisy one, you know, that takes eighteen fellows, nine on a side, and they had only seventeen. 'Oh, here comes another,' I heard some one say as I ran up; but when they saw it was me, there was a sudden silence, and every one of the lot turned away."

"I should say, 'When they saw it was I,' George," observed Mr. Henry, not really to correct his grammar, but to divert his thoughts from the subject.

"Oh, bother," answered George, his large, bright, grey eyes laughing. "But, I say, I wonder what can be the reason?"

"Some little prejudice, perhaps," carelessly replied Mr. Henry. "There exists something of the sort, I fancy, against the out-door pupils. Be brave, and hold on your right course; you will live it down."

"I'm not afraid of that," answered George. "I should like to know, though, what it is the boys have got in their heads. When are you coming to see us again?" he halted to say, as he was hastening away as unceremoniously as he had come in. "Mamma says she has something to ask you that she forgot the other night."

"Does she? I will come one of these first evenings."

George Paradyne vaulted away, and Mr. Henry sat on alone. His jealous eyes — jealous for the welfare of another — had not failed to detect the feeling against George Paradyne; but this confirmation of it fell upon him with a sort of shock, and he was as certain in his own mind that the origination of it was Raymond Trace, as that it existed.

He was right. Mr. Raymond Trace, in his bitter resentment against the Paradynes, was breaking his word of honour in the spirit, if not in the letter. He did not speak of the past, it is true; but by dint of whispers, of insinuations, he was setting the school against George Paradyne, and contriving it in such a way that none could have suspected him to be the originator. He was also fanning the flame against Mr. Henry; and in his self-righteousness he thought he was doing the most natural and justifiable thing.

CHAPTER VI.

Mr. Gall abroad.

AND now, not to make a mystery of it to you, my boys, any longer, I will tell you that it *was* Raymond Trace who had fired the pistol. Mr. Henry was not mistaken in his recognition of Trace; and what's more, he knew that he was not; though at the time he did not know his name, or who he was. Mr. Trace had silently quitted the college after prayers on a little private expedition of his own; in his hurry he caught up Mr. Long's cap, not noticing the mistake; and was rushing through the plantation when the sound of hushed voices caused him to slacken his footsteps and advance

cautiously, lest he should be seen himself. Peeping
through the trees, he discerned Smart and Dick Loftus,
each flourishing a pistol about like two young madmen;
and Trace, making a movement in his surprise, betrayed his presence. You know what followed: the
boys flew off with one of the pistols; the other Trace
took up, and presently fired it off. He fired it heed-
lessly, without thought of harm, never supposing it
was loaded; with an idea perhaps of further scaring
the two decamping boys; neither had he heard the approach of Talbot. When he found the pistol *was*
loaded, and that some mischief had ensued, he was
startled nearly out of his senses, quite out of his presence of mind.

His straightforward course, as everybody knows,
would have been to go up and see who was wounded;
but I'm afraid Trace's was not a very straightforward
nature; and there was also the instinctive desire to
conceal his having come abroad. Not a boy in the
college was more solicitous of appearing to keep the
rules than Trace; and he had grown to be looked upon
as a model to the rest. Dropping the pistol, away he
stole, obeying instinct only, too terrified to be able to
think calmly, and came face to face with the new
foreign master. Up went his hand to his face to hide
it, and away he backed amidst the trees; stealing on
noiselessly for some short distance, and then tearing
back to school helter-skelter. It was only when he
came to hang up the cap that he discovered the mistake he had made in taking out a master's. He glided
into the hall, sat down behind the nearest desk, and
gradually let his presence be noticed. When the news
came presently in, Trace was talking with Irby and

Brown major, and rose up in the same consternation as the rest.

You may therefore imagine what his sensations were when the Head Master subsequently appealed to his honour; to his, in common with that of the rest of the school. He could not declare himself; the time had gone by; it was quite impossible that he, *having concealed it*, could come forth with the avowal at that, the eleventh hour. Over and over again he blamed his folly and his cowardice for having stolen away; he would give all the money his pockets contained — and money was often a scarce commodity with Mr. Trace — to have bravely gone up to the wounded boy and declared the truth of the accident. He called himself a fool; he called himself a coward; he called himself sundry other disparaging names: but that it was not in his habit to do it, he might have sworn at himself. Not for the mere act in itself, the having fired the pistol; that was almost a pure accident; but for having concealed that it was he who did it.

However, his course was entered upon, and all he could do now was to hope and trust that he might never be discovered. While this hope was filling every crevice of his heart, making itself heard hourly in his brain, there came the startling question of the German master — "Was it not you I met?" Trace could only be indignant and say it was not; but the disagreeable doubt, whether he had been positively recognized or not, caused him to fear and hate Mr. Henry with a bitter fear and hatred. He thought it was but a suspicion, not a recognition, for Mr. Henry's quiet and cautious manner deceived him, and he grew to believe that his denial had borne its intended fruit.

So the fear subsided, but the hatred ripened; and it might perhaps bring trouble in the future.

A sunny day towards the close of September, and Miss Brabazon went abroad with Rose. She was about to pay a visit to Mrs. Paradyne; not only because it was her custom to call on the friends of the outdoor boys, but to show, in this instance, all she could of consideration and kindness. The Head Master and Miss Brabazon were in one respect the very opposite to Trace. Trace thought inherited misfortune a legitimate target for lances of contempt, if not of reproach; *they* deemed such people, so blameless and unhappy, should receive all of gentle commiseration that the world can show.

Miss Rose went mincing along in her short petticoats, the tails to her Leghorn hat flying behind, as she turned her little vain head from side to side, looking if any chance college boy might be abroad to cast his admiring eyes upon her. Not seeing one, she darted up to Mrs. Gall's governess, who was walking about the grounds of Mr. Gall's residence with some of the children, and then darted back to her sister.

"There's Jessie and Kate Gall, Emma. Can't you call on their mamma, while I walk about with them? Mrs. Gall is at the window. I know her by the yellow in her cap."

Emma Brabazon looked across the lawn at the handsome house, and saw a yellow silk screen standing near one of the windows. She laughed.

"You can stay here, however, Rose," she said, nodding to the governess. "I will call for you as I come back."

Glad that it had so happened, for Miss Rose had

insisted on accompanying her rather against her will, Emma Brabazon walked on to Prospect Terrace, as the houses were named, perhaps because they faced a brick-field, and inquired for Mrs. Paradyne. A rather faded lady, sitting in a small upper room, styled by courtesy a drawing-room, rose to receive her. She was tall and slender, with a fair thin face, and bright dark eyes. Her cap was of real lace; her gown, a delicate silk, looked faded, like herself; her manners were quiet and self-possessed. At the first glance Miss Brabazon could not fail to perceive that she was essentially a lady.

"It is very kind of you to come," she observed, when they had spoken a little together, Miss Brabazon sitting on the chintz sofa, herself on an opposite chair. "Living in the obscure way my circumstances compel me to live, in these small lodgings, I had not expected of course that any one would call upon me."

"But I am very pleased to do it," said Miss Brabazon, "not only because your son is at the college; and I have brought papa's card," she added, laying it on the table. "He has not time to pay visits himself; but he bade me say he hoped you would come to see us, and that we should be good friends."

"I visit nowhere," said Mrs. Paradyne, a certain fretfulness observable in her tone. "People do not care to invite those who cannot return it to them. Do not think me ungracious," she hastened to add; "I was not speaking in answer to Dr. Brabazon's kind message, but rather thinking of my past experience."

"I hope your son likes the school," observed Emma, rather at a loss what to say.

6*

"He likes the school; he does not like his companions," answered Mrs. Paradyne.

"No!" exclaimed Emma, taken by surprise. "Why not?"

"They seem to shun him; they do shun him, there's no doubt of it. It is making me miserable: I could not sleep all last night for thinking of it. There's scarcely a boy will speak to him, or treat him as a companion; — my dear son, who is so bright and good."

Amidst a mass of confused ideas, two in particular loomed out dimly in Emma Brabazon's mind — that Mrs. Paradyne was rather absorbed in self, and that her son was to her a very idol.

"Can those boys have betrayed him?" she involuntarily exclaimed.

"Betrayed what?" questioned Mrs. Paradyne.

And Emma Brabazon blushed to the very roots of her hair. She had been prepared to offer every kind and considerate sympathy if Mrs. Paradyne herself alluded to the past, but certainly had not intended gratuitously to enter upon it. There was no help for it now; and she spoke a few words of the discovery made by Trace — that he had recognised George Paradyne to be the son of a gentleman who had injured his father.

"Yes," said Mrs. Paradyne, folding her delicate hands in meek resignation on her lap, "I was sure something disagreeable would ensue as soon as George came home and told me that the sons of Loftus and Trace — as the firm used to be — wore at the college. It is most unfortunate that he should happen to have come to the same."

"Yes, it is — for your son's sake," murmured Emma, who felt almost guilty herself.

"I expected nothing less, I assure you, Miss Brabazon, than to find my son come home with a note from the Head Master, dismissing him from the college. I ——"

"Oh, if you only knew papa, you would not think it," she interrupted, gathering her scattered courage. "He would be all the more likely to retain him in it. The only fear was about the others, the Loftus boys and Trace. If their friends had raised any objection — but it has been quite the contrary," she hastened to add, quitting the unpleasant point; "and papa charged the boys on their honour not to breathe a word of the past to the school."

"They have breathed something, or others have; for George is being shunned most unjustifiably. Ah, well; it is but a natural consequence of the miserable past; I said it would cling to us for life, an incubus of disgrace. And so it will."

"Papa would like to tell you how greatly he sympathises with you," said Emma, eagerly. "I hope you will accept our friendship, and let us testify our respect in every way that we can. Unmerited misfortune is so sad to bear."

"I thought it would have killed me," was the answer made by Mrs. Paradyne, her tone one of discontented reproach — reproach for the husband who had gone. "I asked myself what right he had to bring this misery upon me; to entail on his children an inheritance of shame; I asked what he could have done with all the money; and there was nothing to answer me but the mocking word, What? When I look on my darling, I can hardly forbear to cry out against his memory. Pardon me, Miss Brabazon, I think this is the first time I have spoken of it to a stranger, but your words of kindness opened my heart."

"Have you many children?" inquired Miss Brabazon.

"Two sons, — George and an elder one. I have George only with me; the other is out, working for his living. And I have a daughter."

"Is she with you?"

"She is a teacher in a school in Derbyshire. I seem to be quite isolated from friends and family," continued Mrs. Paradyne, in a fretful tone. "It is but another natural result of the wretched past. I suppose my boy in this new college will be equally friendless."

"Your son has one firm friend in our new German master, Mr. Henry," was the reply of Miss Brabazon.

It was intended to be a reassuring one; but Mrs. Paradyne seemed to take it up in quite an opposite light. Her faded brow contracted; her eyes assumed a hard expression.

"I beg your pardon, Miss Brabazon; I would rather not speak of Mr. Henry. When I remember that it is through him we came up to this college, where my boy is being subjected to these slights and insults, I cannot think of him with patience."

"Was it through Mr. Henry you came to Orville?"

"It was. He wrote to us from Heidelberg, saying he had made an engagement with a first-class college in England, and suggested that George should be placed at it. He could give him so much of his time, he said. And this is the result! — that we find Raymond Trace here and the Loftus boys."

"But surely Mr. Henry did it for the best?"

"He intended it for the best, no doubt, but it has not turned out so for George. What I think is this — that Mr. Henry, knowing past circumstances and the cloud they cast upon us, might have made some inquiries as to who the scholars were at Orville College, before he brought George to it, and put me to the expense and trouble and pain of coming here."

The exceeding injustice of the reasoning — nay, the ingratitude — brought to Emma Brabazon a deeper conviction of the innate selfishness of Mrs. Paradyne. She supposed that her great misfortunes had hardened her; and the saying, so keen and true, arose to her mind, — "Adversity hardens the heart, or it opens it to Paradise."

"You knew Mr. Henry well in Germany, I believe? He was professor in the college where your son was a scholar?"

"Yes, he was," replied Mrs. Paradyne.

Miss Brabazon took her leave, and went away, a dim idea resting on her that she had seen Mrs. Paradyne before; or some one resembling her. Ever and anon, during the interview, an expression had dawned over her countenance that seemed strangely familiar. "But it was only when her face looked pleasant that the idea arose," thought Emma Brabazon, as she turned into the avenue and crossed the lawn leading to Mrs. Gall's.

Miss Rose was making herself at home, and had her things off. "I'm going to stay tea, Emma," was

her salutation to her sister. "You can go home without me."

It was her way. She did not say, "May I stay?"
but took will and decision into her own hands. In
great things Emma quietly corrected her; in trifles
Rose was yielded to. Emma looked at Mrs. Gall, a
slight, thin, kind little woman, with a sharp red nose.

"Do let her stay, Miss Brabazon. William is
coming home to go out to dinner with his papa, and
the children and governess are to have a pleasant hour
with me. See how anxious Jessie is that you should
say yes."

Emma laughed and acquiesced. Upon which Rose
waltzed into the governess's room with the news, and
watched her sister away. It was scarcely tea-time yet,
and Miss Brabazon found she had leisure to go round
to Mrs. Butter's, whom she had occasion to see about
some mushroom-ketchup. Mr. Henry was standing at
his low sitting-room window as she passed, dreamily
watching the boys in the playground, for school was
over. They were whooping, halloaing, running, as it
is in the nature of schoolboys to do; and a little army
of them had gathered at the palings, looking this way.
The master's face wore the sad look that had previously
so struck Miss Brabazon, and she turned aside to speak
to him.

"I have been to see Mrs. Paradyne," she said,
thinking the information might give him pleasure, as
she stood at the open window.

"Have you!" he answered, his countenance and
his luminous eyes lighting up. "How very kind of
you, Miss Brabazon!"

"Poor thing! What terrible trouble she must have

seen! She carries it in her face, in the tones of her
voice, in her manner; all tell of it. She says she shall
never overcome the blow."

"But did she speak of it to you, Miss Brabazon?"
he inquired in some surprise.

"Yes, but it was my fault; I inadvertently alluded
to it," replied Miss Brabazon, dropping her voice. "I
was so vexed with myself. Mrs. Paradyne tells me
there is another son who is out somewhere."

"Ah, yes," returned Mr. Henry; and his dreamy
eyes went far away again, as if he could see the other
son in the distance.

"But she seems quite rapt up in this, her second;
it struck me somehow that she does not care for the
elder," continued Miss Brabazon, in a pleasant tone of
confidence. "She tells me it was you who recommended the college to her."

He looked for a minute at Miss Brabazon before
he answered: it almost seemed to her as if he divined
Mrs. Paradyne's reproachful words. She waited for
an answer.

"After I had made the agreement with Dr. Brabazon
to come here, I wrote to Mrs. Paradyne. She wanted,
as I knew, to place her son at a first-class school, and
I thought I might give him some little extra attention."

"Just so. It was very kind of you. Mrs. Paradyne has an idea that the boys are shunning him,"
added Miss Brabazon.

"I believe they are. But why, I cannot find out,
for I don't think they have any clue to the past. I
tell George Paradyne he will live it down."

"To be sure he will. There is a daughter also, I
find — a teacher in a school."

For one moment Mr. Henry turned and looked sharply, questioningly, at Miss Brabazon; as if he would ask how much more Mrs. Paradyne had told her. But it was evident that he shunned the subject; and he made no comment whatever on this additional item of news. An idea flashed over Miss Brabazon that Mr. Henry was attached to this young lady; but why it did so she could not have told.

"Good afternoon, Mr. Henry."

He bowed his adieu, and Miss Brabazon went round to the house-door, and thence to the kitchen. Mrs. Butter was standing there in a fury, surrounded by coils of string and a heap of paper.

"Look here, Miss Emma," was her salutation; and she was familiar with Miss Brabazon from having formerly lived servant in the college. "If those boys don't have something done to them, it's a shocking shame. There comes a railway porter to the door five minutes ago — 'A parcel for you, ma'am,' he says to me, 'fourpence to pay!' Well, I was expecting a parcel from my brother, and I paid the fourpence and took it in. 'What on earth has made Bill tie it up with all this string for, and wrap it round with all this paper?' says I as I undid it. First string, and then paper; then string, and then paper; and curious round holes bored in all of it, as if done with a big iron skewer. But it never struck me — no, Miss Emma, it never struck me; and I went on and on till I came to the last wrap, and was bending over that to see whatever it could be, done up so careful, when a live mouse jumped out in my face. I shrieked out so, that it brought the German gentleman in — he thought I was afire. Between us we caught the mouse, and there

he is, in a pail o' water, which is where them boys
ought to be. The depth of 'em! boring them holes to
keep the animal alive, and getting a railway porter to
come with it, as bold as brass!"

Emma Brabazon, staid lady of thirty though she
was, stood coughing behind her handkerchief. "But
how do you know it was the boys?" she asked.

"Know!" wrathfully retorted Mrs. Butter. "There's
fifty faces turned on to the house now from the playground, if there's one; and all of 'em as meek as
lambs! Just look at 'em!"

Thinking she would leave the ketchup for a more
auspicious occasion, Miss Brabazon went away, leaving
Mrs. Butter fuming and grumbling. Sundry faces
certainly were still scanning the house; but Miss Brabazon appeared to see nothing, and went on her way.
In turning round by the chapel, she encountered the
senior boy.

"Did you send that present to Mrs. Butter just
now, Gall?"

"A present, Miss Brabazon?"

"A live mouse done up in a parcel."

Gall stared, and then laughed. He knew nothing
of it. The seniors were above those practical tricks.
"It was the second desk, no doubt," he said. "Am I
to inquire into it, Miss Brabazon?"

"No, not from me. But they should not tease the
old woman beyond bearing."

"She is of a cranky temper," said Gall.

"And the boys make it worse. Gall," added Miss
Brabazon, her tone changing, and the senior boy
thought it bore a touch of fear, "you have not discovered yet who fired the pistol?"

"Not at all. We begin to think now, Miss Brabazon, that it was not one of us."

"Ah," she said, turning her face away. "What is
the cause of this feeling against the new boy, George
Paradyne?" she continued, and the question seemed to
come abruptly after the pause.

"I don't know," replied Gall, excessively surprised
that it should be asked him. "I perceive there is
some feeling against Paradyne; I suppose because he
is an outsider."

"Gall, you have more sense, more thought, than
some of your companions, and I can speak to you
confidentially, as one friend would speak to another,"
resumed Miss Brabazon. "Ascertain, if you can, the
cause of this feeling, without making a fuss, you
know; and tell me what it is. Soothe it down if possible; make the boy's way easy amidst you. I am
sure he does not deserve to be shunned."

Gall touched his cap, much flattered, and went on
his way. Not into school: he had been invited out to
dinner with his father, as Mrs. Gall had said, and had
leave from Dr. Brabazon until eleven o'clock. This
gave a golden opportunity to the seniors, of which
they were not slow to avail themselves. In recording
the doings of a large school, where truth is adhered
to, the bad has to be told with the good.

Smoking was especially forbidden: nothing was so
certainly followed by punishment as the transgression
of the rule. Not only was it sternly interdicted, but
Dr. Brabazon talked kindly and earnestly to the boys
in private. The habit when acquired early was most
pernicious, he reiterated to them; frequently inducing
paralysis by middle age. He gave Gall special in-

structions to be watchful; and this was well; the
senior boy was faithful to the trust reposed in him,
and, though the vigilance of the masters could be
eluded, it was not so easy to escape his. But on occasions like this, when Gall's back was turned, certain
of the seniors who liked a cigar, or pipe, or screw —
anything — when they could get it, seized on the
opportunity, in defiance of rules and the Head
Master.

They set about the recreation this evening in the
privacy of their chamber. There were seven beds in
it, occupied by Gall, Loftus, Trace, Irby, Fullarton,
Savage, and Brown major. Taking off their jackets
and putting out the candle, they drew the window up
to its height slowly and gingerly, and lighted their
cigars. Not Trace: he had never been seen with anything of the sort in his mouth; and it always made
Brown major sick, fit to die; but he considered it
manly to persevere. There they stood at the window,
puffing away, laughing and talking in an under-tone.
News of Mrs. Butter's present had run the round of
the school, and the seniors, though loftily superior to
such things in public, did not disdain to enjoy that
and other interesting events in private. That lady's
domicile was in full view; her large dog lay in the
garden. It was the fourth dog she had tried, and
those wicked reptiles (one of Mrs. Butter's laudatory
names for them) had made friends with each animal
in succession, and so bribed him to their interests.

"I say, what is it that's up against Paradyne?"
suddenly asked Brown major, glad of any opportunity
to get that miserable cigar out of his mouth.

Nobody answered: the boys were too lazy, or

the cigars too exacting. That Brown major had a trick of bringing up unpleasant topics. He asked again.

"He had no business to be put in our class," said Savage at length.

"Jove, no! But that wasn't his fault."

"An outsider and all," continued Savage. "It's the second desk, though, that are making the set at him."

"What has he done to them?"

"Bother!" said Savage, who was in some difficulty about his cigar.

Brown major was not to be put down; talking was more convenient than smoking just now. "Do you know, Trace?"

"It's no affair of mine," replied Trace coldly, and Irby exchanged a meaning glance with him in the starlight.

"This beastly cigar won't draw at all," exclaimed Savage.

"No, they won't," assented Fullarton, in much wrath; "and I paid threepence apiece for them." For the treat this evening was his. "It's a regular swindle."

"The best cigars—"

"Hist! Who's that?"

The warning came from Trace. Not being occupied as the rest were, his attention was awake, and a sound like a cough had caught his ear from underneath the window. Out went the heads and the cigars, which was a great want of caution. On the gravel walk below, pacing about before the Head Master's study, whose large bay window abutted outwards, was Mr. Henry.

"Take care, you fellows," murmured Trace; "it's that German spy."

In came the cigars. The boys, snatching them from their lips, held them behind, back-handed, and put out their heads again.

"What makes you call him a spy, Trace?" whispered Loftus.

"Because I know he is one. Mind! he saw the cigars: I watched him look up. I wonder what he is doing there."

The idea of a spy in the school — and he one of the masters — was not at all an agreeable prospect, and the smokers felt a sort of chill. "How do you know he is one, Trace?" asked Brown major.

"That's my business. I tell you that he *is*, and that's enough. I'd give half a crown to know what he is walking there for! He can't have any business there."

For the walk was a solitary walk, not leading to any particular spot; of course open to the inmates of the college, but nobody ever thought of going there at night. Hence the wonder. Perhaps its solitude may have made its attraction for Mr. Henry: quiet and still it lay, underneath the stars, but a minute or two's distance from his lodgings. The boys, peeping out still with hushed breath, saw him presently stroll away in the direction of his home, making no sign that he had observed them.

"Mark you," said Fullarton, much put out, "the fellow has stationed himself in those low-lived rooms of Mother Butter's to be a spy upon us. Trace is right."

But not one of them had known that during this little episode Brown minor came into the room on some mission to his brother, and had seen the red

ends of the five cigars, just then held backwards.
Divining that it might not be deemed a convenient
moment for intrusion, young Mr. Brown withdrew
quietly, leaving his errand unfulfilled; went back to
his own room, and there whispered the news confidentially that the seniors were smoking.

CHAPTER VII.

Mr. Lamb improves his Mind in Private.

RATHER to the consternation of the first desk, though
perhaps not very much to their surprise, Mr. Long
brought a charge against them — that they had been
smoking. It was the morning following Gall's holiday;
and Mr. Long waylaid three or four of the seniors as
they were filing into the school-hall after chapel. Gall
of course knew nothing of it. His nose had been
greeted with an unusual scent on his entering the
chamber the previous night, when the boys were all in
bed and asleep, but he was wise enough never to take
cognizance of things that did not fall under his immediate observation. Mr. Long addressed himself to civil
Trace.

"Trace, I charge you, speak the truth. Were you
smoking?"

"No, Mr. Long, I was not. I never smoke."

"I *can't* smoke, sir," put in Brown major eagerly.
"Smoking wouldn't agree with me."

"I beg your pardon, Mr. Long, but I think whoever
has carried this story to you, might have been better
occupied in minding his own business," observed Loftus, boldly. "I wonder you take notice of tales brought
by a rat."

Mr. Long flushed a little, but was not to be put down. He awarded every one that slept in the senior room, except Gall and Trace, a severe punishment: lessons to do out of hours. Gall, from his absence, could not have been in the affair, and the denial of Trace was believed. If Lamb was the sneak of the school, Trace was the Pharisee, and considered by the masters accordingly. But that Mr. Long was conscious of feeling rather small himself on the subject of listening to "a rat" — whom *he* took to mean Lamb — he might have laid the offence before the Head Master: as it was, he dealt with it himself. There was much dissatisfaction rife at the first desk that day.

Had a very angel from heaven come down to tell them the informant was not Mr. Henry, they had scarcely listened. He was their rat. Even Loftus and Irby, the two who had been inclined to like the German master, turned against him. Gall also, in his private thoughts, considered it a gratuitous interference.

"I told you I knew the fellow was a spy," cried Trace, speaking vehemently in his condemning resentment.

A spy from henceforth, in their estimation, and to be looked upon as such: one who would have the whole school armed against him.

But now, the informant was not Mr. Henry — as I daresay you have divined: the real one was Lamb. When Brown minor carried back the news to his chamber of what he had seen, Lamb, who slept there, treasured it up, and whispered it to Mr. Long the first thing in the morning. Not a single boy, save himself, would have told. The whole lot of juniors, from the second desk downwards, would have scorned it: they were too fond of escapades themselves, to tell of the seniors; not to speak of the hidings — to use their own language — they would have been treated to in private. In this instance Lamb was not suspected, the suspicion having fixed itself on Mr. Henry.

Something almost amounting to a rebellion took place in the quadrangle after morning school; and perhaps no man had ever been called so many hard names as the unfortunate foreign master. Paradyne was not there; being an outsider, and not in favour besides, he had gone home at once; or the news of the accusation might have reached Mr. Henry. A cad! a sneak! a German spy! What was to be done? asked the enraged boys, one of another. Well, nothing much could be done, except send him to Coventry. Not being the Head Master, they had not the authority to dismiss him from his place; neither, as the affair had its rise in that forbidden fruit, tobacco, could they be demonstrative in the hearing of the masters.

"Let's go to him," foamed Savage. "Let's have it out."

"Better not," advised Fullarton, who, as purchaser of the cigars, felt a trifle more insecure than the rest, and naturally wished the affair to die away. "There'd only be a row. You know you never can keep your temper, Savage."

"Temper be bothered," cried Brown major. "He ought to be told that we've found him out."

"Then let Trace go. Trace can keep his."

Trace declined. "He'd rather not speak to the fellow."

"I'll go," said Loftus.

Away he went, on the spur of the moment, nearly

the whole lot at his heels.   Brown major walked into
the room with him; Fullarton pushed in also, to see
that peace was kept.   Mrs. Butter, in a hot flurry
banged her kitchen-door in their faces; but their visit
this time was not to her.

Mr. Henry was at dinner.   A snow-white cloth and
napkin, and silver forks; everything of that sort nice,
as befitted a gentleman's table; but the dinner itself
consisted of potatoes, eaten with salt.   A Dutch cheese
was there; bread; and a small glass of milk.   The in-
truding gentlemen stared at the fare, and Mr. Loftus's
handsome nose went up with an air.   Mr. Henry rose
and stood before the table, courteous always; and
Fullarton kicked out behind to keep out the throng.

"You were pacing the gravel walk at the back last
night, Mr. Henry," began Loftus, so calmly that no
human listener could have supposed it the advance
trumpet-blast of war, "and saw two or three cigars
overhead, I think?"

"Both saw them and smelt them," answered Mr.
Henry with a smile.

"Exactly.   Don't you think it was rather dishonourable of you to go and tell the English master of it
this morning?"

"I did not do so."

"*We* think it was," continued Loftus, wholly disre-
garding the denial.   "A gentleman could not be guilty
of such an act.   You have but just come among us,
and in any case the matter was none of yours.   Perhaps you will concern yourself in future with your
own affairs, and not with ours.   The first desk is not
accustomed to this kind of thing."

Except for the stress laid upon the word "gentle-

man," there was nothing offensive in the cold tone:
Loftus could not have descended to abuse. Mr. Henry
looked surprised, rather bewildered.

"I should think you did not hear my denial, Loftus.
I assure you I have not spoken of this."

"That's all," returned Loftus, going out with his
tail, who had not seen cause to interfere. Brown major, however, thought better of it, and turned back for
a parting word.

"Such a nasty, sneaking thing to do, you know!
You might have accused us openly to our faces; not
have gone canting to the masters behind our backs."

Whatever Bertie Loftus's faults might be, he
scorned a lie: and he fully believed the denial of the
German master to be nothing less. So far as the
smoking party knew, nobody else had been, or could
have been, cognizant of the cigars; for Brown minor
and his room had kept their own counsel.

"I knew he'd deny it," exclaimed Trace, when
they got back, his light eyes flashing with a scorn not
often seen there. "You now see what he is."

"I say, what d'ye think he's having for dinner?"
burst out Fullarton. "Potatoes and salt."

"Potatoes and salt? Go along with you."

"Ask Loftus then; ask Brown. He had got nothing else but a Dutch cheese; he was washing 'em
down with milk."

"What else could be expected of one who'd go to
lodge at Mother Butter's?" was the scornful remark of
Savage. "He must be a cad!"

"And an owl," squeaked Lamb, venturing forward.
"Owls go out prowling at night. Nobody else *could*
have told."

Clearly. A master who dined on potatoes and salt, and eat his words with a lie when his villany was found out, was an owl, and all the rest of it.

Mr. Henry meanwhile was unconscious of the storm against him. He rather laughed over the matter, attaching no importance to it. His frugal dinner despatched, he was plodding on with his translation, when a little fellow, to whom he had promised some help in a tormenting French exercise, came in; and he was followed by George Paradyne, who often brought his Greek difficulties to Mr. Henry. George was a good classical scholar, but Mr. Henry was a better. Patiently he gave his best attention to both, putting his own work aside. He was always ready to help the boys out of hours, and encouraged them to come to him, though it was not in his line of duties.

Afternoon school began. A dull, weary afternoon, with inward dissatisfaction reigning. Mr. Henry called up the second desk, and found his pupils careless and troublesome, bordering on insubordination. He promised them punishment if they did not attend better. Master Dick Loftus especially was as scornfully insolent as he dared be. Not very long after they were sent back to their places, Dick lifted the lid of his desk, and fished up a rotten apple.

"Onions, see here. I've a great mind to shy it at him."

Onions glanced round the room; he enjoyed mischief as much as Dick, and was heartily hating and despising Mr. Henry: having nothing of the sneak in his own disposition, he could not tolerate it in others.

"You'll be seen, Dick. Old Jebb's eyes are rolling about."

"They always are, and be hanged to him, when Brabazon's away!" exclaimed Smart from the other side of Dick, as resentfully as if the rolling of the Reverend Mr. Jebb's eyes were a personal affront.

Presently the opportunity came; Dick raised the apple, carefully took aim, and sent it flying. Good aim, for it struck the cheek of Mr. Henry, making on it a great dash and splash, as it is in the nature of a rotten apple to do. But, unfortunately, at the very moment of Dick's giving an impetus to the missile, Mr. Henry happened to raise his eyes; he saw the deliberate aim, saw the throw, and Dick knew that he saw it. The whole room was aroused.

"Who did that?" cried out Mr. Baker, in a passion. "He shall have a good caning, whoever it was."

Nobody answered. The second desk especially, bending attentively over their books, looked up in innocent surprise.

"Who did it, I ask?" roared Mr. Baker, a choleric man, beginning to talk fast and furiously, and to cane his table as kindly as if it had been a boy's back. In the midst, in walked the Head Master. As he took his place the noise sunk to a calm.

"Did you see who flung the apple, Mr. Henry?" inquired the Master, when he was made cognizant of the cause of uproar he had come upon: and his quiet voice of authority presented a contrast to Mr. Baker's.

Involuntarily, as it were, and for a moment only, Mr. Henry's glance met Dick's. Something like shame for the act, something like a piteous appeal for silence, went out of Dick's eyes. It is so very different, you see — the accomplishing a little thing of this sort with impunity, and the being caught in the act. Mr. Henry, replying to the Head Master, said it might have been an accident, and finished wiping his face with his handkerchief. A nice mess the cambric was in.

"Accident or no accident, the boy shall be punished if I can discover him," returned the doctor. "Can't you tell who flung it?"

Mr. Henry merely shook his head very slightly. It was of no consequence, he quietly said, and called up the third class for its German exercises. Dr. Brabazon, letting the matter drop, sat down and began turning the things over on his table in search of his lead-pencil. Not finding it, he took one from his pocket, and, in doing so, let it fall. It rolled along the floor, and one of the boys picked it up.

"Thank you, Jessop," said he, always pleasant with his pupils. "It would not do to lose this, would it?"

The pencil was of gold, with a beautiful diamond set in the top. It had been a present to him from some former pupils. The doctor began to make notes on an exercise.

"I say, Dick, what a blessing the German did not twig you," whispered Smart, speaking with his head bent over his Euripides as if he were steadily conning it.

"But he did," answered Dick.

"I'm sure he didn't. What nonsense! As if he'd not have got you into punishment if he had the chance!"

Dick, for a wonder, did not insist on his own opinion, and the afternoon went on. Dr. Brabazon's man-servant, Dean, appeared at the door and said a gentleman was waiting to see him, and the doctor left

the hall. He only came back again just as the classes
were rising.

Boys and masters poured out indiscriminately as
usual. Mr. Henry walked away quickly, and the boys
went into a state of frantic delight in the tea-room,
ironically hoping he was washing his cheek.

But Dick Loftus had been struck with the amazing
generosity displayed to him; for that Mr. Henry saw
him fling the apple purposely, had been as plain to
him as the sun at noon-day; and he thought he owed
some acknowledgment of the consideration shown.
Dick Loftus was all impulse, and he forthwith went
off on the gallop to Mother Butter's. Mr. Henry was
bending over his table working at the translation.

"I've come to say I'm sorry for what I did, and
to thank you for not telling of me," began Dick, his
face glowing rather more than usual.

"That's right," said Mr. Henry, his luminous eyes
lighting up with a smile as he took Dick's hand and
shook it.

"You saw me fling it, didn't you, sir?"

"Yes."

"Then why didn't you tell?"

"Because I did not wish you to be punished. I
like to make people's lives pleasant to them; perhaps
because I have had very little pleasure in my own."

"Would you never punish any of us?"

"I would if I saw you do essentially wrong. But
for petty spite — retaliation — revenge — oh, Dick,
don't you know Who it is that has warned us against
these? I think we must all try for love and peace on
earth if we would enter into it in heaven."

Dick considered: it was rather an unaccustomed

way of putting matters. He began to work things out in his mind, speaking, as was usual with him, what came uppermost.

"I don't call it at all a heavenly thing to have gone behind their backs, and told about the seniors smoking," said he, practically. "I suppose you think smoking's one of the wrong things."

"It's not very right," replied Mr. Henry. "It injures themselves, and it is flying in the face of orders."

"But why did you not report them openly, instead of the — the other way?"

"I did not report them at all. I did not mention it to any one."

"Is that true?" asked Dick, dubiously.

"Boy! I should never tell you what was not true."

Dick stood puzzled. It was Mr. Henry's word against common sense; against the conviction of the whole school. Nothing would come of arguing the matter, even had Mr. Henry been disposed to argue it, and Dick turned to leave, saying something in a complaining tone about having to get to his lessons in play hours.

"Do you find them difficult?" asked Mr. Henry.

"Difficult?" returned Dick, as if the question were an aggravation. "It's that horrid Euclid. Nothing ever bothers me as that does."

"Bring it to me; I daresay I can smooth your mountains for you by a little explanation."

"Do you mean it?" cried Dick, a spring of gratitude in his voice. "But it is not in your work. You have nothing to do with Euclid."

"Never mind that. Fetch it now."

Dick flew for his books. Mr. Henry did smooth the mountains, patiently, kindly; and he bade him always come to him in the same stumbling-blocks — every evening if he liked. Mrs. Butter made her appearance once, which Dick regarded as an agreeable interlude, for it enabled him to ask affectionately after the shorn cock and the other animals, to the lady's great wrath. She had a pair of new boots in her hand for Mr. Henry; the man, she said, was waiting for the money. Mr. Henry replied that it was not convenient to pay him then; he would send it in a day or two.

Dick, his Euclid difficulty over, went home; and in giving an account to his friends of various matters, mentioned this episode of the new boots and the non-payment — not in ill-nature, but in his propensity to gossip. Trace was contemptuous over it.

"I'll lay a guinea the fellow has not a shilling in the world!"

"But look here!" cried Dick. "I don't really think it was he that told about the smoke. He says he didn't: he's as earnest as he can be."

"That's all your opinion's good for," returned Trace. And the rest gave a slighting laugh at Dick. Dick took his revenge in a most impudent whistle.

The boys were subsequently in the hall at their evening lessons. Lamb, who had contrived to do his quickly, was stealing out to pass the intervening half-hour before prayer-time in his bedroom, which was against rules. In passing the mathematical room, he encountered Mr. Long. Glancing around to see that no one else was within hearing, Mr. Long accosted him in a semi-under-tone.

"By the way, Lamb — there was no mistake I sup-

pose in regard to that matter you mentioned to me?
The seniors *were* smoking?"

"No mistake at all, sir.   Five or six cigars were
alight, and the room was full of smoke."

"They are making a terrible fuss over it — just as
though it were not true."

"It was quite true, sir. My only motive in report-
ing it to you was their own good: I did not want to
get them into a row.   It *is* a pernicious habit."

"Ah," returned Mr. Long, peering rather dubiously
through his spectacles on his virtuous friend.   For he
really did not approve of sneaks as a whole, but there
always seemed some excuse for listening to this one.
What with his near sight, and what with his absent
brain, buried in its calculations and sciences, Mr. Long
was reproachfully self-conscious that he did not look out
for peccadilloes as he ought.   "That's all then, Lamb."

Mr. Long turned towards the hall; Lamb towards
the library, as if he wanted to borrow a book.   But as
soon as the master's footsteps had died away, the young
gentleman altered his course, and stole gingerly up the
stairs.

After Dick Loftus had left with his mathematical
books, Mr. Henry got to his translation, and wrote on
by candle-light, how long he hardly knew.   His head,
which had been aching all the evening, grew worse,
and he suddenly bethought himself to take a mouthful
of fresh air.   The heavy atmosphere was so different
from what he was accustomed to in Germany, that he
sometimes felt three parts stifled. Putting on his trencher,
he strolled across the gymnasium ground, damp this
evening, to the broad gravel walk before mentioned,
leading past the study and the rest of the back win-

dows of the college. Barely had he begun to pace the path, when he encountered a strange man, much to his surprise; for the place was private. Mr. Henry accosted him.

"Are you in search of any one?"

"I have a letter for Dr. Brabazon. I can't find any entrance to the house. This is Orville College, isn't it?"

The words were spoken roughly and impatiently; the tones seemed to be those of an educated man. Mr. Henry tried to get a distinct view of his face, but the speaker turned his back, and appeared to be looking for some entrance to the college.

"You must go round to the front," said Mr. Henry. "The entrances are all on that side."

Without a word of thanks, the stranger went off down the path, looking here and there like one uncertain of his road; but he took the right turning, round by the chapel. Mr. Henry, who had watched him, continued his way to the top of the gravel-walk — he, and his tired brow.

As he was passing underneath the bedrooms in returning, a piece of newspaper, seemingly as large as a whole *Times*, and crumpled into a sort of ball, came down upon his cap.

"Who's that?" he called out, thinking it might have been done to attract his attention. The question brought forth a boy's head from one of the upper windows, and a faint light that was burning in the room suddenly went out.

"Did you throw that down for any purpose?" asked Mr. Henry.

"No, sir. Did it touch you? I beg your pardon. It was only a piece of old newspaper I threw away."

The head went in again. Mr. Henry had not discerned to whom it belonged, and did not care to know. He began to cross slowly back towards home; he could not afford to waste more time, but must get to his work again.

"It was that beast of a German!"

The words came from Mr. Lamb — for his head it was, which had been thrust forth in answer to Mr. Henry. Lamb had gained the bedroom unmolested — you saw him on his way to it — and the first thing he did, after bolting the door, was to light a private taper. He had brought a huge cake to school, with sundry other luxuries, and had been enjoying them systematically, so much each day, as he could get solitary opportunity. The last slice of the cake only remained to be eaten. He gobbled it in rather quickly, licked up the crumbs remaining in the paper, made a ball of that, and flung it out just as Mr. Henry chanced to be passing. When the latter called out, Lamb extinguished the candle with his finger and thumb, and then looked out to answer.

"It's that beast of a German!"

But Mr. Lamb need not have called names. He watched Mr. Henry crossing towards his home, and gave him time to get indoors. It wanted still some twenty minutes to the hour for chapel, and he relighted his taper. Diving into the bottom of his box, he brought forth a favourite book for a little wholesome recreation, and also a choice cigarette, which he lighted. Down he sat on the next box, low, square, and convenient; puffing comfortably away, and improving his mind with the solacing pages of "Jack Sheppard."

CHAPTER VIII.

A Loss.

THE next morning was distinguished by an event that brought pleasure to all. Talbot was amongst them again. He was looking fresh and well; did not limp in the least; and seemed to have grown an inch and a half. Mr. Baker directed him to take his place at the first desk, and this was a surprise to its occupants: but they welcomed him gladly.

"Did you know you were going to be moved here, Shrewsbury?" asked they.

"Not for certain. I thought it likely."

"You are going in for the Orville?"

"Of course I am. I should have done that had they kept me at the second desk. I say, has it never come out who shot me?"

The boys shook their heads. It was a sore subject with them yet.

"I heard that Sir Simon offered a gold watch as a reward."

"So he did. But nothing turned up. Never mind, earl."

"*I* don't mind; why should I?" returned the earl. "No harm has come of it. I say, though, you can't think how kind the doctor and Miss Brabazon have been. If I were old enough I'd marry her."

This caused a laugh. The earl had the queerest way of bringing out things, keeping his own countenance as steady as could be all the while.

Dr. Orville, the founder of the college, had bestowed on it an exhibition at his death. It fell in at the end of every third year; and for three years gave seventy pounds a year to the boy who got it. It was open for competition to all unconditionally, no matter whether they were seniors or not; though of course none but seniors were sufficiently advanced to try for it; and the name of each competitor must lie on the books, *as* competitor, for one year previous to the trial. The boys called it familiarly the Orville Prize; in short, the Orville. The names had been just put down, several, for the probationary twelvemonth was on the eve of being entered; and, to the unspeakable indignation of the school, George Paradyne's was one. A new boy (leaving other things that some two or three of them knew of out of the question) who had but just come in, to thrust down his name indecently amidst the old pupils! This was said from mouth to mouth; and Trace had a sore battle with himself not to disclose the disgrace of the past.

The Head Master came into the hall and called up Talbot. The boy had been at home for a week or two, and only returned that morning.

"Are you feeling strong, my lad?"

"Quite so, thank you, sir. I have been to the sea-side."

"Have you!" returned the Master, some surprise in his tone, for he knew how limited funds were at Talbot's home.

"Sir Simon Orville came to see my mother the day after I got home; he insisted that she should take me to the sea-side," said Talbot with a smile, as if he had divined those thoughts. The doctor understood the rest in a moment.

"I'm proud of Sir Simon; I'm proud to call him a friend," cried he, warmly. "I am glad you've been."

"If you please, sir, I wish my name to be entered for the Orville Exhibition," Talbot stayed to say.

"Do you? Very well. How old are you?"

"Close upon seventeen."

"All right. I don't care how many of you enter. Only one can gain it; but it will get the rest on in their studies. I'll just make a note of your name in pencil now."

He looked for his lead-pencil, and could not see it. Then, remembering that he had missed it the previous day, he put his hand in his pocket for the gold one. But it was not there.

"Why, what have I done with it?" cried the doctor, searching about. "Perhaps I took it into my study and left it there. Very careless of me! Go and see, Talbot: it will be on the table in the large inkstand."

Talbot went and came back without it. "It's not there, sir. This is the only one I could see," handing an old silver one.

"Not there!" Dr. Brabazon sent his thoughts backwards, trying to recollect when he last used it. The fact of the pencil's falling in the schoolroom the previous afternoon occurred to him, and he remembered that he was making pencil marks on a book with it when his man-servant came to call him out. What did he do with the pencil? Did he leave it on his table; or put it in his pocket; or carry it away in his hand? He could not tell. Here, it certainly was not at present; and the Head Master rose and went to his study himself. When called out of school the previous afternoon he had sat there for some time with the visitor, a gentleman named Townshend, who had come on business. Subsequently, he and Miss Brabazon had gone out to dinner: and, in short, his memory showed no trace of the pencil since he was using it in the hall. He could not find it in the study, and went to the sitting-room, interrupting his young daughter; who had quitted her French exercise to drop airy curtseys before the glass.

"Rose, have you seen my gold pencil?"

"Oh, papa," said Rose, demurely, making believe to be stooping down to tie her shoe. "Pencil-case! No, I've not seen it. Why, papa, you are always losing your things."

A just charge, Miss Rose. The doctor, an absent man, often did mislay articles.

"But they are always found again, papa, you know. As this will be."

However nothing seemed so certain about it this time. The search for the pencil went on; and went on in vain. Quite a commotion arose in the house, especially in the hall, where the search was greatest.

"It could not go without hands," said the doctor, after turning everything out of his desk-table. "If I had let it fall in getting up when I was called out yesterday, some of you would have heard it."

One of the boys, and only one, affirmed that he saw the doctor with it in his hand as he left the hall. This was Trace: and there were few things Trace did not see with those drawn-together eyes of his. Dr. Brabazon believed Trace was mistaken. If he had carried the pencil away in his hand, he thought he should not fail to remember it; besides, others of them would surely have noticed it. Trace persisted: he said he saw the diamond gleam.

Well, the pencil was gone. Gone! Dr. Brabazon looked out on the sea of faces, curious ideas hovering around his mind. He did not admit them; he would not have accused any of the boys for the world; no, nor suspected them. But it was very strange.

The boys thought it so. First Talbot was shot, and now a diamond pencil (as they phrased it) was stolen. Had they got a black sheep amongst them? If so, who was it?

But in a day or two Trace's assertion proved to be correct. Dr. Brabazon saw Mr. Townshend, the friend who had called upon him, and this gentleman said he had observed a gold pencil in the doctor's hand when he came into the study that day; and he, the doctor, had put it into the large inkstand on the table, as he shook hands with him. This news, if anything, complicated the affair; but it appeared entirely to exonerate the boys, had exoneration been required. It also drew it into a smaller nutshell: and the hypothesis to arise now was, that some one had come in by the glass window and taken it. Dean, the doctor's private servant, a faithful man who had lived with him for many years, avowed freely that it was unusually late when he went in that night to close the shutters. He found the glass door on what he called "the catch;" that is, pushed close to, but not shut; which was nothing unusual. On the following morning the doctor was in his study by six o'clock, and opened the shutters himself, his frequent custom. That the pencil was certainly not in the inkstand then, the doctor felt sure.

"I say, Trace, do you think the German would take the pencil?"

It was Lamb who put this question. Morning school was over, and the boys were in the quadrangle, discussing the loss and other matters. Trace looked up quickly.

"Why do you ask it?"

"Because he was prowling about before the study window the night of the loss — just as he had been the other night when that stupid tale about the smoking got about. I went up to our bedroom: I like to get a few minutes' quiet for reflection sometimes — it improves the mind," continued candid Lamb; "and in chucking a piece of newspaper out of the window, it happened to touch his head. He called out, and that's how I knew he was there."

Trace drew in his breath: a grave suspicion was taking possession of him. The eager boys, a choice knot of them, had gathered round.

"Nobody's ever there at night, no stranger, as Dr. Brabazon said this morning," observed Trace. "It looks queer."

"You think the German went in and helped himself to the pencil, Trace?"

"Be quiet, Onions; you are always so outspoken. I'd rather not 'think' about it on my own score," was Trace's cautious answer.

"Upon my word and honour, I think it must have been the fellow!" cried Lamb, vehemently; and for once in his life Mr. Lamb spoke according to his conviction. "It stands to reason: who else was likely to be there?"

"I don't say he took it, mind," resumed Trace;

8*

"but of all, belonging to the college — masters, boys, servants, take the lot — the German is the one who seems most in need of money. One may say *that* much without treason. Look at his engaging Mother Butter's cheap lodgings! and living on potatoes and such things!"

"The other day he was dining off a suet-pudding: he ate it with salt," interrupted Fullarton's eager voice.

"How fond he must be of salt!" exclaimed Savage. And the boys laughed.

"He's working at some translation like old Blazes — sits up at night to do it," resumed Powell. "He told Loftus minor it was for a bookseller, who was to give him thirty pounds for it. He'd not work in that way if he didn't need money awfully."

"But where does his money go? His salary — what does he do with it?" wondered the boys.

"He must have private expenses," said Trace.

"What expenses?"

This was a question. They had once had an usher who indulged himself in horse exercise; they had had another who gave forty-five pounds for a violin, and half ruined himself buying new music. Mr. Henry did neither.

"Perhaps he has got a wife and family," hazarded Brown major, impulsively.

The notion of Mr. Henry's having a wife and family was so rich, that the boys laughed till their sides ached. Which rather offended Brown major.

"I'm sure I've heard those foreign French fellows often marry at twenty-one; Germans too," quoth he. "You needn't grin. When a man's got a wife and family, he has to keep 'em. His money must go somewhere. Dick Loftus saw some new boots come home for him the other day, and he couldn't pay for them. What are you staring at, Trace?"

Trace was not staring at Brown major or any one else in particular. The mention of the boots called up a train of ideas that half startled him. This incident of the boots had occurred on the very evening of the loss; the following day (when they were in the midst of searching for the pencil) Mr. Henry had gone by train into London after morning school, and was not back until three o'clock. Soon after he returned, Trace, by the merest accident, saw him take out his purse, and there were several sovereigns in it. The thing, to Trace's mind, seemed to be getting unpleasantly clear. But he said nothing.

"What are you all doing here?" exclaimed Gall, coming up at this juncture. "Holding a council?"

They told him in an undertone: that the German master had been pacing about before the study-window the night the pencil must have been lost out of the room; and they spoke of his hard work, his want of money, of all the rest they had been saying and hinting at.

Gall stopped the grave hint in its bud. The suspicion was perfectly absurd as regarded Mr. Henry; most unjustifiable, he assured them; and they had better get rid of it at once.

It was rather a damper, and in the check to their spirits, they began to disperse. Gall had a great deal of good plain common sense; and his opinion was always listened to. Trace rose from the projecting base of a pillar on which he had been seated, knees to nose, put his arm within Gall's and drew him away.

He told him everything; adding this fact of seeing the money in Mr. Henry's purse, which he had not disclosed to the rest. Gall would not be convinced. It might look a little suspicious, he acknowledged, but he felt sure Mr. Henry was not one to do such a thing: he'd not dare to do it. Besides, think of his high character, as given to the Head Master from the university of Heidelberg.

Trace maintained his own opinion. He thought there were ways and means of getting those high characters furnished, when people had a need for them; he said he had mistrusted the man from the first moment he saw him. "Look at his peaching about the smoking! Look at the mean way he lives, the food he eats!" continued Trace, impressively. "He must have private expenses of some sort; or else what makes him so poor?"

"He may have left debts behind him in Germany," suggested Gall, after a pause of reflection.

"And most likely has," was the scornful rejoinder. "But he'd not make his dinner off potatoes and work himself into a skeleton, to pay back debts in Germany. Rubbish, Gall!"

"Look here, Trace. I know nothing of Mr. Henry's private affairs; they may be bad or good for aught I can tell; but if I were you, I'd get rid of that suspicion as to the pencil-case. Rely upon it," concluded Gall, emphatically, "it won't hold water. Put it away from you."

Good advice, no doubt; and Trace, cautious always, intended to take it. It happened, however, that same afternoon, that the Head Master sent him to his study for a book. Trace opened the door quickly, and there saw Miss Brabazon, on her hands and knees, searching round the edge of the carpet. She sprang to her feet with a scared look.

"A pencil-case will roll into all sorts of odd places," she observed, as if in apology. "I cannot understand the loss; it is troubling me more than I can express."

"It must have been lost through the window, Miss Brabazon," said Trace. "That is, some one must have got in that way."

"Yes; unless it rolled down and is hiding itself," she answered, her eyes glancing restlessly into every corner. "I think I shall have the carpet taken up to-morrow. It will be a great trouble, with all this fixed furniture."

"I don't think you need have it done," observed Trace, who was standing with his back to her before the large bookcase. "I fancy it went out through the window."

"You have some suspicion, Trace!" she quickly exclaimed. "What is it?"

"If I have, Miss Brabazon, it is one that I cannot mention. It may be a wrong suspicion, you see; perhaps it is."

"Trace," she said, laying her hand upon his arm, and her voice, her eyes were full of strange earnestness, "you must tell it me. Tell me in confidence; I have a suspicion too; perhaps we may keep the secret together. I would give the pencil and its value twice over to find it behind the carpet, in some crack or crevice of the wainscoting — and I *know* it is not there."

She spoke with some passion. The words, the manner altogether, disarmed Trace of his caution; and he breathed his doubts into her ear. They were received with intense surprise.

"Mr. Henry! that kind, gentlemanly German master! Why, Trace, you must be dreaming."

Trace thought himself an idiot. "To tell you the truth, Miss Brabazon, I fancied you were suspecting him yourself, though I don't know why I took up the notion," he resumed, in his mortification. "But for that, I should not have mentioned it. I won't eat my words, though, as I have spoken; I do believe him to be guilty."

"I cannot think it; he seems as honest as the day. Just go over your grounds of suspicion again, Trace. I was too much surprised to listen properly."

Trace did so; the huge book he had come for standing upright in his arm, supported by his shoulder. He mentioned everything; from Lamb having seen Mr. Henry before the study that night, down to the empty purse filled suddenly with gold.

Did you ever happen to witness a knot of boys favoured personally with an unexpected explosion of gunpowder on the fifth of November? I'm sure they did not leap apart in a more startled manner than did Trace and Miss Brabazon now, at the entrance of Mr. Henry. He had come to see after Trace and the book; the Head Master thought Trace must be unable to find it. Away went Trace. Miss Brabazon stooped to put down the corner of the hearth-rug, saying something rather confusedly about searching for the pencil, now that it was known to have been lost in that room.

It happened that Mr. Henry, an out-door master, had not heard that that fact was established. Miss Brabazon told him of it.

"Some one must have got in through the un-
fastened window, and taken it," she continued, looking
at him. "It is very curious. Strangers are never
there: the grounds are private."

"Got in through the window," he repeated, as a
recollection flashed across his mind. "Why, I saw a
man on the gravel-path; there," pointing to the one on
which the window opened, "that same night. He was
looking for the entrance to the college, and I directed
him round to the front."

"How came you to see him?" she returned, speaking rather sharply.

"I had been hard at work at my translation, the
one I told the doctor of, and strolled across for a
breath of fresh air. This man was coming down the
path, must have just passed the window, and I asked
him what he wanted. He replied that he had a letter
for Dr. Brabazon."

"Why did you not speak of this before, Mr.
Henry?"

"I never thought to connect it with the loss. It
was believed that the pencil was lost from the hall.
The man did not seem in the least confused or hurried.
I should fancy his business was quite legitimate, Miss
Brabazon; merely the delivery of the letter. I saw
one in his hand."

She went at once to question the servants, debating in her mind whether this was fact, or an in-
vention of the German master's to throw suspicion
from himself. Not any tidings could she get of a
letter having been brought by hand that night. Dean
was positive that no such letter had been delivered:
one came the previous night, he said, for Mr. Baker,

and he took it to him. Miss Brabazon went back to the study, and asked Mr. Henry, waiting there by her desire, whether he had not made a mistake in the night.

"None whatever," was his reply. "I had received a letter from Heidelberg that day, enclosing an order for a little money due to me, and when I met this man I was considering how I could shape my duties on the following one, so as to have time to go to London and get it cashed."

"And did you go?"

"Yes, as soon as morning school was over. I told the doctor what my errand was. When I left, they were searching the hall for the pencil."

This, if true, disposed of one part of Mr. Trace's suspicions. Miss Brabazon thought how candid and upright he looked as he stood there talking to her. "Should you know the man again, Mr. Henry?" she suddenly asked.

"I might know his voice: I did not see much of his face. A youngish man; thirty, or rather more. I thought he walked a little lame."

Miss Brabazon lifted her head with more quickness than the information seemed to warrant. "Lame! *Lame?*"

"It struck me so."

She said no more. She sat looking out straight before her with a sort of bewildered stare. Mr. Henry left her to return to the hall; but she sat on, staring still and seeing nothing.

———

CHAPTER IX.

Christmas Day.

SOME weeks elapsed. Things had blown over, and the Christmas holidays were coming on. Wonders and calamities; and, in some degree, suspicions; yield to the soothing hand of time. Talbot's accident was almost forgotten; the lost pencil (never found) was not thought of so much as it had been, and the gossip respecting it had ceased.

The bitterness had not lessened against George Paradyne. Gall could not fathom its source. There was no cause for it, as far as he knew, except that the boy had been placed at once at the first desk, and had entered his name for the Orville prize; both of which facts were highly presumptuous in a new scholar, and an outsider. It was also known that he was in the habit of flying to Mrs. Butter's house for help in his studies: the boys supposed that the German (as they derisively called Mr. Henry) was paid for giving it: and many an ill-natured sneer was levelled at them both.

"Are you going to coach Paradyne through the holidays?" asked Trace of Mr. Henry, condescending to address him for once in a way: and be it remarked that when Trace so far unbended, he did not forget his usual civility. But Mr. Henry always detected the inward feeling.

"Trace," he said, every tone betraying earnest kindness, "you spend the holidays at Sir Simon's, therefore I shall be within reach. Come to me, and let me read with you: I know you are anxious to get

the Orville. Come every day; I will do my very best
to push you on."

"You are a finished scholar?" observed Trace,
cynically.

"As finished as any master in the college. When
a young man knows (as I did) that he has nothing
else to trust to, he is wise to make use of his op-
portunities. I believe also that I have a peculiar
aptitude for teaching. Come and try me."

"What would be your terms?"

"Nothing. I would do it for" — he laughed as
he spoke — "love. Oh, Trace, I wish you would let
me help you! I wish I could get you to believe that
it would be one pleasure in my lonely life."

"What a hypocrite!" thought Trace: "I wonder
what he's saying it for? Thank you," he rejoined
aloud, with distant coldness; "I shall not require your
assistance." And so the offer terminated; and Trace,
speaking of it to Loftus, said it was like the fellow's
impudence to make it.

One thing had been particularly noticeable throughout the term — that the young German usher seemed
to have a facility for healing breaches. In ill-feelings,
in quarrellings, in fightings, so sure was he to step in,
and not only stop the angry tongues, but soothe their
owners down to calmness. Rage, in his hands, became
peace; mountains of evil melted down to molehills;
fierce recrimination gave place to hand-shaking. He
did all so quietly, so pleasantly, so patiently! and,
but for the under-current of feeling against him that
was being always secretly fanned, he would have been
an immense favourite. Putting aside the untoward

events at its commencement, the term had been one of the most satisfactory on record.

Loftus and his brother, Trace, James Talbot, and Irby were spending the holidays at Pond Place. Sir Simon Orville generally had two of the boys, besides his nephews. They had wanted Irby and Leek this time; but Sir Simon chose to invite Talbot, and gave them their choice of the other two. And it happened that Sir Simon, the day after their arrival, overheard Trace and Loftus talking of sundry matters, and became cognisant of the offer made to Trace by Mr. Henry.

"And you didn't accept it, Raymond?" he asked, plunging suddenly upon the two in his flowery dressing-gown. "If I were going in for the Orville competition, I shouldn't have sneezed at it. This comes of your pride: you won't study with Paradyne."

"No, it does not, uncle," replied Trace; "though I should object to study with Paradyne. It comes of my dislike to Mr. Henry."

"What is there to dislike in Mr. Henry?"

Trace hesitated, making no direct reply. Bertie Loftus moved away. Sir Simon pressed his question.

Wisely or unwisely, Trace, in his ill-nature, forgot his ordinary caution, his long-continued silence, and disclosed the suspicions attaching to Mr. Henry in regard to the lost pencil. It was so delightful a temptation to speak against him! Loftus came back during the recital, and curled his lip in silent condemnation of Trace.

"Look here," said Sir Simon, wrathfully, "I'd rather suspect one of you."

Loftus went away again without making any answer. Trace smiled very grandly compassionate.

"You were always suspicious, Trace," continued Sir Simon; "it's in your nature to be so, as it was in your poor mother's. He's a kindly, honest gentleman, so far as I've seen of him. Steal a pencil, indeed! Who rose the report? You?"

"There has not been any report," said Trace, with composure. "Lamb saw him before the study window that night, and we wondered whether he had come in and taken it. The doubt was hushed up, and has died away."

"Not hushed up as far as you go, it seems. Raymond, I'd ——"

Talbot and Dick Loftus came running in, and Sir Simon changed the private bearings of the subject, for the more open one of Raymond's pride, as he called it, in not accepting Mr. Henry's offer.

"Giving him two hours a day in the holidays!" exclaimed Talbot. "I wish it had been made to me!"

"You do!" cried Sir Simon. "I suppose you hope to get the prize yourself?"

"I shall try my best for it, sir," said the boy, laughing. "Seventy pounds a year for three years! It would take me to Oxford; and there's no other chance of my getting there."

Holidays for everybody but poor Mr. Henry! He was slaving on. He took George Paradyne for two hours a day; he took another boy, one of the outsiders, who was poor, friendless, and very backward; receiving nothing for either; he gave Miss Rose Brabazon her daily lessons, French one day, German the next, alternately; he went to Mrs. Gall's, to drill three of her little boys, not out at school yet, in Latin and Greek; and he worked hard at his translation, which translation was a very difficult one to get on quickly with, necessitating continual references to abstruse works; for Mr. Henry discovered numerous errors in the original, and desired, in his conscientiousness, to set them right in the English version.

He was at home one morning, a few days after the holidays began, buried in his translation books, marking the faults in Miss Rose Brabazon's last French dictation — and he believed nobody else could have made so many — when Sir Simon Orville walked in. The sweet, kind, patient expression in Mr. Henry's face had always struck him: very patient and wearied did it look to-day. It was Christmas Eve.

"Hard at work? But this is holiday time, Mr. Henry."

Mr. Henry smiled and brightened up. "Some of us don't get the chance of any holiday, Sir Simon," he cheerfully said, as if it were a good joke.

"Bad, that! All work and no play, you know — but I'd better not enlarge on that axiom," broke off Sir Simon, "since my errand here is to give you more work. Of the boys whose names are down for the Orville, one comes to you daily, I hear."

"Yes; Paradyne," replied Mr. Henry, feeling rather sensitive at mentioning the name which must be so unwelcome to the brother of the late Mrs. Trace.

"Ay, Paradyne. You made an offer to my nephew, Raymond Trace, to take him also for the holidays, I hear. And he declined."

"I should have been so glad to be of service to him!" returned Mr. Henry, his eyes lighting with the earnestness of the wish.

"The prejudiced young jackass!" explosively cried Sir Simon. "Well, the loss is his. But now, I want

you to make the same offer to another, one who won't
refuse it; and that's Talbot — Lord Shrewsbury, as
they call him. He's staying with me — you know it,
perhaps — and he can come to you daily. The boy
has only his education to look to in life; he does not
possess a golden horde laid up in lavender to make
ducks and drakes of when he comes of age, as some of
the rascals do; and through those other two bright
nephews of mine his studies were stopped for some
four or five weeks. Will you take him?"

"Yes, and gladly, Sir Simon. He — perhaps" —
Mr. Henry paused and hesitated — "will have no objection to study with young Paradyne?"

"He'd better not let me hear of it, if he has,"
retorted Sir Simon. "Why should he? Paradyne and
his people have not hurt *him*. No, no; Talbot's another
sort of fellow to that. And now, what shall we say
about terms? Don't be afraid of laying it on, Mr.
Henry; it's my treat."

"I could not charge," said Mr. Henry, interrupting
the cheering laugh. "Excuse me, Sir Simon; but I
am not helping the boys for money. It would scarcely
be an honourable thing. I am well paid by Dr.
Brabazon; and any little assistance I can give them
out of school is only their due."

"But you are not paid to teach them Latin and
Greek and mathematics. You have the right to make
the most of your holidays."

"I scarcely see that I have, so far as the college
pupils are concerned. Let Talbot come to me at once,
Sir Simon; but please say no more about payment.
Robbing me of my time? No, indeed, not of a minute,
if he comes with Paradyne: their studies are the same.

As to any little trouble of my own, I would not think of accepting money for that. I am too glad to give it."

Sir Simon nodded approvingly; he liked the generosity of the feeling, and shook Mr. Henry's hand heartily as he went out.

"The cocked-up young Pharisee!" he soliloquized, apostrophizing the unconscious Trace, and dashing an enormous gig umbrella, that he had brought as a walking-stick, into the ground. "If ever there was an honest, honourable, good spirit, it's his I have just left. Mr. Trace and his uncharitable suspicions will get taken down some day, as sure as he is living."

Turning into the college, he went straight on to the sitting-room, where Miss Brabazon was, to all appearance, alone. Rose was behind the curtain at the far end of the room, ostensibly learning her German, for Mr. Henry would be due in ten minutes; really buried in a charming fairy-tale book, lent to her by Jessie Gall. And her sister had forgotten she was there.

"What is it that these rascally boys have picked up against that poor young German master?" began Sir Simon, in his impulsive fashion. "Do you know, Miss Emma?"

Emma Brabazon laid down the pretty baskets of flowers she was arranging for the evening; for her married brothers and sisters and their children were coming that day on their usual Christmas sojourn. But she did not answer.

"Trace has been talking to me about the lost pencil," resumed Sir Simon. "But *surely* it is a slander to suspect him of having taken it. Miss Emma,

I'd lay my life he is as honest as I am; and he's a vast deal more of a gentleman."

"It was very foolish of Trace to speak of it," she said. "Pray forget it, Sir Simon. The thing has dropped."

"But did you suspect him? You must forgive me, my dear, for asking you these questions; I intended to ask Dr. Brabazon, not you, but I find he is out."

"And I am very glad he is, Sir Simon, for I have never told papa. There were circumstances that seemed to throw a suspicion on Mr. Henry at the time, but they were so doubtful that it was best not to speak of them; and I desired Trace — who was the one to bring them under my notice — to let them die away."

"Oh, Trace brought them to you, did he? But how do you mean they were doubtful?"

"In so far as that Mr. Henry, if applied to, might have been able to explain them all away. It would have been very cruel to bring accusation against any one on grounds so slight."

"Just so. Well, my dear lady, I'd stake Pond Place against Mr. Raymond Trace's prejudices, that the young man is as upright as he is — perhaps more so. We poor sinners shan't be able to stand in Master Trace's presence with our hats on soon; he must be going on for heaven head-foremost, he must, with all this self-righteousness."

Emma Brabazon laughed, and followed Sir Simon out, talking. Upon which Miss Rose emerged from her hiding-place to escape, her German book in her hand, and the fairy tale stuffed up her frock.

"What did they mean?" debated the young lady, who had but imperfectly understood. "If I could find out, I'd tell him. He is always kind to me with my German, though I am so tiresome. I hate that Trace: he never gives me anything; and he stole one of my letters out of Dick's drawer the other day, and made game of it."

People called Sir Simon Orville an odd man. Mr. Raymond Trace in particular could not understand him; there were moments when that young gentleman deemed his respected uncle fit only for a lunatic asylum. He had surely thought him so this morning, had he been behind him. For Sir Simon, quitting Dr. Brabazon's, went on direct to Mrs. Paradyne's. It was not the first visit he had paid her in her present residence. Deprecating, as he did, the past frauds and crimes of which her husband was guilty, he yet in his benevolent heart thought the poor widow as much deserving of commiseration as were his own relatives; and he chose to show her that he thought it. His errand was to invite her and George to dinner on the next day, Christmas; that day of peace and goodwill to men. Mrs. Paradyne at first declined; but Sir Simon was so heartily pressing, there was no withstanding it, and she at length yielded. He went home, chuckling at the surprise it would be to his nephews, for they knew nothing of it, and he did not intend to tell them.

A surprise it proved. They went for a very long walk after morning service on the following day, and had not been home many minutes when the guests arrived. Trace stared with all his eyes: he thought he must be dreaming. *Was* that Mrs. Paradyne, coming into the room on the arm of Sir Simon, or were his eyes deceiving him? He might be wrong: he had

9*

not seen her indoors for many years. She wore a
handsome silk gown, and a cap of real lace; rather
reserved and discontented in her manner, but essentially a lady. George followed her in, and there could
be doubt no longer. George was free, merry, open,
cordial, as it was in George Paradyne's nature to be,
and he went up to Trace with his hand outstretched,
wishing him heartily a merry Christmas. Trace turned
salmon-coloured: he would not see the hand; did not
respond to it. Bertie Loftus, as if to cover the marked
rudeness, put his hand cordially into George Paradyne's; and Trace would have annihilated Bertie, could
looks have done it.

"Is he mad?" groaned Trace in a side-whisper,
alluding to his uncle.

Bertie laughed. "Let us drop old grievances for
once, Ray. It's Christmas Day."

"If my mother — who died here — could but rise
from her grave and see this!" retorted Trace. He
went and stood at the window, looking out, his bosom
beating with its wrongs.

Dick leaped three feet into the air when he came
in and saw the guests. The more the merrier, was
Dick's creed. It was that of Talbot and Irby. And
now that they met George Paradyne on equal grounds,
away from the prejudices of the school, they all saw
how much there was to admire and like in him —
Trace excepted. Had George Paradyne suddenly cast
his shell as a chrysalis does, and appeared before them
an angel, Trace, in his condemning prejudice, would
have turned his back upon him. It crossed Trace's
mind to refuse to sit down to table. But he feared Sir
Simon: it would not do to offend *him*.

It was at the dessert, when the banquet was nearing its close and Mrs. Paradyne had drawn on her gloves, that Sir Simon told Talbot he was to go and read daily with Paradyne at Mr. Henry's. Mr. Henry's kind offer, he called it; and he spoke a few emphatic words of praise of the hardworking usher. Apparently the theme was not palatable to Mrs. Paradyne. She folded her gloved hands one over the other, said a word or two in slighting disparagement of Mr. Henry, and then resolutely closed her lips. Evidently she had not yet forgiven the mistake which had brought them to Orville. George, as if reading her thoughts and struck with their injustice, glanced reproachfully at her as he turned to Sir Simon.

"Mr. Henry is very kind to me," said the boy: "he is kind to us all. Nobody knows how good he is. He must be very lonely to-day. He was to have dined with us."

Sir Simon gave a start. "I *wish* I had asked him here! The thoughtless savage I was! No more right feeling about me than if I'd never heard of Christmas. I might as well have been born a Red Indian."

Mr. Henry was at home, eating his dinner alone. Not potatoes or suet-pudding to-day: he had learned to keep Christmas in Germany, and was lavish in its honour. As George — a great deal too open-speaking to please his mother — said, he had been invited to Mrs. Paradyne's, but when she arranged to go to Sir Simon's she sent an apology to Mr. Henry. Mrs. Butter cooked him a fowl and made him a jam-pudding. He went to church in the morning and stayed for the after-service. As he sat over the fire after dinner, in the twilight of the evening, he could not help feeling

as if he were alone in the world — that there was
nobody to care for him. At the best, his life, in its
social aspect, was not a very happy one. He had a
great deal of care always upon him, and he saw no
chance of its ever being removed; but he was learning
to live for a better world than this.

Miss Rose Brabazon had let her tongue run riot
the previous day, telling him something confidentially
— he could not make out what. Rose's own ideas
were obscure upon the point, therefore it was too much
to expect they would be clear to him. The young
lady thought that "Trace and Emma and 'some of
them' feared he might have been capable of taking
papa's diamond pencil-case, just as much as the real
thief who came in at the glass doors and stole it." It
had startled Mr. Henry beyond measure; *startled* him,
and thrown him into a mass of perplexity. The impression conveyed to him was, not that he was suspected of taking the pencil, but, that he might be
capable of taking one. What reason could they have
for believing him capable of such a thing?

Later in the evening he strolled out in the cold
starlight air. He felt so very lonely, so isolated from
all the world, that only to look at the gay windows
of other people was company. Every house, poor and
rich, seemed to be holding its Christmas party. Quite
a flood of light streamed from Mr. Gall's — from Dr.
Brabazon's; all but himself were keeping Christmas.
There was neither envy nor rebellion in his heart.
His only thought was, "If they knew I was here alone,
they would invite me in." He pictured the inside
gladness, and rejoiced in it as though it were his own.

"Peace on earth, and goodwill to men!" he murmured gratefully over and over again.

The muslin curtains were before the dining-room windows at Dr. Brabazon's, but not the shutters. It was a large party — all the children and grandchildren. A smile crossed Mr. Henry's lips as he thought of Miss Rose in her element. Save the admiration of the college boys, there was nothing that young damsel liked so much as company. Mr. Henry halted and looked across the lawn, and by so doing apparently disturbed another watcher. A man turned round from the window, against which he had been crouched, and came away.

"What do you want there?" exclaimed Mr. Henry, going forward to confront him.

"Nothing to-night," was the ready answer; "I'll come another time."

All in a moment, Mr. Henry recognized the voice; recognized the low-crowned hat, and the slightly lame step. He placed himself in the intruder's way.

"I saw you here once before, at the back of the house then: you were looking for the entrance, you said, to deliver a letter. Did you — did you enter the house that night and take anything?"

"No; *you* did."

The cool and positive assertion nearly took away Mr. Henry's presence of mind. He had spoken upon impulse. He was quite uncertain what he ought to do in the emergency, whether anything or not. Meanwhile the stranger was walking quietly away, and Mr. Henry did nothing.

The following day he met Miss Brabazon with some of her relatives and a whole troop of children.

She was a little behind the rest, hastening to catch them up.

"Will you allow me to speak to you for one moment, Miss Brabazon?"

"Well," she answered, rather impatiently, as if it were a trouble to remain. It cannot be denied that she had at times treated him with scant courtesy since the suspicion of him instilled into her mind by Trace.

He told her what he had seen; that he recognised the voice to be the same; recognised the man and his lameness. Miss Brabazon's face grew white.

"He was looking in at us, you say?"

"Undoubtedly."

"Are you coming, Emma? What are you about?" called out the party in front, who had turned and halted. "John will miss the train."

"Mr. Henry, oblige me in one thing," she hurriedly said; "*don't speak of this.* I may trust you?"

"Indeed you may," he answered. "You may doubt me, Miss Brabazon; you have perhaps only too good cause to doubt me; but you may at least rely upon me in this."

Emma Brabazon ran on, the curious words ringing their echo on her ears.

CHAPTER X.

A Man in a Blaze.

THE winter holidays soon passed, and the boys came back to college again. "No pistols this time, I hope, Mr. Loftus," was the Head Master's greeting to that gentleman, and it called a mortified expression into the handsome face. Loftus's whiskers were growing, and he had taken to wear a ring in private. Trace smiled pityingly; Dick made fun of both appendages; but their owner knew not which of the two to admire most.

The routine of school set in, and the boys were busy; some few studying hard, chiefly those who were to go up for the Oxford examination in June; others going in for idleness, mischief, and sport; playing football, snow-balling, making presents and writing love-letters to Miss Rose. All the candidates for the Orville prize were going up for the Oxford examination; it was essential they should pass that, or else withdraw from the competition for the Orville.

But none, whether boys or masters, worked on so patiently and persistently as Mr. Henry, for none had so much to do. His private assistance to Talbot terminated with the holidays; but not so that to George Paradyne. Trace was outrageously angry at the latter fact, and spoke his mind: as Paradyne was going in for the Orville prize, it was *disgraceful* to give him an advantage that the others did not get. Trace's opinion carried the school with it: Paradyne was shunned worse than before, and resentment prevailed against the German master.

"You have only to come to me," Mr. Henry reiterated to them; "I can read with a dozen of you just as well as I can with one. I have no wish surreptitiously to get Paradyne on; I would a great deal rather that you should all keep together, and enjoy the same advantages, one as the other; but if you will not come to me, and he does, the blame rests with you."

"Such a thing as coaching a fellow for the Orville

prize was never heard of before, you know," retorted Brown major.

"I am not coaching him for the Orville prize. I am not coaching him at all, for the matter of that. He reads the classics with me, and I explain away his difficulties in mathematics. It is preparatory to the Oxford examination, not the Orville."

"The one implies the other," said the angry boys. And they spurned the assistance for themselves; which, metaphorically speaking, was like cutting off their noses to spite their faces. Talbot would have liked to continue, but could not fly in the teeth of popular prejudice.

"Perhaps I'd better give it up," said George Paradyne one day, throwing himself back in his chair at Mr. Henry's.

"Give what up?"

"Everything. What with the life at college and the life at home, I'm ready to — to — pitch the whole overboard," concluded Mr. George, having hesitated for an expression sufficiently strong to denote his feelings.

"You have only to bear up bravely against the one; you'll live it down in time ——"

"Rather a prolonged time, it seems," put in George, who was quite unlike his own light-hearted self to-day.

"And for the other," continued Mr. Henry, ignoring the interruption, "you should bear it cheerfully, for you know it is born of love for you."

"Ah, but you can't *imagine* what it is," said the boy, leaning forward, his wide-open bright grey eyes full of eagerness. "It has been worse since we dined at Sir Simon's; that called up to mamma all the old forfeited prosperity. The grumbling never ceases; the lamentation's dreadful. We can't make ourselves rich, if we are not rich, so where's the use of groaning over it? It drives me wild."

"Hush, George."

"But I can't hush. Mamma is so ungrateful. There's poor Mary slaving in that school, never coming up for the holidays; and here's ———"

"George, I'll not hear this. Your mother's trials are very great."

"There's an awful bother about the Christmas bills," went on George, paying slight attention to the reproof. "I wish you'd come down and talk with her."

"I! My talking might do more harm than good."

"You might try to smooth things a little — get her to look at troubles in a different light. Won't you? I can tell you it is miserable for me."

"Well, I'll see. Go on with your Greek now."

Mr. Henry, ever ready to do good where it was to be done — to throw oil on troubled waters — went down that evening to Mrs. Paradyne's. His interference was not received graciously. Mrs. Paradyne invited him to an opposite chair, and talked at him from the sofa.

"I *should* like to know what business it is of Mr. Henry's," she exclaimed, her cold resentful manner in full play. And of course he could not reply that it was any business of his; but he spoke of the trouble it was causing that fine boy, George; he spoke a little of the sad past, he spoke cheerily of a future that should be brighter. Mrs. Paradyne was often in a grumbling mood, but never in a worse than that evening.

"I can't pay the Christmas bills. The money pre-

pared for them I have had to encroach upon for other
things. A new silk gown I was obliged to have; I
can't go like an alms-woman. Never before did I
have Christmas bills; I paid as I went on; but the cost
of things in this place is frightful. I did not want
money embarrassment added to my other troubles. It
is all through our having come up here."

Mr. Henry winced at the last reproach, too evidently
directed to him. "I did it for the best," he gently
said. "I was anxious that George should get on."

Mrs. Paradyne lifted her delicate hands with deprecation, and went on with her complaints. They
were wearying and painful, even to him; what, then,
must they be to the high-spirited and generous boy
who was exposed to them always? But Mr. Henry
contrived to accomplish his mission, and he left a feeling of peace behind him when he quitted the house.

He had plenty of work on his hands yet that night,
and ran all the way home. Dashing into Mrs. Butter's
kitchen for a light, a quicker mode than ringing for
that esteemed and rather slow landlady to bring it, he
dashed against a man who was seated on the kitchen
table by fire-light, his legs swaying. No need to wait
for recognition this time; it was the young man he
had twice seen near the college.

"Well?" said the latter, with cool equanimity;
"there's room to pass without knocking me over."

"Who are you?" exclaimed Mr. Henry; "are you
waiting to see Mrs. Butter?"

"I have seen her — cross-grained old thing! Her
temper does not improve with years."

Before anything more passed, or Mr. Henry had in
the least formed an idea as to the aspect of affairs,

Mrs. Butter came in with Miss Brabazon. The latter
had a shawl over her head, and burst out crying as
she spoke to the stranger. "Oh, Tom, why have you
come here?"

"Can I be of any assistance to you, Miss Brabazon?" whispered Mr. Henry, partially comprehending
the mystery. "Will you make use of my sitting-room?"

"Thank you. It is my brother!"

Yes, it was her brother, — the great incubus on
Dr. Brabazon's life. In spite of all that had been
done to reclaim him; in defiance of education, position,
training, Tom Brabazon had turned out a black sheep
amidst the doctor's white flock. Dr. Brabazon had
paid and paid until he could pay no more; Emma
Brabazon never awoke to morning light but a dread
crossed her mind of what trouble in regard to *him* the
day might bring forth. It was not only debt; he had
done worse things than spend; he had been in prison
for three months, and worn the felon's dress, and had
his hair cut close; he had been forbidden his father's
house; he dared not show himself there or elsewhere
in the broad light of day. Mrs. Butter, faithful to the
family, knew about it, and she said a word or two of
explanation to Mr. Henry as he sat on the other side
of her fireplace, while the brother and sister were in
his parlour.

"He wants to stay here," she resentfully cried,
giving her fire a fierce stir, as if she were stirring up
the delinquent. "He is obliged to be in hiding again;
and he avows it with all the brass in the world. I'd
not have gone to Miss Emma with my own will, but
he made me. Ah! the aching heart that she and my
poor master have had with him, that ill-doing Tom!"

Emma came in, her eyes inflamed. "You must let him be in that upper room for a day or two; there's no help for it," she said to Mrs. Butter. "And he must have a bit of supper to-night. I'm going back now, or papa may find out my absence. Of course — you know — his being here must be kept a secret."

"I know, Miss Emma," was the wrathful answer; made doubly wrathful because the gentleman had entered. "He up and told me that the first thing."

"Hold your tongue, Mother Butter," cried Tom Brabazon, laughing as if he had not a care in life. "You have been in scrapes yourself before this, I'll lay. Mind you make me a plum-pudding to-morrow; I've not tasted a piece of one yet. Perhaps you'll introduce this gentleman to me, Emma."

And she obeyed mechanically. In the blow the night had brought, she felt utterly bewildered. "My unfortunate brother, Thomas Brabazon; Mr. Henry."

Mr. Henry acknowledged the introduction slightly; and took up his hat to walk home with Miss Brabazon. She begged him not to take the trouble, but he quietly insisted, and they went out together.

"Is this the same that you have seen near the college?" she asked, as they went along.

"It is."

"Ah, yes; I only inquired to see if you remembered him. He denies, most positively, having entered the study that night; and when I spoke of the pencil, he apparently did not know what I meant. He had written a letter to papa, asking for some trifling temporary assistance, intending to send it in and wait for the answer. But he saw the front sitting-rooms were in darkness, and went round, fearing we were out, to see if the back ones were. That is what he says. We were out, you know, as the want of light showed him, and he returned to London, and was arrested before he could come again. When I mentioned the pencil, he asked whether I thought he had become worse than a common thief to touch *that*. I don't think he took it."

"But why have used an evasion to me — that he was looking for the entrance to the college?" returned Mr. Henry.

"He fears an enemy in every person he meets, and I suppose wished to pass himself off as a stranger. Mr. Henry, I must rely on you not to betray his sojourn at your house."

"Betray him! You little know me. Anything in the world I can do for him, or for you, or for Dr. Brabazon, in this painful emergency, I shall only be too happy to do, faithfully and truly."

"You see now," she said, with a faint smile, "that we have too much trouble of our own to be severe upon others. Every bit of secret pride has been taken out of us, and papa's hair is grey before its time. He is the eldest son."

"The eldest son?"

"Yes, the oldest of us all. He went wrong first of all at Oxford, and instead of retrieving his position, or allowing it to be retrieved for him, as others do who get into debt there, he went on from bad to worse. Good night, Mr. Henry."

She hung her shawl up in the inner hall, smoothed her hair, and went in as if nothing unusual had happened. Mr. Jebb was sitting with Dr. Brabazon; they were in an animated discussion about some popular

question of the day, and her absence had passed unnoticed. Miss Rose had disappeared. Miss Rose, finding
the coast clear, had taken the opportunity to visit her
treasure drawer upstairs. It contained presents and
love-letters; the one of about as much real value as
the other; but the young lady coveted both. Some
fresh parcels had just arrived to be added to the collection: we may as well look over her while she examines
them. And I beg to state, for the benefit of society
in general, that the letters are but copies of genuine
originals.

"Dear Miss Rose, — I hope you will accept of
the enclosed trifle. With my best love, believe me
yours ever affectionately,
                                                "Dick L."

Which stood for Dick Loftus. The enclosed trifle
was a thin paper scent-case, pretty to the eye and
sweet to the nose. Rose gave a few sniffs, and flung
it into the drawer to take up another.

"My dearest Miss Rose, — Will you oblige me
by trying the accompanying? That blue bonnet
you wore on Sunday was charming. Ever yours,
C. Brown."

Meaning Brown minor. A packet of barleysugar
came with this, and Miss Rose began upon it greedily.
Then she turned to the third.

"Ever dear Rose, — I take this favourable oper-
tunity of writeing to you, Our desk got in a row this

morning and I can't go out to buy that broche I told
you of, If Stiggings buys it you fling it in his face,
I send you a few rasons if you'll except of them,
We are going to have a joly lark this week with
Mother Butter, Your affectionate lover, Alfred Jones."

Mr. Alfred Jones was a gentleman of Miss Rose's
own age, thirteen. She put as many raisins into her
mouth as it would conveniently hold, and went on
again.

"Beloved Miss Rose, — *Would* you wear the accompanied box for my sake, I mean its contents, which
Jones minor (that wretched little muff in the fifth
form, you know) said he should buy for you, the im-
pudense of the youngster. I expect some jam to-
morrow and shall send you a pot. Ever your devoted
and respectful admirer, W. Stiggings. P.S. — I hope
you have less bother now with those beastly lessons.
Miss Brabazon's a tyrent."

The box contained a very smart brooch, for which
W. Stiggins, who was a year older than Jones minor,
had given ninepence. Miss Rose stuck it into her
dress and figured off before the glass, eating alternately
the raisins and the barleysugar. Emma had not called
her down, or come to see after her, so she thought she
might write her acknowledgments, and got out a pencil
and some delicate miniature note-paper, straw-coloured
and notched round the edge.

"Dear Mr. Loftus, — Thank you for the scent-
paper, it's very delicious, but not so nice as that

almond-rock you sent me. I've no more time, for fear Emma should come up. Ever yours, Rose B. P.S. — I saw you all riding that donkey on the common, why didn't you look up? I was with Jessie Gall and their governess."

This accomplished, she went on to the next, taking them in rotation.

"Dear Mr. Brown, — The barleysugar's first-rate; I've eaten it nearly all. It's a love of a bonnet. I wanted Emma to let me have a blue mantle like it, and she went and bought a black! Ever yours, Rose B. P.S. — Please excuse the smuge; an old raisen out of my drawer got crushed on it."

And the next was to Jones minor.

"Dear Mr. Jones, — I'm very sorry about the brooch; perhaps you could get me something else. Don't you ever speak to Stiggins — I shouldn't. The raisens are gritty; perhaps you droped them. Do pay out that Mother Butter. She told Emma the other day I was a little minx. Couldn't you steal her cat? So no more at present from yours ever, Rose B. P.S. — You ought to do some dictation."

And then came the last.

"Dear Mr. Stiggins, — The brooch is beautiful; I've got it in my frock now, but daredn't go down in it for fear of Emma. I wonder you could ever mention Jones minor to me. Why do you speak to him? I don't. I like jam, apricot especially. The lessons are worse than ever, and I wish German was buried.

Emma's going to have me put into linear drawing, or some such horrid name, so I mean to break all the pencils. Ever yours, Rose B. P.S. — I'd tell you of something I heard from Jessie Gall, only I'm afraid Emma will be up."

These various missives were directed to the gentlemen, each of them receiving the title of "esquire," and Miss Rose locked up her treasures, the brooch included. A little cousin of hers who was in the junior class, and ran in at will, was made the messenger on either side; otherwise the young men might have found it difficult to convey their offerings to the shrine.

A few days passed. One dark evening Mrs. Butter was in her kitchen, making toast for her not very welcome lodger-guest, who had descended from his room of concealment to talk to her and enjoy the warmth, when there came a sudden and imperious knocking at the casement. Down went the toasting-fork, and Tom Brabazon sprang from the fire into a dark corner.

"Not there, Mr. Tom," she whispered. "Better go upstairs again; it's safest."

One fear only was in the mind of both of them — that this peremptory summons must mean mischief to the fugitive hiding from the law. Mrs. Butter, when he had escaped, drew the heavy red curtain from before the window, and looked out. She expected to see some officers of justice there, or something as formidable; her heart rose to her mouth; he *was* her old master's son, with all his faults and sins, and she would have shielded him with her life.

10*

"Don't open the door on any account," softly cried Tom Brabazon, from the stairs.

Between the light inside and the darkness out, combined with her own flurry, Mrs. Butter could see absolutely nothing. A form in a hat, as of a short, stout man, at last made itself dimly visible to her, but he seemed to be standing with his back to the window; at least, she could discern no features.

"What do you please to want, sir?" she called out, deeming it well to be civil.

Instead of making any answer, the glass was rapped at again, more peremptorily than before. Mrs. Butter drew the casement open; it had upright iron bars on the outside, so there was no danger that any Philistine, above the size of a thin rabbit, could make his way in.

"What is it?" she asked.

But still the man never spoke; and now that her eyes were getting accustomed to the darkness, she saw that he had no face, or if he had a face, it was enveloped and hidden from view. A disagreeable feeling, as of some vague fear, stole over her.

"What is it, sir, I ask? Won't you please to say what you want?"

All in a moment, without warning, the man burst into a blaze. Blazed up as if he had been coated with pitch or stuffed with gun-powder, and had suddenly caught fire. Mrs. Butter, nearly beside herself with terror, darted back from the window, uttering scream upon scream.

For some little time all was confusion. Mr. Henry, and Tom Brabazon, the one brought from his room by the cries and the light, the other forgetting his needful privacy in the interests of humanity, rushed out of doors, each with a bucket of water. But the burning man, who appeared to have arrived on an iron barrow, was suddenly wheeled to a safe spot off the premises, and a set of gleeful savages were dancing and shouting round him, while he blazed away. Tom Brabazon stole indoors again.

Need you be told that this was the work of the college boys? It was the "jolly lark" hinted at by Jones minor to Miss Rose. They had made a straw figure, introducing a modicum of gunpowder, and fired it before Madam Butter's eyes for her especial edification.

Dancing, howling, shouting, the boys did not see the approach of Mr. Baker until that gentleman was close upon them. He had happened to be passing within view, and ran up in terror. They took flight then; and indeed there was nothing to wait for, for the figure had nearly emitted his last spark. Mr. Baker, rather in fear still, perplexed, and outrageously angry, threw out his arms in the dark, but only succeeded in grasping one: the rest eluded him. That one was George Paradyne. Mrs. Butter, in a state of fury, came out with her tale.

"I'll cane *you* at all events," said Mr. Baker to his captive. "Come with me."

"I have not done anything," said George. "I don't know now what has happened."

"I'll teach you, you vagabond, what has happened," stuttered Mr. Baker, still further exasperated by the assumption of ignorance, which he entirely disbelieved. "Come along."

He marshalled George Paradyne away to the hall,

holding his jacket collar. Every boy had got back before them. About twenty were in the fray, and Mr. Baker had not distinguished one. They were seated sedately at their evening lessons now, in common with the rest, and not to be distinguished. The angry master got out his cane.

"One single moment, Mr. Baker, before you strike me," said George Paradyne. "I *declare* that I was not in this. I knew nothing of it: I was going to Mr. Henry's for my usual reading when I came upon the blaze. Surely they will tell you I was not in it! They never do let me join in anything."

Mr. Baker paused, cane in air. George Paradyne had certainly been amidst the throng: he did not believe that he was not joining in the mischief.

"I was not in it, indeed, sir: I had but run up when you came. I was asking what it was."

"Who was in it, if you were not?" asked Mr. Baker. "You saw."

"I saw some of them."

"Tell me who they were. I shall cane you if you don't."

George looked round on the boys, as if to say, "Will none of you exculpate me?" They dropped their eyes on their books, and made no response.

"I shall cane you, Paradyne, if you don't tell."

"I can't help it, sir. I will not tell."

He took his punishment, a very severe one. Pulling his jacket on his stiff and aching arms, when it was over, he once more looked at the lot as he went out. And the boys, in their heart of hearts, felt that George Paradyne, the despised, was made of nobler stuff than they were.

CHAPTER XI.

Only the Heat!

In one of the houses in Prospect Terrace there sat a family at early breakfast. A nice family; the growing up sons and daughters loving and obedient, the father and mother anxiously training them to good. It was the Talbots. They had quitted their close residence in Pimlico, and taken this in the healthy country district; having moved in at the recent quarter. Mr. Talbot was a tall, spare man, rather absorbed in cares; Mrs. Talbot a pleasant woman with a countenance and demeanour serenely cheerful, imparting in some way an idea of peace. James, known to you as Earl of Shrewsbury, was the eldest son. He was at the breakfast table now, for this was the last day of the Easter holidays, which he had been spending at home.

Yes, time had gone on at Orville, as it goes on with us all. April was in, and the Easter holidays were now at an end. There was nothing much to tell of the last term, no particular event to record. Mrs. Butter overcame her fright in time, but not her anger; Tom Brabazon disappeared again; the German master was patiently working; and George Paradyne was battling with the school enmity, and bearing on his own way in spite of circumstances. He would have done it less gallantly but for the ever-constant, daily counsels of Mr. Henry. Over and over again, but for that, the boy would have broken down, for the battle against him waxed fierce and strong. The step taken by Sir Simon Orville, in inviting Mrs. Paradyne and

George to dinner on Christmas Day, meant to be a healer of strife, turned out just the reverse. Trace, powerless to rebel against it, concentrated his indignation within him at the time, to let it loose on the head of the unhappy boy later. Not in a violent way, not in any manner that could be taken hold of: he was civil to Paradyne's face; but he so worked craftily on others, that a regular cabal set in against George Paradyne. Mr. Henry, so to say, bore the brunt for him. He soothed the insults, he talked the boy's resentful spirit into peace, he cheered him bravely on, he encouraged him to persevere and be patient. The Talbots were speaking of this enmity as they sat at breakfast. James suddenly interposed with a question to his father.

"Papa, shall you not be late?"

Mr. Talbot glanced at his watch and smiled. The idea of his son's giving him a caution on the score; he, the most strictly punctual clerk the bank possessed. "It's odd how a feeling of dislike does arise in schools against a particular boy," he observed. "It was so in the school I went to, I remember. There's sure to be good cause for it. These instincts are generally to be trusted."

"Papa, what do you call instinct?"

"What do I call instinct?" repeated Mr. Talbot. "I should have thought you were old enough, James, to know what instinct meant, without my telling you."

James laughed. "Because I think in this case our instinct is *for* Paradyne, instead of against him. I know mine is."

"Then why is he disliked?"

"Well, I don't know. There is something not

square, I believe, known to a few of the seniors only. The feeling against him is very strong."

Mr. Talbot rose, and put his watch in his pocket. He always breakfasted with it on the table. "I don't understand it at all," he said; "but I must be going now."

James went to the front door and opened it. Now that he had risen, you could see James Talbot's height. He was already nearly six feet, almost the tallest in the school. The boys were wont to say that the shots had made his legs grow. Mr. Talbot walked away quickly, and a boy, wearing the college cap, came up and accosted James at the door. At the same moment Mrs. Talbot came out in a commotion.

"Oh, James, my letter! Papa was to have posted it in town. Run and give it to him."

"Allow me," said the stranger, raising his trencher to Mrs. Talbot, and taking the letter from her hand. She looked at him, and was struck with the fine character of the attractive countenance — the open candour of the large grey eyes.

"That's Paradyne," whispered James, watching him as he caught Mr. Talbot.

"*That* Paradyne! Then I am sure —"

But he had accomplished his mission, and was coming back again, laughing at the haste he had made. "Mr. Talbot bade me say he did not know there was any letter to take," he observed to Mrs. Talbot.

"No, I forgot to tell him. Thank you very much."

He lifted his cap to her again as he walked away, and she went in with the earl.

"James," said Mrs. Talbot to her son, "you tell me that the school has a prejudice against that boy?"

"Indeed it has. Something more than a prejudice. We are all against him."

"And your motive — your reason, I should say?"

"I really don't know. The prejudice is there, and we all share in it, and that's all."

"Oh, James! is it right?"

"Perhaps not. I have thought it not quite the thing all along; but one must go with the stream. They are very poor, those Paradynes. Don't look angry, mamma; I am not speaking it as a reproach."

"I hope not. I think a son of mine would scarcely do so. They cannot well be poorer than we are."

"Yes, they are, a great deal. It is our education that keeps papa poor — mine especially. I shall try to repay you for it some day, mother mine. A vision comes over me now and again of gaining the Orville. I should get to college then, and all would be easy."

"You vain boy. The Orville will be for some one of your seniors, sir."

Talbot laughed. "Yes, I fear it is but a vision of dreamland. But oh, mother," — and his tone changed to solemn earnest, — "what a boon it would be!"

"Tell me why you dislike George Paradyne," resumed Mrs. Talbot, breaking the slight pause.

"I don't dislike him. I like him in spite of all. One can't help admiring him for his spirit; he throws off all our shafts so bravely. He is one of the most generous, open fellows possible. I see you don't understand, and I don't understand it myself. Few of us do. There's an awful feeling about his going in for the Orville."

Mrs. Talbot gave it up as a bad job, and opened

the book for the ten minutes' reading to the children, never omitted in the house.

The Talbots had made some acquaintance in the place, and Mrs. Talbot questioned Mrs. Gall and one or two more, what the dislike of George Paradyne arose from. She felt more interested on the subject than she could account for. But none were able to answer her. Mrs. Gall had herself put the same query to her son, and nothing satisfactory came of it.

As the term went on, the uncomfortable feeling in the school grew greater and greater. But there was little time for anything but study, for the Oxford examination was approaching fast.

One hot Saturday afternoon, when the College had holiday, Mr. Henry went to the railway station to inquire after an expected parcel of books. Saturday afternoon was no holiday for him. He had three private lessons to give in it. As he left the station, walking very fast to keep his time at Mrs. Gall's, a sharp, sudden pain seized upon him. He was leaning against the fence of the plantation, white and faint, when Sir Simon Orville passed.

"Why, bless me, what's to do?" exclaimed that hearty gentleman. "Have you been run over?"

Mr. Henry smiled: his colour was coming back again. He said something about a sudden pain.

"Been eating green gooseberries?" asked the unsophisticated man. "I caught young Dick buying a quart. He's crunching the lot."

"It took me here," said Mr. Henry, touching his left side. "It's gone now."

"Why, that's near the heart; it couldn't have been there, I should think," said Sir Simon, peering at him curiously. "Well, we are close at home; come in to Pond Place and rest."

"Thank you, Sir Simon; I am all right now. I must go on quickly to my pupils."

"I'll tell you what it is, sir; you are overworking yourself. That's my opinion."

"Oh, no. Folks can't do too much at my age."

"That depends upon the amount of strength: I could have plodded on night and day; you seem to get more of a lath than ever. What's the reason you never will accept my hospitality? Got any dislike to me? — taken up a prejudice? I know I'm a plain man, without education; but you might put up with that."

"If I could only show you how I respect you, Sir Simon; if I could but live to be of service to you!" was the impulsive answer. "But, indeed, I can never get time for visiting: the little Galls are waiting for me now."

And away he went through the plantation, leaving Sir Simon considerably puzzled, as he had been before, at the earnestness of the words and manner; for they seemed to imply more than was on the surface. That afternoon, in the very midst of explaining to Master Fred Gall an abstruse difficulty in the Latin grammar, Mr. Henry leaned back in his chair and quietly fainted away. With a hullabaloo that might have been heard at the distant college, the children threw open the door and scattered away, pell-mell.

The noise brought forth Mrs. Gall and her eldest son; who had stepped in at home, as he had the liberty to do on holidays. They took off his neckcloth and brought him wine, and were very tender with him.

"Do forgive me," he murmured, in deep contrition for the trouble he was causing. "The heat must have overpowered me; I have been walking fast."

Mrs. Gall would not hear of his continuing the lesson. She made him lie on the sofa and rest. She and her children had grown to like him very much; which the senior boy, in his prejudice, silently shrugged his shoulders at. But there was something about him this afternoon, in his transitory helplessness, his gratitude for the care shown, that appealed to William Gall's better feelings and half won his heart. Mr. Henry could not rest long; he had a German lesson to give at five o'clock, and must go home first for the necessary books. When he went out, Gall went with him, and offered his arm.

"You will walk all the better for it, Mr. Henry. Years back I used to have fainting-fits myself, and know how they take the strength away."

Mr. Henry accepted it, and they walked on together. He had always liked Gall: never a better head and heart *au fond* than his. Leaning too readily, perhaps, to the prejudices of the school he partially swayed; but Mr. Henry allowed for that: others might have done it more offensively. Gall had never taken an active part in the cabal against young Paradyne, or in the contempt lavished on the German master; but he had tacitly acquiesced in it.

Some of the boys happened to be in the quadrangle; and, to describe the commotion when Gall passed arm-in-arm with the enemy — as Trace was in the private habit of calling Mr. Henry — would be beyond any pen. Gall, thoroughly independent always, vouchsafed a cool nod to the sea of astonished faces, and continued his way. If anything could have daunted him, it was the supercilious contempt on Bertie Loftus's handsome face: anything that Gall did was sure to excite that, for there was no good feeling between them. Bertie would have done the same thing himself for Mr. Henry, or for any one else in case of need; but he lost sight of that in his prejudice against Gall. Mr. Henry called for some coffee on going in: coffee was his panacea for most ailments.

"You'll stay and take a cup with me," he said cordially, to Gall. "I feel quite well now. It must have been the heat."

Mrs. Butter brought the coffee and some bread-and-butter, and the two chatted together. Gall had never seen so much of Mr. Henry in all the past months as in this one hour, and he felt ashamed for having turned the cold shoulder on him.

"I hope I shall see more of you, Mr. Henry, than I have seen hitherto," he said, when he was shaking hands to leave. "Is there nothing I can do for you? If there is, tell me. I hope you'll not have a renewal of this."

"Thank you," replied Mr. Henry, looking straight at him with his pleasant eyes. "I wish I could get you to alter one thing — the persecution of young Paradyne."

"Well, it is too bad," observed Gall. "But I can't make the school like Paradyne if they dislike him."

"Can you tell me *why* they dislike him?" pointedly asked Mr. Henry: for times and again it had struck him that the particulars of the Liverpool business must have been privately circulated by Trace or Loftus.

"No, that I can't," frankly answered Gall. "I have

heard Trace hint at some reason for dislike, but he
never said what. Miss Brabazon asked me about it
once, but I did not learn anything. I think they are
vexed that he, a new fellow, should have his name
down for the Orville Exhibition."

"That should not cause them to persecute him."

"True. But, you see, when once a prejudice arises,
it is not easy to allay it."

"Did it ever occur to you to realize Paradyne's position to your own mind?" asked Mr. Henry. "He is
clever, generous, noble, forbearing; wishing to live in
amity with all; and yet he is subjected to this cruel
persecution: and for no cause that I can find out.
Think it over, Mr. Gall, at your leisure; and now
goodbye, and thank you for your company."

Mr. Henry sat back in his chair, listening to the
senior boy's departing footsteps. There were times
when he felt utterly depressed, as if every bit of spirit
and energy had gone out of him. He was in a false
position at Orville College, and he knew it. Since the
first day of his entrance he had been fighting a battle
with conscience; this of itself, with his sensitive mind,
was enough to wear him out; it needed not his hard
work added to it.

"I can't keep it up," he said to himself, as he
rose, caught up some books, and went out to give his
lesson. "And it is not right I should. Once the Oxford examination's over, the end shall come; and then,
if I have to leave the college, why, I must leave it.
I'd rather be back at Heidelberg."

Meanwhile Gall was walking slowly away, and
"thinking over" the matter in regard to Paradyne: not
because Mr. Henry had desired him to do it, but on

his own score. Gall's was a just nature; he felt vexed
with himself for the past; angry with the school in
general.

It was not an opportune moment for Loftus to meet
him, with his supercilious face, his still more supercilious words.   In the middle of the grass, near the gymnasium-ground, they encountered each other.   The under-current of enmity between these two was of long-
standing, and Gall at least had inwardly and bitterly
resented it.   What Loftus said was never precisely
known; some stinging taunt, reflecting on the "new
friendship," meaning little, perhaps; but the other was
not in a mood to bear it.   The next moment, Gall had
knocked him down.

He lay sprawling, the distinguished Loftus, his
golden curls in contact with the base earth, his handsome nose bleeding with the blow.   Gall stood erect,
with compressed lips; the wondering boys were flocking
up, and Mother Butter's dog stood by, barking fiercely,
as if it were a raree-show.

Loftus rose.   Whether he would have struck again
was a question; he was not deficient in personal bravery,
rather the contrary, but these elegant dandies rarely go
in for blows.   No opportunity was given one way or
the other, for Mr. Henry, hastening up, stepped between them.

"Move away," said Loftus to him.   "What business
is it of yours?"

"The business of authority," was Mr. Henry's answer, delivered with calm decision.   "So long as I
hold the position of master here, I shall act as such
when need arises.   Gentlemen," — and he looked at
both equally — "there must be no more of this."

"You need not be alarmed on your friend's behalf," said Loftus, with an ugly stress on the word "friend." "You, Gall," — and he turned to him — "shall answer to me for this, later."

They moved away in different directions, Gall one road, Loftus another, Mr. Henry a third; and the astonished boys stood, looking after them with a vacant stare, hardly able to believe that the transitory scene had been real.

CHAPTER XII.

In the Shop in Oxford Street.

MISS BRABAZON was walking through Oxford Street on that memorable afternoon, taking her time, as befitted the heat of the day, and looking into the shop windows; which, truth to say, bore attraction for her, as they do for most persons who see them rarely.

"I daresay I could get it here," she thought, halting at a jeweller's shop and finally entering it. A double shop with two separate doors, but Miss Brabazon did not observe that. She had broken the key of her watch and wanted a new one, but wished it of a particular pattern. A middle-aged, pleasant-looking man came forward, whom she took to be the master. Yes, he had keys of the shape she described, he said, and reached out a tray.

While he was fitting the key to the watch, Miss Brabazon's eyes went roaming (naturally) amidst the many attractive articles of plate and jewelry. They alighted on a gold pencil with a diamond set in the top. Except that the stone was considerably smaller, it was very much like the one lost from the college.

"That is a beautiful pencil!" she exclaimed.

"Very, ma'am. The diamond makes it also a valuable one."

"Is it not very unusual to see a diamond set in a pencil-case?"

"Rather so," he replied. "I have made them to order before now. We have a better one than that, but it's not for sale. Not yet, at least. It is one of our pledges in the other shop; was left with us some months back."

"Do you mean it was — pawned?" she asked, bringing out the word gingerly, as ladies in general do.

"Yes, ma'am."

"But — is this a pawnbroker's?" she hastily asked.

"The other shop is, ma'am."

A thousand thoughts came crowding over her; a suspicion arose, almost amounting to an instinct, that it was the pencil they had lost. "When was it left with you, do you say?" she inquired.

"Some time last autumn; either in September or October."

"I wish you would let me see it," she exclaimed.

"It is quite against all rule, ma'am, to show our pledged goods," was the reply of the jeweller.

"Is it? But if you would! The truth is — I don't see why I should not tell you — we lost one about that time. I do not wish to claim the pencil, only to see it for my own satisfaction, just to set my doubts at rest. They have been —" dreadful, was the word on her tongue, but she paused in time and substituted another — "tiresome."

The jeweller was an honest man; kind and considerate. It was, as he said, entirely against the rule to show pledges left with them; but the young lady seemed very anxious, and was evidently sincere. He stood in hesitation.

"I am Miss Brabazon," she resumed, drawing out her card-case and showing her cards. "My father is Dr. Brabazon, of Orville College; you may have heard of it and of him. Indeed you may trust us not to make any fuss or trouble about this."

"Orville College," repeated the jeweller. "I am almost sure that was the address given with the pencil. I think the person who pledged it said he was a master there."

A rush of conviction and the image of Mr. Henry came over her together. "Do let me see it," she said; "I am certain it is the same."

He went into the other shop by a communicating door, was away for several minutes, and came back with a box in which was the pencil. She only needed to take one glance at it; the chased gold was bright as ever, the diamond flashed with all its accustomed brilliancy. It was Dr. Brabazon's. "Yes, it is papa's," she exclaimed. "Who was it that pledged it?"

"The name in the book is Henry Jebb; I have been looking. But there seems to have been some doubt whether ——. Here, Simms," broke off the jeweller, "step this way."

"Henry Jebb!" mentally repeated Miss Brabazon, as a young man, running his hand through an amazing head of light hair, came in from the other shop.

"Tell this lady the particulars of the transaction I

11*

have been asking you about," said his master. "When you took in this pencil, you know."

"It was Watson that took it in, sir, not me; but I was standing by and heard what passed. The gentleman came in, mem," he continued, turning to Miss Brabazon, "and said he wanted a little temporary accommodation for a few days, and he pulled the pencil out of his waistcoat pocket, mem, and asked what we'd lend upon it; as much as ever we could, he hoped, for he was hard up till his remittances came. Well, Watson, seeing a pencil like that, with the diamond stone in the top, was rather sharp; he asked whether it was the party's own, and if it wasn't a family relic, and lots more things; he was quite down upon him, mem, in fact, and gave him a look from head to foot as if he didn't think him exactly the one to be offering such an article. 'Hadn't you better call in the nearest policeman and tell him to question me?' says the customer. 'I can go where I'm known if you decline to negotiate.' Well, what with his coolness, and his composed manner, and his gentleman's voice, Watson thought it was all right, mem, and lent him seven pounds upon it. 'What name?' says Watson. 'Henry,' answered he, and stopped. 'Henry what?' says Watson; 'is that the surname or Christian name?' and the stranger stroked his chin for a moment looking at him. 'I suppose I must give it in?' said he, 'Henry Jebb.' 'What address?' asks Watson next. 'Oh, Fleet Street,' said he. 'That won't do this time,' says Watson, 'I should like the real one.' 'Then take it,' said he, picking up the money and putting it in his pocket, and he gave the address that is in the book, sir," — turning to the jeweller — "Orville College. 'I'm one of its masters,' he went on, 'and that pencil was presented to me by the pupils, so you may be sure I shall redeem it. In a week's time from this it will be in my pocket again.' But here it is still," concluded the speaker; "and it often is so."

"You have a good memory, Simms," observed his master, smiling.

"And so I have, sir. I won't take upon me to say that those were the precise words used, but I know they are not far out on either side. Watson said afterwards that he'd lay half-a-crown Henry was the right name, though he put it down as Henry Jebb."

"Was he a young man?" asked Miss Brabazon; feeling how superfluous was the question in her certainty of conviction.

"Oh yes, mem; youngish, that is."

"That's all, Simms; you may go. Has this helped to solve your doubts at all, ma'am?" continued the jeweller, turning to Miss Brabazon.

"It has indeed," she sadly said. "We have suspected him — at least some of us did — from the first. His name is not Jebb. But I would rather not say any more about it. Do not think me uncivil," she hastened to add; "indeed I am sensible of your kind courtesy, and thank you very much. You will keep the pencil safe; and please keep — if you would so far oblige me — the matter secret too."

He came round to open the door for her, assuring her of his discretion, and that the pencil would be perfectly safe.

"Mr. Henry!" she repeated over and over again to herself as she went home. "And I had nearly overcome those doubts of him that so pained me. But the impudence of his using poor, unconscious Mr. Jebb's name!"

And the "impudence" of the thing did strike upon her so forcibly that, in spite of her distress, she stood still and gave way to a burst of laughter, unable to restrain it within bounds.

Dr. Brabazon was alone in his study when she entered, looking over some books just brought in. As if anxious to get the communication over, she sat down at once on a stool at his feet, and told him all. It must be remembered that *his* suspicions had never been directed to Mr. Henry, and for the first few minutes he really thought his daughter was dreaming, or that the day's heat had affected her usually cool brain.

"It is impossible, Emma. Steal my pencil! — Mr. Henry! My dear, you don't know what you are saying."

"Papa, I am very sorry to say it. You must judge for yourself; but I don't see how it can have been otherwise. You have not been listening to me."

"Begin again. Surprise took my listening faculties away."

She untied her bonnet, pushed it off her head, and began again; telling him of Trace's back suspicions and their foundation; of her recent discovery of the pencil, and what passed. "Is there any *room* to doubt, papa?"

"Stay a moment, Emma: why did you not inform me of this doubt of Mr. Henry at the time?"

"Because I thought, as you do now, that it was so very unlikely; and also — I feared — that some one altogether different might have taken it."

"Who?"

"Forgive me, papa; I know how you dislike the name to be mentioned — Tom."

Dr. Brabazon frowned. "How could you possibly have suspected him when he was not near the place? That comes of letting your thoughts run upon him always. You should have told me this about Mr. Henry."

She sat with her finger on her cheek, looking out apparently at the boys in the play-ground, and asking herself whether to tell the whole now — that Tom *was* near the place the evening of the loss. But to what end? To hear of his being near them, always destroyed her father's rest; and the suspicion was now quite removed from him.

"Mr. Henry must have intended to redeem it within a week, as he said, papa; or he would never have disclosed the fact of his being one of the college masters: he hoped, I suppose, to replace it here before it was missed. I wonder why he did not do it?"

"Emma, I could have trusted that young man with untold gold."

"What shall you do about it, papa?"

"I don't know what to do," said the doctor, rousing himself from a pause of perplexed thought. "Look you, child; he *must* stay here until the Oxford examination. To discharge him now might peril the passing of the boys."

"I see. Of course it might. And he is so excellent a master!"

"I wish; I *wish* I had not heard this."

Emma wished so too; wished, rather, there had been nothing to hear.

"His staying on a little while will not make matters worse, papa," she resumed, trying to put the best side of things outwards; "he might stay until the end of the term. We have missed nothing since. And if I had not happened to go into that shop for a watch-key, we should be in just as much ignorance as we were before."

"If!" said the doctor, "if! if! life is half made up of ifs. I'll take a night's rest upon this unpleasantness, Emma; meanwhile keep strict counsel."

"I shall keep that always, poor young man. I can't help being sorry for him; he is so hardworking and so friendless; and, papa, with it all, he is a gentleman. But what about the pencil?"

"Time enough to think of that," said the doctor. "It won't run away."

It was all utterly incomprehensible to Dr. Brabazon. As he said, he could have *trusted* Mr. Henry; not only with untold gold, but with things far more precious. He thought that some great emergency, some urgent need of money must have tempted him; it had tempted others before him, as the world's history tells. It struck the doctor that in this must lie the secret of Mr. Henry's demeanour; there was always a sort of shrinking reticence observable to *him*, not to others. "As if — I declare, as if he were conscious of some acted wrong towards me!" cried the doctor aloud, the new thought striking him. Whatever his degree of guilt, Dr. Brabazon felt certain it was bitterly repented of. To part with him before the Oxford examination, thereby suddenly cutting short the thread of the French and German instruction, was not to be thought of: and the Head Master buried the unwelcome knowledge within his breast, and suffered things to go on as usual.

It was drawing so near now, that all other interests gave place to it. There was a good deal of rivalry amidst the boys going up for it; there was some jealousy, a little disputing. The remoter competition for the Orville prize was lost sight of now. It was at the option of the Head Master to send the boys up for this Oxford examination, or to retain them; according as, in his judgment, they were sufficiently prepared, or the contrary.

The elder ones, those whose age would preclude trial another year, were to go; that was certain; and take their chance: but in regard to the rest it lay with Dr. Brabazon. Only, if they did not go up for the Oxford; or, going up, did not pass; they could not compete for the Orville. And of the candidates, there was not one, Gall excepted, and perhaps Loftus, who did not secretly pray that Paradyne might not be allowed to go up. Altogether there was as much excitement and commotion just now in the college over the coming Oxford examination, as there is in a bribery borough on the eve of a general election.

Mr. Loftus sat in his bedroom at Pond Place, fingering his cherished pistols. It was the day subsequent to his encounter with Gall, and he was spending it at Sir Simon's. Loftus had not been himself since the mishap; he was not one to cherish revenge in a general way, but he did in this instance firmly resolve that Gall should suffer. On all occasions of his visits to his uncle's these pistols were got out, their state ascertained, their shape and points admired. It was Sunday afternoon, but Loftus was rubbing them with wash-leather; he and Leek, who stood by, talking in a desultory manner.

"Loftus, I would not care to possess pistols if I had to keep them locked up out of sight," cried Leek rather inopportunely.

"Ah," said Loftus, "wait until I am my own master. I wish I *might* use them," he added, significantly. "I could put a little bullet into somebody with all the pleasure in life — that is, if he were not too great a coward to meet me; but snobs are always cowards. Give me that oil, Onions."

"You mean Gall," said Onions, handing the phial, and taking out the cork by way of facilitating operations; upon which a strong smell of bergamotte was diffused through the room. Onions gave a sniff.

"I say, Loftus, this is hair oil!"

"It will do; I've got no other. Yes, snobs are safe to be cowards; it's in their blood, and they can't help it," observed he, dropping a modicum of oil on the bright steel and delicately rubbing it. I'd lay you all I'm worth; I'd lay you these pistols, Onions, that if I called out Gall, he'd laugh in my face."

"Bosh, Loftus! Folks don't fight duels now," was the slighting remark of Onions.

"Not on this side the Channel. No; and that's what the fellow would shelter himself under — a custom obsolete. Gall has insulted me, and if I live I'll make him suffer for it. I *should* like to put a bullet into him," continued Bertie, grandly.

"It was too bad," said sympathising Onions. "I should pitch into him, Loftus."

Mr. Loftus threw up his head. "Pitching in" was not in his line, or anything so vulgar. "It was a great mistake to allow duelling to go out," he observed, in his lordly manner. "There's no way left now for gentlemen to resent an insult. You can't fight a fellow with your fists, as if you were a prize-fighter; you can't bring an action against him, and let things be blabbed out to the world."

"You can kick him down stairs," said Onions.

Mr. Loftus scorned a refutation. "Just lay hold of this end, will you, while I rub. Mark my words, Onions, before fifty years have gone over our heads, duelling will be in again."

"I say! is this Sir Simon coming up?" cried Leek, hurriedly.

Loftus listened for a moment, and then bundled pistols and leather and oil into the drawer. Sir Simon was passing to his own room, and there was no certainty that he would not look into this. So, for the time being, the polishing and the discussion were alike cut short.

But on the following morning, Onions, whose tongue was as open as his own nature, got talking to the school. And the matter reached the ears of Gall.

"Says he would like to meet me in a duel! says he is a better shot than I! *Is* he? If I chose to take him at his word and meet him, he'd see who was the best shot."

"And so I am a better shot," affirmed Loftus, coming forward to face Gall. "What should *you* know about shooting? It is an art that belongs to gentlemen."

In point of fact, neither of the two could shoot at all. Gall lifted his finger.

"Look here, Loftus. This is not a time to be taken up with petty interests: I can't afford the leisure for it, if you can; neither shall the school. We'll settle matters, you and I, when the Oxford's over."

"Agreed. Mind you don't flinch from it," was the scornful conclusion.

Gall spoke rather without his host, in saying that the school should not waste its time in disputes. At that very moment, the school was divided into groups, some taking Gall's part, some taking Loftus's, some differing on private matters of their own. After morning study, the various dissensions seemed to have merged into one single outbreak, and that was between Loftus minor and Paradyne. Paradyne had been taunted well that morning, by Dick especially, and he turned at length on the taunter. It was in the quadrangle.

"Because I have borne what hardly anybody else would, you think I *can't* retaliate; you think I am a coward! Try me, Dick Loftus."

Dick — hot, impulsive, passionate Dick — dashed in and struck the first blow. That was his answer. Off went the jackets, the boys closed round in a ring; it was to be an impromptu, stand-up, hand-to-hand fight.

And the very cries would have decided it, could cries decide. Every encouragement was heaped cheerily on Dick, every derisive insult that tongue can utter was levelled at Paradyne: never had the feeling of the school been more palpably displayed than now. Paradyne stood his ground bravely: cool, collected, retaining his temper and his self-possession, he proved a great deal more than a match for Dick, who had very shortly to acknowledge himself beaten. Paradyne had not a scratch upon his face; parrying all blows successfully, to this he chiefly confined himself, and, instead of punishing Dick, had been content to show that he could have punished if he would.

"And now," said he, as he put on his jacket, "as you see that I can fight, perhaps you'll let me alone for the future. I shan't take things so patiently as I have done."

He set off to run home to dinner; and a glow of admiration went out after him from all that were unprejudiced. The boy had half won their hearts with his gallant bearing.

He appeared at his desk as usual in the afternoon. Dick Loftus was at his, a little sore about the arms. Suddenly, amidst the silence that follows the first settling down of a large number of students, a voice was heard.

"Who has done this?"

It came from Paradyne. He was standing with a paper of many sheets in his hand, and had spoken aloud in his shock of surprise. The paper was a Latin essay, to go in that night to the Head Master; it had taken him many days to write it.

"What is the matter?" asked Mr. Jebb.

Paradyne left his place and carried up the paper. It was torn, blotted, soaked in ink almost from beginning to end. The contents of one inkstand could scarcely have put it in the state it was.

"What *is* it?" cried Mr. Jebb, gazing at the black relic.

"It is my Latin essay, sir. I left it clean and perfect in my desk after morning school."

"Your Latin essay! You left it —— Nonsense, Paradyne," broke off Mr. Jebb, "you must have had an accident with it: you have been upsetting the ink."

The whole school was staring and wondering. On the merit of these essays was supposed to lie very much the decision of the Head Master, whether their author should or should not go up for the Oxford. The school denied all knowledge of the affair. The first desk, collectively and individually, protested they had had no hand in it, and a whisper arose that Paradyne had done it himself to hide the poorness of his Latin. There was no time to attempt another.

"He can't go up for the Oxford now," were the first words that greeted Paradyne's ears when the hall rose; and they came from Dick Loftus.

"Did *you* do it?" cried Paradyne, turning sharply upon him.

"No, I did not," answered Dick; his red face and his honest eyes raised fearlessly to Paradyne's. "You beat me this morning in a fair, stand-up fight; but I'd scorn to do a mean trick of this sort."

"I believe you," said Paradyne, "and I beg your pardon for asking."

"And I am sorry that you should lose your chance for the Oxford," added Dick, not to be outdone in generosity. "I have never said either, as some of them do, that you ought not to go up for the Orville: it's as fair for you to compete as for the rest, for what I see."

But all chance for Paradyne, either for the one or the other, was over, in the opinion of the school.

Some of the better-natured felt sorry for him, and said it. Paradyne bore himself bravely before them; not a cloud on his brow, not a shadow on his lips, proclaimed aloud the bitterness of his defeat. But, later, when he was sitting at Mr. Henry's, he astonished that gentleman not a little by bursting into tears.

"I had taken such pride in that essay! I had looked forward to this examination with so much certainty of success. And now to have it all destroyed in a moment!"

"Hush, George! You may go up yet."

"No, I shall not; I can see that Brabazon thinks I did it myself. I might just as well never have worked on for the examination; I'd better not have come to Orville. It's awful treachery!" he burst forth presently, his tone changing as anger superseded the sobs. "I know this has been done by some of them. Oh, what a life it is to lead! And there's another thing — the mother has been counting on my success."

There were rare times and seasons when Mr. Henry was so utterly dispirited himself, that it seemed like a mockery to attempt to impart consolation or preach of patience to another. This was one. The trouble lay heavier on him than it did on the boy. As he sat alone, after George's departure, and took up the Book; more, it must be confessed, from custom that night than from any comfort he thought to find — for, in truth, he felt entirely beaten down, worn, sick, weary; it opened of itself at a part that seemed — ay, that seemed to have been written expressly for him.

"My son, if thou come to serve the Lord, prepare thy soul for temptation. Set thy heart aright and constantly endure, and make not haste in time of trouble."

And by the time he had read on to the end of the chapter, which is the Second of Ecclesiasticus, peace and trust had come back to him.

CHAPTER XIII.

If the Boys had but seen!

The long worked-for Oxford examination was over, and the results were at length known. Irby and Fullarton had not passed; Powell had not gone up for it by the decision of the Head Master; the rest had passed, including Paradyne. All George Paradyne's apprehensions, and the school's forebodings had proved alike mistaken, for Dr. Brabazon had sent up Paradyne in spite of the damaged essay. In his glee, George Paradyne heartily forgave all, and was his own bright self again. The studies went on again vigorously until July: the great prize, the Orville, had to be competed for yet.

In July the school rose for the long vacation, and Dr. Brabazon could no longer put off the explanation with Mr. Henry, which he had deemed it well to defer until the term should be over. To say the truth, he shrank from it. To convict this hardworking, pains-taking gentleman of theft — and such a theft! — was a most unpleasant task to enter on. He let a day or two pass, and while he was seeking for an opportunity to speak, it was afforded by Mr. Henry himself. The heat, or something else, seemed to be retaining its spite against the German master, and on the third day of the vacation, when he was giving Miss Rose her usual lesson, he fainted away without notice, just as he had that other day at Mr. Gall's. He had a short cough occasionally, and symptoms of blood-spitting.

The doctor sent Rose away and sat with him when he was restored, and rang for Mr. Henry's favourite

beverage, coffee. "You shall not go until you have
taken some, and the child's lesson can be continued
another day," said he, peremptorily and kindly, in
answer to remonstrances. "Do you think you can be
very well?" he continued, the weary look of pain on
Mr. Henry's face striking him forcibly.

"Not very; perhaps I have a little overworked
myself," was Mr. Henry's reply. "Sometimes I think
this place — the air, I mean — does not agree with me."

"Have you anything on your mind?" asked the
doctor; and either the nature of the question or its
suddenness brought a flush to Mr. Henry's face. They
were in the study, seated opposite each other near the
large window, the deserted playground, silent now,
lying beyond it in the vista; so that the quick flush
was perfectly perceptible to Dr. Brabazon.

"Now," thought he, "for my opportunity: I could
not have a better. Mr. Henry," he resumed, aloud,
"I have for some time fancied that you had some care
or trouble, that you were concealing especially from
me."

A pause. A yearning look of what seemed like
detection — detection pleading for pardon — crossed
Mr. Henry's countenance. The hour, which he had
been dreading for months, was come; and he was not
ready for it! He sat in uncomfortable suspense, not
knowing how much or how little the master knew,
pressing his thin fingers together, his elbows resting on
the arm of the chair.

"That some unpleasant trouble was on your mind
I have undoubtedly seen," resumed the doctor. "Now
that the opportunity for explanation has come, I think
you must afford it to me."

"I cannot disclose it to you now, sir," said Mr. Henry slowly, and with evident pain. "Perhaps in a day or two —"

"But suppose no disclosure is needed? — suppose I know it already?" interrupted the master.

"Is that so?" asked Mr. Henry, lifting his face.

"It is. The affair has unhappily come to my knowledge; not, of course, the inducement — the — the leading motive for yielding to the temptation. I cannot describe to you how it has pained me. Had you been a son of mine I could scarcely have felt it more. It seemed that I might so fully trust you."

"Since when have you known it?" asked Mr. Henry in a low tone.

"For some weeks now. I did not stir in it at the time," continued the master, brushing a large fly off his black waistcoat, "on account of not interrupting the classes of the boys who were going up for the examination. And, that over, I thought things might remain as they were until the vacation, as they had gone on so long."

"Then you intend to discharge me, Dr. Brabazon?"

The doctor could not help thinking it was rather an *assuming* question. He played with his paper weight on the table.

"What do *you* think about that, Mr. Henry?"

"Of course I have feared so. But yet —"

"But yet what?"

"Oh, sir, I'd rather not go on. I was going to speak of leniency — of consideration; but you might think it only made my offence worse."

"I will show you all the leniency in my power. I think my having delayed the explanation proves that my intentions are not hostile, and I will be your friend if I can. You were, I conclude, led into this by some overwhelming pecuniary pressure, as others have been before you, and then found that you could not redeem your act. This is Emma's view of the case as well as mine. Why did you not make a friend of me, and tell me your difficulty? I would have lent you the money."

"What money, sir?"

"The money you had need of. It was a poor sum to peril one's future for — seven pounds. And why did you use Mr. Jebb's name?"

Mr. Henry had been staring with all his eyes, as if the words bewildered him. "I don't quite understand, sir, what it is you are talking of."

"Of my pencil, that you took from this room and pledged in Oxford Street for seven pounds," returned the Head Master in terse language, nettled at the assumption of ignorance and innocence. "Why do you force me to speak out so plainly?"

Mr. Henry rose up; his whole attitude, his face, one entire questioning astonishment. "Why, Dr. Brabazon, what is it that you would accuse me of?" he exclaimed.

"Of the theft of the gold pencil. Of your having taken it out of this inkstand — this inkstand," laying his hand angrily upon the article — "and making money upon it."

The charge was so exceedingly different from the one feared by Mr. Henry, and seemed in itself so entirely absurd and ludicrous, that he burst into a laugh — laughed, it might be, in very relief.

"I beg your pardon, sir, a thousand times. You

12*

cannot seriously suspect me capable of such a thing. Steal your pencil!"

"Yes, my pencil," replied Dr. Brabazon, feeling rather bewildered. "Did you not come in at this window and take it; and then pledge it the next day in Oxford Street for seven pounds, and say you were a master here, and give in Mr. Jebb's name instead of your own?"

"Certainly not. What can possibly have induced you to fancy it? Oh, sir, don't you *see* that you might trust me better than that?"

"Well, I had thought I could," answered the doctor, feeling in a hopeless maze. "I said so to Emma. You see, one of the boys had noticed you that night walking about before the window; and there were other attendant circumstances — never mind them now. I am very sorry to have said this to you if you are innocent."

"Which of the boys was it that saw me?"

"Trace, I think. It was he who spoke to Emma." And the doctor, feeling a conviction that this accusation was really a mistaken one, gave a summary of the details. Mr. Henry distinctly and decisively denied the charge, and the doctor could doubt no longer. But — that no shadow of uncertainty might remain — Mr. Henry urged him to accompany him at once to the jeweller's shop, that the matter might be set at rest: nay, demanded it.

"A moment ere we start, Mr. Henry," said the master. "If this is not the trouble on your mind, what is that trouble? You cannot deny that there's something. What is its nature?"

"Spare me the question a little while, Dr. Brabazon," came the answer, given in a strangely-impassioned tone. "I have been wishing to tell you all along, but I — I — have been unable; and the conflict has robbed my days of peace, my nights of rest. Perhaps — in a few days — in a day even, I may disclose it to you."

"What can it be?" cried the wondering doctor, gazing at him earnestly. "Have you done anything wrong?"

"Yes, very wrong. But — it is neither theft nor murder," he added, his eyes lighting up with their luminous smile. A smile that so strangely, one could not tell how, imparted a feeling of confidence in him to whomsoever it was cast upon.

They took the first conveyance, and were soon in Oxford Street. The master of the shop was in, as before, and listened to a few offered words of explanation. He called the same young man in — Simms.

"Look at this gentleman," he said, indicating Mr. Henry. "Do you recognize him as one of our customers?"

Mr. Simms ran his eyes over Mr. Henry, and shook his head conclusively. "No, sir; I don't remember ever to have seen him."

"Is he the gentleman who pledged that gold pencil with the diamond top?"

"Oh dear no, sir. That person was older than this gentleman. They are not in the least alike."

"Just so," said Dr. Brabazon. "Will you give me a description of that person?"

Mr. Simms complied. "A party getting on for thirty-five, I should say, sir: rather shabby than not, but talked off-hand like a gentleman. Hair had a

reddish cast; and party walked, I believe, a little
lame."

"Lame!" exclaimed the doctor, in a startled tone.

"You did not mention any lameness the other day,
Simms," interposed the jeweller.

"No, sir; I didn't know it then. When I was
telling Watson afterwards about questions being asked
as to who had pledged that article, he said the party
walked lame; least-ways, that he limped in going out
of the shop. I hadn't noticed it, and so I told him;
but Watson was positive."

Dr. Brabazon looked like a man who has received
a blow. He went home leaning on Mr. Henry's arm,
as if he needed the support.

"Forgive me for having entertained a doubt of
you," he murmured, as he wrung his hand at parting.
"Perhaps when you tell me of this trouble of yours I
may be able to make it up to you. I know now who
it was took my pencil."

And so did Mr. Henry know; for he had recognized
the description and the lameness. Mr. Tom Brabazon
was the culprit; and had no doubt enjoyed amazingly
the joke of giving in the Reverend Mr. Jebb's name,
and taking in the shopmen with his assumption of innocent inexperience. Before the time had expired for
the running out of the pledge, he would probably have
enclosed the ticket to Dr. Brabazon, or to Emma,
with Mr. Jebb's name on it as large as life.

As Mr. Henry was turning from the college gate,
Sir Simon Orville's pony carriage drew up, himself
and Trace in it, the latter driving. Sir Simon ran
after Dr. Brabazon, who was then crossing the lawn;
Trace, conveniently near-sighted to the German master,

remained in the carriage, and turned his head the other way. However, Mr. Henry went up to him.

"Trace, I have a question to ask you. I understand you have been suspecting that it was I who took the Head Master's pencil. Will you tell me what reason you had for this?"

Trace felt uncommonly taken to. He had not a great deal of moral courage. "Oh," said he, shuffling with the reins, "that's an old affair now; past and gone."

"Not quite past and gone yet, Trace. What could have led to your suspecting me? Will you tell me the truth, so far? I have a reason for asking."

"Of course it was only a doubt. Some one must have gone in and taken it, and Lamb saw you there before the window. And — you appear to be always so inconveniently short of money as to make a few pounds an object," candidly added Trace, plucking up his courage. "Pardon my alluding to it."

"Slight grounds. I don't think I should have suspected you on such. Was there no other reason?"

"Except that you are a sneak and a cad," rose to Trace's lips. But he did not consider it would be convenient to speak it, and answered with a monosyllable, "None."

"Then —— was it a kind or a good thing of you to go with these suspicions to Miss Brabazon, my master's daughter? Had the doctor been a different man from what he is, you might have utterly ruined me. A charge of this nature cannot be refuted, in most cases, as easily as it is made."

"Have you refuted this one?" asked Trace, turning full upon him.

"Yes; at once and entirely. I did not know until to-day that it stood against me."

"Then I must tender you my apologies," returned Trace. Not that there was the least sign of apology in his tone; rather, it seemed to have borrowed the haughty ring of his cousin's, Bertie Loftus. "There was no harm done, it appears, so don't let us have a fuss raised now."

"I am not one to raise a fuss. You cannot but be conscious that to you, Trace, I have been especially tolerant — some might say forbearing. I fear it has been lost upon you."

"You have been very kind, no doubt," cynically returned Trace. "I do not wish more tolerance or forbearance shown to me than others get. Neither am I conscious of having received more."

"No? Yet I have been keeping some of your secrets, Trace. Suppose I had betrayed you in the matter of Paradyne's essay?"

"Of Paradyne's essay?" echoed Trace, seizing the whip and flicking the ear of one of the pretty ponies. "I don't think you know what you are talking of."

"Yes I do. And so do you. When I saw the blotches of ink on your wristband that afternoon, and asked what had caused them, that you should be so sedulous to tuck it out of sight, you knew as well as I did that I guessed the secret. I did not tell of you. It would have been a shocking thing, ruining you with the school and with the masters. Not even to forward the interests of Paradyne in a just cause, would I injure *you*. I wonder if you will ever understand me, Trace; or get to learn that I would be your friend and not your enemy?"

Trace cut the air with his whip; but he gave no answer. At that moment Sir Simon came back, holding out his hand in his cordial manner.

"You are not looking fat and rosy, Mr. Henry. Fagged with the term: it has been a heavy one. Why don't you do as we are going to do — take a trip over the water?"

"To Germany, Sir Simon?"

"Germany! — that's your paradise," laughed Sir Simon. "We are going to Boulogne — not much crossing there, you know, which I confess doesn't agree with me. We get over in an hour and a half. You should try it yourself. Good day!"

The pony carriage rattled off, and Mr. Henry turned to Mrs. Paradyne's. He had a little matter of business to arrange with her. But matters of business were not always palatable to that lady; and there ensued an unprofitable argument between herself and her visitor. He sat at the table in the little drawing-room, his elbow on it, his thin cheek resting on his two fingers. Mrs. Paradyne, dropping her work, a glove of George's that she was mending, talked at him from the sofa, and in her quiet, persistent way, allowed no reasoning but hers to be heard. Seated near her mother was Mary Paradyne, a bright-looking girl of twenty, with her brother George's great grey eyes. She had come home in June, having left the school in Derbyshire, and was seeking daily teaching near home. A Mrs. Hill, living near Pond Place, was negotiating with her.

"Where's George?" asked Mr. Henry, when he at length rose to leave.

Mrs. Paradyne would not answer. She was resent-

ing something that Mr. Henry had said. He approached
Miss Paradyne to shake hands, but she left her seat
and followed him out.

"You are right and mamma is wrong," she whispered, with the handle of the closed door in her hand,
and the tears gathering in her eyes as she lifted them
to his. "Oh, I wish she would not be so unjust to
you. George is spending the day at William Gall's."

All the answer Mr. Henry made was to bend down
and kiss her lips. A very suggestive action, and certainly not discreet. If the boys had but seen!

CHAPTER XIV.

Over the Water.

THE fine passenger boat was ploughing its way
across the channel, receding from Folkestone, gaining
on Boulogne-sur-Mer. Sir Simon Orville and his three
nephews were on board. It was a fine, warm, calm day in
August; and as Sir Simon Orville sat on the upper
deck, steadily as he could have sat in one of his own
chairs at home, he thought what a charming passage
that was between the two points, and how silly he had
been never to have tried it before.

For — if the truth must be told — Sir Simon Orville had never made but three water trips in his life:
the one to Ramsgate, from London; the other two, the
short crossing to the Isle of Wight. He had called
them all equally "going to sea;" and as it happened
that the water had been very particularly rough on
each of the three occasions, and Sir Simon terribly ill,
his reminiscences on the subject were not pleasant. To
find himself, therefore, gliding along as smoothly as if

the channel were a sea of glass, was both unexpected and delightful.

The sky was blue over head; the water was blue underneath; the slight breeze caused by the motion of the vessel was grateful on the warm day; and Sir Simon thought he was in Paradise. And now, as they were nearing the French town, there came gliding towards them the steamer that had just put off from it; her deck crowded with merry-faced passengers, congratulating themselves like Sir Simon, at the easy voyage. The vessels exchanged salutes, and passed, each on her way.

And now the harbour was gained and traversed; the boat was made fast to the side, and the passengers began to land. The first thing Sir Simon did on *terra firma* was to turn himself about and gaze around, perfectly bewildered with the strange scene and the strange tongue. It was so new to him: he had never been out of his own country in his life. Bertie Loftus, who knew something of the place, and prided himself on his French, consequently felt obliged to speak it as soon as he landed, drew his uncle to the custom-house through the sea of gazing faces, and said, "Par ici." That passed, and the egress gained, they found themselves in the midst of a crowd of touters, shouting out the names of their respective hotels and thrusting forward cards.

"Hotel du Nord," said Bertie, grandly, waving his hands to keep off the men, with an air of deprecating condescension.

"But what is it? What do they want? What are these cards?" reiterated Sir Simon. "My goodness me, boys, what's *that?*"

"That" was a string of the fishwomen in their
matelotte costume, dark cloth short petticoats, red
bodies, and broad webbing bracers. They were har-
nessed to a heavy truck of luggage, already cleared,
and starting with it to one of the hotels.

"Uncle, we shall never get on if you stay like
this," said Bertie. "That's nothing: the women do all
the work here."

Up came four or five more women and surrounded
the party, bawling into Sir Simon's stunned ears with
their shrill and shrieking voices, evidently asking something.

"What on earth are they saying of, Bertie?"

Now Mr. Bertie's French only did for polite table
life, and Anglo-French intercourse. To be set upon
by a regular Frenchman with his perplexing tongue,
and (as it seemed) rapid utterance, puzzled Bertie always: what must it have been then when these fishwomen attacked him with their broad patois?

"Come along, uncle; they don't want anything.
Allez vous en," rather wrathfully added Bertie to the
ladies, which only made them talk the faster.

"Bertie, I shall not go along: the poor women
must want something, and I should like to know what.
What — do — you — want — please?" asked Sir
Simon in his politeness, laying a stress upon each word.
"Spake Anglish? No spake French, me."

Jabber and shriek, jabber and shriek, all the five
voices at once, for there were five of them. Sir Simon
put up his hands and looked helplessly at Bertie; who
was feeling rather helpless himself just then.

"They are asking if you have any luggage, and if
they may carry it to your hotel, Sir Simon," spoke a

free, pleasant voice, evidently on the burst of laughter.
And Sir Simon turned to behold George Paradyne, and
seized his hand in gladness at being relieved from his
dilemma.

To hear the boy interpreting between Sir Simon
and the women; to note that his French tongue was
ready and fluent as theirs and with rather a more refined sound in it, was somewhat mortifying to Bertie
Loftus. The women disappeared, George talking fast
and laughing after them. "What brings you here?
When did you come?" asked Sir Simon, keeping him
by his side.

"We came yesterday, Sir Simon. I am with the
Galls. They kindly invited me to accompany them.
We are at the Hotel du Nord."

"The Galls here, and at the Norde!" almost shouted
Sir Simon in his delight. "I shall have somebody that
I can speak English with."

"Yes; the Galls had made friends with George Paradyne and brought him to Boulogne with them. Mrs.
Gall, a woman of the kindest and truest nature, had
told her husband, told her son, that she should make
the school ashamed of its prejudice against Paradyne.
William Gall had not accompanied them: he was coming later. Sir Simon had known nothing of their move-
ments: he had been a week and more from home.
The Talbots were coming; the Browns were coming;
Leek and his mother, Lady Sophia, were already there.
As Sir Simon remarked, it seemed like an arranged
party. Such, however, was not the case.

"What a lingo, to be sure!" cried Sir Simon, as
he trotted up the hot and blazing port. "Why, actually those little street urchins are jabbering French!

Halloa! stop!" he added, coming to a sudden halt opposite the goods' custom-house: "Where's Dick!"

Nobody remembered to have seen Dick since the
landing. "He'll turn up, sir," returned Loftus, slightly
annoyed at the unequal progress they were making.
"Dick won't get lost."

Sir Simon did not feel so sure upon the point; he
thought he might get lost himself in that helpless foreign town; becoming, as he was, more strange and bewildered every moment. But Dick came running up
from behind, dragging with him a tall, square-built
man with a thoughtful face and grey hair. Sir Simon
nearly shook his hands off, for it was Mr. Gall.

"What a mercy!" said he. "I never was so glad
in all my life; did not know anything of your coming.
We have been a week at Chatham, staying near my
poor brother Joe, the hop-dealer, who made that sad
failure of it. You know him, Gall. I wanted to see
how he and the wife and chicks were off, poor things,
and we put up at an inn there."

Dick shook hands with Paradyne. Dick listened
to the news that Onions was in the town, and that
Talbot was arriving, with a sort of rapture: the Browns
too, major and minor. Dick would have stood on his
head had there been room on the port to do it.

A few days more, and the different friends and
schoolmates had collected there. It was indeed as if
they had premeditated the gathering. Some went
grandly *viâ* Folkestone, some more economically by the
boat from London: that little muff, Stiggings, who was
fond of writing to Miss Rose, made the trip in a sailing vessel, invited to it by the captain; he was awfully
sick all the way, and landed more dead than alive.

The Galls and Sir Simon's party were at the Hotel du
Nord; the Talbots had small lodgings in the Rue
Neuve Chaussée; the Browns took a furnished house
in the open country, beyond the Rue Royale; and Lady
Sophia Leek, who had no acquaintance with the rest,
and made none with them, was staying at the Hotel
des Bains. And the time went on.

But that Sir Simon Orville was the most unsuspi-
cious of men, he had undoubtedly not failed to detect
that some ill-feeling was rife between his friend Gall's
eldest son, and Bertie Loftus. For three whole days
after William Gall's arrival, they did not exchange a
word with each other; on the fourth, a quarrel, not
loud, but bitter, took place on the sands; and those
low, concentrated, bitter quarrels are worse than loud
ones. People, scattered in groups at only a few yards'
distance, did not hear it; but they might have seen the
white faces raised on each other with an angry glare,
had they been less occupied with themselves, with their
gossip, with the picking up of shells. Bertie Loftus
was cherishing the remembrance of his insult, and
paying it off fourfold in superciliousness now.

Sir Simon's mind was too agreeably filled to afford
leisure for detecting feelings not on the surface: everything was new to him, everything delightful. The
free and easy life in the French town; the unceremo-
nious habits; the sociable salon, where they sat with the
windows open to the street; the passing intimacy made
with the rest of the guests; the sufficiently-well-ap-
pointed meals in the dining-room — the lingering
breakfast at will, the chance lunch, the elaborate
dinner — were what he had never before met with.
Mr. Bertie Loftus considered it a state of things alto-

gether common; but it was after the social, simple-
minded man's own heart. There was the pier to walk
on; with its commodious seats at the end, whence he
could watch the vessels in at will, and revel in the
view of the dancing waves; there was the laid-out
ground before that gay building whose French name
Sir Simon could not pronounce, the établissement, where
he could sit in the sun or the shade, watching the cro-
quet players, and reading his newspaper between
whiles; there was the terrace beyond, with its benches;
there were the sands stretching out in the distance.
An upper terrace also, close at hand, where he could
place himself at a small round table and call for lemo-
nade in the summer's heat. Sir Simon would be now
in one spot, now in another, his *Times* and telescope in
his hand, his friend Gall not far off. And Mr. Gall
was a sensible, shrewd man, looked up to in the city
as the head of a wealthy wholesale business; he was
not despised by his own people, however he might be
by Bertie Loftus. What with the attractions out of
doors and the attractions in, Sir Simon thought Boulogne was pleasant as a fabled town of enchant-
ment.

"A scandal-loving, vulgar, crowded, disreputable,
unsavoury place, sir!" was the judgment some new acquaintance passed upon it one day, to the intense ap-
proval of Bertie. But Sir Simon shook his head, and
could not see it.

Sir Simon stood at the end of the pier one afternoon, his telescope to his eye, ranging the horizon for
the first appearance of the London boat. He was looking in the wrong direction for it, but that was all one
to happy Sir Simon. Young Paradyne put him right.

By that boat he was expecting Mr. and Mrs. Loftus. Some business having taken them unexpectedly to London, Sir Simon had written to say, "Come over here and be my guests." It suddenly struck him that the sight of the boy by his side, Paradyne, might call up unpleasant recollections to Mr. Loftus. Sir Simon had got to like the boy excessively; but that was no reason why Mr. Loftus should tolerate the intimacy.

On came the good ship, "The City of Paris," pitching and tossing, for the waves were wild to-day, and Sir Simon felt thankful he was not in her. She but just saved the tide. Back down the pier he hurried, in time to see the passengers land; Dick and Raymond Trace crowding eagerly against the ropes. Dick leaped them, and had to go through the custom-house for his pains, kissing his mother between whiles. She was like her brother, Sir Simon, in features; simple once, but a little pretentious now. The tears ran down Sir Simon's cheeks when he saw that her hair was grey. Very grey indeed just at present, and her face too, with the adverse wind on deck, and the sickness. Mr. Loftus — a slender, aristocratic-looking man of courteous manners, but with a great deal of Bertie's hauteur in his pale and handsome face — had not suffered, and was ready to greet all friends in his calm, gentlemanly fashion.

There are many ropes about that part of the port, as perhaps some of you know. Mr. Loftus, a very near-sighted man, with an eye-glass dangling, contrived to get his feet entangled in them; he would undoubtedly have fallen, but that some one darted to the rescue and held him up. Mr. Loftus saw a stripling nearly as tall as himself, with a frank, good-looking countenance, and open, bright, grey eyes.

"Thank you, young sir," he said; "I must look to my steps here, I find. Who is that nice-looking lad?" he subsequently asked of Sir Simon.

"Oh, never mind him," cried Sir Simon, evasively; "let us get on to the Norde" — as he always called the hotel. "Eliza looks half dead."

"But where's Albert?" inquired Mr. Loftus, who had been gazing about in vain for his eldest son.

Sir Simon could not tell where he was, and wondered at his absence. He little thought that Mr. Albert Loftus was detained with Gall, the two quarrelling desperately, out by Napoleon's column. Things had come to a most unpleasant pass between them.

Mrs. Loftus went to lie down as soon as they reached the hotel. Mr. Loftus, declining refreshment until dinner-time, was ready to walk about with Sir Simon and be shown the lions. That goodhearted and estimable knight took him to a favourite bench of his on the green lawn — or plage, if you like to call it so — of the établissement, which seemed nearly deserted under the blaze of the afternoon sun. The sea was before them, the harbour on the left, the heights on the right. Here they sat at their ease, and the conversation fell upon Mr. Trace, Raymond's father.

"It is nearly a twelvemonth now since Robert Trace wrote to me," observed Sir Simon; "I can't make it out. We have never been so long before without news. Have you heard from him?"

"No," answered Mr. Loftus. "But my not hearing goes for nothing. I don't suppose we have exchanged

letters three times since we separated in Liverpool four
— nearly five — years ago."

"Is there any particular cause for that?" asked
Sir Simon.

"Well, I can hardly say there is. We did not
agree in opinion about the winding-up of affairs at
that unfortunate time, and I was vexed with Robert
Trace; but we parted good friends."

"He took too much upon himself, I have heard
you say."

"Yes. He would carry out his own opinions;
would not listen to me, or let me have a voice; and
he did it so quickly too. While I was saying such a
thing ought to be done in such a manner, he *did* it,
and did it just the reverse. I have always thought
that if Robert Trace had managed properly, we might
have gone on again and redeemed ourselves. The
fact is, his usually cool judgment was stunned out of
him by the blow. But it is of no use speculating now
on what might have been. How was he getting on
when you last heard?"

"I don't know."

The words were spoken in a peculiarly emphatic
tone, and it caused Mr. Loftus to glance inquiringly
at Sir Simon. The latter answered the look.

"He was at Boston, you know; had got together
some sort of an agency there, and was doing well. In
one of his letters to me, he said he was in the way to
make a fortune. Some capitalists, whom he named
were establishing a great commercial enterprise, a sort
of bank I fancy, and had offered the management of
it to him, if he could take shares to the amount of
two thousand pounds, which must be paid up. He

could furnish the one from his own funds, he said, and
he asked me to lend him the other. In less than a
twelvemonth it should be repaid to me with interest."

"And what did you do?"

"Lent it. I was willing to give him another help
on to fortune; and Trace, as you know, was a long-
headed fellow, the very last to be deluded by any
trashy bubble not likely to hold water. So I despatched him the thousand pounds by return mail."

"You were always too liberal, Simon."

"Better be too liberal than too stingy," was the
rather impulsive answer. "I should not like to remember on my death-bed that I had refused assistance
to friends in need, for the sake of hoarding my gold.
What good would it do me then?"

"And how did it prosper him?"

"I don't know. I got an acknowledgment from
him of its receipt — just a line. I believe I can re-
peat the words, 'Dear Simon, my best thanks to you
for what has now come safe to hand. Will write by
next mail.' The next mail, however, brought me nothing, nor the next, nor the next. After that came
a letter, dated New York; in it he said he had left
Boston, and would give me particulars later. They
have never come."

"That's strange. How do you account for it?"

Sir Simon did not answer for a minute. "I think
the projected enterprise failed," he said at length; "and
that Robert Trace lost his own money and mine too.
I think he is trying to redeem his position in a measure
before he writes and confesses to the failure. It is no
good reason for maintaining silence; but Robert Trace
always was sensitive on the subject of pecuniary losses,

especially of his own. I suppose the Americans were more clever than he, and took him in, and he does not like to confess it."

"What are you going to do with Raymond?" questioned Mr. Loftus.

"I don't know. I shall be in a dilemma over it, unless we speedily hear from his father. Should he gain the Orville prize he will go to the university; but as to what he is to be — of course, it lies with his father to decide. I propose business to him — any sort he'd like; but he turns his nose up at it, just as disdainfully as Mr. Bertie could do."

Mr. Loftus smiled. "Bertie wants to read for the Bar; but I fear it will be up-hill work. He — there's the fine lad that saved me from stumbling," he broke off, as Paradyne and another shot across the sands. "You did not tell me who he was. He has a nice face."

"I'll tell you if you like; but your prejudices will rise up in arms like so many bristles. That's young Paradyne."

"Paradyne! Not Arthur Paradyne's son?"

"It is."

"But what brings him here — with you?" returned Mr. Loftus; his voice taking a cold, haughty, reserved tone.

"There, I knew how it would be," said Sir Simon, with a short laugh. Turning round to make sure there were no listeners, he told the particulars to Mr. Loftus: of George Paradyne's happening to enter Orville College, of Raymond's discovery, and of the Head Master's appeal to himself. "The lad is as nice a lad as ever lived," he concluded, "and why should his father's fault be visited upon him?"

A moment's pause, and Mr. Loftus's better reason
asserted itself. He was of a generous nature when
his pride did not stand in the way: or, as Sir Simon
put it, his prejudice.

"Certainly. Yes. I should have said the same,
had Dr. Brabazon consulted me. Let the boy have a
chance. But, Simon, how does he get supported at
that expensive college? The widow protested she had
but the merest pittance of an income left."

"I don't know how. Somebody, perhaps, has
taken them by the hand: I can't tell what people of
misfortune would do without. I show the boy kindness, not only because I like him, but that I promised
something of the sort to Mary."

"To Mrs. Trace?" exclaimed Mr. Loftus.

"I did," affirmed Sir Simon, to the evident surprise of his brother-in-law. "Mary Trace had been a
hard, cold woman, as you know; but the light broke
in upon her when she was dying. It changed her
nature — as of course, or it had not been the true,
blessed light from heaven — and she got anxious for
others. More than once she spoke to me of the Paradynes; their fate seemed to lie like a weight upon her.
'If ever you can lend them a helping hand, Simon,
do it,' she urged; 'do it for our Saviour's sake.' I can
see her blue, pinched lips now, and the anxious fever
in her eyes as she spoke," he added dreamily, "and I
promised. But I would help the lad for his own sake,
apart from this."

Mr. Loftus made no comment: to confess the truth,
he could not quite understand why Mrs. Trace should
have done this. He raised his double eye-glass.

"Is not that Albert?" he asked. "There, in the

distance, with one or two more young men." And
Sir Simon turned his long glass in the direction to
which he pointed.

Close against the water they stood; three of them
— Bertie, for he it was, and Gall, and Leek. The
tide was nearly out, and Bertie and Gall had found
their way round the point, from the heights down to
the sands, a long round, wrangling all the way. Had
Mr. Loftus and Sir Simon but possessed an ear-glass
as well as an eye-glass, they might have heard more
than was meant for them. That Bertie Loftus was
bent upon aggravating Gall by every means in his
power, short of vulgar blows, was indisputable; each
word he spoke was an insult, a derisive taunt; and
Gall, who had rebelled against this kind of treatment
from Bertie, even when it was implied rather than expressed, was nearly stung into madness.

"Why don't you have it out, and have done with
it?" he passionately cried, stopping short as they came
round in view of the établissement and its frequenters.
"If you keep on like this, you'll provoke me to kick
you to ribbons."

Bertie smiled derisively. Kick *him* to ribbons!
His legs were twice as long as Gall's, if it came to
kicking. Not that Bertie would have played at that.
"There's no chance of having it out with *you*," came
the coolly contemptuous answer. "The only way
which gentlemen use to 'have things out,' you don't
understand. And you can't be expected to."

Leek espied them from a distance and came
running up. It was at this moment that Mr. Loftus's
glasses happened to fall upon them.

"Look at him, Onions," cried Bertie, indicating

Gall by a sweep of the hand that was the very essence of insolent scorn. "He is asking me to go in for a game of kicking."

"I am saying that I'll kick *you* if you don't stop your row," cried Gall, his very lips white with passion. "And so I will."

"I never did see two such fellows as you," was Leek's comment. "You can't meet without insulting each other. What's come to you both?"

Bertie Loftus wheeled round on his heel in the soft sand, and confronted Gall closely, face nearly touching face. "Look here, here's a last chance — will you meet me?"

"Meet you?"

"Yes, meet me. Don't pretend to misunderstand. I have my pistols at the hotel."

"Perhaps you brought them on purpose," said Gall, with an unmistakable sneer.

"Perhaps I did," coolly avowed Bertie. "Will you make yourself into a gentleman for once, if you can, and meet me?"

"Why, you don't think I should be such an idiot as to go out to fight a duel, do you?" wonderingly cried Gall, while Leek burst into a laugh. "People don't do that now, Mr. Loftus."

"Gentlemen do. Ask Leek: he's one. Of course, you can't be expected to understand that. Others shelter their cowardice under plea of the law — of custom — which is so much sneaking meanness. I knew how it would be, and that's why I said nothing before. Why, if you did agree to meet me, you'd steal off by dusk, and give notice to the police."

"Loftus, I am no more a coward than you; but I know what's right and what's wrong."

"Just so. And shelter yourself under the 'right.' Cowards can but be true to their nature."

Gall lifted his hand as if he would have struck, but let it fall again. He was by no means so cool in temper as Bertie Loftus; and a cool temper is sure to win the day in the end. It is of no use to pursue the quarrel further; the harsh and abusive words interchanged would not tend to bring edification; but the result was a very deplorable one.

They separated: Bertie going one way with Leek; Gall remaining on the sands. Mr. Loftus and Sir Simon came forward to meet Bertie, and both of them thought him singularly pre-occupied.

That evening Leek went into the Rue Neuve Chaussée, to call upon James Talbot, and took him out in the moonlight. "Come on the pier," he said: "it will be quiet there, and I want to speak to you. Have you seen Gall?" he asked, as they walked along.

"No, but I have had a note from him," answered Talbot. "He says in it he relies upon me to be his friend. I can't make it out."

They went on to the quiet pier and paced it slowly, the bright moon dyeing the scene with her lovely light. An open-air concert was being held in the garden estrade, its coloured lamps flickering, its numerous listeners flirting and promenading. The garish windows of the ball-rooms flung their light abroad — what a contrast to that pure light riding in the sky! Away they pressed to the top of the deserted pier, out of sight and hearing. The tide had turned and was coming in; the wind was rising; the waves roared and leaped against the end of the pier. There Leek told his story: that Gall and Loftus were about to fight, and he had promised to be Loftus's second; Talbot was to perform that office for Gall. Talbot could not believe his ears.

"Fight — a — duel!" he uttered, in blank astonishment, leaving a pause between each word. "Surely they'd not be such fools."

"They will, earl."

"Not with my help, then. I'd put the police on the track first."

"It would do no good," returned Leek, shaking his head: "they'd evade the police. Look here, Shrewsbury, when fellows are determined to go in for a thing of this sort, be assured they *will* go in for it, by hook or by crook. Loftus, it seems, has been bent on it for some time, and he has so managed to stir up Gall, that I don't know now which is the more eager for it of the two."

"And suppose either of them should get killed? — or both?" debated the earl. "I say, Leek, this is an awful thing."

Leek nodded gravely. A little fishing-boat lay alongside the pier in the harbour, stranded there in attempting to come in when the late tide was nearly out; she was just getting afloat now, and two men on board her were making some bustle, talking in loud tones. Leek and Talbot stood looking down upon her as if attracted to interest; in reality they were absorbed in their own thoughts.

"I told them it was an awful business," spoke

Leek, in answer to the last remark, "but I might just as well have said it to the wind. Well, let us talk it over, old fellow. We must be men for once, and do the best we can."

Talbot held out no longer. And the two paced about, settling preliminaries, planning and devising. A matter of this nature seemed to carry them beyond their years; to take them out of young men into old ones. Returning to Leek's room at the Hotel des Bains, they got out the pistols, which Loftus had re-signed to Leek, and examined them preparatory to their being loaded later. By some untoward fate, while the weapons were in their hands, Brown major, making a call on Leek, burst into the room. Talbot hurried the pistols out of sight, but the gentlemen were both so confused that Brown could not help suspecting something extraordinary was in the wind, and said so. In the irresistible attraction that gossip presents, they imparted the secret to him. Mr. Brown sat down on Leek's portmanteau, while he digested the news.

"I'd not have believed it of Gall," he said at length.

"Nor I at one time," returned Talbot. "Loftus has taunted him into it."

Brown major sat nursing his leg, and revolving possibilities. "Suppose bad comes of this, Shrewsbury? — what about you two?"

"What do you call bad?"

"Why, if they should get shot — killed. You might be taken up and put in prison."

Of course it was not a pleasant suggestion. "They'll not give it up," said Leek, with a rueful look.

"Suppose *you* gave up, Onions; you and the earl?"

"They'd get other fellows for seconds, and call us cowards."

"I don't like those French prisons," gloomily observed Brown major. "If once you get in, you never know when you'll get out. We knew a man who was put in one for ten years."

"What had he done?"

"He owed some money; nothing else. When he had been in about two years, his friends in England clubbed together and got him out. My father was one. You should hear what he says of the place. They serve up the soup in a bucket."

"Nice!" cried Leek.

"*I'd* not run the risk of getting into one," resumed Brown, who was evidently of a prudent turn. "They should fight their duel without me, first. Why, Onions, what would your mother say?"

Onions turned his head quickly towards the door with a somewhat scared look, as if he feared Lady Sophia might be coming in then.

"All you have to do, Brown, is just to hold your tongue, and respect the confidence we've given you," returned Leek. "Whatever consequences come of it, you won't be called upon to answer for them."

"Right, old fellow," cheerfully answered Brown, who was really one of the last to interfere unpleasantly. "You know I'm safe; I was only thinking of you two. The thing shall go on without any interruption from me."

And the thing did go on. As you will find if you read further.

"Somewhere on the heights out beyond Napoleon's

column, I think," suggested Leek in a whisper to Talbot, as they were separating for the night. "I'll go with you to pick out a snug spot to-morrow. You'll not fail us at the last, earl!"

"I'll not fail you, Onions. Good night."

CHAPTER XV.

Dick's Bath.

NOT on the exposed heights by Napoleon's column, but a short way beyond it, down in a non-frequented hollow, the meeting-spot for the duel was fixed. Onions and the earl went out when breakfast was over the next day, and chose it after due deliberation. They explored some fields over at Capécure, beyond the lines of rail; but, for some reason known only to themselves, rejected that side of the town. Gall and Loftus appeared not to care where the spot might be, provided it were somewhere. The time was to be sunrise on the following morning, or as soon after it as they could get out of the hotel and make their way to the spot.

Does it not seem ridiculously absurd to be recording this? But I can only relate what took place; and college students come to the age of these had accomplished such an end before. You may deem that Leek or Talbot ought to have warned the police; but they did not. I think that day added some years to the experience of their lives.

And the two principals — Gall and Loftus — what kind of sensations do you suppose were theirs? Did they look forward to their possible fate — death — with calmness? Was the unruffled exterior, shown to the world, a type of the unruffled mind within? No, you cannot suppose it. Loftus was perhaps the least troubled of the two, for his was the more composed and easy nature; but each had his share of — anticipation.

Why, how could it be otherwise? Try and realize the situation to your minds, my boys; to make it your own. With the rising of the morrow's sun, you are going out to be shot at yourself and to shoot at another. Before that sun sets, you may be lying cold and dead; your life in this world over; your soul before its Maker. It is very solemn; almost too solemn to write of. When men go out to fight duels, they are represented to be full of inward bravery, as poets have sung and friends have boasted. Never you believe it. Or, if it be so, they have been living without God in the world, callous to the never-ending future. Ah, no! Physically brave, as to the possible flesh wound, perhaps; but *not* brave as to the consequences it may involve — a sudden rush into eternity, uncalled.

Leek and James Talbot were here and there and everywhere — men of importance that day. The fixing upon the meeting-spot took them the whole of the morning. Next they had an interview with the two principals conjointly, and, to give them justice, did all that argument could do to induce the affair to be abandoned. Mr. Brown, fit to burst with the great secret confided to him, and of which he could not talk, went to every conceivable corner of the town in search of the two other sharers of the secret, and went in vain. He found them at length, when the afternoon was passing, at the Hotel des Bains, in Leek's chamber. As on the previous night, they had the pistols out, and this time they did not hurry them away.

"Well, how's it going?" demanded Brown, breathless with the wind and his own haste.

"How should it be going?" retorted Leek, not pleased at being pursued by Brown major like this.

"Is it off?" resumed Brown, wiping his hot face. "It's such a wind, Onions."

"No, it's not off, and it's not likely to be off. Lock up the pistols for now, Shrewsbury."

"But it's awful, you know," continued Brown, mounting the foot-rail of the bed, and placing himself astride it. "When I got up this morning it seemed to me too improbable a thing really to take place. Suppose one of 'em gets killed? I say, Shrewsbury, couldn't you persuade them off it?"

Lord Shrewsbury gave his head an emphatic shake. "We have been at both of them, Gall and Bertie, and tried everything tryable. You might as well speak to two posts. Let it drop, Brown; it's of no good bothering us."

Brown let it drop, and did it with a good grace: he was powerless. "Have you engaged a surgeon?" he asked.

"A surgeon? No."

"But you'll have to take one. A surgeon's a necessary appendage to duels. Sometimes each side takes its own."

Singular perhaps to say, this "necessary appendage," as Brown major put it, had not been thought of by the seconds. They looked at one another in the pause that ensued. Onions broke it, more emphatically than politely.

"To speak to a French doctor might blow the whole thing. He'd go right off to the police."

"But you can't take two fellows out to shoot at each other without having a surgeon at hand," debated Brown major, opening his eyes in his simple manner. "Don't you see it, Shrewsbury? Suppose they got wounded. While you were running to find a doctor, one of 'em might bleed to death."

"Both might, for the matter of that," acknowledged Lord Shrewsbury, tilting himself against the tall secrétaire, taller even than himself. "Brown's right, Onions. It's odd we never thought of it."

Onions turned to the window, open to the unsavoury harbour, and stood there in silence. He did not see his way clear on this new point. Not a single doctor in the town was known to him; every one of them might prove a traitor. And, moreover, he had some private doubts of his French, did it come to a delicate negotiation.

"Look here," exclaimed Brown major, briskly, a happy thought striking him; "would not my brother Bob do to go out with you? He is at St. George's Hospital, you know, takes his turn to go round with the surgeons as a dresser. He has his case of instruments over here, and I know he'd be true."

The suggestion was seized upon, and Brown major flew off and brought back his brother. Mr. Robert Brown — a young man of twenty, with a fresh, good-natured, round face — affirmed that he could bind up wounds and restore fainting patients to life with the most skilled hand at St. George's; ay, and extract a bullet, if it came to that. He gave his promise to keep the secret, and seemed to look forward to the affair as a piece of delightful fun, rather than one of solemnity and danger.

This settled, Leek and Talbot went down on the port, deeming it well to show themselves to their friends, lest suspicion should be excited. When we have a momentous secret on hand, you know, we are apt to fear the world may miraculously discover it. Gall and Loftus were both there, on the plage, before the établissement. Indeed it seemed that half the town had gathered on the port, here and in various other parts, to watch the turbulent sea. None could have discerned anything unusual in the demeanour of the two young men, soon to be the combatants in a great tragedy. Both were a little silent, but that was all.

The wind had been rising higher and higher since the previous day. These London inland people called it a hurricane, and gazed on the sea with an interest that partook of awe. It was indeed very rough — sailors might have said half a gale; but the boat from Folkestone had ventured out, and, after a long and difficult passage, was trying to make the harbour. On the pier, people unused to this could not stand without difficulty, and chose rather the safer watching parts on the plage. Some of the boys were gathered on the sands, near to that little yellow house, the Maison de Sauvetage — rather an ominous name to-day.

"I'll bet you five shillings that she gets in, and that I take my bath," said Dick Loftus, hot in dispute; for they had been telling him he could not attempt that dangerous sea to-day, and different opinions existed as to whether the steamer would or would not get in. "And here's the five shillings to deposit," added Dick, proud of having so much riches to display, a most unusual thing with him. "Come now, *you*, Onions; you needn't laugh like that."

Onions was laughing to show his ease. He had an important rôle to maintain, and the eyes of the world were upon him.

But for the white fleecy clouds dashing after each other across the blue sky, the day would have been particularly bright and clear. The waves of the receding tide were coming in with a high white froth, breaking ere they touched their extent of way, and lifting their foaming heads aloft. George Paradyne was talking to a man belonging to the "Société de Naufrage," and the rest were listening to the boy's pure French.

"You have not got the boat out to-day," he observed, alluding to the rescue boat that is always in close attendance during bathing hours.

"She's not needed," crustily returned the man, who seemed a crusty subject. "What bathers would venture into this sea?"

George Paradyne glanced at Dick, as much as to say, Hear that. But Dick chose to take no notice, and the society man walked away.

"If this wind does not go down the meeting will have to be put off," whispered Leek, in an undertone, to Bertie Loftus. "The charge might be blown off at a tangent, and take us seconds instead of you."

"Don't be fool enough to talk of it here, Onions," came the rebuking answer; and Bertie caught up a glass and looked at the boat. She was labouring hard; her two white funnels throwing themselves, as it seemed, from side to side, her nose pitching aw-fully.

But she made her way, and drew near the port at last. People changed their places to watch her in. Mr. Dick Loftus, in secret connivance with himself, was left alone, and he seized on the opportunity. "Danger in bathing to-day indeed!" contemptuously thought Dick. "I'll teach them better."

Not very many minutes, and all at once a cry of anguish broke from the treacherous waters. The boys turned at it; they came running from far and near. Mrs. Loftus, Mrs. Gall, who had much ado to keep their petticoats down over their crinolines, looked in the direction and wondered what the cry meant; and Mr. Loftus came sauntering up. Like his son Bertie he rarely hurried. Sir Simon trotted in more quickly. Another cry! — a cry as from one hopelessly drowning.

"It's Dick! it's Dick!" shrieked Bertie. "Where's the boat? Where's the man?"

Ah, then was commotion. Dick it was, who had been experimenting on the waves on his own account. They ran hither and thither, shouting for the man, calling for the boat; but the man did not answer, and the boat was not on service to-day. While they were running like madmen, all in confusion, Mr. Loftus stood in helpless despair — a very incapable man, he, in any sudden emergency.

But see! While they have been crying and calling, another has been doing. Some one who threw off his superfluous clothing, plunged into the waves, and is nearing the drowning boy. He gains — he gains upon him! He has him in his hands now, and is turning to battle back to shore again; and a silent prayer is going

14*

up from many a heart to heaven. There ensues a
pause of agonized suspense; and then a low murmur
of thankfulness, gradually rising into a shout of admiration, breaks out from the spectators. Sir Simon
Orville fairly dances in his glee, while the tears run
down his cheeks.

"Who is it that has saved him?" asked Mr. Loftus,
feeling as if the one half of his substance, the whole
gratitude of his remaining years, might well be given
in recompense. The beaming, generous grey eyes of
the rescuer met his in answer, and he knew them for
George Paradyne's.

Mr. Dick was conveyed in rather an ignominious
fashion to the yellow Maison de Sauvetage, followed
by a long tail, who were shut out unceremoniously.
Brown major's brother, announcing himself in obscure
French as a "doctoor," was allowed to enter. The
attendants placed Dick in one of the beds that the
room contained, and a French surgeon, springing it
was hard to say whence, appeared upon the scene.
But no vigorous means of resuscitation were resorted
to, simply because the patient, who was not very far
gone, revived without them. George Paradyne, meanwhile, was quietly dressing himself, throwing off thanks
and homage as he best could. Sir Simon Orville, however, would not be thrown off. He took possession of
him and carried him back in triumph to the Hotel du
Nord to dinner.

George was shown to a chamber to brush his still
wet hair, when Mr. Loftus came in, and held out his
hand.

"How can I show my gratitude to you for what
you have done?"

"Oh, sir, thank you; but it does not deserve any particular gratitude," was the boy's laughing answer, as he resigned perforce his right hand, while his left held the hair-brush. "I am so very glad I happened to be there."

"Where did you learn to swim like that?"

"In the West Indies, when I was a little fellow. Papa's regiment was quartered there. We had an old black servant, who taught me. He used to carry me to the water, and let me sport in it like an alligator. Few can swim as I do."

"I have been very distant to you since I came here. You cannot but have observed it," resumed Mr. Loftus, making the confession as an atonement in his impulse of generosity; and indeed he had very markedly held himself aloof from the boy in his pride and condemnation. "This has made me ashamed of myself."

"Don't say anything, sir. I quite understood it. If my father had been the rogue you believed, it was only what I, his son, deserved."

"As I believed," repeated Mr. Loftus, sad commiseration in his tone. "All the world believed it, George."

"I know they did, sir."

"Well, it is not what I can enter upon with you; and I begin now to see how unjust my feeling to you has been. I —"

"But I wish you would enter upon it, sir; I wish you would let me say how *certain* I am that my father was innocent," interrupted George, his face becoming flushed with a crimson glow, his eyes raised full and earnest to those of Mr. Loftus. "I was only a young lad when it happened, between twelve and thirteen; but I was old enough to judge. Why, Mr. Loftus, but for feeling myself free of that inheritance of guilt, could I have gone on bravely as I have, and done battle with the difficulties thrown in my path — the contempt I have had to stand? At Orville College there has been a dead-set against me from the first — an awful opposition; and I am quite sure that past charge against my father is the foundation of it, though it may not be generally known to the school. When I feel inclined to give in, beaten and hopeless, I say to myself, 'He was innocent, and I'll bear up in spite of all this for his sake;' and that gives me pluck to fight on again."

"Did you know the particulars of the case?" asked Mr. Loftus, admiring the brave and hopeful nature, in spite of his wonder that any such opinion on the late Captain Paradyne's case could for one moment obtain, even with his son.

"Yes, every one of them," replied George. "I don't suppose there was a single item that did not fix itself on my heart. The sudden discovery — made first of all by you, sir — that something seemed wrong, and then the looking into it privately by yourself and Mr. Trace, and your finding out the frauds, and the arrest of my father. If he had only lived out the investigation, he would have disproved the charge."

"You wish me to speak of this unreservedly to you, I see, as if you were a stranger," observed Mr. Loftus; in answer, as it seemed, to the boy's vehemence.

"Yes, sir, if you please. I used to wish I might

speak to you of it at the time, and get you to look at it in the light I saw it."

"Then, knowing the details, *how* could you, and how can you, fancy your father was not guilty? Remember, my boy, you have asked for this, and I wish to speak with all kindness. He was the only one connected with the office who could have done it. The clerks had not the opportunity."

"Who did do it I can't say, though I have a doubt; but my father it was not," answered George. "I'll tell you a little matter that happened, sir; not much, you'll say. A week or so before the explosion, I was doing my Latin exercise one evening in the study at home, when papa came in and sat down behind me. He was very quiet, and I forgot he was there; but when I got up to put my books away I saw him. He was leaning forward with his elbow on his knee, pulling at his whiskers, as he would do when in deep thought; and he must have been like that, quite still, all the time. 'What are you thinking of, papa?' I said; 'what's the matter?' He came out of his reverie then, and put his hand upon my shoulder in his fond manner. 'The matter's this, George,' he said, 'that I have a suspicion something wrong is going on in the office, and I cannot make out how, where, or what. I am not up to business, and that's the truth. Either of my partners would find it out in no time.' 'Why don't you tell them, papa?' I asked. 'I am waiting till the sixth of next month, George,' he said; 'that may put things straighter than, to my mind, they are. If it does not, I shall speak to Mr. Trace.' But, you know," added George, his great eyes suddenly becoming wet, "that before the sixth of the next month —

September — he was dead. Mr. Loftus, I could stake my own life that he was sincere when he said that."

Mr. Loftus made no comment. It was the sixth of each month that they used to balance up their accounts.

"After he was taken back to prison the day of the examination," continued George, "they let me go in to see him. I was with Mr. Hopper, and he took me in. I burst out crying. Papa laid hold of my hand, very grave and kind; "George, I am perfectly innocent,' he said, 'do not distress yourself. I am a little bewildered at present, it's true; and I must understand what the frauds have been, and how committed, before I can refute them. You remember my saying to you, George, that I had a doubt; I wish I had spoken at once, instead of waiting to see whether I was right or wrong. I wish I had telegraphed to the Isle of Wight for Mr. Loftus, and had the whole thing investigated. But that must be done now. Tell your mamma from me, that it is all right; tell her it is a mistake, or something worse, on the part of those who have charged me. My boy, you have never had cause to blush for your father, and you have none now.' I was sent out then, Hopper telling me to wait outside for him, while he spoke with papa. He came out soon, and I went home, and —"

George Paradyne broke down. He leaned his head on the dressing-table and fairly sobbed. Mr. Loftus touched him gently, and said a soothing word.

"In an hour or two after that, word was brought that he was dead," presently resumed George. "He died with the suspicion of the guilt upon him, and nobody cared to refute it. I talked to Hopper till he said I worried him, asking him to take it up. I went and saw Mr. Trace, and told him all this, but he only shook his head, and spoke kindly to me, and said there was no doubt. I knew there was no doubt, but it was the other way; no doubt of his innocence."

"Will you let me ask you one question, George? If your father was not guilty, who, in your opinion, was?"

"I don't much like to say," was the answer. "And at the best, it is but a doubt."

"I think you had better say it."

"I fancied it was Hopper."

"Hopper!" repeated Mr. Loftus, lifting his head quickly. "No; that was impossible."

"His manner made me doubt him at first: it was very singular. I am sure that he knew who was guilty; and I think it was himself. And then, sir, you know he disappeared very soon after."

"Yes; that is, he disappeared from Liverpool. He may have taken a clerkship in some London house. But Hopper could not have been guilty. There's the dinner bell. Once more, let me thank you for the service you have rendered my boy Richard."

George Paradyne followed Mr. Loftus down stairs, conscious that his words had made no sort of impression upon him. It was always so: himself against the world. Even his own mother, his father's wife, had never listened to this persistently expressed belief in the innocence. Mr. Loftus knew the theory to be a mistaken one; but he thought none the worse of the boy for entertaining it.

CHAPTER XVI.

The Duel.

THE dinner-table was full. Old Felix, the head waiter, had caused a separate table to be laid for the party of which Sir Simon Orville was regarded as the head; it included the Galls, the Loftus's, young Paradyne, and a friend of Mr. Gall's, named Bouncely, just arrived by the train from Paris; all, in fact, save the resuscitated Dick, who had been brought home, and was upstairs between a few hot blankets.

It was a very singular thing that the conversation at this side table of theirs should turn on duelling. Bertie Loftus, recounting it later to Onions, called it a "droll chance." But nothing happens by chance in life. Mr. Bouncely, a ponderous gentleman in black, with gold spectacles, a huge bunch of seals hanging down from a chain in a by-gone fashion, and who was an alderman or sheriff, or something grand and great of that nature in the City, had recently been enjoying a brief sojourn at Frankfort-on-the-Maine. He was brim-full of a duel just fought there; had not, as he expressed it, got over the horror yet.

"It arose out of a quarrel at the gaming-table; as quite three parts of these duels do arise," said he, tasting his fish. "Two young fellows of most respectable connections, students yet, one training for medicine, the other for the bar, went out with their seconds in the early morning, and shot each other. One died on the spot, the other is lamed for life."

"Ugh!" exclaimed Sir Simon. "One can hardly believe such a thing in these sensible matter-of-fact days." And Gall and Loftus, seated at opposite corners of the table, glanced accidentally at each other, and dropped their eyes again.

"The one, killed, was an only son — an only child — and his mother is a widow," continued Mr. Bouncely, bending his spectacles on something just placed before him, if by good luck they could distinguish what the compound might be. "She has been nearly out of her mind since; all her enjoyment in life is gone. It is very awful when you reflect upon it."

"Poor thing; yes, it is indeed," interposed Mrs. Loftus with compassion. "Every mother must feel for her."

"Ma'am, I spoke of the thing itself; not of the poor mother. *That* is not the awful part of it."

William Gall, passing the water, which somebody asked for, happened to catch sight of his mother's bent eyes; bent to hide the tears that had gathered in them.

"I was alluding to *him*, ma'am; the young man himself," resumed Mr. Bouncely, willing that Mrs. Loftus should be fully enlightened. *What is his future fate to be?* Where is he now? *now*, at this very time, let us ask, when we are left on the earth here, eating a good dinner? God placed him in the world to do his duty usefully and faithfully, and to fit himself for a better; not to hurry himself out of it at his own will and pleasure, a suicide."

"A suicide," repeated Mrs. Loftus, who was apt to take things literally. "I thought the other killed him."

"Why, dear me, madam, what can you call it but a case of suicide; what else is it?" asked the City man. "They stand up deliberately, the pair of them, to shoot, and be shot at; each one, no doubt, hoping and striving to get the other dead first. *I* should not like to rush into the presence of my Maker uncalled for, with murder on my hand, and passion in my heart."

"Ah, no!" shuddered Mrs. Loftus. "It is very dreadful."

"He was about half an hour dying; perfectly sensible and conscious that life was ebbing away fast, past hope," resumed Mr. Bouncely. "What could his sensations have been as he lay there? — what awful despair must have reached him; what bitter repentance! It makes one shudder to think of it."

It seemed as though Mr. Bouncely were imparting somewhat of his own strong feeling on the subject to the table. And, in truth, such reflections were enough to make even the careless shudder.

"What would he have given, in that one half hour of agony, to undo his act of folly, that poor young dying man!" he continued. "He was a Lutheran, and had been religiously trained: 'the child of many prayers,' said a friend of the mother to me. Ah, what petitions of imploring anguish, as he lay in his remorse, must have gone up to his Saviour for pardon! for grace even for him."

And so the conversation continued, this duel being the topic to the end of dinner. It seemed to Gall and Loftus that Mr. Bouncely kept it up on purpose: when anybody strayed to a different subject, he recurred to this. As they were crossing the court-yard after rising, to go into the public drawing-room, or to their rooms up stairs, as inclination led, some one touched Gall on the arm. It was Talbot, who had been waiting under the porte-cochère. Gall stepped aside with him, apparently just taking a look at the street and at the library windows opposite, lighted up.

"I thought I'd come and tell you, Gall, that the wind's gone down," whispered Talbot. "I have been on the pier with Onions, and it's nothing like as high; so there will be no impediment on that score. We got talking to an old fisherman, and he says it will be calm by morning. How's Dick?"

"Oh, he's all right," answered Gall, speaking more as if he were in a dream than awake. At least, it sounded so, and Talbot glanced at him.

"Are you going to the ball to-night?" asked Talbot, the whirling by of a carriage with flashing lamps probably suggesting the remembrance of the ball to him.

"No," said Gall; and for the life of him he could not have helped the sudden sense of the general unfitness of things that just then came over him. Balls in one place, duels and death in another.

"Onions is gone. His mother made him go. At least he's gone in to dress for it. She wants to be there once, just to see what it's like, she says. Onions was very mad, but he couldn't get off it."

"Ah, yes," answered Gall, thinking how much happier Onions was than himself. "I must go in, earl; I promised Dick I'd sit with him after dinner. Good night."

Talbot put out his hand; an unusual occurrence, for the college boys were not given to ceremony between themselves, either at meeting or parting. Gall responded to it mechanically.

"I say, Gall," he said, as he held it, and his voice

dropped to a sort of solemn, concerned tone, as if *this*, that he was about to say, were serious and what had gone before was froth, "must this go on?"

"Must what go on?"

"The business of to-morrow morning."

"Why you know it must."

"I don't like it."

"Neither do I particularly."

"Then put an end to it before mischief comes."

"How?"

"Why, shake hands; you and Loftus. You are both good fellows, as all the world knows. It's a miserable thing that you should quarrel and bring things to this pitch."

"I have not sought the quarrel. Loftus has forced it upon me."

"Well, you did knock him down, you know. Go to him and apologize for *that*, and perhaps between you things may be made up."

"And be branded by him afterwards as a coward— as no gentleman!" was Gall's irritable and indignant answer. "Talbot, there's not another word to be said. This was forced upon me in the first instance; but I have taken it up, and, having done so, there's no retreat."

"Then of course I can say no more; but I wish it were otherwise. At five o'clock in the morning, I'll be at the door here waiting for you. Good night. I've got a bet with Onions that he oversleeps himself. What fun if he should! He brings the pistols."

Talbot walked away in the direction of the Hotel des Bains; he had to see Leek yet; and Gall went up stairs to Dick's chamber in pursuance of his promise.

Dick, however, proved to be in a sound sleep, so he turned to his mother's sitting-room. Mrs. Gall was seated at one end of the crimson-velvet sofa, complaining of a headache.

He had a headache, too, or perhaps it was a heart-ache; and he sat down on the sofa by her, and let his head fall upon her shoulder. Mrs. Gall was a little shrimp of a woman, with a great deal of love for her children and gentleness for the world in general, although the end of her nose was so sharp and red.

"Are you not going down to the salon, mother?"

"No, dear. They will send me some tea here."

"Nor to the rooms?"

"Not to-night, William. Papa's going, I think, with the rest. You are going too, I suppose?"

"No; I'll stay at home with you."

"Nay, my dear," remonstrated Mrs. Gall, supposing his motive was to keep her company; for she was accustomed to much consideration from her children, as a gentle, loving mother is sure to get. "I shall be quite well alone. You must not deprive yourself of the evening's pleasure for me. This ball to-night is the chief one of the season."

"I am not going," he answered. "I did not intend it, mamma."

She lifted her hand as he lay there, to push the hair from his brow, with a fond movement, and stooped to kiss him.

"How hot your forehead is, William! Have you the headache, too?"

"Not much. A little."

"I think the wind brought on mine to-day," observed Mrs. Gall. "That, and the fright connected with Dick Loftus. William, that's a brave boy, that young Paradyne. I'm so glad we brought him."

"First-rate."

"I cannot think why the college should dislike him: it gets more and more of a puzzle to me. He is very good-looking. Did you notice his beautiful eyes and his flushed face when Mr. Bouncely was giving us that narrative at dinner? He was quite a picture then. By the way, William, what a most shocking thing that was!"

"Not pleasant."

"Not pleasant!" repeated Mrs. Gall, rather shocked at the apparently light tone. "Can you imagine anything more dreadful? A mistake, or calamity, so long as it is confined to this world, is not beyond the pale of remedy; but — when it comes to rushing into the next! William, I am sure that thinking of that poor mistaken youth has made my head worse."

William Gall gave no particular reply; his mother thought he was sleepy, and said no more. Sleepy! with the consciousness on his soul of what he was about to do! with the awful amount of responsibility, already making itself heard, that was weighing him down! There was no such blessing as sleep for him.

It might be the last time he should ever, in life, be thus with his mother. It might be his last evening on earth. Oh, life looked very fair, now that he was possibly about to quit it. Scenes of the past and present, pleasant realities of existence, seemed to come tumbling into his mind with strange persistency. The "old house at home," with its home comforts and home affections; the days at Orville College with their hopes and interests; the future career he had been rather given in anticipation, to carve out for himself. Why, what a mockery it seemed! Here was he, a candidate (though he had never much thought he should get it) for the Orville prize — long before the time for bestowing it came, he might be cold in his grave, half forgotten! What a mockery seemed all things, if it came to that: his education at all; his training; nay, even his having been born — were this to be the ending! The more serious, solemn part that Mr. Bouncely had enlarged on in the other case, of what might come after death, William Gall simply dared not glance at. No wonder that his brow grew hotter and hotter.

"I'll go to my room, I think," he quietly said, rising, as his reflections became keen and more keen, his assumption of calm equanimity simply intolerable. "Good night, mother, dear."

She was surprised at the abrupt salutation; at the long, passionate kiss he pressed upon her lips; at the yearning, singular love in his eyes. But before she could say anything, he was gone. Gone to shut himself in his own room, with his troubles and his fear. Not fear of the shot itself or the pain it might bring; William Gall was of a sufficiently brave nature; but fear of the results that might follow in its wake — of the ETERNITY he might be flying into. And yet, so powerful upon him was received custom, the conventionalities of the world; so great a dread had he, in common with others, of being pointed at as a coward, that he let the thing go on, and would not stop it. An almost irrepressible wish had come over him, while he was with his mother, to tell the truth to her; but that might not be, and he thrust it back again.

And so good night to you, Mr. William Gall! Pleasant dreams!

Bertie Loftus was getting over the evening in a different way. Bertie, in full dress, was exhibiting his handsome self at the rooms. He talked, he laughed, he danced; he was so unusually active, so unusually gay, that Raymond Trace, with his unfailing discernment, wondered what Bertie had been about, and knew he was only killing care. Bertie denied it when Trace asked; *there* was his care, that split he had made in his left-hand glove. "Wretched kid that it must be," he said, with a light laugh. With a light laugh; with an assumption of careless gaiety: but nevertheless every pulse in Mr. Bertie's inward heart was beating with something that was more akin to pain than pleasure; and the loud notes of the music seemed to be so many pistol-shots banging off in the air.

"Be on the ground in time, Loftus," whispered Mr. Leek, as he passed in the wake of the Lady Sophia's scarlet cloak, who had soon had enough of it, and was leaving early. "Five o'clock sharp, mind."

"All right, Leek." And subsequently when Bertie Loftus himself took his departure, he and his party, a couple of coachfuls, and rattled along the port, he looked out at the glistening water and wondered whether he should ever see it again. He might wish the morrow over; he might wish what was to take place in it could be stopped; but that was impossible. Pride was in the ascendant with both him and Gall, you see; and of course gentlemen cannot act against the *convenances* of society.

The morning rose; warm, bright, clear; with a

stiffish breeze yet, but nothing to intercept work or
pistol shots. Gall found his way out of the hotel, and
saw the faithful Talbot waiting, his back propped
against the shutters at the parfumeur's opposite. Gall
felt in better spirits than he had been last night, as
most of us do when light has chased away the darkness. And, perhaps, he was willing to show himself
gay.

"Good morning, Shrewsbury! How long have you
been there?"

"Only five minutes. I say, is it not a glorious
morning? Couldn't have a better," cried the earl. He
seemed in spirits too. It was well to put a good face
on what could not now be avoided.

They walked to the appointed place, commencing
the route by the Rue d'Assas, and so upwards. It
was a good step, even when they had left the town
behind. Carriages had been proposed the previous day;
but they were afraid to engage any lest the affair
should get known. These two were on the spot first.
Certainly the seconds had chosen well; the place was
appropriate enough to what had to be done on it. It
was a bit of flat, low ground, where the grass was
short, lying rather in a hollow, and sufficiently
secluded. The sea sparkled in the distance over the
heights; the open country was stretched out on the
other hand; Boulogne lay below. A very few minutes,
and Mr. Leek appeared in full spirits, carrying the
case of pistols.

"How are you, Gall, old fellow?" he asked,
gingerly depositing the case on the ground. "I'm not
long after you, you see, Shrewsbury. Where's Loftus?"

"Not come yet," answered the earl. He put his

15*

arm within Leek's, and drew him off a little way,
talking of the preliminaries in an undertone; not so
low, however, but that Gall might have heard had he
chosen to listen. Gall sat down on a gentle ridge of
the land, and waited. Soon the others came back
again; Onions remarking with an off-hand manner, as
if he wanted to show himself at ease, that they should
have a broiling day.

They waited on; waited and waited. Expectation
grew into wonder. Loftus and Mr. Bob Brown had
arranged to come together, but neither came. Had
Loftus's valiant courage deserted him at the eleventh
hour? Hardly; but Gall felt gratified that he was not
the one to be tardy.

As the clocks were striking six, a shout was heard,
and three figures bounded on to the heights. Brown
major was the first — and *his* company had not been
bargained for; on the contrary, he had been expressly
told by the seconds he was not to come. But the
meeting was a great deal too tempting to be withstood:
as Brown major remarked, he might never have the
luck to get such a chance again. Bertie Loftus, in a
white heat, began explaining their unfortunate deten-
tion. He shared a double-bedded room at the hotel
with Dick, and just as he was about to get up and
dress himself, Sir Simon Orville, anxious for Dick's
health, walked in without ceremony, sat himself down
on Dick's bed, talking, and never (as Bertie phrased
it) went out again.

"I *couldn't* get up while he was there," cried Bertie,
speaking savagely in his mortification; "it might have
betrayed the whole thing. You should have seen the
Guy he was; he had on grey drawers, with a white

stripe across 'em, and a long tassel hanging behind from his cotton nightcap."

There was no time to be lost. It was already too late by a good hour, and Leek and Talbot bestirred themselves with a will. The only one of the party who looked grave, somewhat unwilling, was Mr. Robert Brown. What had been great fun in prospective, was very serious now that the time for action came; and the young doctor felt the responsibility that his two or three years of seniority gave him. Putting out of view the possible consequences, he saw that a large share of the blame might afterwards rest upon him.

"I wish you would make it up, gentlemen," he urged.

Nobody listened to him. The seconds were busy pacing the ground, looking to the pistols, holding communion in an undertone. Gall and Loftus were exchanging a civil sentence now and then, to show their indifference. Both were outwardly calm, though perhaps it strained their nerves to appear so; Brown major, with a scared look in his round eyes, went dodging about restlessly, and rather wished, than otherwise, that he had not come.

"All's ready," cried the seconds, returning to them. Of course they knew very little, if anything, of the executive of such meetings, but were doing things according to their best judgment. "We are putting you sideways to the sun, or else one of you must have had it right in his face," said the earl.

"Do we keep our hats on?" asked Gall.

Now here was a poser. Nobody could answer the question, or say what the custom was. Talbot thought they should be on, Leek thought they should be off.

While the duellists stood in indecision, the young surgeon settled it.

"Keep them on," said he. "What does custom signify one way or the other?"

"You must shake hands," said Onions. But he had no sooner spoken than Lord Shrewsbury whispered to him that it was prize-fighters who shook hands, not duellists. However the thing was done; and, as Mr. Brown remarked by the other doubt, it could not matter.

They were placed facing each other, twenty paces between them, and a pistol handed to each. Ah, how little Bertie Loftus, when he bought those pistols in his pride a year ago, dreamt of the grief they would bring him to! Both of them, Gall and Loftus, were now as white as chalk. The surgeon stood on the side with a rueful face and compressed lips; Brown major removed himself to a safe distance: with those in-experienced shooters there was no knowing what direction the bullets might take; and the seconds as yet were standing close, each behind his man.

"Present!" said Leek, in so low a tone that the doctor did not hear it. Onions might be nervous.

"Fire!" came the next word, after a moment's pause; and that was called out loud enough.

"Not yet! not yet!" shouted Robert Brown in an agony, for the two inexperienced seconds had not re-moved themselves from the place of danger. "Come away first for the love of heaven!"

He spoke too late. The combatants had fired, each his pistol; the reports crashing out loud enough in the morning air. There ensued some momentary confusion, and Robert Brown's eyes were, so to say, dazzled by anxiety and fear. When his sight came to him, he

saw that the rash seconds were uninjured; but the
duellists had both fallen, and were lying on the ground,
their white faces turned up to the full blaze of the
August sun.

CHAPTER XVII.

Mr. Leek in Convulsions.

YES: both the duellists had fallen, and lay on their
backs, their white faces upwards, and the pistols beside
them. The seconds were standing over them with long
chins of horror, and the surgeon came striding up. Gall
was nearest to him, and he halted there first.

"Where has it struck you?" he asked, very gently.

Gall, just able to speak, faintly said he did not
know. He thought in the small of the back.

But this was impossible according to the doctor's
views. The bullet might have come out at the back,
but it certainly could not have gone in that way. As
Gall lay there, hardly knowing whether he was dead
or not, and the glorious sun shining right into his eyes,
an awful remorse came over him. Now that it was
too late, he saw how easy it would have been to refuse
to fight, even at the risk of being called a coward.
While some cast that reproach on him, others would
have lauded him for his plain good sense. How fair,
how very fair the world looked, now that he was about
to quit it!

"Let's see," said Mr. Robert Brown, intending to
turn him on his face, but attempting it slowly and
gingerly. Truth to say, the operator in embryo felt
himself in a bit of a predicament: he had never ex-

tracted a ball in his life, and was rather undecided which way to begin. Gall groaned.

"Why, there's no sign of any injury here," exclaimed the doctor, in a tone of surprised pleasure, as Gall went over in a lump. "The coat's not touched. See if you can get up."

It was what Gall, beginning to recover the shock and his senses together, was already doing. Mr. Brown took his hand to help him, but there seemed no need for it. He was up, and stood as well as ever he had stood in his life. He walked a few paces and found he *could* walk. The surgeon critically passed his eyes and fingers over him, and came to the conclusion that — he was not injured.

"You are not hurt; you were not struck at all," he cried, and the tears actually came into Mr. Bob's Brown's eyes, so glad and great was the relief. "The bullet must have passed you."

He, Robert Brown, flew off to the other wounded man, Bertie Loftus. Bertie was on his feet too, under convoy of Onions and Brown major. Very much the same ceremony had been gone through with him. A moment or two he had lain as one dead, he also having been struck (as he believed) in the small of the back, but had got upon his feet without help, though with much condolence.

"Why, you are not hurt, either!" shouted Mr. Robert Brown, in his astonishment. "Where on earth can the bullets have gone?"

It was quite true; they were *not* hurt. As to the bullets — they must have gone somewhere.

"What made you fall?" reiterated the surgeon, whose delight at this result caused his face to glow

with a red like the early rising sun. Neither of them
could say. Each thought he had been struck in the
back; each had felt the shot there. Bertie repeated
this aloud: Gall said nothing. Gall was wondering
how he could ever be thankful enough to Heaven that
he was in the world yet. How fair it was! how lovely
looked the line of horizon over the dark-blue sea!

"I — don't — think — there — has — been —
any — duel," slowly spoke Mr. Robert Brown, when
he revolved matters. "Did they forget to load the
pistols?"

"If there has been no real duel they must be put
up again," volubly interposed Brown major, quite forgetting, in this agreeable termination, his recent fears.
"Where was the good of all the bother? Where's the
use of going in for satisfaction if you don't get satisfaction? My heart alive, who's this?"

Who indeed! Brown major's startled question was
caused by the appearance of a stranger on the scene.
He came puffing up at a sharp pace, and Bertie nearly dropped into his shoes at the apparition: for it was
his uncle, Sir Simon. And Sir Simon had heard the
report of the pistols too, and took in the truth at a
glance. The young surgeon, some view perhaps of
self-exculpation in his mind, explained the affair in a
few brief words, and dwelt upon the fact that no harm
had come of it.

"You two wicked ones!" exclaimed the really
shocked and scared Sir Simon to Gall and Loftus.
"Give me up those pistols, sir," he sternly continued
to his nephew. "They shall never be in your possession again."

It was easy to say, Give me the pistols. But the

pistols had disappeared, and Bertie's second with them. Before Sir Simon was seen, or thought of, Mr. Leek had hastily shut the pistols into their case, and glided quietly away with them, unobserved.

"Where are the pistols?" roared Sir Simon.

"Onions must have gone off with them," cried Brown major, who seemed more at his ease altogether than any of the rest.

Lissom and surefooted as any cat, Onions was then making his way down the almost perpendicular descent between Napoleon's column and the sands, the case of pistols safe in his hands. When the descent was effected he sat down, partly to recover breath, partly to burst into vehement, laughter. Swaying his body from side to side it seemed that he never would leave off, to the intense astonishment of a fisherman going by with three mackerel dangling in his hand from a string, who stopped to gaze at him.

Never, sure, did a pair of duellists take their way off the field more ignominiously than ours! For nothing to have come of the meeting was sufficiently crest-lowering on the surface, whatever the inward satisfaction might have been; but to be exposed the whole way to the fire of Sir Simon's tongue — now thundering forth its condemning anger, now sunk in ironical raillery — was hardly to be borne. He treated them like a couple of children. In the first place he made them walk arm in arm, and march before him; himself, the acting surgeon, Brown major, and Lord Shrewsbury, bringing up the rear like so many policemen. Thus they made their way home, taking the route through the Upper Town and down the Grande Rue, for Sir Simon would go no other way. Arrived at the hotel, the others having dropped off on the road, he marshalled them into his own room, shut himself in with them, and talked to the two; not in the angry or ironical strain he had been using publicly, but in a solemn, severe, and yet kind tone, with the tears of emotion running down his cheeks.

"Shake hands, and be thankful to God," he wound up with, "for a great mercy has been vouchsafed to you both this day. But for that, you might just as well have been lying stark upon the heights now."

He never supposed but that the pistols had been loaded with bullets. Any doubt to the contrary had not been whispered to him. And the fact, as to whether they had or not, remained yet to be proved.

But the occurrence spoilt the pleasure in Boulogne. It was looked upon in a very grave light by both the families concerned, and they resolved to cut the visit short and return home. Sir Simon made a call upon Onions, and demanded the pistols, which were given up to him. Never again were they seen by Bertie Loftus; and what Sir Simon did with them Bertie could not get to know, but always thought he dropped them into the waves of the receding tide, and let them drift out to sea.

Onions was back in London before they were. Lady Sophia Leek, grown tired of her visit, as it was natural to her to grow, wherever she went, crossed over the day before the large party. It was quite the same to Onions whether he stayed or returned home. He made himself happy anywhere.

Let us take a look at Mr. Henry. While they and others had been amusing themselves, he was working as usual. He gave his private lessons, he finished his translation, he accomplished certain work that Mr. Baker had asked him to do as a favour — the working out of some difficult problems in Euclid. "You are as capable as I am, Henry," said the mathematical master, "and I want to go into Wales and see my poor old father." And Mr. Henry had accepted the task with a patient sigh.

Yes, the translation was finished at last. It had been a stupendous labour, considering the little time Mr. Henry could give to it and the many abstruse books he had been obliged to consult. Had he fore-seen what the task would be, he might not have entered upon it. And he had made too light, by anticipation, of his legitimate work in the college, for that had been greatly added to by the ill-will of the boys. All the trouble and labour they possibly could give to him, they did give. Many and many a night, when he might have been at his translation, was he detained over their wretchedly false exercises; rendered purpose-ly as incorrect, and also as illegible, as it was possible for the malice of schoolboys to render them. Mr. Henry had felt ill for some time now. It was hot sum-mer weather, and yet a sort of ague was upon him; but he did what he could to shake it off.

And that was a red-letter day when, the translation completed, he set out with it for London. It happened to be the same day that Sir Simon and his large party were crossing over from Boulogne; but that had no-thing to do with Mr. Henry. The sun was bright, the skies were clear; his ailments and his weakness, the weary night vigils, and the past fatigue in his labours, all were alike forgotten, as he bore on to the publisher's house in Paternoster Row, and passed at length through its swing doors, carrying his heavy parcel.

"Would you like to receive the money now?" inquired the publisher, after he had talked with him.

"If you please. If not inconvenient."

Not inconvenient certainly to pay thirty pounds; and the money, in five-pound notes, was given into his hand. "We shall send the proofs to you, Mr. Henry; no one but yourself must correct them."

"Very well. You will present me with a copy of the book for my own use?"

"One copy, sir! You shall have more than that, and be welcome to them. Half a dozen if you like."

"Thank you very much. Then I can give a copy to Dr. Brabazon, and send over another to my old university."

He went out, his eyes quite luminous with the pleasure. The money in his pocket; the learned book (it might almost be called *his* book, so great had been his labour) coming out immediately; copies to give to his friends! For once Mr. Henry forgot his care, and seemed to tread on air.

But he could not live on air; and hunger was very powerfully reminding him of that fact when he reached the Strand. He looked out for an eating-house, and turned into Simpson's. Ordering a plateful of lamb and peas (recommended by the waiter), he went out again to a shop close by, to buy some trifle he wanted. As he was bounding back into Simpson's, he found his coat-tails seized, and turned to see a boy in the College cap. It was Leek.

"Why, Onions!" he exclaimed, calling him, in his surprise, by the more familiar name, "I thought you were in France. George Paradyne wrote to me a day or two ago, and mentioned you."

"We came over yesterday; Lady Sophia got tired of the place," answered Onions. "The rest are crossing to-day: I mean Loftus and Gall's lot," he went on to explain with the customary scant ceremony of the College boys. "Oh, Mr. Henry, we have had the jolliest lark! I should like to tell it you."

"Do so," said Mr. Henry. "I am going to have some dinner: will you take some with me?"

"Don't care if I do," returned Onions. "Lamb and peas! That's good, after the kickshaws we've had in France. You'll laugh yourself into a fit when you hear what happened there."

Seated at a table in the corner, Onions recounted his story, and eat his lamb and peas between whiles. Mr. Henry treated him also to some cherry tart. Onions eat and talked, and exploded into bursts of laughter, contagious to see and hear. The diners in the room turned and looked; there seemed some danger of his going into a fit himself. It was the duel he was telling of, and Mr. Henry, when the boy first began, truly thought he was recounting a fable: though it is possible, having been acclimatized to Germany, that he did not feel so shocked at the idea of the duel as the other masters might have felt; say the Reverend Mr. Jebb, for instance, or Dr. Brabazon.

"You see, when they asked me and Lord Shrewsbury to stand seconds, we didn't much like it. Suppose one of them had got killed? But it was of no use our saying a syllable: Gall and Loftus are both just as obstinate as pigs, and a comet with a fiery tail wouldn't have turned either of them. They thought their honour was involved, you see. Oh, and what do you think? Dick went into the sea during a gale, and was all but drowned."

"Dick was!"

"And Paradyne saved him," continued Onions, having got out of one tale into another. "Nobody saw Dick go in, or knew he was in, until his cries were heard. It was too rough for bathers to venture that day, and the Sauvetage boat was not on duty, but Dick thought he'd try it on the sly. And there he was, drowning without help! While the rest of us were rushing about wildly to find the men, Paradyne quietly threw off his jacket, plunged in, and went swimming after him — and a deuce of a long way Dick had drifted out with the tide. He is a brave fellow after all, that Paradyne. You should have heard the cheers when he came in with Dick!"

Mr. Henry was leaning back in his chair, absorbed in the narrative — a hectic flush on his cheeks, a glowing light in his eyes. Praises of George Paradyne stirred every fibre of his heart.

"George never said a word of this in his letter to me."

"Oh, I daresay not; he's not a fellow to talk of himself," was Mr. Leek's answer. "You never saw such a swimmer. Well, Dick was saved. We wondered afterwards whether, if he had been drowned, it would have stopped the duel."

"And the duel really took place? It seems past all belief," continued Mr. Henry. And Onions, his mouth full of pie, went into convulsions again, and upset the beer. When the choking was over, he continued his account.

"I and Shrewsbury laid our heads together; we

didn't want, you know, to aid them in going in for such a chance as *death*. Besides, duelling is over, let Bertie Loftus say what he will. We agreed *not to load the pistols;* but that fool of a Brown major got putting his tongue into it, saying we must take a surgeon. We couldn't say we'd not, for fear of exciting suspicion, and he proposed his big brother who is at St. George's, and we took him. What we feared was, that he might get looking to the pistols; which would have spoilt the game. He didn't though, and was in an awful fright all the time. He placed our men at the distance of twenty paces — you should have seen the combatants; the two were as white as this table cloth — and gave the signal to fire. At the moment the pistols went off I gave Loftus a smart knock in the back with some pieces of brass that jangled frightfully; Talbot gave Gall the same, and down the two went, thinking they were both shot. Oh my goodness! I shall never get over it to the last hour of my life," broke off Onions, struggling and spluttering. "Mr. Henry, if I were in church, — if I were watching somebody dead, — if I were before the examiners for the Oxford, and thought of it, I must laugh."

It seemed so, by the way he was laughing now.

"They thought they were shot, and there they lay; and Bob Brown came up with a long face, getting out his case of instruments. 'Where are you struck?' says he, beginning with Gall who was nearest him; 'whereabouts has the bullet gone into you?' 'I think it went into my back,' says Gall, with a groan. 'Let's see,' says Brown, delicately turning him a little, 'perhaps it came out there? No, there's no hole in your coat at the back. Why, you're not shot at all!' he shouts out, as Gall got up and felt himself. Oh my stars, but it was rich! I and the earl had to keep our countenances, and nearly died of it."

Mr. Henry was laughing quietly; and the crowded room turned round once more and gazed at the College lad.

"I made off with the pistols. That had been arranged. Oh, I assure you we laid the programme well, and rehearsed our parts over and over. My mother walked me off to a miserable ball the previous night; but Lord Shrewsbury came to sleep in my room, and we were practising the thrust upon each other's backs till daylight. We got a brass candlestick out of Lady Sophia's chamber and battered it up for the pieces; the hotel people, finding it had disappeared, thought my Lady must have swallowed it. I've got the brass yet."

He laid his head down on the table, not exactly after a public fashion; shaking and convulsed. "Go on," said Mr. Henry.

"There's no more fun to tell. I made off with the pistols, for fear they should find out the trick, and fight in earnest — but they must have gone to the town for bullets first. Sir Simon Orville came on the scene then, and ——."

"Who had warned him of it?"

"Nobody. His coming was accidental. He went in early to Dick's room, to see how he was, and dressed himself afterwards to take a walk, instead of getting into bed again like a Christian; and somehow arrived at the spot by chance. Wasn't there a row? Shrewsbury says he never heard any old fellow go on so. He made Gall and Loftus shake hands, and marched them

home again before him arm in arm. That same day
he came to me, demanding the pistols, and threatened
to tell Lady Sophia of me unless I promised never to
help in such an affair of iniquity again: that was what
he called it, 'an affair of iniquity.' So I gave him up
the pistols, and told him the truth at the same time —
that I and Talbot had not put any charge in them.
You should have watched the change in him! He
called me all sorts of charming names, and shook my
hand, turning himself about with delight in his funny
fashion, and said he'd be my friend always and Talbot's
too; and then he put his hand into his pocket and
gave me — what do you think? — five golden sovereigns. But he took the pistols; and Loftus's belief is,
that he pitched them, case and all, into the harbour.
Oh, it was a lark, that duel! I don't believe I shall
ever get in for such another."

It was the conclusion of the tale. The company,
who had remained at the different tables, as if fas-
cinated, began to move. They had caught but a word
here and there, and rose up impressed with the idea
that a peer of England, the Right Honourable the Earl
of Shrewsbury and Talbot, had been one of the principals in a duel; which news they forthwith carried to
their friends. There are people who believe to this
day that his lordship was the culprit. Mr. Henry paid
for his dinner, and went out with Leek. They were
parting, for their way was not the same, when the
master laid his hand upon the young man's shoulder.

"I wish I could get you to do me a favour, Leek."

"That I will," was the ready answer. "What is it?"

"Make my duties easy to me next term, instead of
difficult. That is, help to make them so. No one but

myself, Leek, knows what I have to battle with. Sometimes I think it is wearing me out."

"Are you ill?" exclaimed Leek, suddenly noticing, now that they were in the sunlight, the peculiarly worn look on the quiet and refined face.

"I am not very well. Perhaps I may give up my post in the College."

"I say, though, you don't mean that! Are we boys driving you away?"

"That, and other things. I don't know how it will be yet. But if I remain, I must get you all to behave differently."

"And so we will," cried Leek, in a generous fit of repentance, and some shame; as he remembered the impediments it had been their delight to throw into the way of the foreign master, and how patiently he had borne it all. Leek could not help being struck with the look of *goodness*, of truth in the face before him, though it might never have struck him particularly before; and it suddenly occurred to him to wonder whether they had been mistaken on sundry little matters. A man who has just treated us to a good dinner can't be a bad man.

"Mr. Henry, was it you that told of the seniors smoking, when there was that row last autumn term?" he asked impulsively.

"It was not. I answered this at the time."

"Then I'm blest if I don't believe it was Lamb, after all! He's a beauty. And I daresay other things that they said of you were as untrue?"

"I daresay they were," replied Mr. Henry, smiling.

"What a jolly shame! Don't go away because of us, Mr. Henry. It was all Trace's fault."

16*

"Ay. Good bye," he kindly added, as he walked away to catch an omnibus that would take him to Orville.

He went to Mrs. Paradyne's on his arrival there. That lady was alone, evidently in a very aggrieved temper. She sat in her usual place on the sofa, in a once handsome but now faded muslin gown, garnished with seagreen ribbons. Her bonnet lay on the table.

"What is the matter?" inquired Mr. Henry.

"The matter is, that Mary has not come home, and she knows she was to have gone out with me," was Mrs. Paradyne's fretful answer. "I can't think what is keeping her. Mrs. Hill should not do it."

He sat down by her on the sofa, reached out his pocket-book, and gave her five of the bank-notes lying in it. "I took my translation in to-day," was all he said. Mrs. Paradyne began counting them. She looked up.

"I thought you were to receive thirty pounds for it. You have always said so."

"I did receive thirty. But —"

"You have given me only twenty-five," came the quick interruption; and the tone was not a pleasant one.

"I have kept one of the notes. I am sorry to have to do so, but I want it."

"Want it for *what?*" she asked with a surprised stress upon the word. "But a day or two ago you informed me you had no need of money just now."

"True. I will tell you if you wish particularly to know," he continued; for she was looking at him questionably, and evidently waiting for the information, as one might who had a right to it. "You have heard me speak of Carl Weber?"

"That great friend and fellow-professor of yours at Heidelberg. Well?"

"I had a letter from him yesterday, telling me how much worse he is, and that his malady is now confirmed beyond doubt — consumption. I had another letter; it was from young Von Sark, who happened to write to me. He spoke of Weber in it; of the sad state of privation he is in, of the inroads the disease is making, and of his almost utter want of friends. He has been ill so long that people have grown tired of assisting him. A five-pound note will lighten his way to death."

Mrs. Paradyne made no dissentient answer; but she was evidently not pleased. Taking out her purse with almost an unlady-like jerk, she shut the five bank-notes into it with a sharp click.

"I cannot help it," said Mr. Henry in a low tone. "He is in great need, and friendless. It seems to be a duty placed before me."

"Has he been improvident, that he should have saved no means?" asked Mrs. Paradyne.

"No; his salary was small, and he had his mother to keep," was Mr. Henry's reply, looking away from Mrs. Paradyne for a moment. "She died two months ago; the last of his relatives."

"Well, your giving away a bank-note more or less is of little consequence," resumed Mrs. Paradyne, in a displayed sort of resignation, but which bore a sound of irony to initiated ears. "You will not earn many more bank-notes, if you persist in your insane resolution of speaking to Dr. Brabazon."

"I have told you why I must do that," he gently said; "do not let us go over the matter again. As soon as he returns from Malvern, I shall declare all. I have no resource but to do it, and no argument can now change my resolution."

"Or bring you to your senses," retorted Mrs. Paradyne.

"I have something to tell you that will please you very much," he resumed, quitting the other subject.

Mrs. Paradyne lifted her delicate hands in dissenting deprecation, as if nothing could ever please her again.

"It is a story of George's bravery. He has been saving the life of young Loftus."

CHAPTER XVIII.

Told at Last.

In passing the College gates on his way homewards, after quitting Mrs. Paradyne, Mr. Henry, very much to his surprise, saw Dr. Brabazon going in. No further explanation had taken place between them; for the doctor had been staying at Malvern with his daughters. He held out his hand to the young German master.

"You are looking as much astonished as if you thought I was my own ghost," cried he, jestingly.

"Well, sir, I should almost as soon have expected to see it. I thought you were at Malvern."

"A little matter of business brought me up. I go back to-morrow."

"To-morrow!" echoed Mr. Henry. "Can you let me speak to you before you go back?" he continued on sudden impulse.

"Certainly. Come in with me now if you like."

Dr. Brabazon led the way to his favourite room, the study, and they sat down there in the subdued light of the summer's evening. The sun had set; a crimson glow lingered in the west, and the evening star shone in the clear sky. Perhaps Mr. Henry was glad of the semi-light; it is the most welcome of all for an embarrassing interview.

"I have been anxious for you to return," he began in a low, distinct tone. "I did not like to make my communication to you by letter, and yet there was little time to spare."

"Why was there little?" interrupted the master.

"Because, sir, you may have occasion to look out for some one to replace me in the College."

"Are you going to leave?"

"Not of my own accord; but you will in all probability dismiss me when you have heard my confession."

He made a pause, but the doctor, waiting for more, did not break it. They were, as usual, near the window, and what light there was fell full on Mr. Henry. His hands lay on his knee listless; his face was bent, in its sad earnestness, towards the master. A strange look of contrition was upon it.

"I hardly know which you would deem the worse crime, Dr. Brabazon," he resumed; "the theft you were led to suspect me of, or the real offence of which I am guilty. I have not stolen property; but my whole life since I came here has been one long-acting deceit."

"Why, what can you mean?" exclaimed the doctor, who had nearly forgotten that there remained anything to explain, and was again putting full trust in his German master.

"Deceit especially to you, and in a degree to others," came the reply. "I am not Mr. Henry. Henry is only one of my Christian names. I am Arthur Paradyne."

The doctor sat staring. "You are ——; I don't understand," he cried, breaking off in hopeless bewilderment.

"I am Arthur Henry Paradyne, son to the unfortunate gentleman who was associated with the firm of Loftus and Trace in Liverpool; son to Mrs. Paradyne; brother to Mary and George."

"Why, bless my heart!" slowly exclaimed the master, when he had taken in the sense of the words; and then he came to a full stop, and fell into his sea of bewilderment again.

"I never intended to deceive you — never;" resumed the young man. "When I came over to enter on the situation here, I fully meant to disclose to you that I was Arthur Paradyne. The name had not been concealed by any premeditation; but — if I may so express it — in the ordinary course of things. I was always called 'Henry' at the university, and in the town of Heidelberg. My father at one time was living there; he was Mr. Paradyne with the Germans — for they often forgot to give him his title of captain — I, by way of distinction, was called Mr. Henry. It is a foreign custom. In my case it grew into entire use; and before I left Heidelberg, I believe three parts of the people there had forgotten I possessed any other name. I was willing it should be so forgotten; after that terrible calamity in Liverpool, Paradyne was a

tainted name, and I took no pains to recall it to any
one, friend or stranger. Can you wonder at it, sir?"

"Go on," cried Dr. Brabazon, giving no direct answer to the question.

"The negotiations for my coming here were made
between you and Professor Von Sark, one of our chiefs.
You wrote to request him to supply you with a master
who could teach French and German. He knew I
was wishing to do better for myself, in the point of
remuneration, than I was doing in the university, and
proposed it to me. It was what I had long wanted,
and I begged him to accept it for me. Until the negotiations were concluded, I did not know that he had
throughout written of me by the name of Henry, and
by that only. It did not much matter, I thought; I
could explain when I came."

"And why did you not?"

"Ah! there lies my sin," was the somewhat emo-
tional answer; and the Head Master thought the young
man before him was taking almost an exaggerated view
of his offence. "The first evening of my arrival, there
was no opportunity: many were coming and going,
and you were fully occupied; but when I heard myself addressed in my own tongue as 'Mr. Henry,' when
you introduced me to your daughter and to the masters
as such, my face flushed with shame: it was so like
premeditated deceit. I should have told you that
night but for the bustle that arose in consequence of
the accident to Talbot: it took all opportunity away.
The next morning the bustle continued; Talbot's friends
came; the doctors came; it seemed that you had not a
minute for me. In the afternoon arose that unpleasantness connected with the discovery that George Para-

dyne was — who he was; rendering it all the more essential for me to declare myself. But still I could not get the opportunity: the story would have been a long one; and I wished to consult you as to whether I might not still be generally known as Mr. Henry. Do you recollect, sir, my meeting you in the stone corridor just after tea, and asking if I could speak with you?"

"I think I do. I was in a hurry, I know, at the moment; for I had business at the railway station."

"Yes; you were going out, and said quickly to me, 'Another time, Mr. Henry, another time.' I went down to Mrs. Paradyne's that evening, and she — my mother — utterly forbid me to disclose it. 'Did I want to ruin everybody?' she asked; 'herself, me, George.' Was it likely that I, Arthur Paradyne's son, should be retained at my post to *teach* the College boys, when a question had arisen whether George might be even allowed to study with them? It was a doubt that had never before struck me; it staggered me now. My mother took a different view of it. The fact of my being a Paradyne could not make any difference to the boys, or render me less efficient as a teacher, she urged, so long as they were in ignorance of it. It was only by the knowledge that harm could come. Well; I yielded. I yielded, knowing how mistaken the reasoning was, utter sophistry; knowing how wrong a part I should be playing; but she was very urgent, and — she was my mother. There's my secret, Dr. Brabazon."

"A secret truly," observed the Head Master, leaning back in his chair, while he revolved the tale.

"The weight of it has half killed me," returned

Mr. Henry, lifting his hand to his head, as if he felt a pain there. "At any moment discovery was liable to fall, bringing disgrace in its train. It was not so much *that* that I felt — or feared — as the actual deceit in itself. My life was a long living lie, every moment of it one of acted duplicity: I, set up in a post of authority to guide and train others! When the school broke up for Christmas I begged my mother to withdraw her embargo, and let me speak then, but she would not. She would see about it when George had passed his Oxford examination, she said, not before. It is not with her full consent that I speak now; but I laid the two only alternatives before her — to declare myself, or leave the College — and she allowed me to speak as the lesser evil. In any case I may have to leave."

"We'll see: we'll see: I think not. Why should you?" added the master, apparently putting the question to himself, or to the four walls of the room, but not to Mr. Henry. "I am glad to see young men respect the wishes of their mother."

And Mr. Henry's respect for his — that is, his sense of the law of filial obedience — was something ultra great. But he did not say it.

"What a trouble that past business of your father's must have been to you!" exclaimed the doctor, whose thoughts were roving backwards.

Trouble! Mr. Henry shrank at the word, as relating to it, even now. "It took every ray of sunshine out of my life," he breathed.

"No, no; not every one," said the master, kindly.

"For a long, long time every ray of hope — of *life* I may say — went out of me. And now my —

my hope lies elsewhere; there's not much of it left for daily use."

"Where does it lie?" questioned the Head Master, rather puzzled.

The young man gave no answer, unless a sudden hectic that flushed his face, and was discernible even in the fading light could be called such. ONE, looking down at him from beyond that tranquil sky, grey now, knew where it lay, and what it was vested in.

"I had revered my father as the most honourable, just, good man living," he resumed, in a low tone; "a Christian man, a brave officer and gentleman; and when the blow came it seemed to stun me — to take away everything that was worth living for."

He spoke only in accordance with the truth. The blow was great; his sensitiveness was exceeding great, and the shock had cut off all hope for this life. His spirit was by nature a proud spirit; his rectitude great; to do ill in the eyes of the world — and such ill! — would to him have been simply impossible; and the awful disgrace that seemed to fall upon him, to have made itself his, struck to every fibre of his inward life. Never more could he hold up his head in the sight of men. Added to this, was the terrible grief for his father, whom he so loved — for his father's fall, and his father's death. This, of itself, would have gone well nigh to break his heart.

"Have you been assisting your mother?" asked the doctor, remembering the stories carried to him of Mr. Henry's saving habits.

"Oh yes."

"Ay," said the master, as if this explained all.

Few young men have their hopes blighted on the

very threshold of life as his had been. His prospects came suddenly to an end with the shock. Not a doubt of his father's guilt had penetrated his mind. The particulars, as written to him circumstantially by Mrs. Paradyne, did not admit of doubt. He had been working for them ever since. Mrs. Paradyne had a very small income of her own, not much more than enough to find her in gloves and ribbons and a new silk gown once in a way. Arthur (with what little help her daughter could give) had to do the rest. And she was not kind to him. Perhaps it was the long separation — he over in Germany, she in England — that estranged her affections from him, her eldest son. In time he wrote word to her that he had accepted an engagement in England, at Orville College, and suggested that George should be moved to it. He had two ends in view — the one the advantage of the boy; the other that he might get some intercourse with his mother and sister. He knew how he should have to toil and pinch to meet the additional expenses, but that seemed nothing. A shadow, of what the future was to be, fell over him before he had quitted Heidelberg; for on the morning of his departure there came a letter from Mrs. Paradyne warning him *not to make himself known as George's brother or as her son*, at first, until they should have met and talked the matter over. They did meet. On the evening following that of Mr. Henry's arrival he went to her house, as perhaps may be remembered, since Mr. Raymond Trace chose, in a sense, to assist at it. During that interview he had a lesson taught him — that the future was to be estrangement, or something akin to it, between him and his family. He was to continue "Mr. Henry," never to disclose himself as a Paradyne, lest the authorities at the college should carp at it; in which case his means of assisting them at home might cease. He saw how it was — that he was valued only in the ratio he could contribute to their support. His generous love was thrown back upon him; his impulses of tenderness were repulsed; he was to be an acquaintance rather than a son. Mrs. Paradyne was resentful at his having counselled their removal to Orville, now that it was found Trace and the Loftus boys were in the College, which, of course, was manifestly unjust. Something very like a dispute took place about the proposed concealment of name. He refused to conceal it from Dr. Brabazon; she insisted that he should. He yielded at last: she was his mother: but he went away from the house wondering whether he had not better return to Germany. Thus it had gone on. Mr. Henry — or Arthur Paradyne, if you would prefer to call him so — bearing his burden as he best might, and toiling patiently to fulfil the obligations he cheerfully accepted as his own; obligations he never thought of repining at. His heart felt crushed; his mind had a weight upon it; but he only feared lest his health should fail and the dear ones suffer.

"Look you," interrupted Dr. Brabazon, arousing himself from a reverie; "you must remain as 'Mr. Henry' for the present. The fact that you are Arthur Paradyne does not hurt the boys; but the declaring it thus suddenly would cause a commotion that might lead to — I don't know what. Until Christmas, at any rate, things shall go on as they have done. The competition for the Orville will then be over; and really, for my part, I don't see why you should not drop the name of Paradyne, if it pleases you to do so. No, I don't," added the doctor, contesting the point with himself aloud, as if he were disputing it with an antagonist; "and I don't see what business it is of other people's, or why anybody should carp at it. So that's settled. You are Mr. Henry still. But I wish you had disclosed the truth at the beginning. It would have made no difference."

"I wish I could have done it, sir," he said, rising to take leave. "The concealment has told upon me. Thank you ever for your kindness to me this evening, Dr. Brabazon."

"I call that young man the victim of circumstances," thought the master, "It's a good, and true, and earnest nature, I am sure; and ———"

Dr. Brabazon's words came to a standstill, as he followed into the hall. There was Mr. Henry propped against the front door, instead of letting himself out of it according to the custom of everyday mortals.

"Why, what's the matter?" exclaimed the startled doctor, as the rays of the houselamp fell on a white face of suffering.

Mr. Henry rallied himself, and apologized with a smile. He had only felt a little faint: it was over now.

A little faint! But he did not mention that sharp pain, that strange fluttering of heart, which seemed so often to follow any extra emotion or exertion; and this day had brought plenty of both for him. However, it was gone now.

"Here, don't start off in that haste," cried the doctor, going out after him. "Don't you think you ought to have advice for that faintness?" he asked, as Mr. Henry turned.

"Yes, perhaps I ought."

"I should. You have been working your strength away. Good-night."

Mr. Henry hastened home, wrote a short letter to his sick friend Weber, enclosed the bank-note, and went out to post it. As he emerged from the short shrubbery, skirting round by the chapel, and gained the road, he saw, to his surprise, Dick Loftus.

"Why, Dick! Are you home again?"

"Got home to dinner," equably answered Dick, whose mouth was full of some crunching sweetmeat he had come down from Pond Place to buy. "We had a stunning passage: the boat pitching like mad, and Uncle Simon and old Gall fit to die. Will you have some?" he asked, exhibiting the stuff in his hand. "It's Gibraltar rock."

"Not I, Dick, thank you. I should have thought you too old to eat that."

"Am I, though?" said Dick, biting a huge morsel of the tempting compound. "It's jolly. I say, how's Mother Butter?"

"*She's* jolly," replied Mr. Henry, laughing.

"Give my respectful compliments to her, and tell her I've come home. Do, please, Mr. Henry."

Dick disappeared with a careless good-night, that rang out joyously in the evening air. Mr. Henry, having missed the opportunity to ask about his perilous bath at Boulogne, went on to the railway station, and dropped his letter into the box. There was a popular superstition obtaining, that letters posted there went quicker than if posted at the grocer's in the village. He was taking the middle of the road back, Sir Simon's grounds on one side, the plantation on the other, — when fleet footsteps came running behind, and a pair of light hands were laid upon his coat. He turned to see his sister.

"Mary! What brings you here so late as this?"

She laughed as she explained: she was in a merry mood. Mrs. Hill had taken them out a little way in the country, and they missed the train they ought to have come back by, and had only now got in. She could not help it, and she was running home to mamma and mamma's displeasure.

"You *will* catch it," said Mr. Henry, with comic seriousness. "Mamma had her things on in the afternoon, waiting for you to go out with her. Is that safe, Mary?"

"Yes, yes. Just for once, Arthur."

For she had linked her arm within his. Mr. Henry looked round on the lonely road. "All right," he said, "there's nobody about. I have not had you on my arm for a long while."

Was there nobody about? Indeed and there was an inquisitive pair of eyes peering after them. Mr. Raymond Trace, finding Pond Place insupportably dull on his return, had come forth by way of a diversion, to see any little thing there might be to see. And was thus rewarded. Raymond Trace was in an ill-humour with the world. Certain events in Boulogne — the presence of George Paradyne there in the first place, and his elevation in the favour of not only Sir Simon and the Galls, but of Mr. Loftus — had been insufferably offensive to him. And this girl was George's sister!

Crossing the road with soft steps, as if he were treading upon eggs, he followed them, keeping well under the shadow of the hedge. He could see they were talking earnestly together, and he'd have given one of his ears to be able to hear. Truth to say, the evident intimacy astonished Mr. Trace not a little; he thought he had come upon a mighty secret, not creditable to the assistant master at Orville College, or to any other subordinate individual, that might indulge in such.

"The worst is over, Mary," Mr. Henry was saying. "Dr. Brabazon is at home, and I have told him."

"Oh Arthur!" she exclaimed. "But I am thankful it is done at last. What is the result? — your dismissal?"

"Quite the contrary. He was all kindness. I am to remain on as Mr. Henry. He says he does not see why I should not adopt the name for good, and discard the other one. Will you tell mamma this?"

"Yes, I'll tell her. It will be a relief; she has been dreading the communication with a sort of nightmare. And so you will stay on?"

"If my strength shall permit me. Sometimes I have doubts of that."

A sharp pang darted through her. "Arthur, it grieves me that you should labour as you do, and yet meet with no reward. Mamma is not what she ought to be to you; I have told her so."

"Hush, child! it is the pleasure of my life to work for you all. I wish I could do more."

"I wish we were more grateful," came Miss Paradyne's impulsive answer. "George and I feel it terribly, Arthur. You should hear him break out every now and then to mamma."

He interrupted her: he never would allow a word

of reflection on his mother: and began the story of George's bravery, as related to him by Leek. They did not meet a soul: the road was always lonely at night. Miss Paradyne stopped when they drew near its end, when the lighted shops were in view in the distance.

"You must not come any farther with me, Arthur. I shall run home in no time."

She withdrew her arm, but he stood yet a minute talking, holding her hand in his. Then he bent his face on hers for a farewell kiss (not a soul was about, you know), watched her away, and turned towards his home.

Mr. Trace came out of the hedge's friendly shade, trencher first, in a glow of virtuous amazement. He had seen the signs of familiar intercourse; he had certainly seen the kiss; and his indignant feelings could only relieve themselves in a burst of unstilted words that might have been more characteristic of Dick.

"Well, this *is* a go!"

CHAPTER XIX.

A Visitor for Sir Simon.

ONCE more the school had met, and were at work with a will. Ah, this was the real trial — that could occur but once in three full years — the competition for the great Orville prize. Masters and candidates were alike on their metal, making stern preparation for it. It was no child's play. Gall, Loftus, Trace, Savage, Brown major, Whitby, Talbot, and Paradyne, were going up for it.

Who would win? Some thought one would, some

17*

another; opinions were divided, a whisper of bets reigned. Gall openly avowed he did not expect to get it, Bertie Loftus made no secret of not really trying: they chose to go up for it as the seniors of the school, but they were regarded as virtually out of the contest. The more general impression was that the real contest would lie between Trace and Paradyne.

And none were more conscious that this was likely to prove a fact than Trace himself. He was afraid of Paradyne. In spite of Trace's large and vain self-esteem, there was a disagreeable conviction within him that in the trial Paradyne's scholarship might weigh down his own. A bitter pill of anticipation for Trace to swallow from any competitor: but from Paradyne — words could not express his angry indignation: and he felt inclined to question the divine ordering of events that should have brought that one miserable unit of creation in this offensive antagonism with him. With *him*, Raymond Trace!

Ten times a day he said to himself that it *ought not* to be. He was quite honest in thinking this: he believed he was just; for he saw things with a jaundiced eye. The son of the man who had so signally failed in his duty to the world in general, and to his father and Mr. Loftus in particular, was out of place in Orville College, the associate of honest gentlemen. It had however pleased Dr. Brabazon to keep him in it, and Trace thought himself worthy of a gold medal at least for having buried the secret of the past from the school. The far-famed duel in Boulogne had become public property, to the raging mortification of the two duellists, who were chaffed unmercifully, and grew to wish that duels had never been invented. The rescue

of Dick Loftus also spread from mouth to mouth, and
Paradyne was lauded as some young god descended
from Olympus. All so much heartburning for Trace.
He had bitterly rebelled at the favour shown to
Paradyne in Boulogne, asking what brought him there
at all; what right he had there. He seemed fated to
be haunted by this Paradyne everywhere: a second
case of Faust and Mephistopheles. All that was bad
enough, but Trace, doing violence to his own feelings,
had passed it over. What, he began to ask himself
now, was — ought this fellow, this waif of ill-descent,
to be allowed to go in for the great Orville prize —
the prize that all were burning to gain, either for the
honour or the money. Trace pondered the question
very seriously, and meanwhile fanned the ill-feeling
against Paradyne, which had been buried, into a
smouldering heat, that might burst at any moment up
in a flame.

He fanned something else — and, that was, a
vague rumour reflecting on Mr. Henry. That gentleman's name became connected with Miss Paradyne's
in anything but a pleasant manner: but as yet only
by hints and innuendoes; the school had got hold of
nothing tangible. Bertie Loftus asked Trace what the
matter was, but Trace did not define it. "A bad lot,
those Paradynes," he answered, drawing down the
corners of his respectable lips: "and the German is in
league with them." A terrible score had Trace against
Mr. Henry, if only from the fact that he continued to
assist, or, as Trace phrased it, to coach Paradyne: but
for that, Paradyne had never stood a chance of wresting
the Orville prize from deserving fingers. And so, in this
uncomfortable and uncertain state, the time went on.

One afternoon when October was passing, and the great day of decision, the first of November, was drawing near, it happened that in a very difficult Greek lesson, Trace did badly, Paradyne markedly well. They were before the Head Master, and he said a few rather sharp words to Trace, whose failure he attributed to carelessness, about allowing one younger to outstrip him. "You'll stand no chance against him, Trace, if you can't do better than this," added the doctor. Perhaps he spoke lightly, without much thought; but Trace took the words to his heart and let them rankle there.

When tea was over, he went out alone, debating with himself whether he should disclose the past disgrace relating to Paradyne, and so stop his going up for the Orville. Trace was of a concentrative nature, and liked this self-communing. Pacing the plantation, he thought over the question in all its bearings, and came to the conclusion that, to speak, was a duty he owed to society, and would be a righteous act in itself. This so far settled, he was about to leave the tree, against which his back had been propped for the last five minutes, and to go home, when he saw a man come stealthily forth from a dark side-path, and look out as if he were waiting for some one. Trace had no objection to a bit of private adventure, especially if it related to other people's business, and remained where he was, on the watch.

Up came Mr. Henry, making directly for the stranger's hiding-place. That he had come to meet him, was apparent; and Trace stared with all his eyes into the obscure light. He could not make out much: they passed him very close once, as they were talking together, and he heard a few words from the stranger.

"I shall stop here, I tell you. The voyage —— "

Those were all the distinct words Trace caught then. When they came back again, Mr. Henry was speaking.

"Of course, if you are determined to remain, I cannot say you shall not: but I fancy you will not succeed. And then, you know, there will be the risk of —— "

So far only, this time, before they were out of hearing again. Trace's ears were strained to the uttermost, but he caught only two words more, and that from the stranger as they were parting: "Mother Butter's." Mr. Henry walked quickly towards home, the man disappeared amid the trees the other way, and Trace stayed where he was, revolving the mystery. But he could find no clue to it.

Clashing footsteps sounded now. One of the boys was tearing home from the railway station. It was Lamb, with a parcel in his hand, and Trace went out to meet him. How it came about Trace never exactly knew, but while he was saying to himself "Shall I tell, or shall I not?" he *told*, and Lamb was put in possession of the real facts relating to Paradyne: all the past trouble; the past disgrace; that he belonged to a family of fraud, and never ought to have been at Orville. Nuts for Mr. Lamb to crack. But, strange to say, no sooner had the secret escaped Trace's lips, than a voice within seemed to warn him that he had done wrong. It was too late to repent; Lamb went whispering the poison about with his stealthy tongue, and the school listened eagerly.

A few days passed on without explosion. The boys met in secret knots to take counsel, and felt half paralysed at their own audacious words. They talked of mutiny, if Paradyne were allowed to go up for the Orville; they whispered of rebellion, if subjected longer to the authority of a master so ill-doing as Mr. Henry. *But they did nothing.* Not one would undertake the responsibility of commencing hostilities, or of speaking to the Head Master: it was a practical illustration of the old fable of the mice proposing to put the bell on the cat. And November was close at hand.

The rumours, connecting Mr. Henry's name with Miss Paradyne were by no means pleasant rumours; not tending to exalt either of them in public opinion. When a young lady could be guilty of stealing evening walks with a school usher, and very familiar walks indeed — as Mr. Lamb could testify on Trace's private authority, and *did*, turning up the whites of his eyes — of course there was no more to be said for her.

So long as these rumours were confined to the boys, they did not affect Miss Paradyne personally; but circumstances led to their being whispered beyond the college. Mrs. Hill, the lady with whom she had the daily engagement as governess, had gone unexpectedly to Torquay for the winter months, in consequence of the ill-health of one of her children, and Miss Paradyne had made another engagement with Mrs. Talbot. On the evening previous to the day she was to enter on it, the Earl of Shrewsbury dashed home for a minute, and told his mother confidentially that she must not have Miss Paradyne for the girls; that it "wouldn't do."

"Why will it not do?" questioned Mrs. Talbot in surprise.

"Because it won't."

"James, to say so much, and no more, is nonsense. You must tell me why."

But Talbot could not say why. Things had not been made very clear to his understanding. All he knew was, that something was "up" about Miss Paradyne and Mr. Henry. He supposed they were privately engaged; but the school was in arms against Miss Paradyne, saying she went out walking with him at night, and — oh, all sorts of things. She must not be let go there as governess.

"Don't you think, James, that this is arising out of the ill-feeling entertained for Miss Paradyne's brother?" quietly asked Mrs. Talbot.

"No, I don't think it is. Oh, but there is a row about him! — going to be, at any rate," broke off the earl in a parenthesis. "Well, I can't stop, mother mine, but don't you admit Miss Paradyne."

"Upon what plea can I refuse? I have engaged her. James — wait a moment. Upon what plea can I refuse, I ask."

James Talbot looked puzzled and rueful. "I'm sure I don't know," he answered, twirling his trencher round and round. "I thought I'd better tell you. I'm afraid they must be a bad lot. Queer things are coming out about the father: and Paradyne is not to go up for the Orville."

"Why?" she exclaimed, half-startled, and beginning to think the affair must be serious. "Not go up for the Orville!"

"The school would be in mutiny."

"James!"

"It would. And Trace may make as certain of the prize now as if he'd got it."

"Is there no chance for you, James?" she asked, rather wistfully.

He laughed, and shook his head. "I have done my best, but there's not a bit of hope for anybody against Trace. Had Paradyne gone in for it, there'd have been a close struggle between the two — and I don't think victory would have declared for Trace. About the father? oh, I can't stay to tell you," — preparing to dash off again. "Queer rumours they are."

Queer indeed, and various; as whispered about from boy to boy. The exaggerations were something ludicrous. "Paradyne's father had been hung for murder," "been transported for forgery," "was now serving out his time at Portland Island," and so on. Perhaps Talbot did well not to mention such to his mother.

He left her in a comfortable state of uncertainty. She did not like to disregard the warning altogether, and yet did not like to act upon it. Neither did she see how she could act upon it; and sat on much perplexed.

"I will put a question or two plainly to Miss Paradyne, when she comes to-morrow, as to whether there is any private acquaintance between her and Mr. Henry," decided Mrs. Talbot at length. "I am convinced the Paradynes are as nice as they can be: and I don't believe a word against the daughter. It's all the work of those envious boys."

Utterly unconscious of the storm that was brewing,

Mary Paradyne looked forward to her engagement; and when the morning and hour dawned to enter on it, she got ready with alacrity. The young are always so full of hope.

"If the remuneration were but a little better," exclaimed Mrs. Paradyne, in her semi-fretful, semi-resigned way. "Three hours a day, and luncheon and thirty-four shillings a month! What is it?"

"Dear mamma, it is better than nothing a month," was the cheering answer. "When I first knew that the Hills were going away, I feared I might be unemployed for the winter. Something better may arise later: and I am sure I shall like Mrs. Talbot. Miss Brabazon dropped a hint to me the other day that perhaps they might engage me for Rose."

She tied her bonnet, kissed her mother, and went forth with her bright face. It was not far to go; only a few doors. Mrs. Talbot came to her directly, and entered on her task, which did not seem an agreeable one — that of putting a few questions in regard to her intimacy with Mr. Henry. But, instead of meeting them — as Mrs. Talbot had anticipated she would — in a calm spirit of refutation, the young lady turned red, grew confused, and flung her hands up to her disturbed face with a faint cry of dismay. It had come upon her so suddenly.

"Believe me, I do not wish to pain you," said Mrs. Talbot, speaking gently in the midst of her surprise. "Neither would I think of inquiring into any particulars that you may prefer not to disclose. Only tell me that there is nothing in the rumour; that you and Mr. Henry have no — no — acquaintance in common; that will be quite sufficient."

"But I cannot tell it you," replied Miss Paradyne in her straightforward truth.

"What the college boys have got hold of, I'm sure I am unable to say," resumed Mrs. Talbot, thinking she could not have been understood. "Nothing very grave: the most tangible charge I can make out is, that you have been seen walking with Mr. Henry. There is, of course, no harm in that; the harm lies in its being done in secret. Can you refute it, Miss Paradyne?"

No, she could not: and she was growing sick with fear. Not fear for herself: the reproach that might ordinarily be supposed to arise from such a thing, she never so much as glanced at. Her whole thought was for her brother Arthur, lest the concealment of which he had been guilty in regard to his true name, was becoming known. Mrs. Talbot, feeling both grieved and surprised, pressed the question.

"I daresay I may have been seen with Mr. Henry: I did not know it," answered Miss Paradyne, forced into the avowal, and beginning to shiver. Had it only occurred to her to say "My mother is cognisant of all I do," Mrs. Talbot might have been satisfied: but it did not.

There was nothing for it but to part. Mrs. Talbot reluctantly said she could not carry out the engagement, and Mary Paradyne went away, to bear home her unhappy tale. As she stood at Mrs. Talbot's door, the bright sun shining full upon her, she became aware how long the interview had lasted, for the outdoor boys were quitting the college after morning school. George was nearly the first of them, and she drew him into the middle of the road.

"Whatever is the matter?" cried he, perceiving something strange in her countenance.

"George," she whispered, "you must go to Arthur —"

"To Mr. Henry," interrupted George, correcting her. "You are not half so prudent as I am, Mary. I've told you of this before."

"To Mr. Henry," she mechanically resumed, her heart beating with a great pain. "Tell him to be on his guard, lest he should be taken unawares. Something is oozing out, I am sure; and Mrs. Talbot has declined to receive me."

"Declined to receive you!" repeated George, his honest grey eyes flashing anger.

"She was very kind in the midst of it, but she said there were rumours abroad connected with Mr. Henry, and if I could not refute them, I must not enter on the engagement. I did not quite understand her," added Mary Paradyne, speaking to herself rather than to George: "but you had better go at once and warn Ar— warn — you know."

George laughed at the slip, pushed his trencher jauntily aside, and turned back whistling. Knots of the outdoor boys were advancing. Some shot past him with a bound; some stole by sheepishly, as if ashamed to cut him; others walked on deliberately and looked straightforward; a few gave him a hard, bold, insolent stare of non-recognition; and as he went by the quadrangle, the juniors, gathered there, turned their backs upon him.

"It's an awful shame that they should send me to Coventry like this," soliloquized George. "If I thought any one of them set the rest on, wouldn't I leather him! Never mind, gentlemen, if I do get the Orville, you'll be more civil to me."

He was dashing into Mr. Henry's room, when Mrs. Butter interposed, rather less crusty than usual. Mr. Henry was engaged at the moment; he must call again.

"I'll wait in your kitchen, Mother Butter," said George, who rarely stood on ceremony.

"Then you can't," answered Mother Butter, with more haste and decision than the case seemed to warrant. "I've got my saucepans on the fire, and you'd be upsetting of 'em. There. Be off."

As if to end the colloquy, Mr. Henry's parlour door opened, and Miss Brabazon came forth.

"Rely upon me," Mr. Henry said to her in a low tone: and George wondered.

They went into the parlour together, the two brothers, and George delivered his sister's message, adding a comment of his own. "I'd give a guinea to know what's up."

Mr. Henry pondered over it for a few minutes in silence, leaning his head upon his hand. His face was turned to the searching light of the meridian sun, and something unusually wan in its aspect struck George.

"The better plan will be to declare all; to put away this semi-concealment altogether," observed Mr. Henry. "Mary must not be subjected to unpleasantness."

"Only let me get the Orville," observed George, with a vain schoolboy's light boasting. "I'll crow over some of them then."

"George!"

"I know; you are all for meekness and peace. I

should like to pay off some of those fellows. Will you believe that I met half the classes coming here, and not a soul of the whole lot spoke to me? Something new is arising. I've seen it this week past."

"I h ve seen it, too," was Mr. Henry's reply. "George, I used to say you would live this down by dint of time and patience; I thought just after you got back from France that the time had nearly come. But I have my doubts now. I wish I could have helped you better. Well, I'll think about this matter, George, and decide on something. You go home to your dinner now."

Nothing loth to obey, for dinner was as welcome to him as it is to most schoolboys, George was quitting the room, when Mrs. Butter entered it, with a small tray, a basin of bread and milk on its white cloth. She put it before Mr. Henry and went out again.

"I say," cried George, "that's not your dinner, is it? Why it's nothing but bread and milk!"

"My appetite is going strangely," observed Mr. Henry. "Slops seem to suit me best now."

George's great grey eyes flashed out a look of yearning. "Arthur! you have been starving yourself for us — that we may have plenty!"

"Don't be indiscreet; there's no Arthur here," returned Mr. Henry, with a light smile. "I am eating bread and milk to-day, George, because I feel ill: that's all. Run home."

Easily reassured — as it was in his age and nature to be — George Paradyne went flying off. In turning the angle by the chapel at a sharp canter, he came full tilt against Sir Simon Orville, who was walking towards his home.

"Holloa, young sir! Don't run me down. I am not a ship."

George laughed, begged his pardon, and was passing on, when Sir Simon stopped him.

"Here, George; don't fly off again as if you were wound up to go on wheels. What is this matter about your not going up for the Orville?"

"I don't understand you, Sir Simon."

"Are you going up for it?"

"Of course I am, sir. I should like to get it, too. And I don't say I shan't," he concluded, laughing.

"Why, what did those young simpletons mean, then?" cried the knight. "I met a lot of them just now, and Dick Loftus whispered to me you were not going up for the Orville."

"It is a mistake," said George. "Not that I should go up if the fellows could prevent me. But they can't, you know, sir. Good-bye, Sir Simon."

Sir Simon went on, the matter passing from his mind. Turning into his own grounds, he had been busying himself for some time amidst his cherished autumn flowers, when a servant came out, having apparently just seen him from the house.

"A gentleman is waiting to see you, Sir Simon."

"Bless me," cried Sir Simon, who was too kind-hearted, too simple-minded ever to keep people waiting unnecessarily, gentle or simple. "Who is it, Thomas?"

"I don't know, sir. He came in a cab with a portmanteau. He looks like a traveller."

Sir Simon went trotting off as fast as his short legs would go. The servant went after him.

"It is not Mr. Loftus, Thomas, I suppose? You'd know him."

"Oh dear no, sir, it's not Mr. Loftus. It is some-body older than Mr. Loftus."

Thomas went forward and held open the door for his master to enter. In the tesselated hall, with its bright painted windows gleaming in the sunlight and throwing out their rich colours, Sir Simon saw a port-manteau and a cloak. He turned to the door on the right, and entered. The traveller sat in the shade of the spacious room, the green blinds being closely drawn behind him, and for a moment Sir Simon did not recognise him. The stranger: a slight elderly man, wearing silver-rimmed spectacles: rose quietly and offered his hand.

"Don't you know me, Simon?"

"Why — my goodness me! It's Robert Trace!"

CHAPTER XX

As if Ill-Luck followed him.

THEY sat alone, knees together, talking of the present and the past. Sir Simon had never been very fond of his brother-in-law; but to see him alive, after so long a period of no news, was a great relief; and he gave him a cordial welcome. Mr. Trace spoke of his unfortunate losses in the United States, but did not go into details; at least, into details that Sir Simon could make much of. The great scheme, about which he had been so sanguine, had failed, miserably failed, almost before it was organized: and the thousand pounds, so generously sent out to him by Sir Simon, had been swallowed in the vortex, together with his own funds. After that, he had gone to New York, trying, trying ever since, to redeem his position. He could not do it, and had now come home to Europe, penniless.

"I thought that Boston affair was a good one, or I should not have sent the money out," observed Sir Simon. "How came it to fail?"

"Mismanagement partly; partly ill-luck," was the answer of Mr. Trace, curtly delivered.

"Not your mismanagement, surely?" cried Sir Simon, who had the highest opinion of his brother-in-law as a business man.

"Mismanagement altogether. It was a great deal that Hopper's fault. I was a fool ever to have made him secretary to the affair, or to give him power," added Mr. Trace, with unmistakable animus. "Set a beggar on horseback and we know where he'll ride."

"What Hopper?" asked Sir Simon, struck with the name.

"What Hopper?" was the tart retort, as if Sir Simon's question were superfluous — as indeed the hearer thought it. Mr. Trace had never been a good-tempered man.

"Surely you don't mean the young man who was clerk to you in Liverpool!" cried Sir Simon. "What took him to America?"

Robert Trace raised his eyes from their moody stare on the ground and glanced at his brother-in-law. "You knew Hopper was at Boston with me!"

"Not I. How should I know it? I have never heard of the young man from the time of the break-up at Liverpool."

A minute's perplexed gaze, and then Robert Trace dropped his eyes again. He had made a false move. But that he had supposed Sir Simon knew of his ex-clerk's presence in America, he had certainly not mentioned him.

"Hopper told me, more than once, that he wrote to you from Boston, Simon."

"He never did — to my knowledge. What took him out there?"

"I don't know" — and Mr. Trace's tone changed to quiet civility, the same tone that used to strike on Sir Simon's ear with a false ring. "He walked into the office one morning in Boston, to my great surprise, and asked me if I could help him to employment. It happened that I had been wishing for a clever secretary, or sub-manager, under myself, an Englishman if I could get him; and I put Hopper in the place. He was sharp, intelligent, up to the work, and had served us well in Liverpool."

"And by way of rewarding you, he made ducks and drakes of your money and mine!"

"He turned out as great a rogue as ever stepped," exclaimed Mr. Trace, an acrimonious red tinging his cheeks. "I was obliged to go away from Boston to avoid him. The man nearly worried my life out. He made out a claim, and wanted to enforce it. When he discovered that I had gone to New York, he followed me there. I had a world of trouble with him."

"A claim for what?" asked Sir Simon. But Mr. Trace did not answer at once.

"Past salary," he presently said, rousing himself out of a reverie. "I had a great deal of trouble with him. The fellow stuck to me like a leech. He claimed a hundred pounds. I would have given it to him willingly, if I'd had it, to be rid of him. Three several times did he tell me he had written over to you."

18*

"But why should he write to me?"

"I conclude for assistance," replied Mr. Trace after another pause. "I know he said he did write, and it never occurred to me to doubt him. He knew of the money you had kindly sent me in answer to my appeal, and possibly thought he might make one on his own score. He was a great rogue."

"I think it possible that he was," returned Sir Simon; somewhat significantly to Mr. Trace's ear, who had applied the epithet in more of a general sense than a particular one. "Did it ever occur to you, Robert, to suspect that Hopper might have been the guilty man at Liverpool? Hopper, and not Paradyne."

"No," cried Mr. Trace in an accent of surprise not mistakable.

"That sharp young son of Paradyne's thought it at the time," observed Sir Simon, who was speaking in accordance with what had been related to him by Mr. Loftus in Boulogne, touching the conversation with George Paradyne. "*I* don't cast suspicion on the man, mind. I have no cause to do so."

"Nor has anybody else," quietly returned Mr. Trace, taking off his spectacles to wipe them. "A clerk could not have played the game for an hour; I should have found it out at once. Not but that Hopper was villain enough for it."

"Where is he now?"

"Dead."

"Dead!"

Mr. Trace nodded, and broke into a quiet laugh. It jarred on the ear of Sir Simon, and his brow contracted.

"Don't deem me unfeeling, Simon. I am not

laughing at Hopper's death: which was sad enough: but at a mistake he made. Never mind that now."

"I do mind. I want to hear all this."

"I had taken a berth on board the 'Cultivator,' a New York vessel, bound for London. Hopper discovered this, and took one also, with the view no doubt of renewing his worry on the passage. I did not sail in her. He did; and was drowned."

"Mercy upon us!" cried Sir Simon.

"You heard of the calamity, I daresay," continued Mr. Trace, putting on his glasses again. "She went down with every soul on board. We got news of her loss at New York just before I left. Laugh at that? No. It may be my own fate in going back."

"Shall you return to the New Country?"

"If I can get you to help me once again," boldly answered Mr. Trace. "I came home for the sole purpose of asking you. I shall do better if I get another start. I ought to have done well before, but —"

"But what?" asked Sir Simon, interrupting the sudden pause.

"But for ill-luck. Over and over again the chances slipped through my fingers. It was as if ill-luck followed me. We'll talk further of this another day, Simon."

Sir Simon nodded acquiescence, and rang the bell for Mr. Trace to be shown to a chamber.

A message was despatched to the college for Raymond, and he arrived in the evening. His astonishment when he saw his father was something ludicrous, so entirely was he unprepared for it, and the pleasure proportionately great. Cold and cynical to the general world, Raymond cared for his father. Raymond poured

out his budget of news of the past and present; it was
of various kinds and degrees of interest: and Mr. Trace
the elder had his ears regaled with the current history
of the Paradyne family, and George's presumptuous
aspirings to the Orville prize.

"But we shall do him," cried Trace, with a self-
satisfied nod. "Where's Uncle Simon?"

Sir Simon's absence had passed unnoticed in their
own absorption of self-interest. Mr. Trace could not
say where he was.

Truth to say, there was a something beating on
that estimable knight's brain: a little scrap of news
that he had read, or seemed to have read, in the newspapers some days before. He thought it related to
the ship spoken of by Mr. Trace, "The Cultivator:"
and he was now hunting in every corner of the house
for old newspapers, which he scanned attentively. But
without success. He went back to the room, nodded
to Raymond, and sat down in silence, drumming on
the table and ransacking his treacherous memory. It
was so unusual a mood for Sir Simon, that Raymond
remarked upon it, asking if anything was amiss.

"I am trying to recollect something," was the reply.
"Your father has told you, I suppose, Raymond, of
Hopper's sailing for home in the ship 'Cultivator,' and
her sinking with her passengers —"

"No. I have not told him," interrupted Mr. Trace,
so sharply as to startle Sir Simon. "Why bring it
up to him?" he more calmly added, appearing to recollect himself. "The ship was lost with every soul
on board."

"But that's just it — that I don't think every soul
was lost," explained Sir Simon. "I read an account

lately of the landing of some passengers at Cork, who were supposed to have been lost. They were picked up at sea in an open boat, having put off from a foundering vessel. It strikes me the vessel was 'The Cultivator.'"

"If you are speaking of 'The Cultivator,' from New York, some of her passengers have been saved, and are now in England," interposed Raymond. "Mr. Batty, old Gall's partner, had a son on board; the news arrived of the ship's loss, and the Battys went into mourning; but, a day or two ago, young Batty walked in. Father, what's the matter?"

Mr. Trace was standing up, looking like a man scared out of his senses. "Is — Hopper — saved?" he gasped, rather than asked.

"I don't know," answered Raymond. "Who is Hopper?"

"And if he is? — you need not be afraid of him over here!" cried Sir Simon, wondering at the emotion displayed. "It is your father's former clerk at Liverpool that we are speaking of, Raymond," he added to the son. "The man went over to Boston, got put into a good thing there by your father, which failed; and then he began to worry him for money. Let him come and worry here! We'll teach him that England is not without laws, if America is."

Raymond, all curiosity, questioned further, and Mr. Trace could not put a stop to Sir Simon's answers; though it seemed that he would have done it, had there been a decent plea. There was not time for much; Raymond was unable to stay: but for the peremptory message, he would not have come out at all that busy evening. Mr. Trace put his hat on to

walk part of the way with his son. They struck into
the plantation, arm in arm: it was the shortest way;
and the moon glimmered cheerily through the trees.

"You are as tall as I am, Raymond," observed
Mr. Trace.

"And that's not very tall; I hope to shoot up yet,"
answered Raymond. "You should see Bertie Loftus.
But it seems to me that you have grown shorter."

"As we all do, when age and care come upon us,"
remarked Mr. Trace. And, with that, he relapsed into
silence.

"I hope you have come back rich, sir," resumed
Raymond presently, in a tone of half jest, half earnest.

"I have come back not worth a shilling, Raymond," said Mr. Trace, momentarily halting as if to
give emphasis to his words. "All I had of my own,
all I borrowed from your uncle, is lost."

Something like an ice-shaft shot through Raymond
in his bitter disappointment. During this many, many
months' silence of his father's, fond visions had dawned
over him of his coming back a millionaire.

"How is it lost?" he asked, when the shock allowed
him to speak.

"Oh! in those American securities, and in unlucky
speculations. I was not clever enough for the Yankees,
you see."

"What was my uncle saying about Hopper? I did
not understand him."

"He says that Hopper's saved; whereas I had
thought he was drowned."

"I meant, sir, about his worrying you. But he
did not say Hopper was saved; only that he might be."

"Raymond, as surely as that I see those trees around us, so surely do I see that the man's saved."

"And what if he is?"

"Why, he has it in his power to do me injury."

"Of what nature, sir?"

Mr. Trace looked upwards, as if searching for an answer. It was a remarkably bright night, and the moonbeams sent a radiance on the glass of the spectacles. "He says I owe him money, Raymond; he might pursue me for it, I suppose, in this country, and give me a world of trouble. Do you recollect him?"

"Pretty well. I have a sort of general recollection of him."

"Raymond, do you look out for him;" and Mr. Trace pressed his son's arm, to give emphasis to the charge. "A middle-sized man of two-and-thirty, or thereabouts, with a pale face, and a reddish shade on his brown hair. He was looking shabby when I last saw him, perhaps is more so now. If he *is* saved, the first thing he'd do would be to come here and watch for me by stealth. Keep your eyes open, and warn me."

"But, sir, do you really owe him money?"

"No; I do not," was the positive answer. "I don't legally owe him a farthing. Nevertheless, I should" — Mr. Trace paused — "I should have some difficulty in proving that here. Were he to press his false claim upon me to the extent of arrest, which is just what he'd like to do, I might languish in prison longer than I care to think of."

"I will look out," murmured Trace. "I think I should know him. I wish we were not so busy with the Orville. But in a couple of days that will be over."

"Shall you get that prize?"

"If Paradyne is put out of it. You heard me say so, father?"

"Yes, yes," was Mr. Trace's laconic answer, as if the very mention of the name were offensive to him.

A silence ensued. Raymond's spirits were down at zero; his father's were not much higher. As they passed the spot where Mr. Henry came out to meet the stranger, the fact was naturally recalled to Trace's mind: he had not yet succeeded in fathoming the mystery. All in a moment a question darted through him — could that man have been Hopper? That man was shabby, that man was pale; that man had a reddish cast in his hair, and looked about two or three and thirty; and Trace had heard him speak of a voyage. A conviction that it was Hopper, and no other, took instant possession of him. With his brain beating at the discovery, his heart shrinking with an apprehensive fear, Trace halted in his walk, and rapidly told the news.

"When was this, do you say?" questioned Mr. Trace in a covert whisper, as if afraid the very trees might hear.

"It was last Friday. Five days ago."

"Had the saved passengers been landed then?"

"Oh dear yes, and had come from Cork to England. Young Batty had."

"Then, Raymond, it was Hopper," said Mr. Trace, who was looking at matters through his own suspicious glasses; and his face seemed to turn of a grey hue. "Rely upon it, he was trying to ferret out whether I was in the neighbourhood. Who is this Mr. Henry?"

"Our German and French master. He's an awful

rat. Just the fellow for a sneak to apply to for any dirty information."

"You must try and get the truth out of him — whether it was Hopper or not, and if so, where he is now. I'll wait for you here."

"What — now?" exclaimed Trace. "I — I don't suppose he'll tell me. I am not friendly with him."

"Make yourself friendly for the nonce, and worm it out of him," said Mr. Trace imperatively. "Raymond, *I must be at some certainty.* This is almost a matter of life or death."

Raymond went forward without another word; and with a curious sinking of the heart to which he was totally unaccustomed, and did not know what to make of. This sort of coming home of his father's was so very different from those past lofty visions of his. As to the possible arrest, hinted at, Trace went hot when he thought of it. *His* father consigned to an igno-minious debtors' prison in the face and eyes of the college where he had played first-fiddle? Why, in ap-pearance it would be half as bad as the back disgrace of that miserable Paradyne!

Conning his lesson as he went along — a civil re-quest to Mr. Henry to satisfy him upon some German terminations that hopelessly puzzled him — Trace at length found himself in Mrs. Butter's garden, and closely contiguous to a young damsel who was dancing in the moonlight. Trace raised his cap: child though she was, the school treated her with due respect as their Head Master's daughter.

"Miss Rose! What are you doing here?"

"I am dancing to keep myself warm."

"But why are you here at all?"

"I came after Emma," she whispered confidentially, with a suppressed laugh. "She is always going to Mother Butter's after tea now, and she'll never let me go with her; it's cold she says; so I just ran after her to-night. I think there's somebody staying here that Emma comes to see," continued the incautious girl in a lower whisper: "some friend of Mr. Henry's that dare not go out in the day-time."

"Some friend of Mr. Henry's that dare not go out in the day-time!" echoed Trace, repeating the words mechanically, his whole thoughts full of the man who *might* be there, and *might* be Hopper. "Why do you think so, Miss Rose?"

"Never you mind," returned the young lady, with scant ceremony. "I overheard Emma say something to Mr. Henry the other day; but it's nothing to you."

At that moment the house door opened, and Miss Brabazon appeared at it, attended by Mother Butter with a candle in her hand. "You will tell Mr. Henry, then, when he comes in," Miss Brabazon was saying to the woman, the words reaching Trace's ear distinctly, as he stepped aside out of view.

"I will, Miss Emma. He'll be in directly now, and I'll tell him as soon as he comes."

Miss Brabazon walked away quickly; Rose allowed her to go some distance, and then ran after her with a shout. A few words of surprised reprimand echoed on the night air, and they went on together. Trace followed quietly: it was just possible he might catch a stray word, touching the "friend" of Mr. Henry's: and he knew now the latter was not in. In the dwarf shrubbery that wound round near the chapel, between the cricket field and the gymnasium ground, they met

Mr. Henry. Trace stepped outside it, behind the bushy laurel trees, and there, rather to his surprise, found himself close to his father, who happened to have strolled to the spot as he waited for his son. Mr. Henry raised his hat as he spoke to Miss Brabazon, and the bright moon lit up his features with perfect distinctness to the view of the gentlemen watchers.

"I have left a message for you with Mrs. Butter," said Miss Brabazon. "You will be kind enough to attend to it for me."

"I will," answered Mr. Henry. "Is that you, Miss Rose?"

"She ran after me, naughty child! I am taking her home for punishment," returned Miss Brabazon, in a tone between jest and anger. "Good-night."

They parted. Raymond Trace was hastening after Mr. Henry, when he found his arm detained by his father in a firm grasp. "Let me go," whispered Raymond. "That's Mr. Henry. I can fall into conversation with him more naturally as we walk along, than if I made a formal call at his rooms."

"Who do you say it is?" breathed Mr. Trace.

"The German master, Mr. Henry."

"You are mistaken, Raymond; the moonlight is deceiving you. It is some years since I saw that young man's face, but I should recollect it amidst a thousand."

Trace stared. "My dear father, I assure you it *is* Mr. Henry. I ought to know him; I take my lessons from him daily."

"Do you! It is Arthur Paradyne."

"Who?" almost shouted Trace.

"Arthur Paradyne; the eldest son. In the summer

preceding the crash at Liverpool, business called me to Heidelberg. I took a letter of introduction to young Paradyne from his father; he was then a junior master in the university, and I saw him often. He used to act as my interpreter."

"Then he has been amidst us under a false name!" exclaimed Trace, with considerable animus.

The father gave a slight laugh. "He has found it convenient to be so, no doubt. You must still ask him about this man."

Trace darted off. He thought he had got a great hold upon Mr. Henry in this strange secret, and scarcely could persuade himself to make any show of courtesy while he entered on the question of the "German terminations."

"I could show you with the book in two minutes what it might take me five to explain without it," said Mr. Henry, with his usual ready kindness. "Perhaps you will come in-doors with me."

"Have you any visitor?" asked Trace, rather abruptly.

"Visitor? — no. I am quite alone."

"I — fancied — there — was a visitor at Mother Butter's," returned Trace in a hesitating manner, not being sure of his best policy, whether to speak of the visitor openly, whether not. "A friend of yours, somebody said."

"Who said it?"

"Really I cannot charge my memory with that. I saw you meet some — gentleman — in the plantation a few days ago: I thought it might be he."

"What a fine night it is!" observed Mr. Henry, courteously ignoring the suggestion, and letting his pupil see that he intended to ignore it. "It is clear and cold enough for a frost."

"Mr. Henry, would you mind telling me the name of the person you met?" resumed Trace, perceiving that if he wanted information he must ask distinctly for it.

"I cannot tell it you. I cannot tell you anything about him," was the reply. "We will quit the subject, if you please, Trace; it is neither yours nor mine."

"Where is he now? Will you tell me that? Is he in this neighbourhood?"

"Let the subject drop, Trace;" reiterated Mr. Henry, with quiet authority. "I say that it is no concern of yours or of mine."

Trace felt himself checkmated; he feared he had not gone to work in a sufficiently crafty manner, which vexed him. "It may be better that you should satisfy me on this trifle," he resumed, rather scornfully. "You are in my power."

"In what manner?" quietly asked Mr. Henry.

"I know your secret. I could go to the Head Master this moment and say, 'We have a wolf in sheep's clothing amongst us; a man with a false name.' If he has glossed over other things, do you think he would gloss over that?"

"You can try him."

The equanimity of the voice was so entire, the manner so unruffled, that Trace began to feel doubtful of his grounds. "Can you deny what I say?" he asked. "I accuse you of being — not Mr. Henry, but Arthur Paradyne."

"I am Arthur Henry Paradyne: as the Head

Master knows. Though I wonder how you came to find it out, Trace. In what way does the fact affect you?"

"The *contact* has affected us," foamed Trace, giving way to temper for once in his life, for the cool tone nearly drove him wild. "Is it fitting that you, the son of — of — you know who and what — should be placed over us? I wonder you could dare to stay, knowing you were a Paradyne."

"Knowing I was a Paradyne and that you were a Trace, it has made me all the more solicitous to do my duty by you," came the low answer of emotion. "Oh, Trace! have you never marvelled *why* I was so uniformly lenient to you, so anxious for your advancement, so solicitous to hide your faults; always striving to do you good, to get you on, to make your life at college easy? That bitter debt my father left, the wrong on you and yours, has been ever on my mind: I have been trying to work a tithe of it off, because I am his son, Arthur Paradyne."

Trace was not in the least softened; his strong prejudices did not allow him to be so. That this long-disliked master should turn out to be Arthur Paradyne, seemed like a personal and positive insult to himself. But he thought he might turn the discovery to present account.

"You can work a portion of the debt off this instant, if you will, by disclosing to me the name of the man you met."

"That I cannot do. Ask me anything else, Trace."

"Say you will not."

"The terms are almost synonymous. I *may* not."

"That's enough," retorted Trace, turning on his heel. "Good evening to you, Mr. Arthur Paradyne."

CHAPTER XXI.

The Outbreak.

IT was the morning following the arrival of Mr. Trace. The boys filed out of chapel: but instead of hindering, lingering, dallying, as it was generally their pleasure to do, those of the first desk threw off their gowns with remarkable haste, and rushed into school. As sheep follow their leader, so do boys mostly go in the wake of their fellows; and George Paradyne, who appeared to be the only one of the class not acting in concert, and who had rather wondered wherefore the bustle, hastened in also. But he found no place for him. His seat was occupied. By dint of sitting wide instead of close, the first desk contrived to fill the whole space. Brown major was before Paradyne's particular compartment, had got it open, and was disposing his own books and belongings in it.

"What are you doing with my desk, Brown major?" demanded George. "Move down lower, will you."

Paradyne's place now was next to Trace. It had been curious to note in the past weeks the tacit antagonism of the two boys, sitting side by side; Trace ignoring Paradyne always, Paradyne having no resource but to be ignored. Brown major took no heed to the request, and did not move down.

"Will you go down, I say, Brown? I shall have to pull you out if you don't."

Not a word of answer. The boys had their books out now, and were bending over them, putting up their backs as if some great draught were behind. George

Paradyne laid hold of Brown to swing him out, when Loftus major interposed. Gall was at home with a temporary indisposition, or it might not have occurred, since the senior was expected to keep peace. Bertie Loftus acted in a degree for him, but assumed little authority.

"Take your hands off him, Paradyne; we cannot have a disturbance here."

"He is in my place; he is taking my desk," cried George.

"Look here," drawled Bertie; "as good be open about the matter. The class tell me they don't intend to let you occupy your place again: and if the Head Master insists that you should, there'll be a rebellion. But it's thought he won't insist in the face of things. I am not speaking for myself," he continued, idly running his fingers through his luxuriant curls with a cool indifference that might have been laughable but that it was so real, and so characteristic of him. "Being, as may be said, a remotely interested party, I hold myself neuter: I have neither counselled this, nor do I join in it. But I can't have a disturbance, you know. Brown, pass me that Homer."

"Just disclose the meaning of this, will you?" cried George, speaking to the class collectively, "before I pull Brown major out of my place."

"Tell him, some of you," drawled Bertie.

For a moment there was silence: nobody seemed inclined to respond. Paradyne lifted his arm to begin aggression, when Brown major turned round; speaking however civilly.

"There'd better be no row over this, Paradyne. If you flung me out of the place — which perhaps might turn out to be a bit of mistaken boasting, if we came to try it — another would fill it up. You ought never to have come among us, and that's a fact; there has been a feeling against you always, but it's only since a day or two that we've known the cause. If I were you, I'd go quietly out at that door and through the college gates, and have done with it for good. And upon my word and honour I say this for the best: it's the only thing left for you to do."

"If you don't tell me the meaning of this, I'll fling you out, I say," repeated George. "I give you three seconds. One! two! ——"

"The meaning is, that you can't be tolerated here any longer," interrupted Brown. "Neither may you go in for the Orville."

"That's not the *meaning* — that's the result. I ask you for the meaning — the reason — the cause. Are you stupid?" added George, stamping his foot.

"Well — you know what your father was."

"What was he?"

Brown major hesitated. He was of a civil nature, and really did not like his task. To say to a college friend in his teens — your father was a swindler — or a forger — or a felon — is not pleasant. There was no time to lose, for the under-masters were coming in.

"I don't know the rights of it as well as some of them, Paradyne," said Brown at length. "Of course I'm sorry for *you;* but we are gentlemen here. Ask Trace the particulars — or ask Lamb."

Before another word could be spoken, the hall had to rise at the entrance of the Head Master. Instead of taking his seat when he reached his table, he remained standing, and addressed the first desk.

19*

"Gentlemen, in consequence of the absence of Mr. Henry this morning, the order of studies has been changed. You will go at once to Mr. Baker's room for mathematics."

There was a moment's lingering; either in surprise at the command, for it was completely out of routine, or for some other purpose. Could it be that the boys were deliberating, each in his heart, whether *then* to declare their feud against Paradyne? If so, nothing came of it. Bertie Loftus led the way through the room, and the rest followed him, including Paradyne.

Mr. Baker was waiting for them. Mr. Baker was an irascible sort of gentleman who might have settled any dispute, any incipient rebellion, by caning around him indiscriminately. The room was large too, the table spacious, the diagrams on the walls were plentiful, and there was no chance of shutting out George Paradyne from a seat here. So the class had to bottle up its resentment for the present.

Trace had not outwardly joined in the movement by word or look. Not in obedience to the advice given by his father the previous evening, but in accordance with his usual policy. Mr. Trace had casually remarked, "I'd not interfere with young Paradyne, Raymond, to oppress him. What passed was no fault of his, you know." Advice which Mr. Raymond had not the slightest intention of following. Some inward speculation was arising in his mind, touching the cause of Mr. Henry's absence, as just announced. Had he been dismissed? Had the boast — that the Head Master knew who he really was — been a false one, and had Mr. Henry, in consequence of the discovery, forced himself to declare his deceit, and been met by an abrupt dismissal? Trace would have given his two ears — as they say in France — for the knowledge, but did not see his way clear to get at it. As if to gratify him, Mr. Baker suddenly inquired of the class generally, if they knew why Mr. Henry was absent. George Paradyne, who was standing before one of the slates, following out its diagrams, turned round to answer.

"Mr. Henry is gone out, sir. I went round this morning to borrow Ollendorf's key from him, and found him away. Mother Butter thought he had gone off somewhere by train."

"I feared he might be ill," remarked Mr. Baker. "He has looked ill lately."

"His wicked conscience smited him,
He lost his stomach daily,"

sang Whitby in an undertone, quoting the lines from a once popular song that Mr. Lamb carolled on occasion for private benefit at bedroom festivals, and protested it had been composed by Tennyson.

"Mr. Henry had another of those fainting-fits last night when I was reading with him," said George, in answer. "Mother Butter came in, and asked him what he meant by not getting advice for himself."

"Attend to your business," roared out Mr. Baker by way of acknowledging the information. And they did it, one and all; bottling up their private grievances, as previously remarked, for a more auspicious opportunity. Which did not arrive until the close of morning school, so cross-grained and inconvenient a turn did the order of studies take that morning.

Mr. Henry had taken the train to London, to pay a visit to a great physician. Not in obedience to Mrs.

Butter's remonstrance, as disclosed to us by George, but because the time for doing so was come. He had been intending to see a doctor, long and long; had put it off in a sort of vague dread, as many of us do; and now it could no longer be delayed; no, not for a day. As George said, he had another fainting-fit the previous night; but, instead of recovering from it blithely, as was usual, he had lain all night in pain, his heart fluttering strangely. Medical aid, and that of the best, was necessary now, although he felt well again in the morning.

The dread was not for himself, but for those dependent on him. Who would help them if his help failed? The whole night long he lay awake, tormenting himself. With morning light — daylight does not come early when November is on the dawn — he rose and took his breakfast. Dropping a note to the Head Master, explaining the cause of his absence, he went off by train to London, doing all in a quiet manner. Times and again it had been in his thoughts to go to this gentleman, who was one of fame, especially in diseases of the heart. Very nearly an hour did he wait in the anteroom, before his turn came.

He was examined, questioned, talked to: and then the doctor sat down to his table and took up a pen. But he laid it down again.

"I am about to write you a prescription; but I tell you candidly it is not medicine you want. One thing may do you good; and one thing only."

"What is that?"

"Rest. Rest both of mind and body. I do not mean tranquillity only, but entire rest from all kinds

of exertion. Great or sudden exertion might be —— "
the doctor paused; and, as it struck Mr. Henry,
seemed to change the word he had been about to
speak — "prejudical to you, excessively so. You
must avoid alike fatigue and emotion."

"I gather, then, that my heart is not sound."

"Not quite as sound as could be wished."

"Is it so unsound as to place me in danger?"
questioned Mr. Henry, his luminous eyes bent earnestly
on the physician. "You need not fear to speak freely
to me. I have come here to ask you to do so."

"In a case such as yours there is no doubt danger,"
replied the doctor. "We can do little. It lies chiefly
with the patient himself."

"What does?"

"Well, I had almost said life or death. So long
as he can keep himself perfectly tranquil, the danger
is comparatively very little."

"But it is always there, nevertheless, even with
tranquillity. Am I to understand that?"

"It is. In a degree."

"I had a friend once; a fellow-student at Heidelberg, who had heart-disease. The German doctors recommended perfect tranquillity — as you do to me.
He followed their advice; he was of wealthy family,
and could do it; but the disease made rapid strides,
and shortly killed him. He lay ill less than a week."

"Ah, yes," replied the doctor, evincing no surprise.

Mr. Henry, who displayed and felt entire calm
throughout the interview, then proceeded to mention
the strides his own sickness had been making. He
was quite aware of the nature of his (possibly) in-

herited malady; recent symptoms had brought the knowledge to him. But, had he been differently circumstanced, in the enjoyment of past immunity from work and care and fear, it might not have shown itself for years and years. As it was — he frankly spoke of what the ending must in all probability soon be. The physician did not say much; it is not customary to do so; but when Mr. Henry went, he had gathered that death sooner or later must come to him. It gave him no shock: he had seemed to know beforehand what the fiat would be.

Notwithstanding, it was altogether a very serious vista, and yet a sensation of strange peace seemed to fill his heart. How he had shrunk from ascertaining the true nature of his disease, from the consequent absolute cessation from toil, which he knew would be imposed, he alone knew. All for the sake of his mother, her home, her interests. Over and over again he had asked himself, who would work for them when he could not. As if the delay would alter the evil, it was for this he had put off seeking to know the truth; he had dreaded it as one, unprepared, dreads death; and now that it was spoken, instead of the torment and trouble it might have brought, he felt nothing but resignation and sweet peace.

It was but another great mercy, this feeling, from the loving and merciful Father: and Mr. Henry had learnt to trust Him in all things, with the simple, reliant, undoubting trust that a child feels in its earthly parents; in darkness as well as light; in gloom as well as brightness. Oh, my boys, how I wish I could make you understand what this trust is, and how to acquire it! It is the one great blessing in life; the only true peace; a pearl of great price. It is a sure and safe refuge; an ever-present comfort in sunshine and in storm; a resort that is never closed. Every grief, every care, every doubt, had Henry Paradyne learnt to carry THERE, and he knew that it could not fail him. "Things seem dark and dreary; I cannot see my way; undertake for me, Lord!" had been latterly the burden of his prayer. He never failed to rise up comforted, to *know* that God had been with him, lending His gracious ear, listening compassionately to his cry: there were times when he seemed to have been talking with Him face to face, a joy so heavenly was diffused throughout his spirit. My boys, you perhaps hold an idea that religion (as it is very commonly called) is but a gloomy thing; let me tell you that the real religion, as experienced by those who live thus near to God, is as a very light of happiness. It will not come to you all at once; but it will surely come with time if you earnestly desire it. Think what it is to possess a refuge *always*, one that cannot fail! In danger and sorrow, in doubt and difficulty, in trouble and storm, there you may go, and kneeling say, "I cannot see my way; I am threatened on all sides; my fears overwhelm me. Oh, Father of mercies, I put myself into Thy hands; guide me, act for me, love me!" I tell you that, to those who have learnt it, this trust is as a ray direct from heaven, a glimpse of it before its time. With the necessity for comfort, comfort had come, and Mr. Henry was at rest.

He made his way home again. Just as he was entering his house, he heard himself called to, and turning saw Sir Simon Orville.

"I've come on a fishing expedition," cried the

knight, who seemed all in a flurry with the haste he had made.

"A fishing expedition!" repeated Mr. Henry with a smile and air as tranquil as though — as though he had not been on a visit to the great physician, and brought that knowledge home with him. Sir Simon glanced around, wishing to make sure that nobody was within hearing.

The facts were these. Raymond Trace returned to his father the previous night with the account of what he had been able to do with Mr. Henry: or, rather, what he had *not* been able to do. Mr. Trace, by some logic of reasoning, adopted the information as a proof that the stranger was undoubtedly Hopper, and went home to Pond Place in a state of mind not to be envied. The chief torment was the uncertainty. If the man in hiding was *not* Hopper, the inconvenience of going away from him was not to be thought of pleasantly; for, truth to say, Mr. Trace did not possess so much as a handful of silver to go with: if the man *was* Hopper, go he must, whatever the cost. He imparted his doubts to Sir Simon, just relating the story told by Raymond — that there was somebody in hiding at Mrs. Butter's, who might, perhaps, be Hopper — and no more. Sir Simon, detecting the anxiety, and a little wondering at it — for, as he reiterated over and over again to his brother-in-law, rogues could not threaten gentlemen in England with impunity — undertook to appeal to Mr. Henry himself the first thing in the morning, and get the matter set at rest.

"This is the third time I have come here this morning, Mr. Henry. You've been gadding about

London," good-humouredly added Sir Simon, in supreme
unconsciousness of what the "gadding" had been. "And
now, as I say, I am come fishing, and I hope you'll
not let me throw out my line in vain."

Mr. Henry led the way indoors. Nobody was
about; Mrs. Butter's kitchen door was shut, and Sir
Simon talked on, believing they were alone, as soon
as he was in the passage.

"My nephew, Raymond Trace, was questioning
you, last night, Mr. Henry, as to some man he had
seen you with in the plantation. You thought it was
impertinent curiosity, no doubt, and very properly refused to satisfy him; but I want you to tell me. Is
there anybody staying here in private, or is there
not? And if there is, what's his name?"

Mr. Henry laid his hat and gloves on the table,
rubbed his handkerchief across his damp brow: it was
strange how a very little exertion would put him into
a heat now: and led the way to his parlour. "I wish
I could tell you, Sir Simon," he answered, with a
smile. "I would have told your nephew had I been
able."

"Can you assure me that there is nobody staying
in the house?"

What was Mr. Henry to answer? To say There
is not, would have been untrue: to say There is, might
bring somebody trouble.

"Let me tell you why I ask," cried Sir Simon,
who was by far too open-minded a man to succeed in
any matter that required craft. "A friend of mine, at
present in this neighbourhood, has an idea that he is
being looked after for a debt he owes: he got to hear,
by hook or by crook, that some rather suspicious-

looking stranger had been seen talking to you, might even be in this house; he thinks it may be his creditor, and seems to be pretty near out of his senses with fright. That's just the truth."

"I wish with all my heart I had got a debtor in this part of the world," cried the voice of a strange head, putting itself in at the door: and the interruption was so unexpected that Sir Simon backed a few paces in surprise.

"Why, Tom!" he exclaimed. "Is it you?"

"Yes, it's me," answered Tom Brabazon; forgetting his grammar. "Excuse my having listened. I am not afraid of you, Sir Simon, but what are you asking questions about me for?"

"It was not about you I was asking. Is *this* the friend Raymond saw you speaking to?" continued Sir Simon, turning to Mr. Henry.

"Yes it is. You perceive it was not my own secret."

"Tell your friend, Sir Simon, that I've more need to run away from him than he from me," interposed Tom Brabazon. "Here I am; under a deuced cloud; tormenting Mother Butter out of her daily wits, frightening my sister at odd and even hours, worrying Mr. Henry to fiddlestrings. They are getting up a scheme of emigration for me, Emma, and the doctor, but funds run scarce with him just now, and he thinks I'm in Whitecross Street. The safest place going, he says, for me. It won't do to tell him I'm here."

"I'll contribute to the emigration, Tom," cried Sir Simon, his benovolent eyes glistening. "I'll try and make things straighter for you with the doctor. Mr. Henry has been keeping your secret, I see."

"In first-rate style, too! He has done all sorts of things for me: borne with my temper when I've invaded his room at night; gone to and fro with messages for Emma; bought my smoke for me, for old Butter said she'd not, and stands to it. What a droll man that friend of yours must be, to be afraid of *me!*"

"But, you see, Tom, we thought it was somebody else," returned Sir Simon, who really understood less than ever his brother-in-law's anxiety. But the relief to that gentleman would no doubt be very great.

Sir Simon, ever good natured, trotted off home to impart the welcome news, and Mr. Henry, not staying to take anything, but saying he would be back immediately, went his way to the college. His object was only to report himself back, for he intended to take his duties in the afternoon. Not until the following day should be over — the great one of the Orville examination — would he disturb Dr. Brabazon with his ailments. The sky was blue and somewhat wintry, the leaves were falling, the air seemed to strike upon him with a chill. But that sweet peace, diffusing itself within, was whispering comfort: he might be taken, but his mother — he saw it with a sure prevision — would be sheltered under the good care of God.

Not redolent of peace, certainly, were the sounds that greeted his ear as he came to the quadrangle, or the sight that met his astonished gaze. His back propped against a pillar, his honest grey eyes flashing with anger, his arms outstretched to ward off blows, was George Paradyne.

It has been said that no opportunity occurred for an outbreak on Paradyne during morning study. That over, the row began. He was caught up in passing through the quadrangle, on his way home, and surrounded. Yelling, shouting, kicking, hitting, a hundred inflamed faces were turned upon him at once, a hundred arms and legs put out their aggressive strength. The seniors, who first raised the storm, had not intended it to take this turn, but they were powerless to stem the torrent now, and so some of them went in for it. The boy put his back against a pillar, and stood his ground bravely, fencing off blows as he best could, hitting back again, his whole face glowing with scorn for his assailants, and for the unequal conflict. Suddenly Bertie Loftus appeared: he had been indoors, and knew nothing of it: and stood for a moment in surprised astonishment. Pushing through the crowd with his great strength, great when he put his indolence off and his metal on, he took up a position side by side with Paradyne.

"Look here, you fellows, I'll have no more of this. You ought to be ashamed of your manners: I am, for you; disgracing yourselves in this fashion! Trace! Brown major! Talbot! Whitby! — all you strong ones — I call upon you to beat the throng off. Dick, you young fool, be a man if you can!"

He spoke with the authority of the acting senior, but he was not obeyed as the real one. The boys' passions were up. None of them saw that a stranger who happened to be passing, had halted at the great gates to look on, and was standing in amazement. Bertie's words made some temporary impression, and there came a lull in the storm.

"Now then," he cried, taking advantage of the silence, "wait, all of you. Let us bring a little reason to bear, and don't go in for this row, as if you were so many Irish jackasses met at a fighting fair. Trace, the affair is yours if it's anybody's; you raised it; suppose you explain to Paradyne what the matter is."

"Suppose you explain yourself," retorted Trace, terribly vexed at being thus publicly called upon.

"It is not my business," said Bertie. "You know, you all know, I have not joined the cabal."

"Let Paradyne take himself off, and have done with it," roared a voice: and a Babel of tongues followed, each one taking the explanation on itself. The late Mr. Paradyne was called everything but a gentleman, some of the names being remarkably choice. George, with flashing eyes and earnestly indignant words, denied the truth of the charges, and stood up as bravely (morally) for his father, as he did physically for himself. He kept his place and defied the lot, Bertie protecting him.

"Wasn't he a sneak? Wasn't he a swindler? Didn't he go in for everything that was low and bad and dishonest, and then poison himself?" roared the malcontents, hustling and jostling each other.

"No; he was neither a sneak nor a swindler; he went in for nothing that was bad, and he did not poison himself," retorted George. "Look here — you, Lamb — when you were accused of firing off the pistol that shot the earl, were you not innocent?"

"Of course I was innocent," roared Lamb.

"But your innocence did not prevent your being accused. When that straw man was set ablaze to frighten Mother Butter, I had nothing to do with it, as you are all aware, I did not even know of it, but

Baker accused me, and gave me the cane. Well, it was just so with my father. He was accused, being perfectly innocent, and before the proofs of his innocence could be brought forth, before almost he had time to deny it, before he well understood what the charge was, he died: the excitement killed him. Loftus — and I thank you for standing by me now, and I know you have never worked against me as some of the rest have — I told your father this in Boulogne, and I think he grew to believe me. If you have anything to bring against me, you fellows, bring it; but you shall not traduce my father. What have *you* to say, Trace?"

"I am sorry you force me to speak, Paradyne," returned Trace, his quiet voice, civil still, rising above the hubbub. "I say that your father *was* guilty, and that you had no right to come here amidst honest men's sons. We have put up with the companionship; the Head Master forced us to it; and have kept your secret from the rest; and should have kept it to the end but for your attempting to go up for the Orville. It was pure audacity, that, and you were exceedingly ill-advised to think of it. No fellow whose father had dirty hands —"

George Paradyne laid his hand on Trace's mouth, sharply enough, though it was not a blow. It was the signal for renewed hostilities. Trace drew away, but many of the others hit out; Bertie Loftus and George being on the defensive. It was at this moment that Mr. Henry came up; he interposed with more authority than Bertie possessed; but the boys turned their derisive backs upon him, and kicked out behind. Mr. Henry was not to be put down: never was authority more uncompromising than his, when he chose to exert it. He pressed forward and stood before the assailants; he stopped the blows with his firm but gentle hands, he spoke words of calm good sense, his soothing voice hushed the noise and rancour. It was as if magic were at work, or some expert mesmerist: the angry feelings subsided; the boys' passions were allayed: the fierce storm had become a calm.

"Enough of this for now. George, you go home. Gentlemen, make way for him if you please. As to the Orville, which, as I gather, is the bone of contention, his going up for it, or the contrary, is for the decision of the Head Master; not for yours. Disperse quietly, every one."

In after-days, when the boys should think over this little episode in their school life, some wonder might arise in their minds how it was that they had so implicitly obeyed. It is true Mr. Henry made a slight allusion — it was nothing more — to certain divine mandates, that clearly do not enjoin quarrelling and fighting and evil passions, rather, peace and love: but the boys did not at the moment seem to think much of that. It was ever so: come upon what scene of conflict he would, Mr. Henry was sure to turn it into peace. The boys flitted indoors, one and all, Bertie Loftus bringing up the rear; and Mr. Henry went inside the cloisters and sat down on the narrow base of a stone pillar as if his strength or his breath failed him. George Paradyne, looking round from the small gate, happened to catch sight of his face, and came back, asking if he felt ill.

"It's nothing," said Mr. Henry; but the wan face, the panting breath seemed to belie the words. "Wait a moment, George: I want to speak to you. I think you had better withdraw your name for the Orville."

"Not I. Look here, Arthur — and I'll be hanged if I care, though they hear me call you so — this attack upon papa makes me all the more resolute to go in and *win*. Good-bye; 1 shall be round this evening."

George ran on. At the great gates stood the stranger still, looking and listening. A man of thirty, or thereabouts, with reddish hair. As George rushed by, a thought arose that he had seen the face somewhere before: but he was in a hurry and took no particular notice.

"A nice row, that, for college gents," cried the stranger, ignoring ceremony. "And so you are George Paradyne! How you have grown!"

George stopped, naturally; and devoured the face with his eyes. As the light of recollection dawned upon him, he darted close to the man, and cried out with a great cry.

"You are Abel Hopper!"

"Just so. But I didn't expect to see you in these parts."

It was indeed Hopper, the ex-clerk at Liverpool. The coincidence was curious; had we time to follow it out — that the real Hopper should make his appearance just as the fears of Mr. Trace should have been set at rest as to the false one.

"You see the life that is mine; the disgrace that clings to me," panted George, in his impulsive emotion. "If you have a spark of manly feeling, you will speak out and clear my father's memory, even though at the cost of criminating yourself."

Hopper stared at George with a questioning gaze. "I don't know what you mean," he said. "You must talk plainer, young sir."

"Yes, you do know. You know — don't you — that my father was innocent?"

"I do know it. He was innocent."

"And that you were guilty."

"No; that I swear I was not."

The accent wore a sound of truth, and George paused. "Then who was guilty?"

Hopper laughed as he crossed the road to the plantation. "We may come at that, perhaps, Master George, by-and-by. All in good time."

"But it is not all in good time," cried George, pursuing him. "Oh, come with me to my mother! She has believed him guilty; and it has embittered her heart, and changed her nature, and made a misery of our daily life. Only come and show her that he was innocent!"

But Hopper only went on all the quicker, and the sound of George's voice died away in the distance. Mr. Henry had seen and heard nothing of this. Some of the boys were coming out again with bats in their hands. Trace was one: but he carried a book, not a bat. They wondered what the German was sitting there for. Trace went up to him, and spoke.

"The part you acted just now was uncalled for, though I did not stop it before the school. Interference on Paradyne's behalf from you is particularly out of place."

"I think not, Trace."

"You think not! When you know who you are! A man who is here under a false name; whose life is a lie; is not one to ——"

20*

Trace stopped. The boys had been nearer than he thought, and were listening with eager ears. Mr. Henry got up and walked away.

"Trace, what did you mean?" came the eager questioning voices. "Who *is* he?"

And Trace told them. Betrayed out of his usual civil prudence, or perhaps tired of concealment, at last he disclosed the secret he had so recently learnt. It was another Paradyne.

Another Paradyne! Another of the bad brood! Trace, giving his nose a contemptuous twist, pointed a finger of scorn after the receding master: and the boys stared in stupid wonder. Another Paradyne!

CHAPTER XXII.

Before the Examiners.

THE great day had come, big with the fate of the Orville, All Saints' Day, the First of November. In the large hall, made ready for the occasion, wearing their gowns, their trenchers laid beside them, sat the candidates, before the gentlemen who had come from other parts and schools to preside with the masters of the college. It might, on the face of things, have been almost called a solemn farce, this sitting there in conclave, this great examination, confined to one day and to the formal routine of questioning, but that it was known the true adjudicator of the prize was Dr. Brabazon, who had probably decided beforehand upon the victor. Essays and papers on various subjects had been prepared and given in previously by the candidates; these had been examined, and their respective merits adjudicated upon by the masters in their several departments, whose opinions as to individual merit were conveyed to the Head Master in sealed notes. It had been impossible for Mr. Henry to assign the palm in his branches, French and German, to any other than Paradyne; but the just impartial tone of his mind might be seen by the fact that he had appended to his decision a memorandum, calling the Head Master's attention to the fact of George Paradyne's partly foreign education; thus leaving it to Dr. Brabazon whether the proficiency should be allowed to weigh in the contest. He need not have troubled, for, after all, now that the trial had come, Paradyne did not go up for it.

A sort of disturbance took place the previous night about Paradyne. Mr. Jebb, made acquainted with the cabal in the quadrangle, had carried the grievance to the Head Master, and the candidates were called into the study, Paradyne excepted. Gall, who had come back, made one of them. Sir Simon Orville was sitting with the Master — which was unexpected. The question to be decided was this: was Paradyne, with his burden of inherited disgrace, to be allowed to compete for the Orville with themselves, who had no such inheritance, and repudiated all possibility of disgrace on their own score, present and future, and for their forefathers in the past. The matter was settled by Sir Simon, who scarcely allowed the Head Master to put in a word edgeways, even to acquiesce. He said that if Paradyne was excluded from the trial, his nephews, Loftus and Trace, should not go up for it, nor Gall either, for he should take upon himself to act for his friend, Gall the elder, who was a very particular enemy to oppression in any shape. It decided the question.

Gall and Talbot at once spoke up, saying they had never wished Paradyne not to try; Loftus said the same; Brown major, with round eyes, avowed an opinion that it would be horribly unfair to Paradyne to deprive him of the chance, and he had always privately thought so, though he *had* gone in for the row against him. Dr. Brabazon dismissed the lot with a covert reprimand, and Trace, speaking a private word with Sir Simon, learnt that the man whom he had seen with Mr. Henry was not the dreaded Hopper. The news consoled Trace in some degree for this unwelcome decision, and he was uncharitable enough to hope that individual had been drowned.

But on this, the eventful morning, a note had been delivered to the Head Master from George Paradyne, saying he withdrew from the contest. And perhaps the master was not in his heart sorry, for it put an end to a matter of strife that had been somewhat difficult to deal with.

How had George Paradyne been won over to do this? you may be asking in surprise. In the first place, Hopper had — so to say — eaten his words. George had found out where he was staying, at a small obscure inn beyond the station, and went to him in the evening, pressing the man to say who was really guilty. Hopper could only be brought to respond in a joking, derisive sort of way; but insisted that the guilty man was really Captain Paradyne. "You know it was your father, after all," he said emphatically to George; and his look and tone were so sincere, that George's heart sunk, for the first time, with a doubt that it had been. In this frame of mind, his spirit subdued almost to despondency, George went round to Mr. Henry's; and when the latter urged him again to give up the Orville, George received the advice in silence.

"You think it right, then, that I should yield to this cabal against me?"

"It is not altogether that, George," said Mr. Henry, who was lying upon three chairs, and spoke slowly, as if in pain. "They are all against you, and perhaps it is not right that one should hold out in opposition to the many. Not on that account would I so strenuously urge it, but on another. There is little doubt that the real contest will lie between you and Trace."

"And as little doubt that I shall beat him in it," added George.

"Yes, I believe you would. Well, George, do a generous action and withdraw from it for his sake. Let Trace get it. That past wrong upon him can never be wiped out by us; but we, you and I, may do a trifle now and then of kindness to him, perform some little sacrifice or other in requital of it. *I* have been ever seeking for the opportunity since I came here; it is one reason why I have been always urging you to peaceful endurance, rather than active resentment; George, be generous now."

And George Paradyne was at length won over to this view. His mother, in her haughty resentment against the school for their treatment of him that day, had already urged it. The note of renouncement was written to the Head Master, and one candidate's chance for the coveted prize was over. It was made known just before the examination began, after the morning service in the chapel.

"It will be Trace's now," cried the boys with

shouts of victory. "Trace, old fellow, here's wishing you joy! The rest might as well give in at once."

"It is not for the sake of the benefit," disclaimed Trace, his cheeks wearing their salmon-coloured tinge of satisfaction, "but for the honour it will bring. It would have been out of the order of just things for that tainted fellow to gain it over me."

Of course. But nevertheless there was a feeling on some of them — led to, perhaps, by a word of Gall's — that it was an unfair thing for Paradyne to have been put out of the trial.

The long table was removed from the middle of the hall — the sweating hall it was called that day — and the candidates sat across it, before the masters and the gentlemen. One of the masters was not there — Mr. Henry, and it was supposed he was resenting the defeat of Paradyne. Let us leave them to their work.

The rest of the boys had a holiday, and highly agreeable they found it; although an order had been appended to the privilege that no noise whatever should be made within bounds, to the disturbance of the examiners. This rendered them a little uncertain what to do with themselves, until it entered into the bright head of Brown minor to propose to "have it out with Mother Butter." About ten of them started on this laudable errand, chiefly second-desk boys. But when they arrived at that estimable lady's residence, they found that she was abroad and her kitchen locked up.

It was a disappointment. There was no paint convenient to paint the door green, as they had the cow, or they might have tried their hand at it. They stood disconsolate.

"Let's take a look at old Henry in his sulks!"

cried Mr. Smart, briskly. "Fancy his not showing at the examination!"

"And ask him how he relishes Paradyne's being put out," added Lamb.

"Won't it be jolly!" said Dick Loftus, beginning to dance.

They turned to the door. Mr. Henry's assumed sullenness at Paradyne's defeat was set down partly to the special fact that he had coached that gentleman, partly to his mortification at the disclosure that he was not himself but somebody else. Trace had favoured the school with all particulars. This would be almost as good fun as Mother Butter.

"Let's give a postman's knock, or he mayn't open it," whispered Leek.

A postman's knock they gave; so far as fists upon a parlour door could imitate that sound. It was not so distinct as it might have been, from the fact that too many hands gave it in too many places. Mr. Henry's voice called out, "Come in," not very distinctly. And in they went. The room was empty, but in the small bed-chamber opening from it, the door thrown wide, they saw their master. He was in bed, sitting up in it, not lying, leaning back against some cushions.

Ah yes, the incapability had come, all too soon. Had he seen the physician to-day instead of yesterday, there had been no need of the injunction, to give up work, to stay away from the college. The disease had shown itself rapidly and unmistakably; the power of exertion had left him. And there he lay; a desperate pain at his heart, and the crimson of hectic on his cheeks.

Appearances were so unlike "sullenness," or anything else they expected to find, that the invading crew stood in sudden discomfiture of spirit. Two or three of them began to back out; but Mr. Henry held out both his hands with a sweet smile of welcome.

"I hoped some of you might come to see me this holiday, when you knew I was ill. Thank you all, my dear lads."

"But we didn't come to see you because you were ill; we didn't know it," cried truthful, open Dick. "I'm afraid we came for something else. We thought you were stopping away in vexation, sir, because Paradyne was not going up for the Orville."

Mr. Henry gently shook his head. "It is by my advice that Paradyne does not go up. I should have been vexed if he had. And now tell me how you are spending your holiday."

He seemed to speak with a slow, faint voice, and breath that did not come so freely as it ought. The boys made no answer. They were taking in everything, and had not yet regained their audacity. Lamb had fully meant to address him as Mr. Paradyne, and go in for a sneer, but somehow could not readily get the name out, and felt crestfallen in consequence.

"Are you staying away on account of illness, Mr. Henry?" asked Leek.

"Don't you see that I am?"

"But the examination's on!" cried Leek, who could not understand any illness to be as important as the trial for the Orville.

"I wish I could have gone," Mr. Henry replied. "I lay very still all night hoping to get strength to appear, but it proved useless."

"When shall you be well enough to come back to

college?" asked Dick Loftus, in rather a subdued tone.

Mr. Henry took one of Dick's hands in his; with the other he clasped Leek's. He did not reply at once, only looked out at them all with a strangely affectionate gaze.

"Should you miss me very much if I were never to come back again?"

"But you *are* coming back?" exclaimed Brown minor, leaning forward on the foot of the bed.

"I think not. I fear not. I have thought for some little time now that this might be the ending. But it has come on very rapidly."

"You — don't mean," hesitated Brown, "that you are — going to die?"

"I fear it may be so."

The boys stood awe-struck. Their hearts seemed to have stopped beating.

"But, Mr. Henry — what a dreadful thing!"

"Oh, boys, it may be a happy thing. God knows what is best for me."

"Why don't you have a doctor?"

"Your friend Mrs. Butter's gone for one now," he answered, with a smile. "And I went into London yesterday morning and saw a great physician. It was the cause of my absence from class."

They remembered the absence quickly enough, and also the row in the quadrangle afterwards, which he had quelled. — Had that disturbance anything to do with this sudden increase of illness? The physician might have said it had.

Going to die! A terrible shadow, as of remorse for unkindness rendered, fell upon them as they stood.

They called to mind how they had treated him; how uniformly kind and forgiving and generous he had been to them in spite of it, and of the peace he had contrived to shed.

Leek's conscience began to prick him. "Is your illness caused by the trouble you have had with us boys, Mr. Henry?" he asked, remembering the promise he had given that day in the Strand, and how soon he had forgotten it.

"No, no. It may have helped it on a little: I can't tell."

Dick Loftus's heart was collapsing more than anybody's; it was one of the tenderest breathing. "I wish the time would come over again!" cried the boy, in his flood-tide of repentance. "I've been worse than any of them. I hope you'll never forgive me."

"Not forgive you!" cried Mr. Henry, regarding him tenderly with his luminous eyes. "There's nothing to forgive. It seems that you have always been kind to me. You have let me give you many a private lesson, and take your part in many a dispute. Thank you for it all, Dick."

"But that has been doing kindness to me," debated Dick.

"And to do you kindness, Dick, is one of the things I have lived for," said Mr. Henry, softly. "I am a Paradyne, you know; I have had a great debt upon me."

Dick could not see the argument, although Mr. Henry was a Paradyne. Brown minor interposed with an opportune question.

"Does the Head Master know of your illness, Mr. Henry?"

"Yes. He's coming round when the day's work's over."

"Trace will have the Orville."

"Oh, yes, I hope so."

The boys began to back out. Illness that might be about to terminate in death, nobody knew how soon, was what they were not accustomed to. It seemed to strike upon them as disheartening; not to mention a sense of awkwardness in the manners that was anything but agreeable. They had gone in, impudent and noisy; they went out humbly on tiptoe. At the garden gate they encountered Mother Butter, and did not molest her, or pay her a single compliment; to that lady's infinite astonishment, who came to the conclusion that they must have been "cowed" by a flogging all round.

Dick Loftus sat down on the stump of a tree in the playground. Dick, for the first time in his life, was supping sorrow. He did not look at the past in the light Mr. Henry appeared to do, when he spoke of the debt left on him by Captain Paradyne; but he remembered what the universal kindness (about which he had never previously thought) had been, and he knew that he who had shown it was passing rapidly away.

With an aching of the heart that Dick had never felt, — with the consciousness of that bitter sin, ingratitude, breaking its refrain on his brain, Dick started to his feet again, and dashed after Brown minor, taking a knife from his pocket as he ran. It was a recent acquisition, bought with some money that Dick had been saving for the purpose, and prized accordingly. Mr. Brown was astride on a gymnastic pole.

"Look here, Brown: you wanted to buy my knife for three shillings the other day, and I laughed at you. You shall have it now. It cost four-and-six-pence."

Brown minor, a regular screw at a bargain, took the knife in his hand for a critical examination. "I'd not give that now, Dick. You've used it."

"I've not hurt it," answered Dick. "I haven't a penny in my pocket," he continued ruefully; "I want money for something, or I'd not sell it. What will you give?"

"I don't mind two shillings."

Dick tossed over the knife and held out his hand for the money. Brown gave eighteenpence; it was all he had about him, he said, and promised the other six-pence later. Dick took the available cash and started off to the shops. Half an hour later Mr. Henry was disturbed by his sudden entrance with a cargo of trea-sures.

Three sour oranges, but the best Dick could get; an apple as large as a child's head; some almond rock; two bath buns; an ounce of cough lozenges; and Cap-tain Marryat's novel "Snarley Yow," which he had gone in trust for. These several articles he tumbled out upon the bed.

"If you will try an orange, or a piece of the rock, Mr. Henry, you'll be sure to like them," said Dick earnestly. "And the book's beautiful. You'll laugh yourself into fits over it."

Mr. Henry caught the boy's hands, his eyes glistening with dew: "Thank you very much, Dick! God bless you. This kindness does me good."

He did not damp the generous ardour by saying that the purchases would be useless to him: rather did he seem to make much of the collection in his grateful

good nature. And Dick Loftus, wringing the delicate
hand, turned tail and bustled out again: for his eyes
were glistening too.

CHAPTER XXIII.

Falling from a Pinnacle.

You might decidedly have thought that Mr. Raymond Trace was treading upon air. But that it was
almost dark — for the examination had only terminated
when the shades of evening fell — his bearing might
have excited the admiration of his fellows. His back
was upright, his face was lifted; pride and self-suffi-
ciency puffed him out. He had come out well before
the examiners, and there could be no moral doubt that
the prize would be his. Talbot had also done well —
they were about upon a par; but Trace and everybody
else knew that Talbot, his junior in the college, would
not be preferred to him. The examiners had compli-
mented him; the Head Master had shaken hands with
him; Trace felt elevated to the seventh heaven, and
was walking forth to impart the glorious news at Sir
Simon's.

Treading upon air. His gown was thrown back
from his shoulders, his trencher sat jauntily on his
head, his boots creaked, his feet seemed not to touch
the ground. Just before he turned in at Sir Simon's
gate, he saw two people turn out of it, and recognized
George Paradyne and his mother. Trace vouchsafed
no notice whatever, and thought it very like their impudence to be there. George, who did not recognize
him at the first moment, ran after him inside the
grounds.

"Have you gained the prize, Trace?" he asked, as he caught him up.

"It has not pleased the Head Master to proclaim who has gained it or who has not," answered Trace, turning, and speaking with the same sort of accent he might have used to a dog.

"But I suppose you feel sure of it?"

"I have felt that all along. I *am* sure now."

"That's right," cried George heartily. "I am glad I gave up to you! If I have been secretly chafing over it all day, I'm only thankful now."

"Glad you gave up to me!" retorted Trace. "You did not give up to me; you were forced to give up because you couldn't help yourself."

"I gave up to you indeed, Trace; that you might get it. It was through Mr. Henry; he persuaded me: and I'm heartily glad of it as things have turned out. Good-bye, old fellow! I won't keep you now; but I'll stand by you through all, Trace. Mind that."

Scarcely according a moment's thought to the ambiguous words, except to resent their insolence, Trace gave his shoulders a shake, metaphorically shaking off George Paradyne, and went on his way of triumph. Ah, boys! how often when we are at the very height of prosperity, is a fall near! as you go through life you will remark it. That was the last hour of pride to Raymond Trace.

He rang grandly at the hall-bell — as became a senior fellow who was above the ordinary run of mortals, and had just gained the Orville. "Is Mr. Trace in the dining-room?" he asked of Thomas, rubbing his shoes on the inner mat, and handing him his gown and trencher.

A simple question, however lordly put, but Thomas answered it in a peculiar way. He dropped his voice to a confidential whisper, and laid his fore-finger on Trace's shoulder, as if there were some mystery in the house.

"He's not here, Mr. Raymond. He is safe off."

"Safe off!" exclaimed Trace. "What do you mean?"

"He is gone, sir. I let him out at the back-lawn window, with his carpet-bag, as soon as it was dusk."

Trace stared at the man. "What is he gone for?"

"There's some trouble afoot, Mr. Raymond, and your father has gone away out of it. He was looking like a ghost. Mr. Loftus is telegraphed for, and we think he may get here to-night by a late train."

"But what is the trouble?" asked Trace, a strange feeling of vague dismay stealing over him.

Thomas shook his head. "I don't rightly know what it is, sir. A man of the name of Hopper brought it, I fancy, and he's in there now with Sir Simon" — pointing to the dining-room. "I dare say you can go in, Mr. Raymond," he added, advancing to open the door. "Mrs. Paradyne has just gone."

It had been an eventful day. While Raymond Trace was flourishing his acquirements and his proficiency before learned men, fate, so cross-grained at times, was working elsewhere no end of ill. On the hearthrug, when he went in, stood Sir Simon and Hopper. Hopper left them, and Sir Simon prepared to enter upon an explanation. Trace set himself to listen; a moisture as of some awful dread, breaking out upon his brow.

It appeared that Hopper had been dodging about the neighbourhood the past day and part of this, stealthily looking after Mr. Trace, and endeavouring by covert inquiries to ascertain whether or not he was in it; which plan he adopted for certain private reasons, rather than apply boldly at Sir Simon's, and make open inquiry. He could learn nothing. Nobody had seen any such person about, as he described Mr. Trace to be. This afternoon, he met Mrs. Paradyne close to her house, and she caused him to enter. Full of her griefs and grievances, she spoke out unreservedly, especially of this latter grievance of George's treatment about the Orville Prize; that he should have been forced to put himself out of it that young Trace might win.

Hopper listened. He seemed struck with the injustice dealt to the boy. He could but sympathize with Mrs. Paradyne — who had been kind to him in the days gone by, when he was a poor friendless clerk — and her misfortunes; with her changed face, with the tears that she once in her life let fall, overcome by the old associations his presence brought; and in a rash fit of generosity, he avowed solemnly to her that the misfortunes were unmerited, for her late husband was *not the guilty man*. He appeared to repent of this confidence almost as soon as given, and went away, asking her to keep it strictly to herself.

Keep it to herself! not Mrs. Paradyne. The disclosure had fallen on her in the light of a revelation; the belief maintained in her husband's guilt swept itself from her mind at a single stroke, and she marvelled at her credulous blindness. It seemed to change the current of her life's blood, the knowledge; to restore to her the energy she had lost. Never so much as giving a thought to Hopper's request for secresy, deeming it wholly unreasonable, Mrs. Paradyne took her way to Sir Simon Orville's, requested a private interview, and told her tale. Sir Simon, impressed by the energetic words, caught up the conviction that the unfortunate Captain Paradyne had been really innocent. He could not call Mr. Trace to the council because that gentleman had gone to London by train and was not yet back.

"And who was guilty? — who was guilty, my dear lady?" cried Sir Simon. "Did Hopper tell you that?"

"No; he would not say. I pressed the question urgently on him," continued Mrs. Paradyne; "but could get no answer. All he said was, that it was inconvenient just yet to disclose it."

"The guilty man was himself," said Sir Simon.

"I do not think so," answered Mrs. Paradyne. "His manner did not strike me as that of a guilty man."

Sir Simon nodded, but did not by words maintain his opinion. He quitted the room, took prompt measures, and in a very short while, Mr. Hopper found himself under convoy to Pond Place, somewhat against his will.

There, very much to his surprise, he was accused by Sir Simon of the past frauds. At first Hopper laughed at it; but he soon found it a matter all too earnest; that he was about to be consigned to the protection of the law. In self-defence he made a clean breast of the truth, and avowed that the real culprit was — Robert Trace.

Sir Simon Orville felt something like a stag at bay. He listened to the particulars like a man in a dream:

never, never had his doubts touched on this. And Mr. Trace, who returned home during the recital, and was told by Thomas that Sir Simon was engaged on business, went straight to his chamber, all unconscious that the business concerned him, and that he had been seen to enter and was recognized by Hopper.

"I suspected Mr. Trace from the very first," observed Hopper, continuing his story to Sir Simon. "A singular occurrence, though trifling enough in itself, led to my doing so: and I thought it was beyond the range of probability that Mr. Paradyne, so simple-minded and honourable, could be guilty. But Mr. Paradyne died before anything could be proved or disproved, and the guilt was supposed to have died with him. Mr. Trace hushed the matter up. People said how lenient he was; but I looked upon the leniency, which was foreign to his usual mode of doing business, as another reason for doubting him. I was not sure, but I quietly set to work to track out my clue; I had one to go upon; and I tracked it out surely and safely. The result was what I had anticipated — Robert Trace was the guilty man. Never, sure, was one so lucky before! had Mr. Paradyne but lived four-and-twenty hours, the farce could not have been kept up. Ask him, Sir Simon, whether I am right or not," concluded the worthy Hopper. "I know he is here."

"If you knew all this, why did you not denounce him at the time?" growled Sir Simon, who was feeling terribly scandalized by the whole thing.

"Because he had sailed for America before I had finished tracking it out."

"And you followed him there! And worried his life nearly out of him, trying to make your own game,

I see now; I understand it all," added the aggrieved knight, his thoughts going back to the semi-explanations of Hopper's conduct and claims, given him by Mr. Trace.

"Anybody else would have done the same in my place, sir," was the self-excusing answer. "It was better for him that I should keep the affair hushed up, than proclaim it."

"And the Paradynes to have lain under the guilt all this while!" groaned Sir Simon. "What on earth did he do with the money?" he added, the problem striking him.

"Ah well, that's best known to himself," cried Hopper. "He *had* it. He went into ventures under another name, for one thing."

"Into ventures?"

"Speculations, and that," explained Hopper. "Lots of folks do the same nowadays, more than the world knows of. If successful, they grow into millionaires, and their friends can't make out how; if non-successful, there comes a smash. Ask him, sir, whether it's not all true that I have told you. I saw him come up that path a few minutes ago."

Sir Simon Orville had no need to ask. A conviction that the man did indeed speak truth was within him, sure and certain as a light of revelation. He followed Mr. Trace to his chamber and accused him, speaking quietly and sadly; and Mr. Trace finding that Hopper was below, felt scared out of his senses. The time for denial was past: Robert Trace, believing himself overtaken by the destiny that seemed so long to have been pursuing him, did not attempt to make any. Sir Simon, locked in with him, saw how it was

— that the hunted man was, and had been all these years, at his ex-clerk's mercy.

"I never intended to accuse Paradyne," said Mr. Trace with abject lips. "Loftus got meddling with the accounts, a thing he had not done for years, and found something was wrong. For appearance sake, I was obliged to go through the books with him; and then to agree with him that fraud must be at work. It was Loftus who accused Paradyne; there was no one else whom it was possible to suspect; it was Loftus who ordered him to be taken into custody: and I could not say the man was innocent without betraying myself. Then came Paradyne's sudden death, and I let the onus of guilt rest upon him."

Sir Simon interposed with but one question. "What became of the money?"

"Private speculations," answered Robert Trace. "There you have the whole."

Yes; Sir Simon had the whole, and now, a little later in the day, Raymond Trace had it. Mr. Trace had made his escape from the house at the dusk hour, while Hopper was still detained with Sir Simon. Hopper showed every wish, as far as hints could show, to compromise the affair; meaning, that for a sum of money he would hush up Mr. Trace's part in it. Sir Simon dismissed him when Raymond entered: Mr. Hopper gave his address at the inn, and went away in confidence; leaving, as he supposed, Mr. Trace the elder and Sir Simon to talk over any offer they might feel inclined to make him.

Sir Simon disclosed the whole to Raymond: there was no possibility of its being kept from him. The boy — if it be not wrong to call him so — sat very

still on a low chair, feeling as if the world, and everything in it bright, and honest, and desirable, were
closing to him. If ever a spirit was flung suddenly
down on its beam-ends from an exalted pinnacle, it
was that of Raymond Trace.

"You cannot go in for the Orville now, Raymond,"
said Sir Simon to him in a low tone, breaking a long
and miserable pause.

Raymond glanced slightly up. "I have gone in
for it. And gained it."

"My boy, you know what I mean. You must give
up the gain."

The same thought had been beating itself into
Trace's conscience. A bitter struggle was there. "You
would have let Paradyne gain it and wear it, Uncle
Simon, when you thought *his* father guilty!"

"True. But there is a difference in the cases."

As Raymond Trace saw for himself. He sat with
his pale face bent, his cold fingers unconsciously pressing his hair off his brow. Sir Simon, sorry to his
heart for the signs of pain, laid his own hand compassionately on the cold one.

"Raymond, this disgrace is no more your fault
than it was young Paradyne's. Take my advice: look
it in the face, now, at first; do your best in it; in time
you may live it down. Let it be the turning-point in
your life. You have not gone in — I use the language
of your college fellows — for a strictly straightforward
course: begin and do so now. It will be as certain
to lead you right in the end, as the other will lead
you wrong. Begin from this very hour, Raymond."

"I'll do what I can," was the subdued answer.
"Where's my father gone?"

"I don't know where until he writes to me. Raymond! your mother, poor thing, knew the truth of this."

Raymond looked up questioningly.

"I am sure of it. I can understand now her bitter sorrow, the shivering dread that used to come over her, her anxiety that I should be kind to the Paradynes. She seemed always to be living in a sort of fear. The knowledge must have killed her."

Trace shivered in his turn. Yes, the knowledge of her husband's guilt, and the fear of its coming to light, must have killed her.

"Have you sent for Mr. Loftus, Uncle Simon?"

"Hours ago. Thomas telegraphed for him."

Raymond rose. It was time for him to go. He must show himself at college, and attend evening service at chapel as usual. On festivals especially there might be no excuse, and this was All Saints' Day. The great examination had not done away with duties, neither did this private blow of his own. A thought crossed his mind to write a note to the Head Master, and never go back to college again: but it was not feasible. Better, as Sir Simon said, face it out. If he could bring himself to do it!

The contrast nearly overwhelmed him — between this walk out and the recent walk in. He placed his back against a tree in the long avenue, wondering if any misery since the world began had ever been equal to this. As he stood there, the cruelty of his behaviour to the Paradynes came rushing over him in very hideousness. Mr. Henry had once put an imaginary case to him — "Suppose it had been your father who was guilty?" — and that now turned out to be reality. Trace's line of conduct was coming home to him; all its hard-heartedness, all its sin: a little forgiving gentleness towards the Paradynes, a little loving help to bear their heavy burden, would have cost him nothing; and, oh! the comfort it would have brought to him, now, in his bitter hour. As a man sows so must he reap.

They were filing into the robing-room when he got in. Gall said something about his being late, but Trace took no notice. He had his gown on already, and stood near the door to take up his place.

"Have you heard the news?" asked Gall.

"What news?" was the mechanical response.

"About Mr. Henry. He is dying."

"Dying! Mr. Henry! Who says it?"

"It is quite true, unhappily; he will never get up from his bed again," answered Gall. There was no time for more explanation: the masters were approaching, and the organ was already playing in the chapel.

Once more Trace sat in his place, listening to the lessons as one in a dream. How applicable the first of those lessons was to his present state of mind, he alone could feel. Gall read it, with his soft, clear voice that in itself was music. It was the fifth chapter of Wisdom to the seventeenth verse. The following are the parts that struck Trace particularly, but you can look out the whole for yourselves, and see whether it was or was not likely to come home to one acting as Trace had done, suffering as he suffered, repenting as he repented. Mr. Henry, dying, was in his mind throughout; or rather, not Mr. Henry, but Arthur Henry Paradyne.

"Then shall the righteous man stand in great boldness before the face of such as have afflicted him, and

made no account of his labours. When they see it
they shall be troubled with terrible fear, and shall be
amazed at the strangeness of his salvation, so far beyond all that they looked for. And they, repenting
and groaning for anguish of spirit, shall say within
themselves, This was he whom we had sometimes in
derision, and a proverb of reproach: we fools accounted
his life madness, and his end to be without honour:
now is he numbered among the children of God, and
his lot is among the Saints! . . . .

"What hath pride profited us? or what good hath
riches with our vaunting brought us? All those things
are passed away like a shadow, and as a post that
hasteth by: and as a ship that passeth over the waves
of the water, which when it is gone by, the trace
thereof cannot be found, neither the pathway of the
keel in the waves.

"Even so we in like manner, as soon as we were
born, began to draw to our end, and had no sign of
virtue to show; but were consumed in our own wickedness. For the hope of the ungodly is like dust that
is blown away with the wind: like a thin froth that is
driven away with the storm; like as the smoke which
is dispersed here and there with a tempest, and passeth
away as the remembrance of a guest that tarrieth but
a day. But the righteous live for evermore; their
reward also is with the Lord, and the care of them is
with the Most High. Therefore shall they receive a
glorious kingdom, and a beautiful crown from the
Lord's hand: for with His right hand shall He cover
them, and with His arm shall He protect them."

Gall's voice ceased. And Trace thought verily
that lesson had been specially appointed by Fate to

bring his works home to him. In a few minutes there came another shock: one "in grievous sickness" was solemnly prayed for: and he knew it was Mr. Henry. Caring little now whether he were discovered breaking the rules, or not, Trace went after chapel to pay a visit to Mr. Henry. Before he escaped, the boys were upon him with their congratulations. It was the first opportunity afforded them since the day's examination. Trace winced awfully. He wished to respond, "I shall not avail myself of the Orville, though I may have gained it," and thus begin at once to herald in the blow of exposure. But his heart and his voice alike failed him; he *could not* speak the words to that sea of faces.

Sitting up in bed, as he had been all day, his prayer-book open, and a candle on the stand by his side, was Mr. Henry. He put out his hand and drew Trace near; his face lighting up with the happiest smile.

"You have come to tell me the good news! Thank you for thinking of me. I am so glad that you have gained it!"

"No," said Trace, in a voice half husky, half sullen, "I did not come for that." And there he arrived at a pause. His task was very unpalatable.

"I have been reading the First Lesson for the evening," remarked Mr. Henry. "What a beautiful one it is! A real lesson. One of those that seem to speak direct to our hearts from God."

A colour as of dull salmon tinged Trace's cheeks. But for the loving light thrown on him from the earnest eyes, larger and more luminous than of yore, he might have thought there was a covert shaft intended for him.

"I came to speak to you, Mr. Henry: perhaps I ought now to say Mr. Paradyne. Circumstances have occurred which — Have you heard any particular news?" broke off Trace.

"Only the good news that you have gained the Orville. Dr. Brabazon has been with me, and he whispered a little word in my ear. I seem to feel so thankful. George will not have given up in vain, either. He said to me last night — with a rueful face, as an argument against what I was urging — 'But suppose one of the others should get it, and not Trace?' It is all as it should be."

Trace recalled George Paradyne's recent words; he understood them now. He understood, unhappily, the other words — "Mind, Trace, I'll stand by you through all." George had come forth from Sir Simon's, having learnt what he, Trace, was then in blissful ignorance of. "Why did you urge Paradyne to give up to me?" he asked of Mr. Henry.

"Knowing me now for Mr. Paradyne's son, you will understand how heavily that past calamity, entailed upon you, has lain on me. If I could but have wiped it off! I was always thinking; have atoned for it in any way! And I could do nothing. It was but a slight matter for George to withdraw from the Orville. And besides, you know the cabal was so great against his trying for it."

The words went down into Raymond Trace's uneasy conscience; that debt seemed as nothing, compared to the one now thrown on him. He dashed into his explanation.

"Circumstances have occurred which show me how very wrong and mistaken my resentment against you and George has been. I will not allude to them; I'm not up to it to-night; but you will hear soon enough what they are. And I came round to say that I am sorry for it; that I repent of it in a degree which no words could express. — You were prayed for in chapel to-night;" continued Trace, after a pause. "The report in the school is that your case is hopeless."

"It is quite so, I fear."

Trace paused, as if to get up his voice, which seemed like himself — very low. "You will say you forgive me before you die?"

"The need of forgiveness lies on my side," said Arthur Paradyne, pressing the cold hand with a grateful pressure. "If you were a little resentful, it was but natural. Say you forgive my poor father!"

"Don't!" cried Trace, with a sort of wail. "I'll come in again another time, when you have learnt to understand better."

"One moment," said Mr. Henry, detaining him. "You seem to have some great sorrow upon you to-night. Is it so?"

"Sorrow!" bitterly echoed Trace. "Ay; one that will last me my life. A sorrow, to which yours has been as nothing."

"I have been picturing you as so full of joy this evening. Trace, you *have* gained the Orville. I know it."

"Yes. But I shall give it up to-night."

"Give up the Orville!"

"I cannot help myself. Good-bye."

Mr. Henry was curious, but he would not question further. Trace's hand was still a prisoner. "When pain is too fresh to be spoken of, Trace, there is only one thing to do," he gently whispered. "*I* learnt it."

"Yes. What?" asked Trace, rather vacantly.

"*Carry it to God.* And then in time you will learn that it came down to you from Him; came in love. One of those mountains that lie in the road to Heaven, so sharp to the feet in climbing them, so good to look back upon when the summit is gained, the labour done. Good night."

The low persuasive accents lingered on Raymond Trace's ear as he went out into the night; the suffering, kind, gentle face rested on his memory. God help him! God pardon him for the additional thorns he had gratuitously cast on this young man's already thorny path. What a wicked spirit had been his! He had sown thorns and nettles and noxious weeds; and in accordance with the inevitable law of Nature, they had come up to sting and pierce him.

CHAPTER XXIV.

In the Quadrangle.

Almost sooner than perhaps even Trace anticipated, was Mr. Henry (one can't help adhering to the familiar name) to be enlightened; for, as Trace went out of Mrs. Butter's, Mrs. Paradyne went in. Ah, could he ever forget his astonishment at what then took place. She fell on her knees at the bedside; and, pouring out the news she brought, besought him, with tears and kisses and heartfelt lamentations, to forgive her. To forgive her for her conduct to him!

That past calamity, five years ago, falling on her with the fury of an avalanche, seemed to have suddenly changed Mrs. Paradyne's nature. The sense of disgrace had warped every kindly feeling of her heart, to have brought out all there was within her of selfishness.

She had been a proud woman, secure in the self-esteem that arises from a consciousness of ever striving to do well. The blow seemed to have dried up all affection, except for George, her youngest-born, whom she had ever passionately loved; and her time was spent in silently, sometimes openly, reproaching the husband who had so wronged her. Her letters to her eldest son in Germany grew few and cold; she accepted as her due what aid he could send, returning scant thanks for it. When, four years later, he came to Orville, she scarcely received him patiently. She resented his having advised the removal of George to Orville College, now that it was known the Loftus boys and Trace were at the same; and she, from motives of policy, forbade him to own relationship with them, or to call her mother. Were it disclosed that he was a Paradyne, he might no longer be able to work for them. He must go to the house but once in a way, and then as an acquaintance. But for the ordeal of sorrow he had been passing through for four years, these cruelties might have well nigh gone to break Arthur Paradyne's heart. As it was, they were but additional drops in the cup of bitterness he was draining.

But when the astounding news, that her husband had been innocent, burst upon Mrs. Paradyne, she woke up from her nightmare. With the lifting of the stigma from their heads, all her former kindly nature (it had not been very great) returned; the hard scales fell from her eyes and heart, and she saw how selfish, nay, how cruel, had been her treatment of her eldest son. In nearly the selfsame hour, she received tidings that his sickness — in which she had previously only half-believed — had increased alarmingly; she heard the report that it might end in death. And here she was on her knees at his bedside; the tears streaming from her eyes, kisses from her lips, pouring forth the blessed news, just heard, and beseeching him to forgive her; to love her as of yore. It seemed to him that he was repaid for all.

Morning rose. Standing in the quadrangle, that favourite place of theirs, under the early November sun, were the college boys, George Paradyne making one. Strange and startling tidings had just been disclosed to them. The gainer of the Orville, so universally assumed to be Trace, might probably turn out to be somebody else.

For Trace had thrown up the prize, and quitted the college!

Thrown up the Great Orville Prize? Quitted the college? The throng stared stupidly at one another, unable to understand it. And yet it must be true; for the announcement had come to them from the Head Master.

The truth was, poor Raymond Trace, after a whole night's battling with his mortified spirit, had found himself utterly unable to face the disclosure that must be made. If not made at once, it must inevitably, as he knew, come out later. At six o'clock that morning he was with the Head Master; and before seven he had gone out of the college gates, never to return. At present the boys were in ignorance of any ill; and would be kept so as long as was possible. A report arose, its origin not altogether clear, that Trace was called thus suddenly away by some stupendous business in which his father was engaged in America.

The boys were repeating this over to each other, in full belief of its veracity.

The substance of their conversation reached the ears of two gentlemen who were advancing unobserved, arm-in-arm: Sir Simon Orville and Mr. Loftus. "Called away on sudden business!" repeated Sir Simon. "Let 'em think it. As good, that, as any other passing plea. Poor Raymond!"

Bertie Loftus was the first to catch sight of his father. Bertie was as ignorant of recent events as the youngest boy there. He went up with a glow of pleasure on his face, hardly believing the vision could be real. Dick, dashing in, got the first question. "Papa! papa! what have you come for?"

Mr. Loftus, his tall, slender figure and handsome face presenting a contrast to Sir Simon's, made a sign for the boys to gather round him, and drew George Paradyne to his side. "Sir Simon telegraphed for me on a matter of business," he said to his sons. "But" — turning to the throng — "I have come here this morning to perform an act of justice: one which has been delayed so long through ignorance on my part and fraud on another's, that it seems to me as if vengeance must cry aloud to Heaven. Gentlemen, you have heard of the frauds that George Paradyne's father was accused of perpetrating. Within a few hours we have discovered his innocence. He was innocent as I; and more so: for I, by my culpable negligence, and mistaken trust in another who was guilty, con- tributed to the mistake. This boy" — laying his hand on George's shoulder — "has been reproached by you as the son of a man of crime: let me tell you, as I do before Heaven, that his father was a good and

honourable gentleman; a brave soldier of his Queen's;
a faithful servant of One who is higher than any Queen."

"He has been treated like a dog amidst you," impatiently broke in Sir Simon, drowning the more
temperate words of Mr. Loftus, and turning himself
about in his own fashion. "You have behaved cantankerously to him, like a cross-grained set, as you are!
And now you'll have to eat humble-pie and be ashamed
of yourselves. I'd not own any of you; I wouldn't."

In spite of the hard words, there was a humorous
sound of excuse in them; the boys detected the good-feeling, laughed, and began to cheer. Mr. Lamb put
on his meekest face and drew a little away; and then
called out that the college would not have known anything about Paradyne, neither have thought of being
hard upon him, but for Trace.

"Just so," cried Sir Simon. "Trace is ———"

Mr. Loftus laid his hand upon his impulsive brother-in-law, who might have been about to declare more
than was necessary. It was not noticed. The excitement was rising; the hubbub was great. A hundred
hands were held out to shake Paradyne's, in atonement
for the past; a contrast to the scene of the previous
day when the same hands were put forth to strike
him. They shouted, they threw their caps in the air:
they felt, and with shame, how ill they had behaved
to him throughout, how mistaken they had been. George
met the hands with his own ready one, with his frank
and generous smile; not a bit of malice entertained he.
But there was a world of pride in the self-sustained
movement with which he threw back his head; in the
quiet, self-reliant only words he spoke:

"I always said, you know, that my father was innocent."

CHAPTER XXV.

Very Peacefully.

HE was dying very peacefully and quietly, very happily, surrounded by his friends. Sir Simon Orville went in perpetually, blustering rather at first, because Mr. Henry — as they still, from old custom, mostly called him — would not be moved to Pond Place, to be made much of for the closing period of his life, and depart out of it in luxury.

"The exertion might be too great for me," he said, clasping Sir Simon's hand gratefully. He sat up in bed still; most likely would to the last. "I am better here in my own poor home, where the boys can run in and out at will. Thank you ever, Sir Simon."

"But I can't make up to you for the fraud, I can't do the slightest thing towards it," remonstrated Sir Simon, who was altogether in a state of repentance for the past, and what it had brought forth — as if it had been any fault of his. "But for that miserable brother-in-law of mine, you might have been hale and healthy now, and flourishing in the world."

"God knows what is best," was the cheering answer of Arthur Paradyne, the same he had made to Trace. And Sir Simon saw that it must be best: for there was a serene light of peace in the eyes, in the face altogether, that worldly honours, be they great as they will, can never bring.

"He has been leading me through the wilderness in His own way," continued Mr. Henry, scarcely above a whisper. "But for the dreadful trouble that fell upon me, I might not have found my road thus early: and then where should I have been now? The doctors

22*

think, you know, that under the most prosperous auspices I could not have lived to be thirty. Oh, Sir Simon, God sees and knows what we do not see, and He has been guiding me home."

"You could be surrounded by so many more comforts at Pond Place," resumed Sir Simon, when he had overcome a troublesome cough.

"But not with more love. I have everything I want, and see how my friends come round me. Not an instant am I left. Before one goes, another comes. Sometimes," he added, with a gay smile, "they arrive as if it were a levée, and we have to borrow Mother Butter's kitchen chairs. My mother and Mary are here nearly always; Dr. Brabazon and his daughter come, my pupil Rose comes, the masters come, the boys come, and you come, you know, Sir Simon. How could I be better off?"

"I should have liked you to get well and live, that I might do something for you; set you up in a coach-and-four, or some little thing of that sort," contended Sir Simon, with an expression of face half cross, half piteous.

Mr. Henry shook his head with a smile: coaches-and-four don't always bring happiness with them, or drive their owners on the best road to it. "Could any one have been more bountiful than you, Sir Simon? You have —"

"Tush!" crossly interrupted Sir Simon. "Is it not my duty to do it, as Robert Trace cannot? 'Twould be a second fraud on my part if I didn't."

The allusion was this. Sir Simon Orville had hastened to announce his intention of refunding to Mrs. Paradyne, and with interest, the three thousand pounds her husband had put into the Liverpool firm, and which had been lost in the vortex. Not only that: he avowed that George's future education and career should be his care.

"Why did you not confide in me?" cried Sir Simon. "Why did you not tell me you were a Paradyne. I'd have helped you on."

"Tell you, Sir Simon! It seemed to me always a species of fraud on my part to receive the many little favours you were ever wishing to show me."

"The odd thing to me is, that you should have so fully put credence in your father's guilt," observed Sir Simon. "Knowing him as you did."

A slight flush, as of remorse, shone in the fading cheeks. No opportunity had been given him of believing otherwise. His mother, so impressed with it herself, had succeeded in imparting her impressions to him, beyond possibility of doubt.

"Where is Raymond Trace, Sir Simon?" he asked in a whisper. "I should so like to have seen him again. He said he would come, but he did not."

"Well, I'll tell you," said Sir Simon confidentially. "Robert Trace is in hiding about twenty miles off, and Raymond with him: they are not out of England, as some suppose; Hopper for one. When the explosion arose, we were all confused together; as was but natural. Robert Trace thought he must escape from Hopper; and I — to say the truth — winked at it. It was not my place to show 'em up to the Lord Mayor; and if a thousand pounds or so — But never mind that now. When we came to talk matters over sensibly and coolly, I and Mr. Loftus, we saw that he could not be made criminally responsible, except Mr. Loftus

chose to do it, for the frauds had been against the
firm; and other liabilities were all paid. We have
privately seen Robert Trace (mind, this is between
ourselves) and advised him to face it, and I think he
will. He says he'll be made a bankrupt."

"And Hopper?"

"Hopper will be floored — as he deserves to be.
Not a single penny shall he get out of me."

"But he will make Mr. Trace's fraud known, out
of revenge, Sir Simon!"

"It is known already, known by this time to the
very length and breadth of the land. You don't suppose Mr. Loftus would suffer your father's name to lie
a day under its obloquy! Not he: if Loftus has a
proud nature, it is a just one. And so is Bertie's."

"And generous too," cried Mr. Henry, his face
flushing with its old pleasant light. "Bertie never
once insulted George by a look or a word; but stood
by him quietly in many ways, smoothing things for
him. He will make a good and brave man. He
comes here every day to sit with me. I think the
duel did him good. It took some of the assumption
out of his spirit."

Down sat Sir Simon with a burst of laughter.
That duel, now that he had overcome the horror it
brought to him at the time, was a rich joke. Gall
and Bertie winced at its remembrance still. But they
had been firm friends since.

The days went on. Mr. Henry had more visitors
than he sometimes knew what to do with. His mother
was there often; Mary occasionally, as she could spare
time from her occupations with Miss Rose Brabazon,
whose resident governess she was now. Mrs. Paradyne

was eating the bitter bread of repentance: the mistaken line of conduct she had pursued to him, her eldest and dutiful son, grew harder and harder to reflect upon. She could not say so; it distressed him too much, and she sat mostly in silence, letting him hold her hand, yearningly wishing she might recall the past. Too late; too late. She could not stop the course of the rapid disease; she could not prolong his life, or bring back the isolated days he had been condemned to pass, or the weary nights of labour in which he had wasted his delicate frame: the sensitive spirit had been wounded to the quick; the tender heart flung back upon itself. It had been all good for him, no doubt; necessary adjuncts to that process of purification his spirit had been unconsciously undergoing for its coming flight to a better world, but which Mrs. Paradyne could never forgive herself. The deceit she had forced him to observe in regard to his identity had told upon him, there was no doubt, more than any other untoward circumstance: and Mrs. Paradyne had the comfort of knowing that she had helped — on the end. He was, so to say, living a lie; it was altogether wrong, unjustifiable, little better than a fraud on the Head Master; and neither his health nor his natural integrity could bear up against it. And so, Mrs. Paradyne sat by his bedside in silence; she and her aching heart. Now that the relationship was known, people could trace the likeness in their faces; which had once puzzled Miss Brabazon.

And there was another who would come and sit by him, and take his hand; and, closing the door, read to him words from the Book of Life — and that was Dr. Brabazon. The doctor saw the prize that he was losing: he knew now, if he had never known it before, how valuable Mr. Henry's precepts had been in the school, and the peace he contrived to shed around amidst warring elements. Other things were known to the doctor now: the sojourn of his ill-doing son in the house, and the kind friend Mr. Henry had been to him. It seemed to have made Tom into a better man; and he went off to Australia in a spirit of reformation that Mrs. Butter, in a satirical spirit, "hoped would last."

Rose ran in and out at will, bringing him flowers. One day she came to him with a great trouble — Emma had found her love-letters, and she was never, never to write or receive more. Well, Mr. Henry said smiling, as he pushed her pretty hair off her brow, she was certainly getting too old for it.

Emma Brabazon would come sometimes, and lift the little table to the bedside, and make tea at it. She was cheerful now, gay even, for a great care had been removed from her; she would call him Dr. Henry, or Professor Paradyne, and laugh over that back suspicion connected with the gold pencil, now safe in the Head Master's pocket. She confessed to him that she had had great fears, at the time Lord Shrewsbury was shot, that it might be her brother who had fired the pistol. "Not intentionally, to do harm, you know," she added; "but he was often down here, wandering about the plantation, in the hope of meeting me and getting money from me, and it was so easy for him to have picked up the pistol."

"Be at rest," said Mr. Henry. "It was not your brother."

Miss Brabazon was surprised at the assured tones. "You know who it was?"

"It was one of the college boys. Do not ask me more, for that is all I can say." He intended to carry the secret with him to his grave. And might have done it, had it lain alone with him.

Of all his casual visitors, he liked best to see the boys. He would cause them to sit close to him, and talk pleasantly of the journey of life on which, after this half-year, some of them would be entering. Not one but treasured his words; not one but would remember them to profit in the busy battle to come.

CHAPTER XXVI.

The End.

A DAY in December. The fine old hall was decorated as for a festival. Ordinary signs and appurtenances were put out of it; desks were not; books, slates, ink, canes, all had disappeared. The boys wore their gowns; the masters were all suavity; and James Talbot, Earl of Shrewsbury, had a bit of blue ribbon in his button-hole, the badge of the Orville Prize. From his chair of state the Head Master had just announced him as the victor, and decorated him with its sign. It had been virtually known for some weeks that Talbot would have it, but this was the formal investiture.

The term was drawing to its end: Mr. Henry, in his proximate dwelling, was drawing near to his. On the day but one following this, the school would disperse. Gall, Loftus major, Brown, Talbot, and others who have less concerned us, were quitting the place for ever. Mr. Henry had been considerably better for some days; he had been up, and even walked in the garden. It was the flickering of the candle's flame before going out.

Mr. Trace had just sailed for America, taking Raymond with him. The full particulars of the past frauds had been for some time known; and the unhappy man had never come out of hiding. He had nothing to fear, legally or criminally, but he could not face the world. Not until this morning, when the news of their sailing for New York reached the boys, had they given up the hope that Raymond might come up to say farewell. And Mr. Lamb, as you will see, intended to take advantage of the fact of his departure. Hopper had disappeared from Orville; nobody knew or cared where. Sir Simon had made short work of his refusal to give him money: though it was very generally suspected that he had again substantially assisted his brother-in-law, Robert Trace.

The ceremony of formally investing Talbot with the bit of blue ribbon was over, and the masters left the hall. Up rose the boys with their shouts of congratulation.

"Long live the Earl of Shrewsbury!"

The earl laughed, and held his hands above his head. "Don't hail me," said he jestingly, "I have but stepped into another's cast-off shoes. Trace gained the prize."

"If hailing goes by deserts, you should hail Paradyne," interposed Gall. "But for his withdrawal, Trace would have come off second-best. I know it."

"I'll shake hands with the whole of you with pleasure as Trace's deputy," heartily called out George Paradyne.

Lamb stepped forward. Never had his face been more virtuous, his voice so candid. "I can't let the opportunity pass without declaring a thing that is in my keeping," he smoothly began. "In that matter of the pistol, fifteen months ago, when Lord Shrewsbury was shot — you all remember it well. It was Trace who did it."

Gall wheeled round on Lamb. The rest stood in wonder, listening for more.

"And it was Trace who inked that Latin essay of Paradyne's," continued the estimable young man. "I *saw* him do that, and I know he did the other. As he is gone, it's as well the truth should be known. Trace was a sneak."

A good swinging blow in the chest, which sent Mr. Lamb staggering backwards. It came from Bertie Loftus. Never before had Bertie been seen to strike gratuitously.

"You are the sneak," he said to Lamb. "Can't you let a fallen fellow alone? Trace is in misfortune, and absent. But for that, you'd not have dared to traduce him, you coward."

"It was he who fired off the pistol," roared Lamb, smarting under the blow. "I swear it was. There! It's only lately I got to suspect it, and I taxed Trace with it the morning he left, and he couldn't deny it: he didn't seem to care to; he was too down. You hold your row, Loftus major."

In dodging away from Bertie, Mr. Lamb contrived to back amidst the throng, and tread upon their feet. It only wanted that to set them on. This last announcement, so exceedingly characteristic of him, was as the climax of his sins, and they thought the time had come to pay him out. Trace had never been a favourite; and perhaps he really had something of the sneak about him; but this did not make Lamb less of one. Hissing, pushing, striking, calling him every derisive name they could lay their tongues on, buffeting, kicking, the lot set to on the miserable Lamb. And Bertie helped in it.

His ears were tingling, his hair was pulled, his eyes were smarting. One whacked him here, another kicked him yonder; his back was already growing blue; his voice, poor wretch, was raised in a howl, piteously shrieking for quarter. Suddenly the onslaught was interrupted. Somebody had interposed to part them, and so stopped the fray. One look round, and the boys fell back in very astonishment.

It was their dear old master, Mr. Henry — for dear in truth he had become to them. A little worn, shadowy, looking taller than he used; but with the same kind and gentle face, the same loving gaze from the luminous eyes. Sir Simon stood behind.

"I thought I would try and get as far once more; and my good friend, Sir Simon, helped me with his arm," said Mr. Henry, speaking so very quietly that a sudden hush seemed to fall upon the room. "But I did not expect to find you *thus.*"

As if in excuse, and perhaps a little ashamed of the turmoil, a score of voices avowed the cause. Lamb stood to his creed; and Sir Simon's ears were regaled with Raymond Trace's private misdoings in the past. Perhaps it did not much surprise him.

"It does not excuse Lamb," said Gall, his eyes flashing indignation on the latter, who stood cowering behind.

"It was Lamb who told about the smoking that time," called out Leek with indignation.

"He's a wretched coward." And the boys began to hiss again.

"Forgive him for my sake," said Mr. Henry, throwing oil on the troubled waters. "Next term he will do better perhaps; he will have learnt a lesson."

"He'd better not come back! he'd better not show his face here again!" growled the boys.

"I'm not coming back," retorted Lamb.

"But to think that Trace ——"

"Hush, hush," interrupted Mr. Henry. "We must have peace and pleasantness to-day. How can we expect mercy for our own faults if we do not show it to one another? If you only knew how pleasant it is to do a kindness instead of an injury! Try it, Lamb, in future."

Lamb's only answer was to steal out of the room surreptitiously, as quickly as his stiffness allowed. He had not enjoyed his bonneting. Sir Simon Orville went up to Talbot, and fastened a gold watch and chain to his waistcoat.

"My present comes opportunely," he remarked, "since you were on the subject of the pistol. You may remember that I offered a gold watch and chain to whosoever should track out the shooter of Talbot. But what do you think I did, boys? — I'm nothing better than a plain old goose, you know. — I went and bought the watch and chain, never supposing but somebody would turn up to win it the next day. He didn't turn up, and I've had it by me ever since, lying useless. It crossed my mind once to give it to my friend Onions here," — with a nod to Mr. Leek — "for his services in a certain duel you've heard of;

but I hadn't got it with me in Boulogne; and, besides, he has a handsome gold watch of his own. So then I determined to keep it for the winner of the Orville; and I've brought it. It seems consistent with poetical justice that it should be Talbot's at last, since he was the one damaged by the shots. Long life to you, my brave earl, to wear it out!"

"Not to me, sir," said the earl, flushing with delight, but just and generous in the midst of it. "It is true I have got the Orville, but Paradyne merited it. He gave up the contest voluntarily — and he has not a watch any more than I have."

"I'll take care of Paradyne," said Sir Simon, with a significant nod. "He'll miss neither the watch nor the Orville, and he goes to Cambridge when you go to Oxford. I'm a plain man and like Cambridge best. Wear your watch with content, my boy: your name is on it, and you have deserved it."

A deafening cheer followed Sir Simon as he went out. Mr. Henry stayed behind. Sitting down on a bench, he gathered them round him, his low clear voice echoing on their ears and hearts with a strangely peaceful echo, as he talked of the journey he was so close upon; of the one they must all take in their turn, and of many little things that would speed their packing up for it. In the middle of this, to the general consternation, Dick Loftus broke into sobs, and dropped his head upon Mr. Henry's arms. Dick came to himself in a few moments. Feeling intensely ashamed, he made a feint of carrying off things with a careless hand.

"Don't you go and die yet. We shouldn't like it, you know. Wait till we are off. And couldn't you leave us something as a legacy?"

"Oh yes! leave us a legacy," cried the rest, ready for any suggestion of that sort.

"A legacy?" repeated Mr. Henry, smiling. "Very well. What kind of legacy?"

They ran over different articles, each in his mind, from a gold watch and chain like Lord Shrewsbury's, to a lock of Mr. Henry's hair. But nobody mentioned one thing in particular. "Anything you like," said the boys.

He smiled still, and rose; shaking hands with each of them, saying a tender word of encouragement to all; and went out, leaning on Gall's arm, Bertie walking on the other side. Ah, what a contrast it was! They, so full of life, of its interests and passions; he, so near its close.

Nearer than they thought. On the following morning when they were at breakfast, crowing over the premature departure of Mr. Lamb, who had declined to face the school again, the Head Master walked in and imparted the news.

They were allowed to go and see him. He lay on the bed where he had died. His face was perfectly beautiful from its look of intense peace, almost as if a halo of glory were around it. No wonder: he had gone to the God and Saviour whom he served. With hushed breath and softened hearts, they stood gazing on him, very conscious just then that their time must also come. He had but gone on a little while in advance — as he told them the previous afternoon in the college hall.

They were returning to their homes that day or the following: to their Christmas festivities, the puddings, the games, the gaieties, all to be merry; just as you are at this very present time. Some few would never come back to Orville College; they were about to be launched forth on their several ways of life. A tempting prospect to look forward to: but a conscious voice within them was whispering that *he* was happier in his early death, than they who had yet the battle and the strife to encounter. God defend them in it, and keep them for Himself! As He had kept him, who lay there.

And the promised legacy? As they filed noiselessly out, a folded paper was put into Gall's hand. It was headed "The legacy to my dear friends and pupils." He had sat up in bed the previous night to write it. It proved to be a small portion of the thirteenth chapter of St. John, in his own beautiful handwriting, and signed with his full name, "Arthur Henry Paradyne."

"*A new commandment I give unto you, that ye love one another: as I have loved you, that ye also love one another. By this shall all men know that ye are my disciples, if ye have love one to another.*"

Gall reverently folded the paper, and they passed out of the house, putting on their trenchers. "We'll have it framed," said he, "and hang it in the hall. Us senior fellows will be gone, but we can come in sometimes, and look at it."

Oh, boys! my dear young fellow-workers for whom I have written this story! Do you strive, earnestly and patiently, to do your duty in this world; and take that legacy home to your hearts!

THE END.

PRINTING OFFICE OF THE PUBLISHER.